PET SIMULATOR™

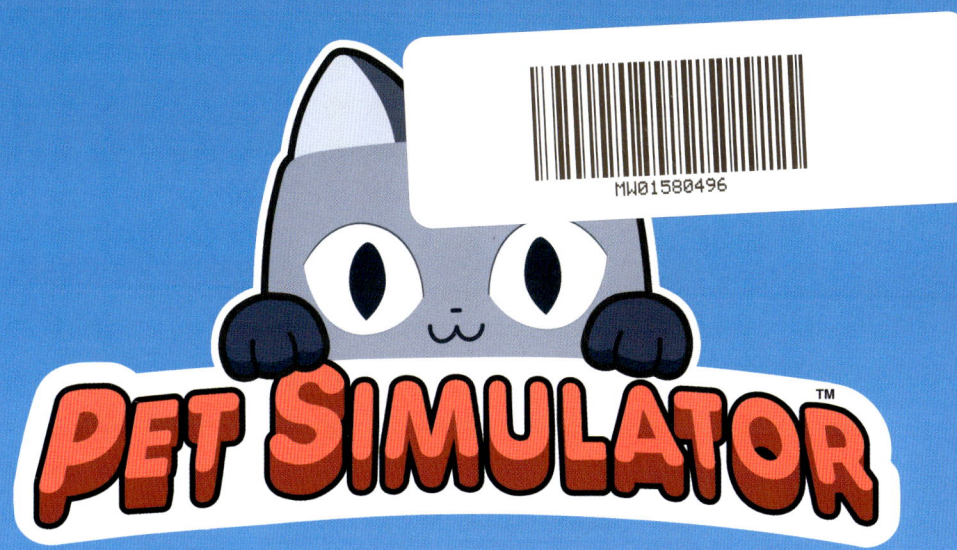

FRIENDSHIP UPGRADE

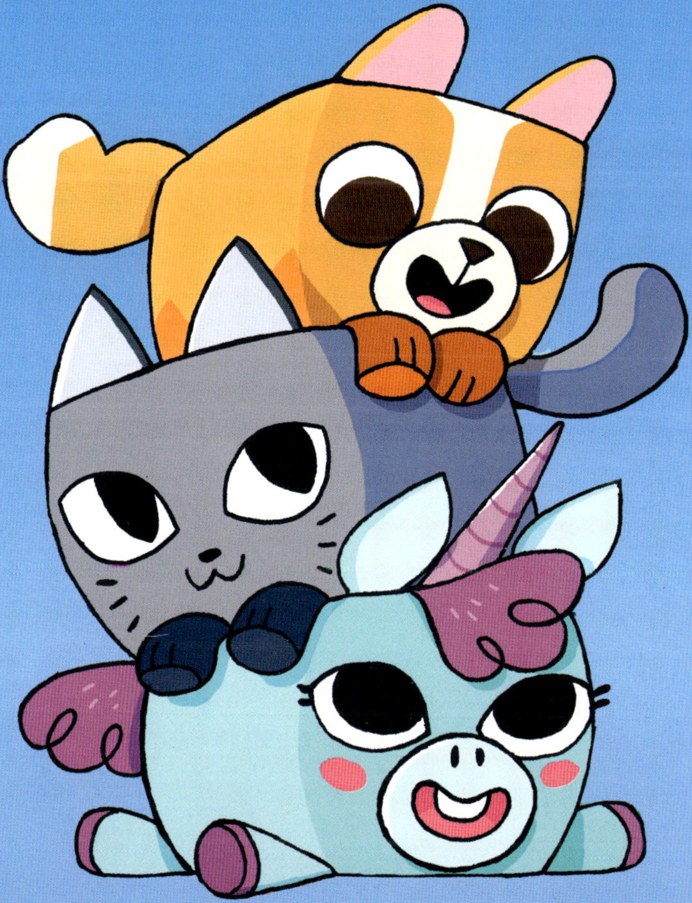

© 2025 BIG Games, LLC

All rights reserved. Published by Graphix, an imprint of Scholastic Inc., *Publishers since 1920*. SCHOLASTIC, GRAPHIX, and associated logos are trademarks and/or registered trademarks of Scholastic Inc.

The publisher does not have any control over and does not assume any responsibility for author or third-party websites or their content.

No part of this publication may be reproduced, stored in a retrieval system, or transmitted in any form or by any means, electronic, mechanical, photocopying, recording, or otherwise, or used to train any artificial intelligence technologies, without written permission of the publisher. For information regarding permission, write to Scholastic Inc., Attention: Permissions Department, 557 Broadway, New York, NY 10012.

This book is a work of fiction. Names, characters, places, and incidents are either the product of the author's imagination or are used fictitiously, and any resemblance to actual persons, living or dead, business establishments, events, or locales is entirely coincidental.

ISBN 978-1-5461-6933-8 (paperback)
ISBN 978-1-5461-9828-4 (hardcover)

10 9 8 7 6 5 4 3 2 1   25 26 27 28 29

Printed in China   62

First edition, October 2025

Artwork by Mike Laughead and Keaton Kohl
Edited by Lori Wieczorek
Lettering by Matt Krotzer
Book design by Martha Maynard

FRIENDSHIP UPGRADE

WRITTEN BY
STEVE FOXE

ILLUSTRATED BY
**MIKE LAUGHEAD
AND KEATON KOHL**

An imprint of
SCHOLASTIC

PART 1
ENTRUSTED EGG

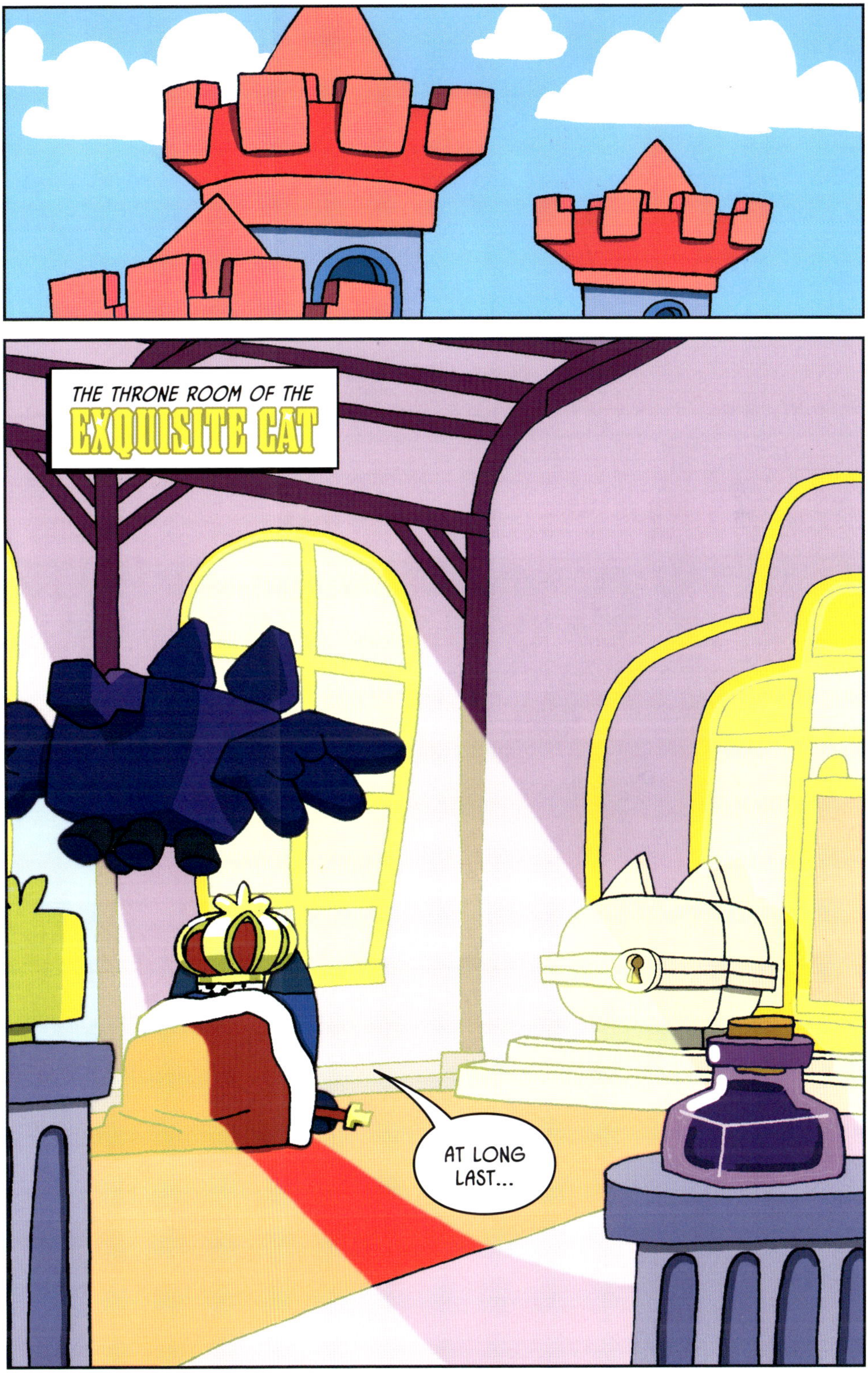
THE THRONE ROOM OF THE
EXQUISITE CAT
AT LONG LAST...

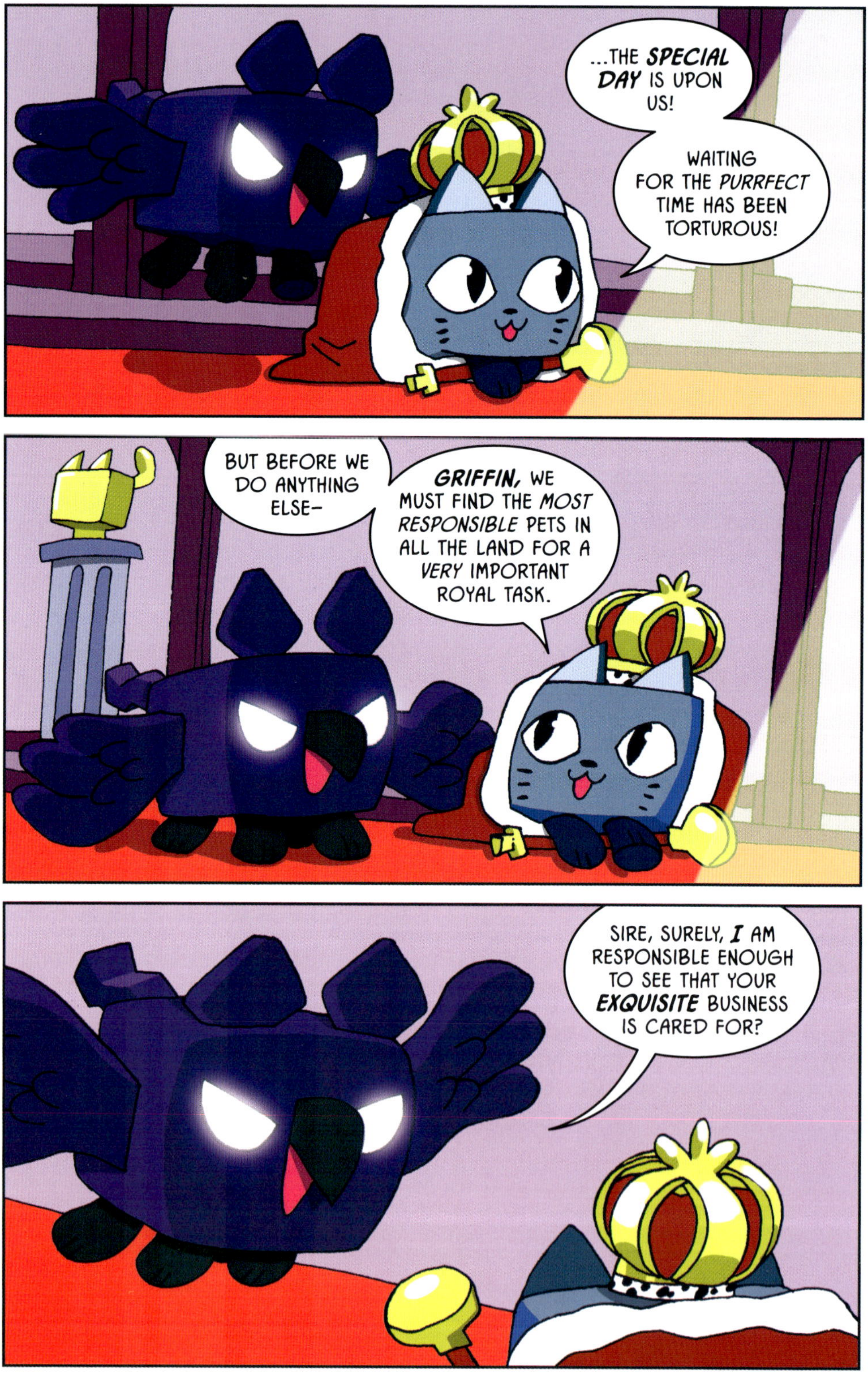

...THE SPECIAL DAY IS UPON US!
WAITING FOR THE PURRFECT TIME HAS BEEN TORTUROUS!
BUT BEFORE WE DO ANYTHING ELSE–
GRIFFIN, WE MUST FIND THE MOST RESPONSIBLE PETS IN ALL THE LAND FOR A VERY IMPORTANT ROYAL TASK.
SIRE, SURELY, I AM RESPONSIBLE ENOUGH TO SEE THAT YOUR EXQUISITE BUSINESS IS CARED FOR?

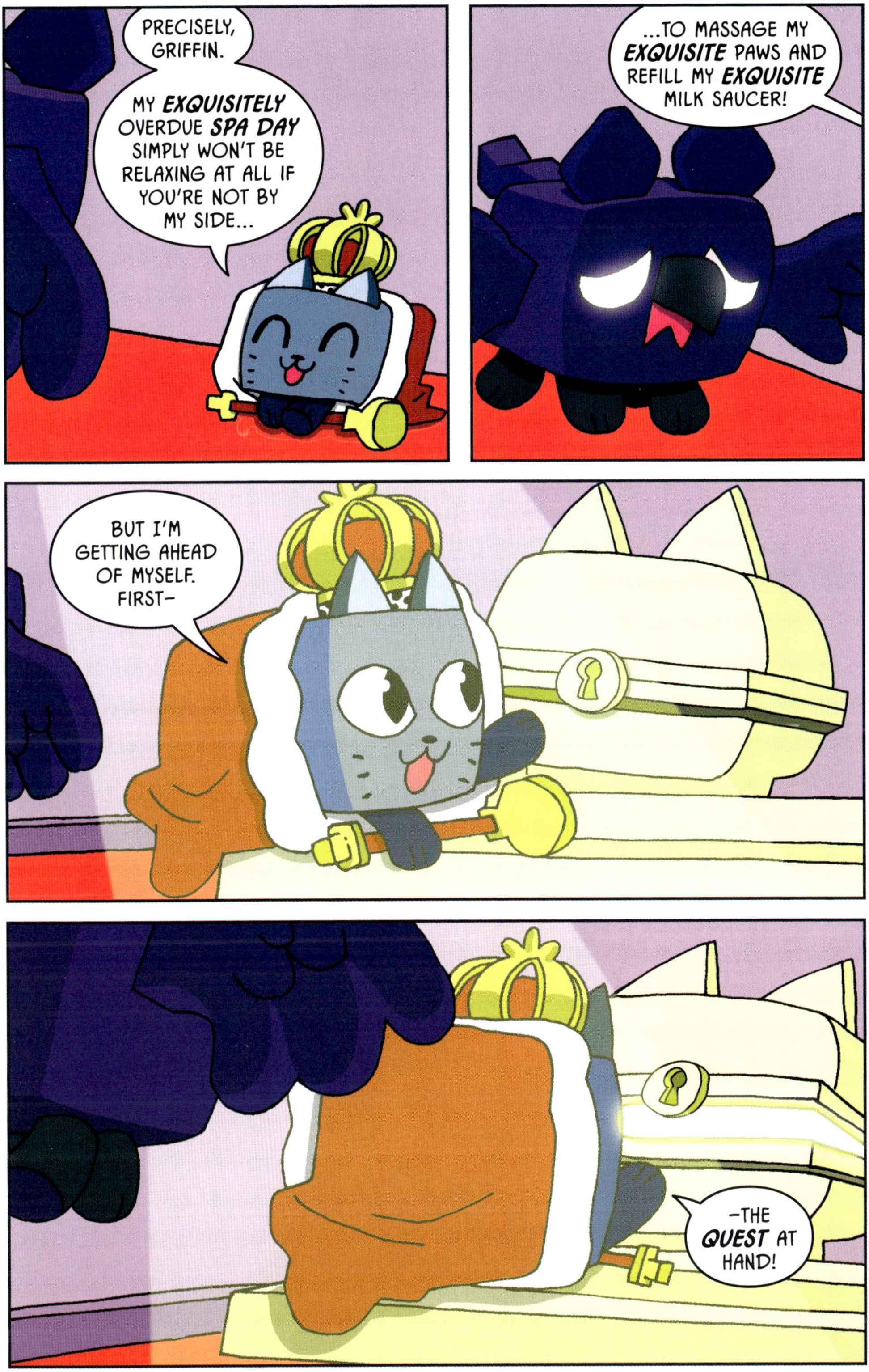
PRECISELY, GRIFFIN.
MY **EXQUISITELY** OVERDUE **SPA DAY** SIMPLY WON'T BE RELAXING AT ALL IF YOU'RE NOT BY MY SIDE...
...TO MASSAGE MY **EXQUISITE** PAWS AND REFILL MY **EXQUISITE** MILK SAUCER!
BUT I'M GETTING AHEAD OF MYSELF. FIRST–
–THE **QUEST** AT HAND!

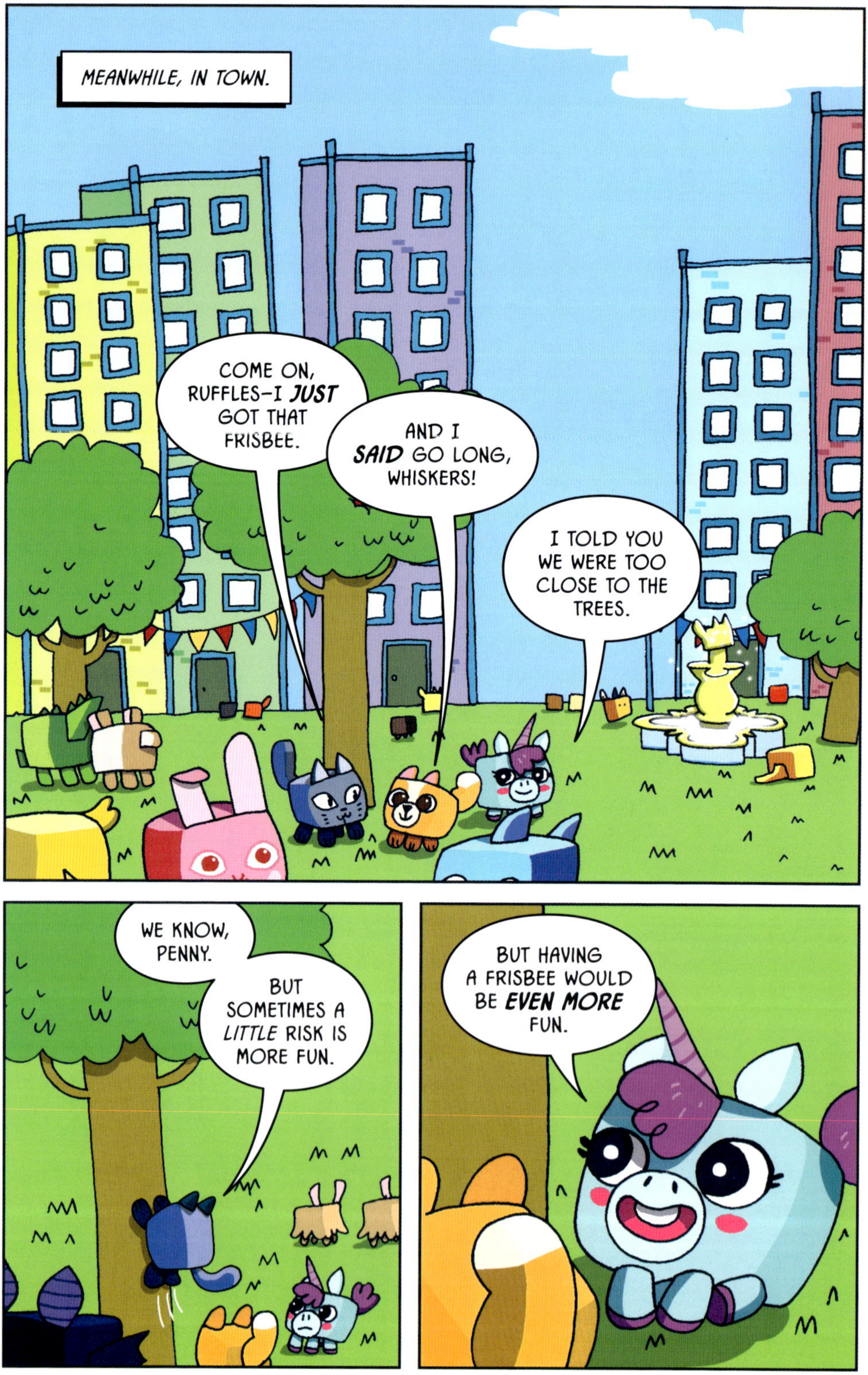
MEANWHILE, IN TOWN.
COME ON, RUFFLES—I *JUST* GOT THAT FRISBEE.
AND I *SAID* GO LONG, WHISKERS!
I TOLD YOU WE WERE TOO CLOSE TO THE TREES.
WE KNOW, PENNY.
BUT SOMETIMES A *LITTLE* RISK IS MORE FUN.
BUT HAVING A FRISBEE WOULD BE ***EVEN MORE*** FUN.

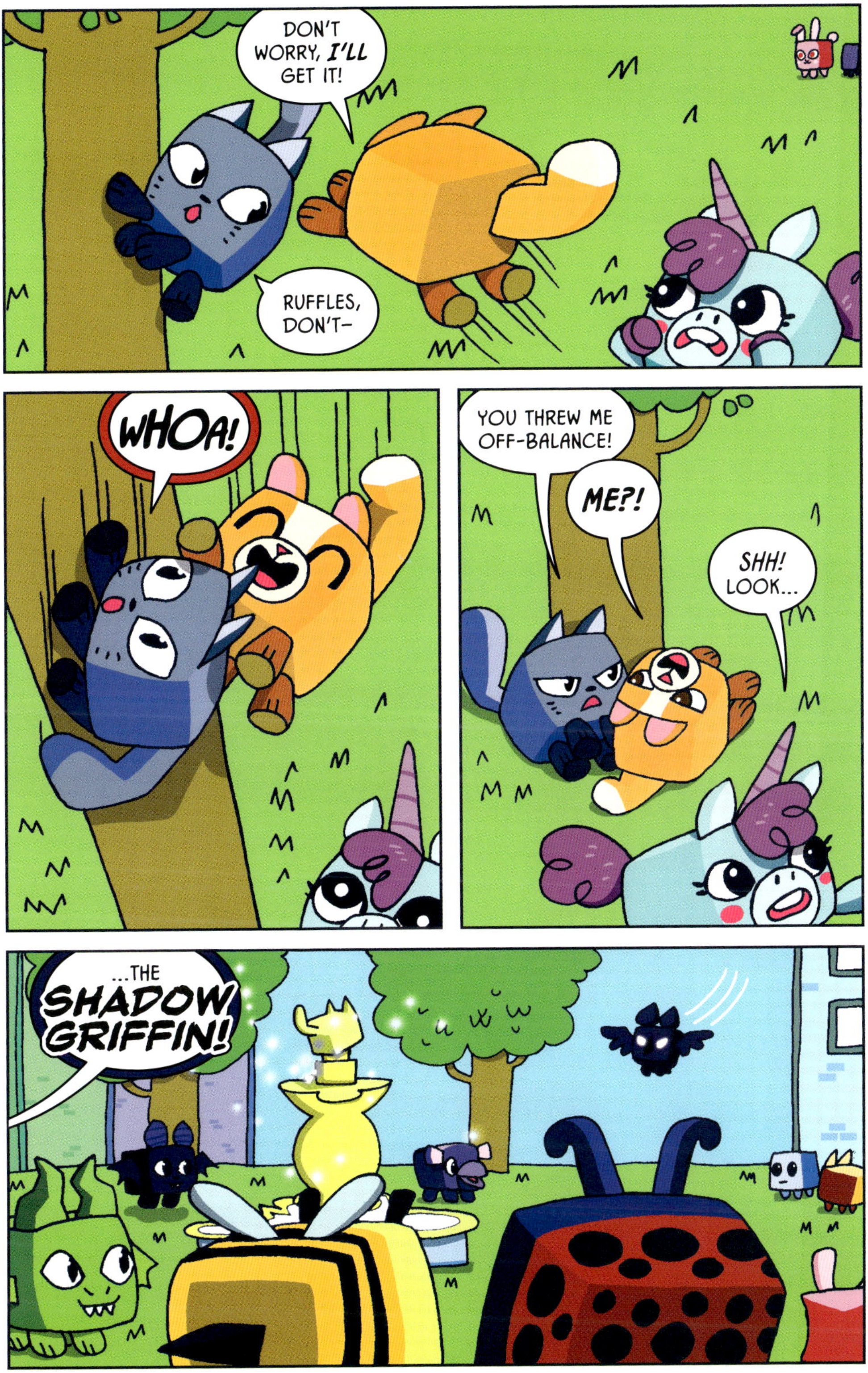
DON'T WORRY, *I'LL* GET IT!
RUFFLES, DON'T-
WHOA!
YOU THREW ME OFF-BALANCE!
ME?!
SHH! LOOK...
...THE SHADOW GRIFFIN!

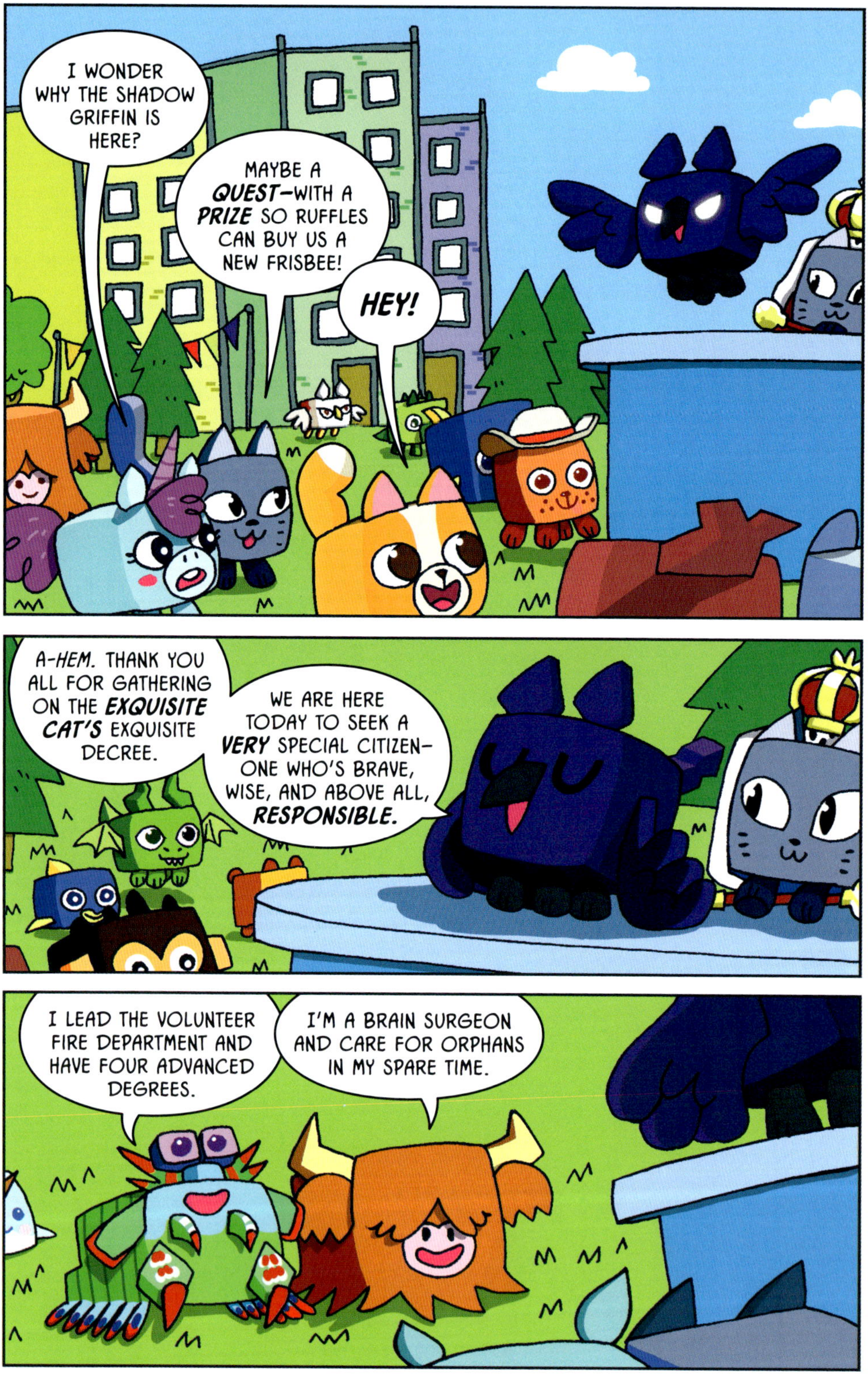

I WONDER WHY THE SHADOW GRIFFIN IS HERE?
MAYBE A QUEST—WITH A PRIZE SO RUFFLES CAN BUY US A NEW FRISBEE!
HEY!
A-HEM. THANK YOU ALL FOR GATHERING ON THE EXQUISITE CAT'S EXQUISITE DECREE.
WE ARE HERE TODAY TO SEEK A VERY SPECIAL CITIZEN—ONE WHO'S BRAVE, WISE, AND ABOVE ALL, RESPONSIBLE.
I LEAD THE VOLUNTEER FIRE DEPARTMENT AND HAVE FOUR ADVANCED DEGREES.
I'M A BRAIN SURGEON AND CARE FOR ORPHANS IN MY SPARE TIME.

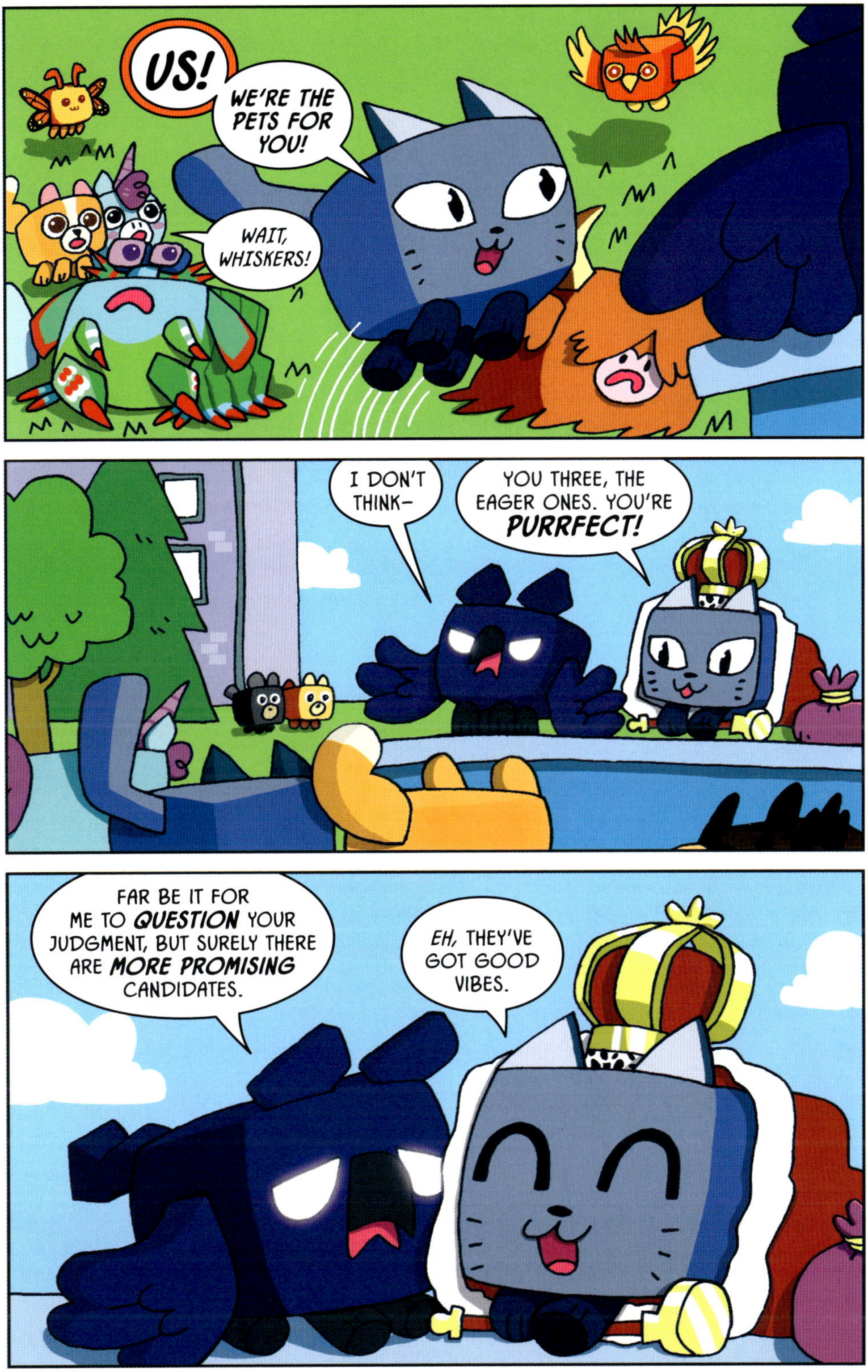
US!
WE'RE THE PETS FOR YOU!
WAIT, WHISKERS!
I DON'T THINK–
YOU THREE, THE EAGER ONES. YOU'RE PURRFECT!
FAR BE IT FOR ME TO QUESTION YOUR JUDGMENT, BUT SURELY THERE ARE MORE PROMISING CANDIDATES.
EH, THEY'VE GOT GOOD VIBES.

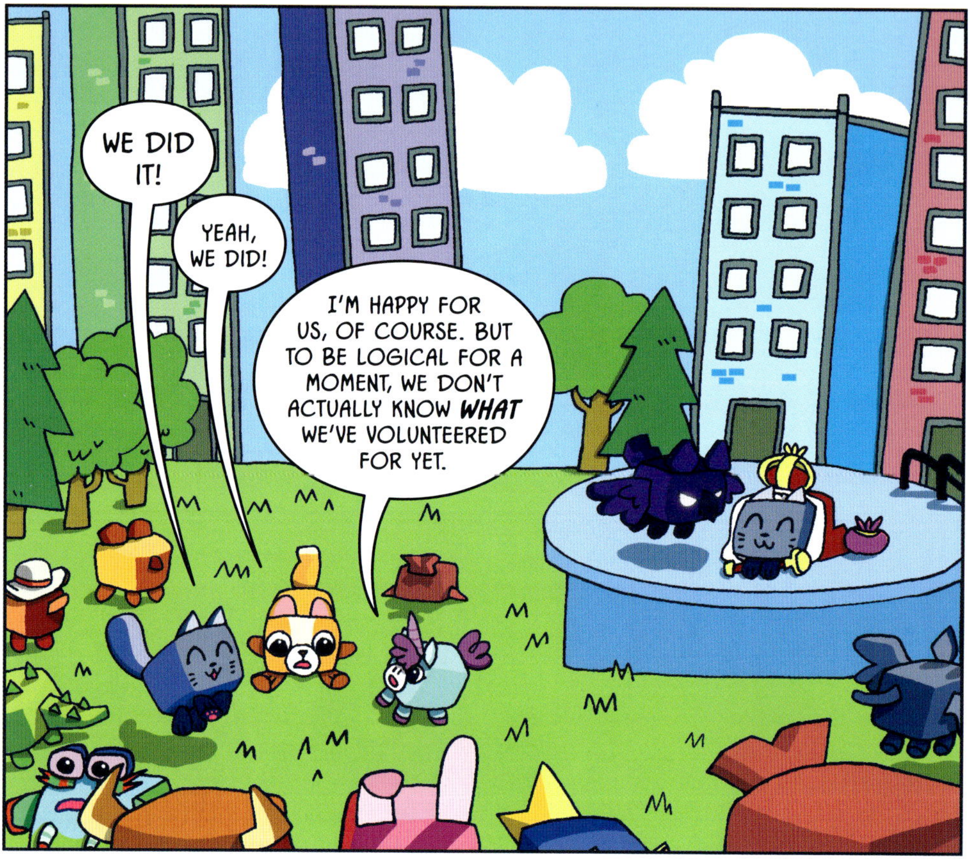
WE DID IT!
YEAH, WE DID!
I'M HAPPY FOR US, OF COURSE. BUT TO BE LOGICAL FOR A MOMENT, WE DON'T ACTUALLY KNOW WHAT WE'VE VOLUNTEERED FOR YET.

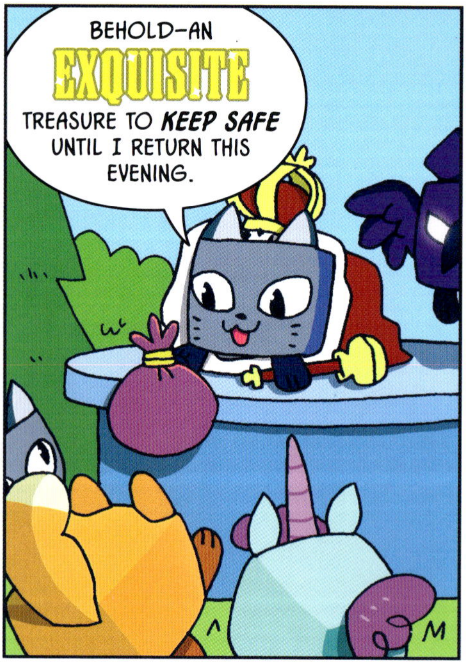
BEHOLD—AN EXQUISITE TREASURE TO KEEP SAFE UNTIL I RETURN THIS EVENING.

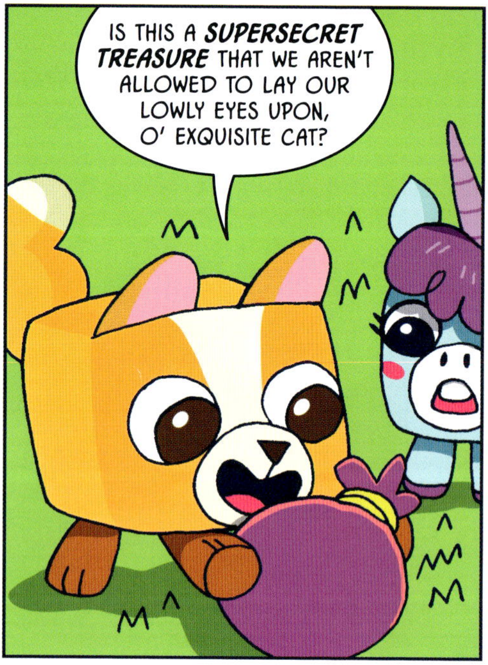
IS THIS A SUPERSECRET TREASURE THAT WE AREN'T ALLOWED TO LAY OUR LOWLY EYES UPON, O' EXQUISITE CAT?

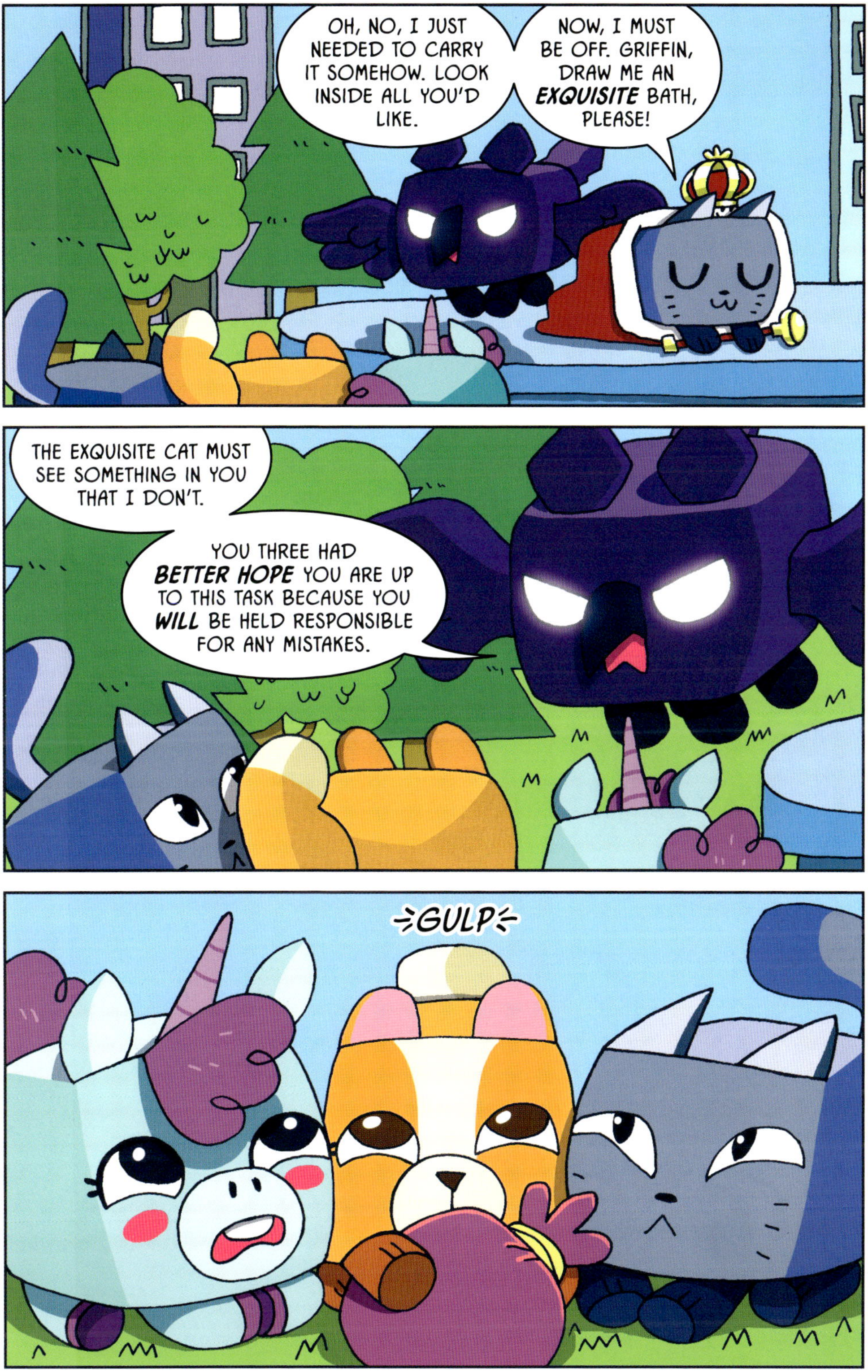
OH, NO, I JUST NEEDED TO CARRY IT SOMEHOW. LOOK INSIDE ALL YOU'D LIKE.
NOW, I MUST BE OFF. GRIFFIN, DRAW ME AN ***EXQUISITE*** BATH, PLEASE!
THE EXQUISITE CAT MUST SEE SOMETHING IN YOU THAT I DON'T.
YOU THREE HAD ***BETTER HOPE*** YOU ARE UP TO THIS TASK BECAUSE YOU ***WILL*** BE HELD RESPONSIBLE FOR ANY MISTAKES.
GULP

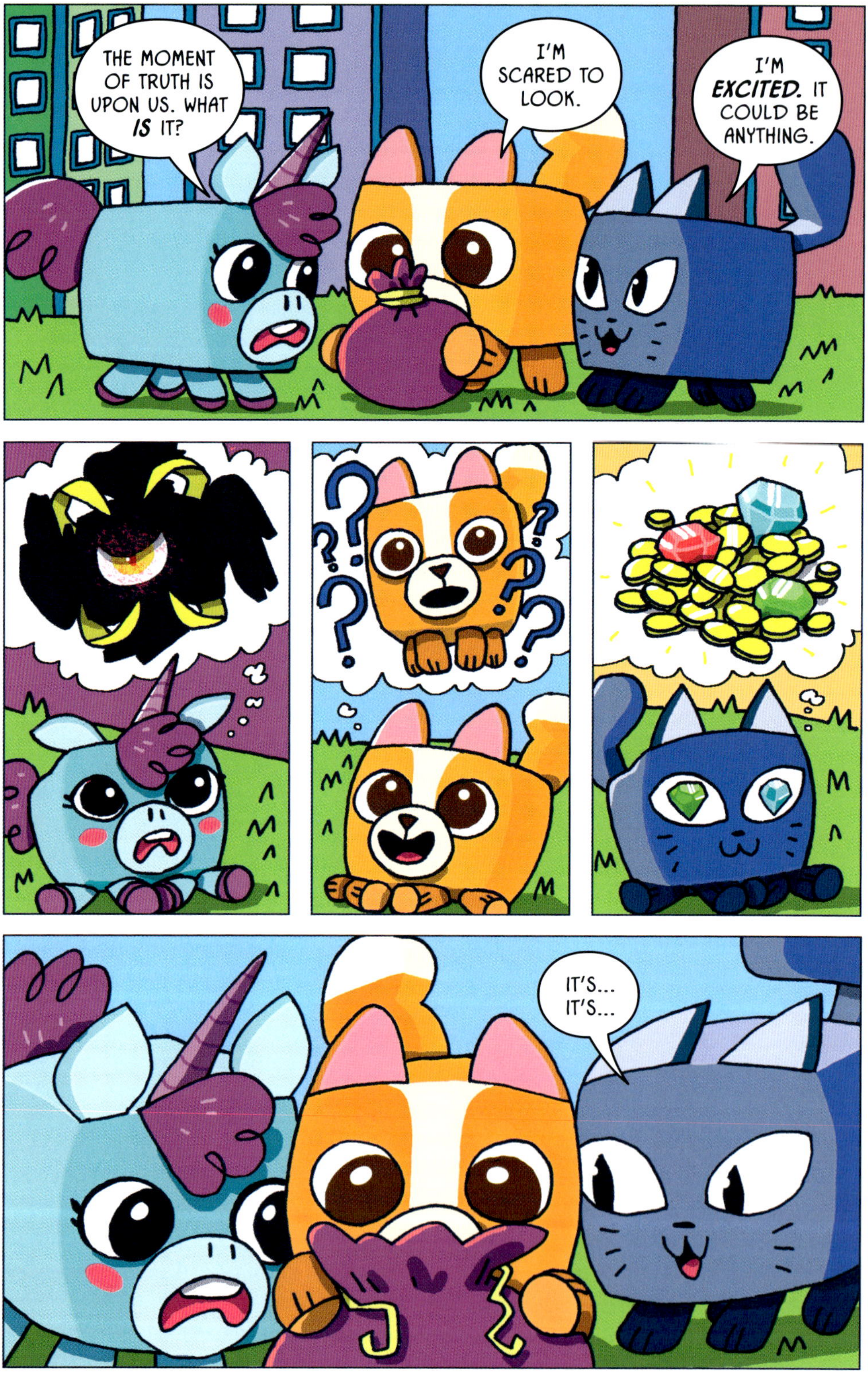
THE MOMENT OF TRUTH IS UPON US. WHAT *IS* IT?
I'M SCARED TO LOOK.
I'M ***EXCITED.*** IT COULD BE ANYTHING.
IT'S... IT'S...

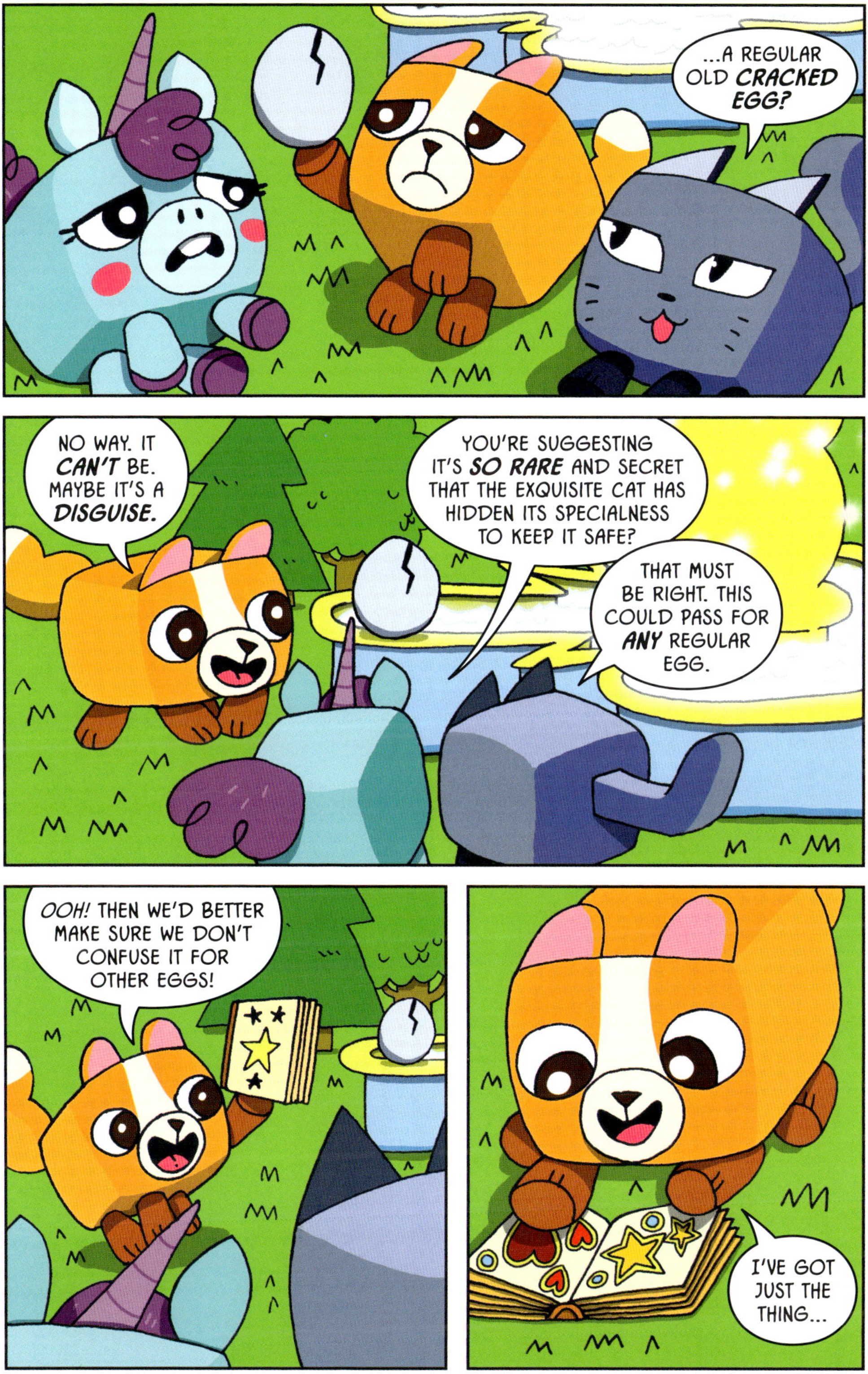
...A REGULAR OLD **CRACKED EGG?**
NO WAY. IT **CAN'T** BE. MAYBE IT'S A **DISGUISE.**
YOU'RE SUGGESTING IT'S **SO RARE** AND SECRET THAT THE EXQUISITE CAT HAS HIDDEN ITS SPECIALNESS TO KEEP IT SAFE?
THAT MUST BE RIGHT. THIS COULD PASS FOR **ANY** REGULAR EGG.
OOH! THEN WE'D BETTER MAKE SURE WE DON'T CONFUSE IT FOR OTHER EGGS!
I'VE GOT JUST THE THING...

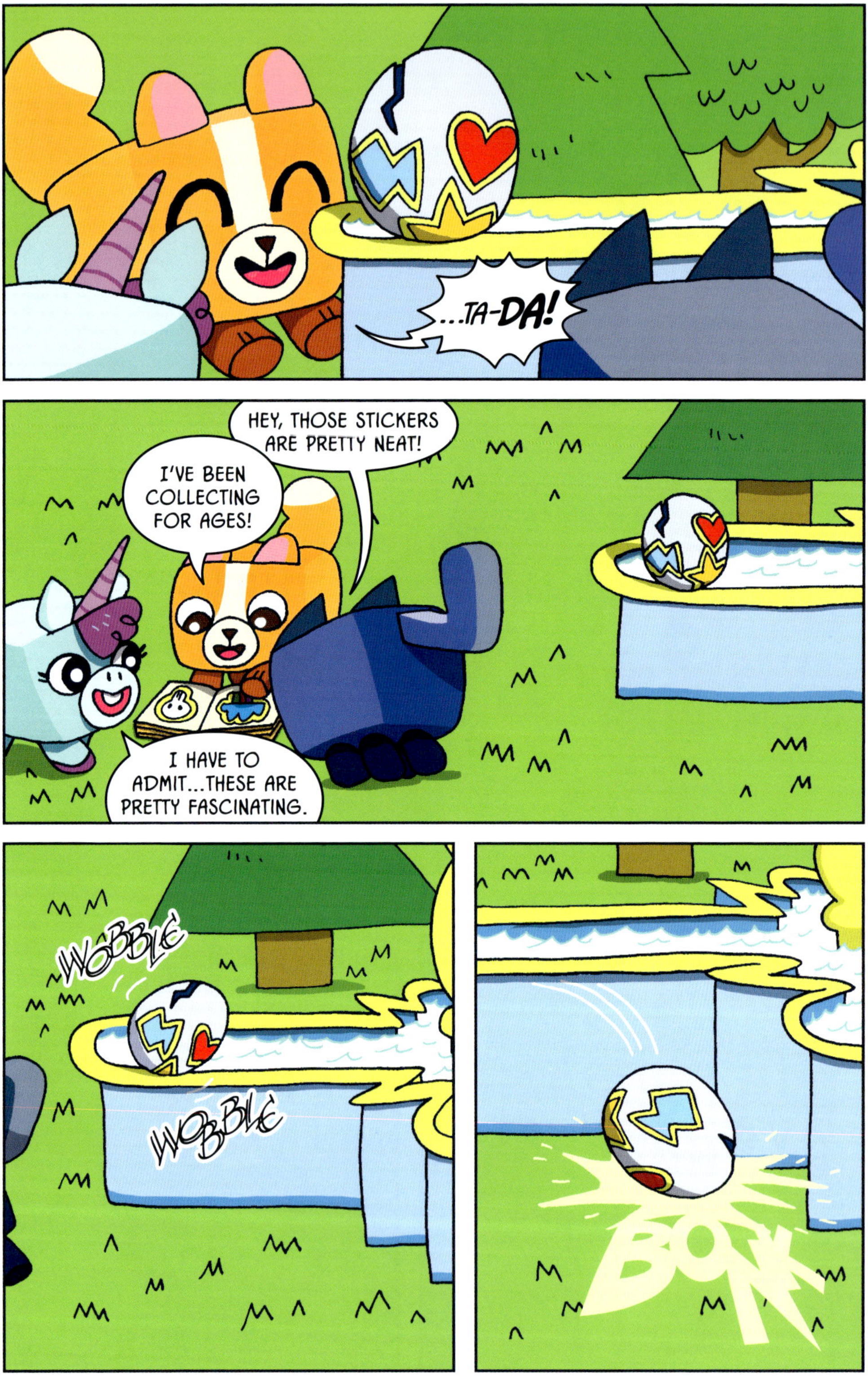
...TA-DA!
HEY, THOSE STICKERS ARE PRETTY NEAT!
I'VE BEEN COLLECTING FOR AGES!
I HAVE TO ADMIT...THESE ARE PRETTY FASCINATING.
WOBBLE
WOBBLE
BOK

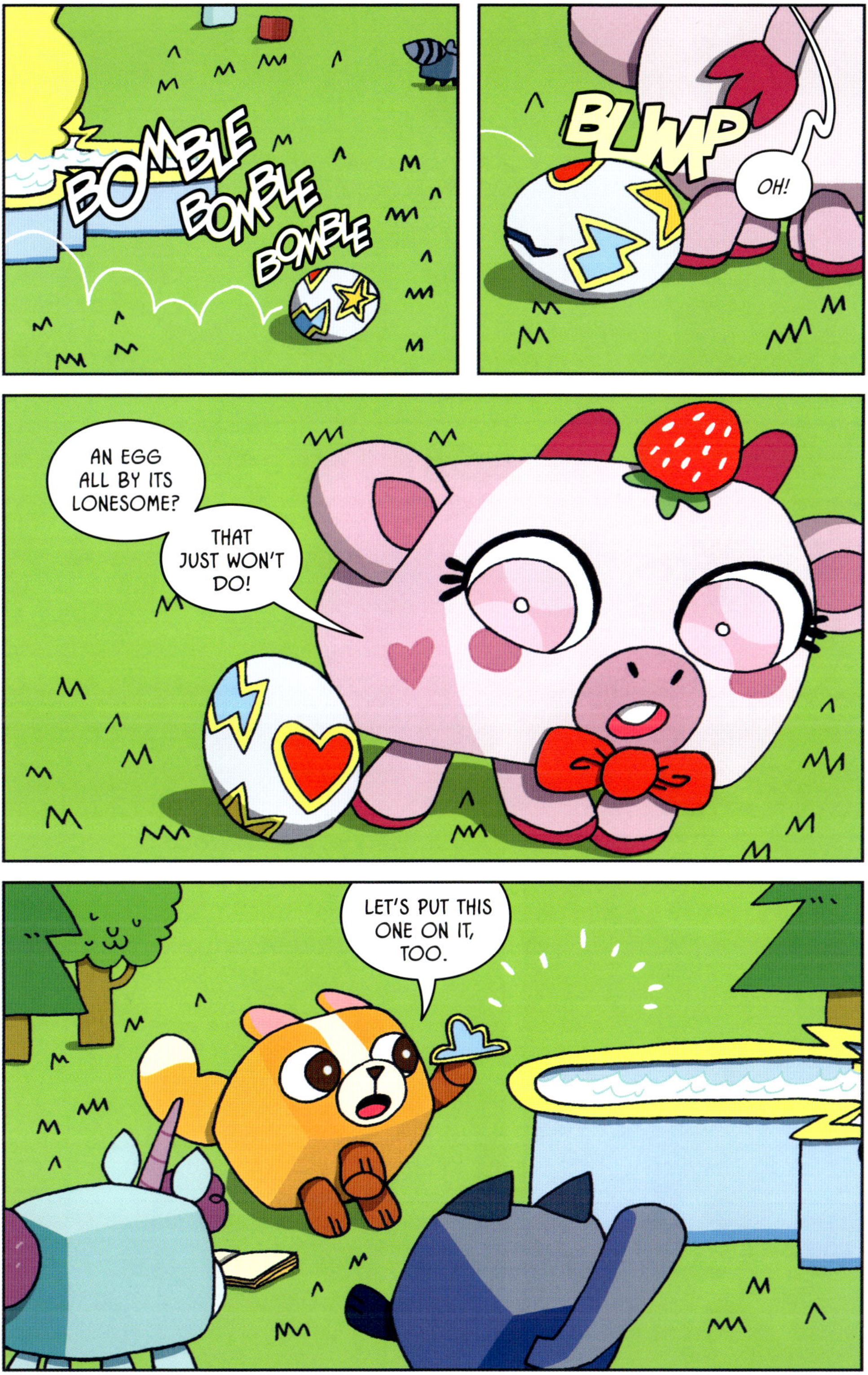
BOMBLE
BOMBLE
BOMBLE
BUMP
OH!
AN EGG ALL BY ITS LONESOME?
THAT JUST WON'T DO!
LET'S PUT THIS ONE ON IT, TOO.

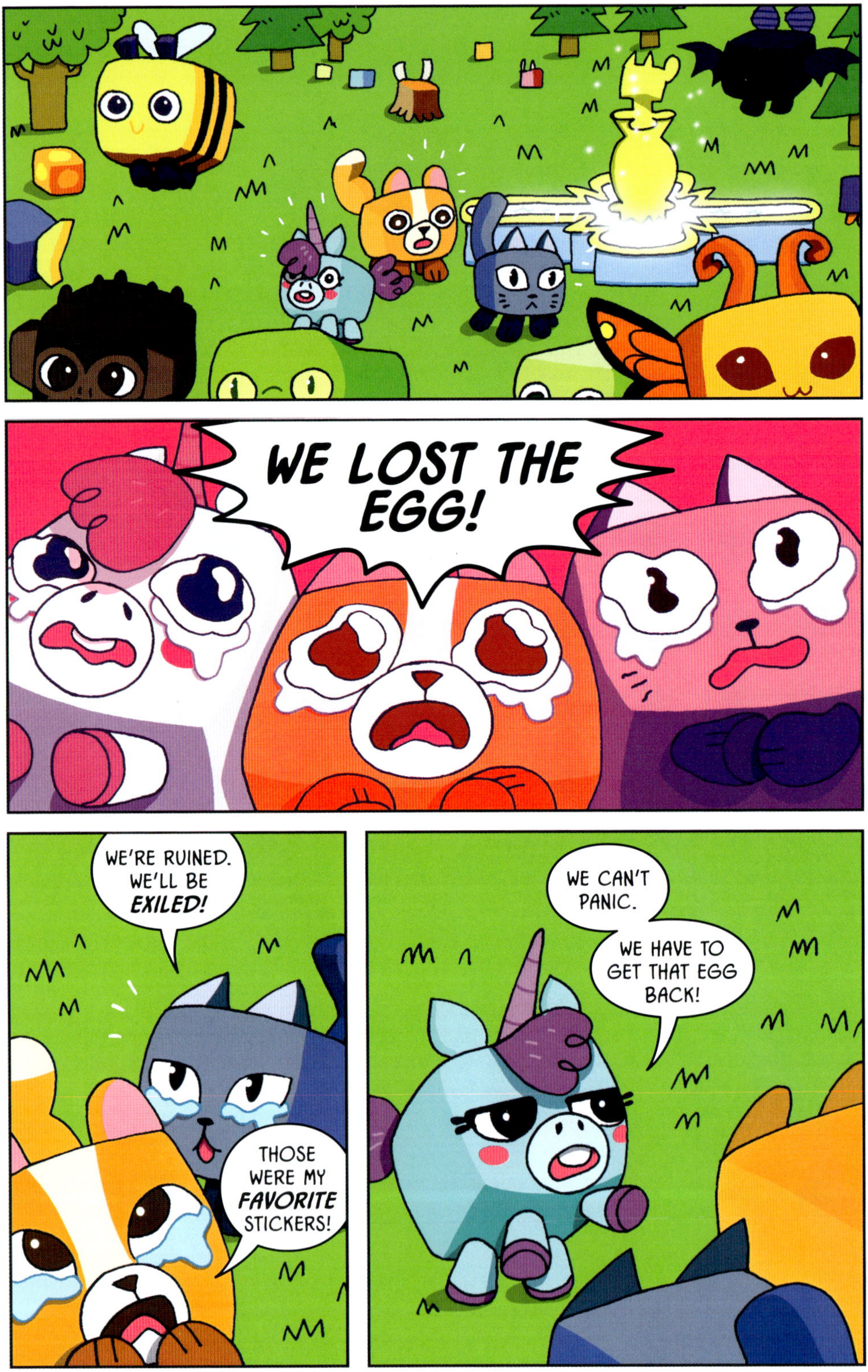
WE LOST THE EGG!
WE'RE RUINED. WE'LL BE *EXILED!*
THOSE WERE MY *FAVORITE* STICKERS!
WE CAN'T PANIC.
WE HAVE TO GET THAT EGG BACK!

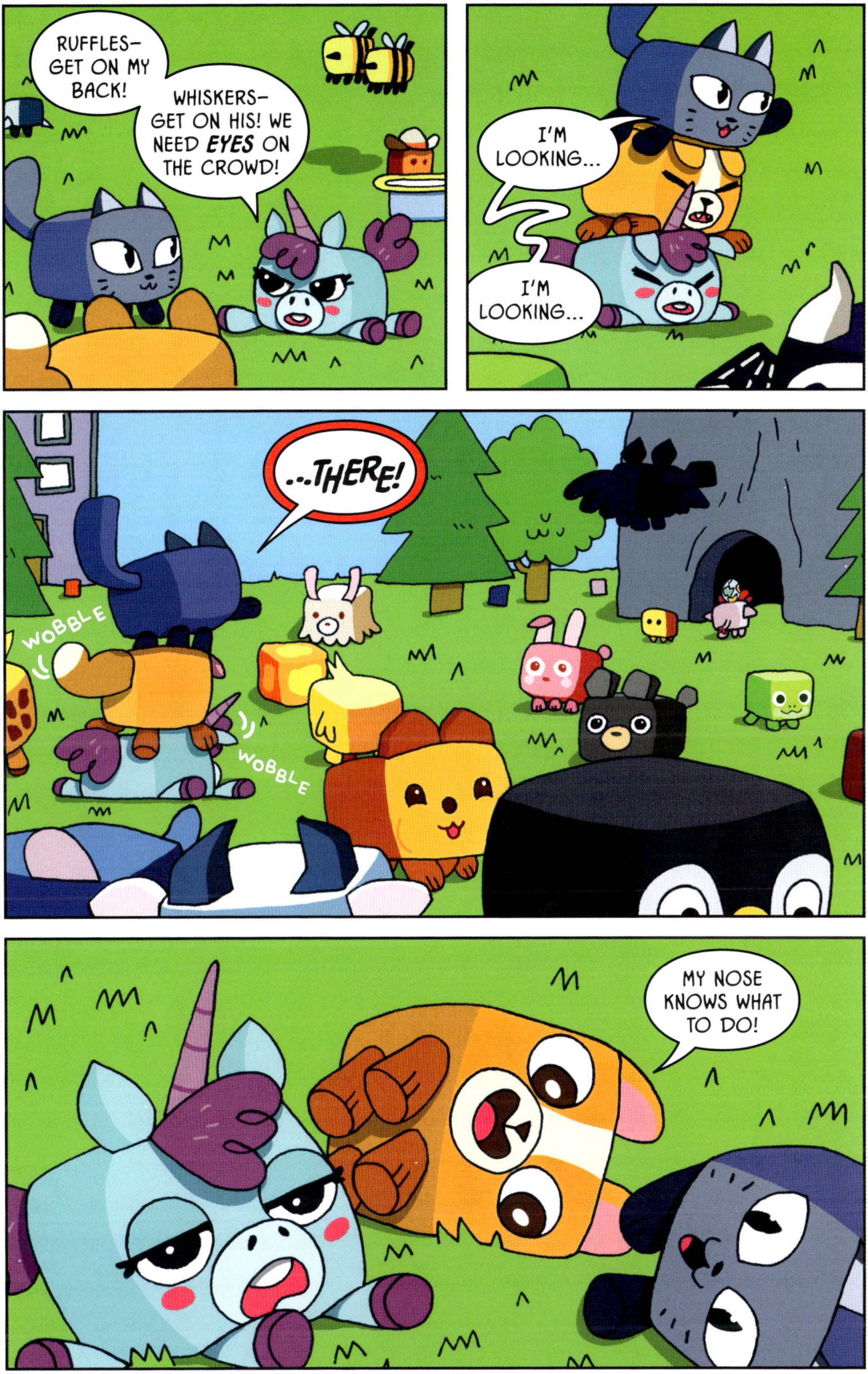
RUFFLES—GET ON MY BACK!
WHISKERS—GET ON HIS! WE NEED ***EYES*** ON THE CROWD!
I'M LOOKING...
I'M LOOKING...
...THERE!
WOBBLE
WOBBLE
MY NOSE KNOWS WHAT TO DO!

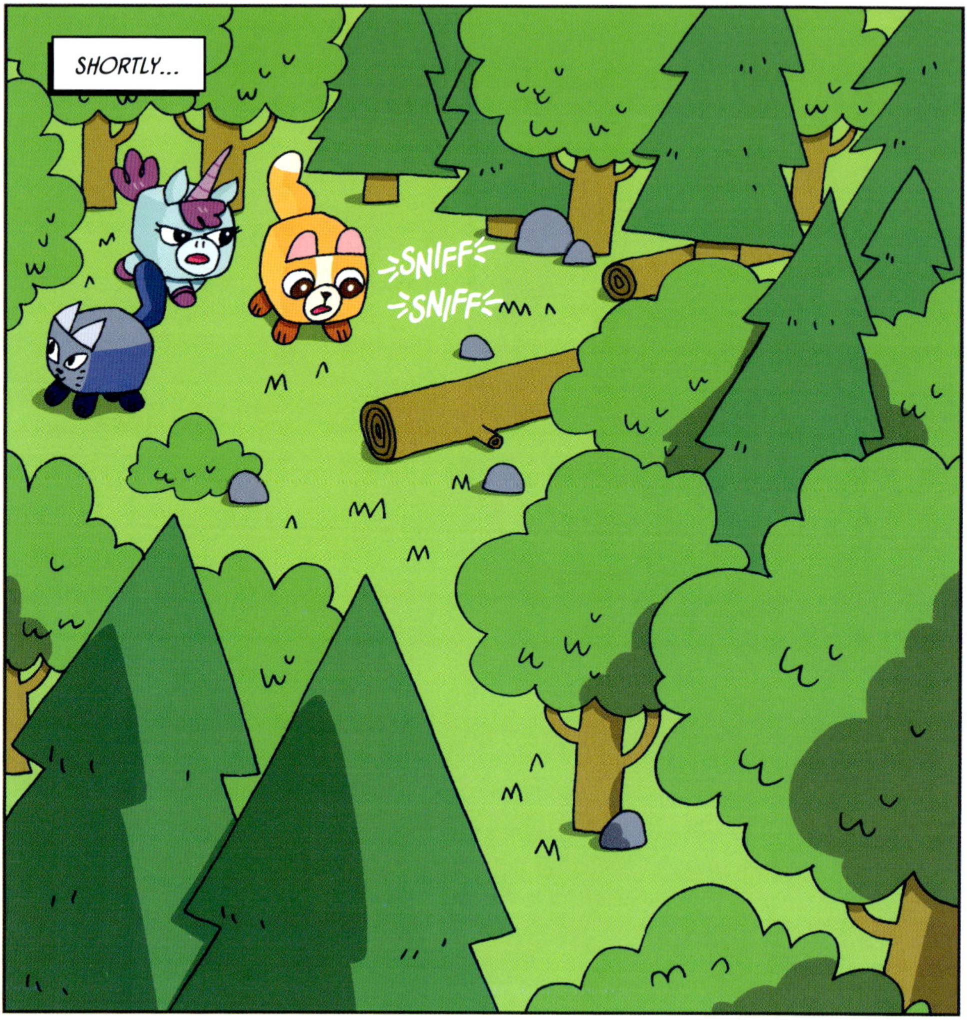
SHORTLY...
SNIFF
SNIFF

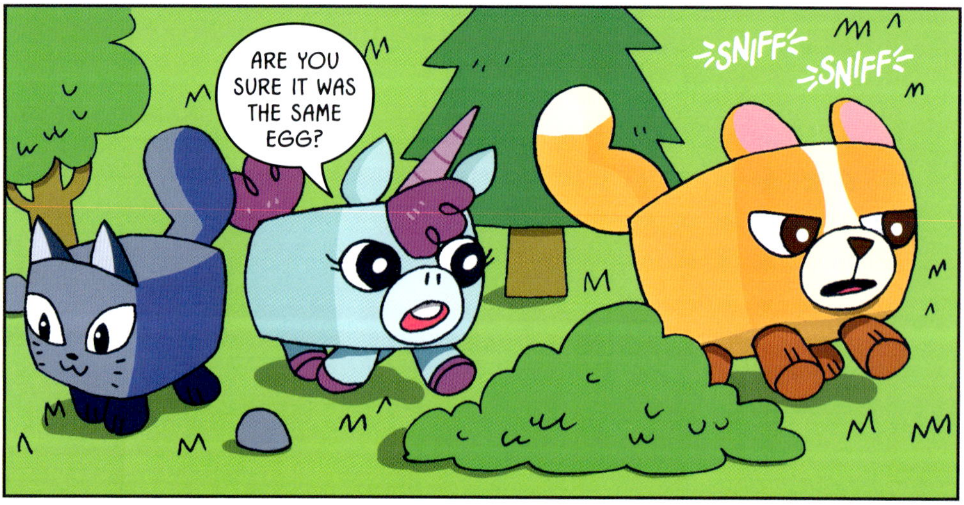
ARE YOU SURE IT WAS THE SAME EGG?
SNIFF
SNIFF

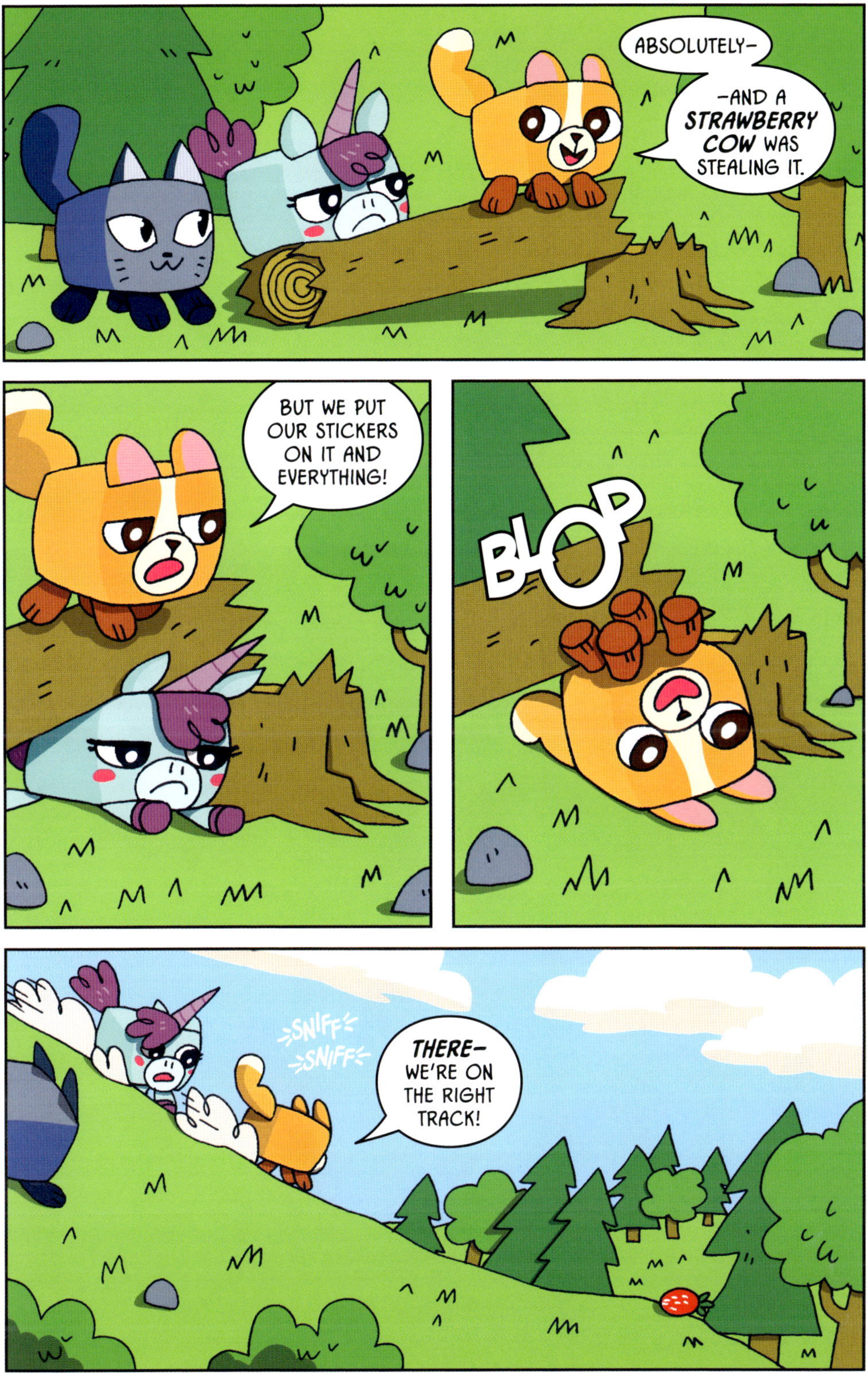
ABSOLUTELY-
-AND A STRAWBERRY COW WAS STEALING IT.
BUT WE PUT OUR STICKERS ON IT AND EVERYTHING!
BLOP
SNIFF
SNIFF
THERE- WE'RE ON THE RIGHT TRACK!

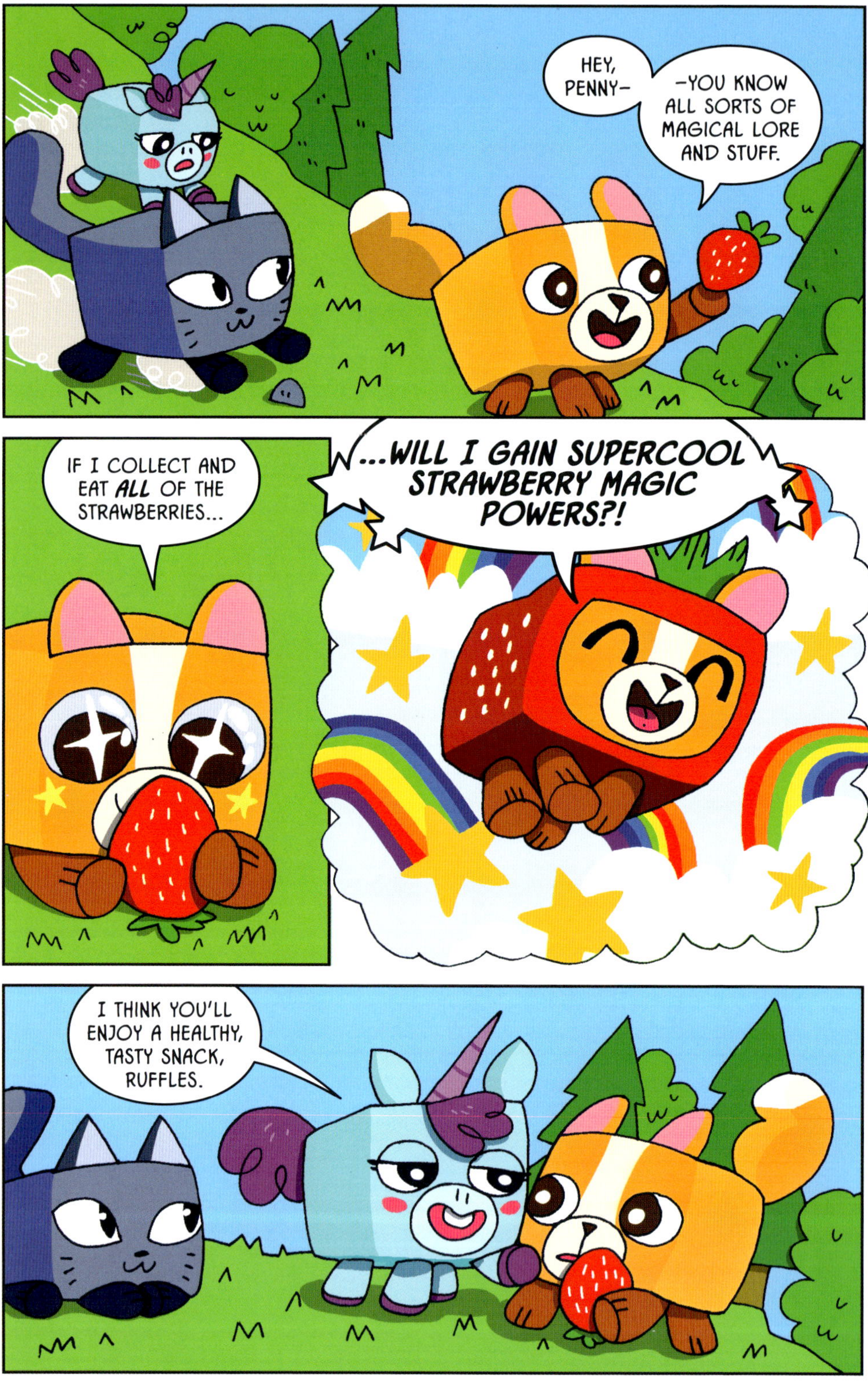
HEY, PENNY—
—YOU KNOW ALL SORTS OF MAGICAL LORE AND STUFF.
IF I COLLECT AND EAT ALL OF THE STRAWBERRIES...
...WILL I GAIN SUPERCOOL STRAWBERRY MAGIC POWERS?!
I THINK YOU'LL ENJOY A HEALTHY, TASTY SNACK, RUFFLES.

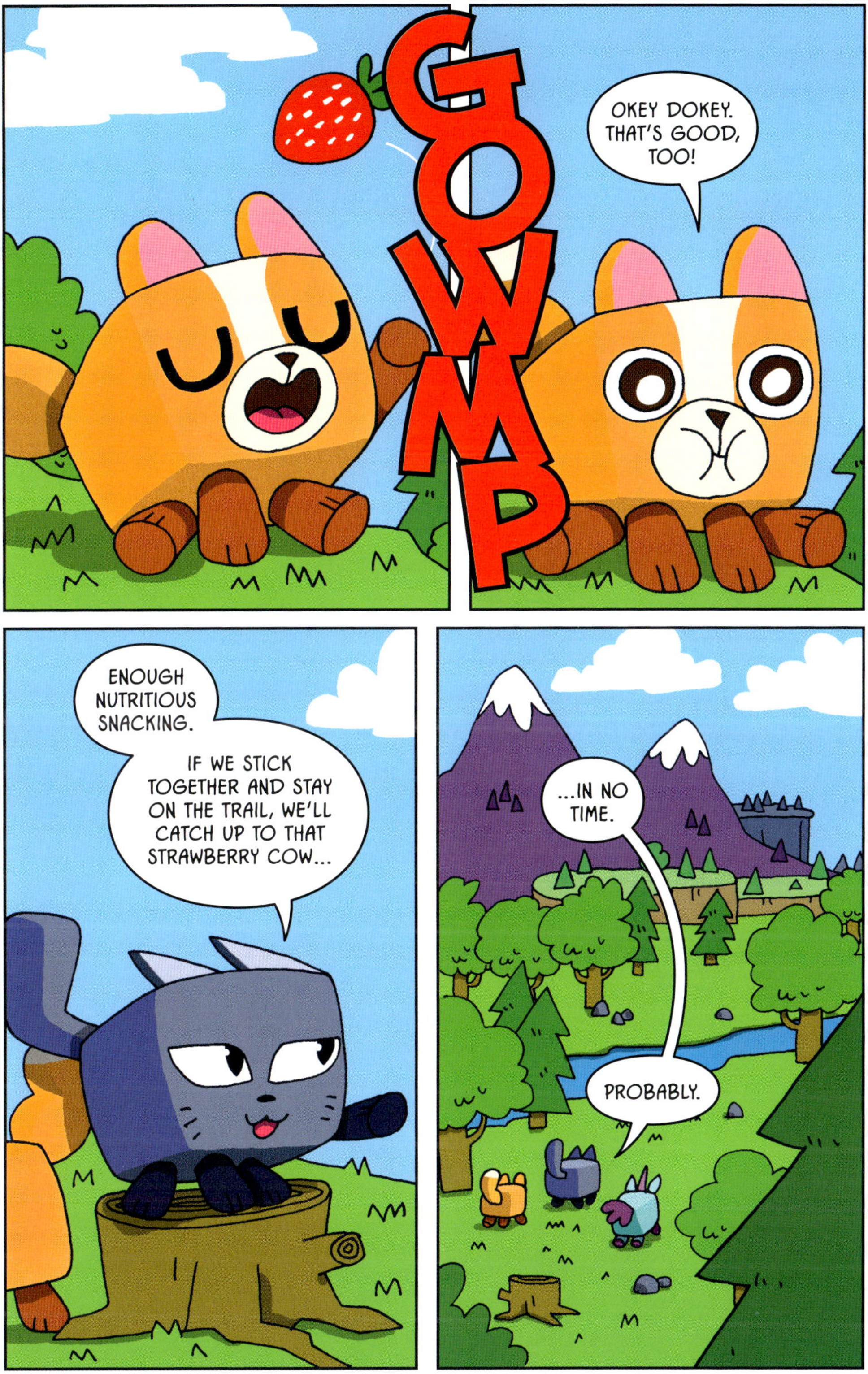
GOWMP
OKEY DOKEY. THAT'S GOOD, TOO!
ENOUGH NUTRITIOUS SNACKING.
IF WE STICK TOGETHER AND STAY ON THE TRAIL, WE'LL CATCH UP TO THAT STRAWBERRY COW...
...IN NO TIME.
PROBABLY.

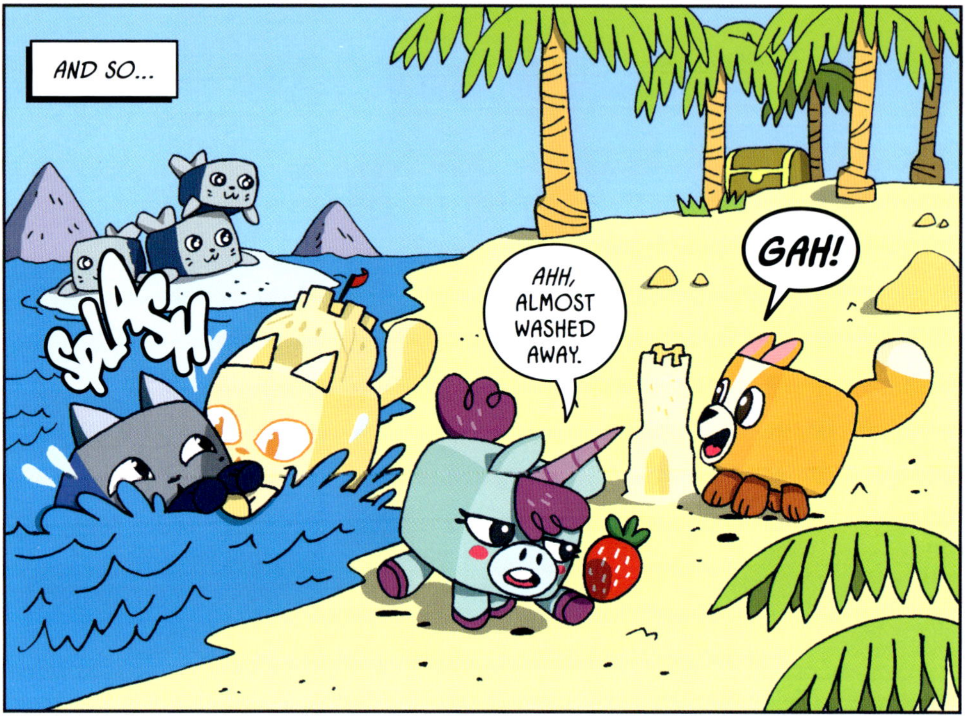
AND SO...
SPLASH
AHH, ALMOST WASHED AWAY.
GAH!

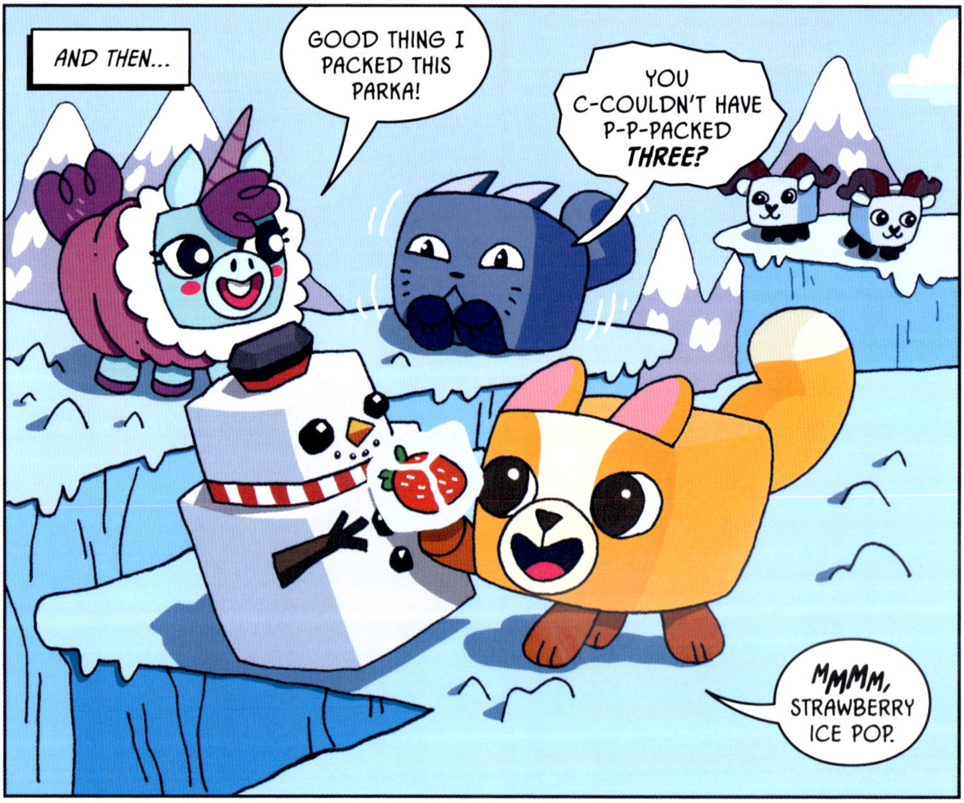
AND THEN...
GOOD THING I PACKED THIS PARKA!
YOU C-COULDN'T HAVE P-P-PACKED THREE?
MMMM, STRAWBERRY ICE POP.

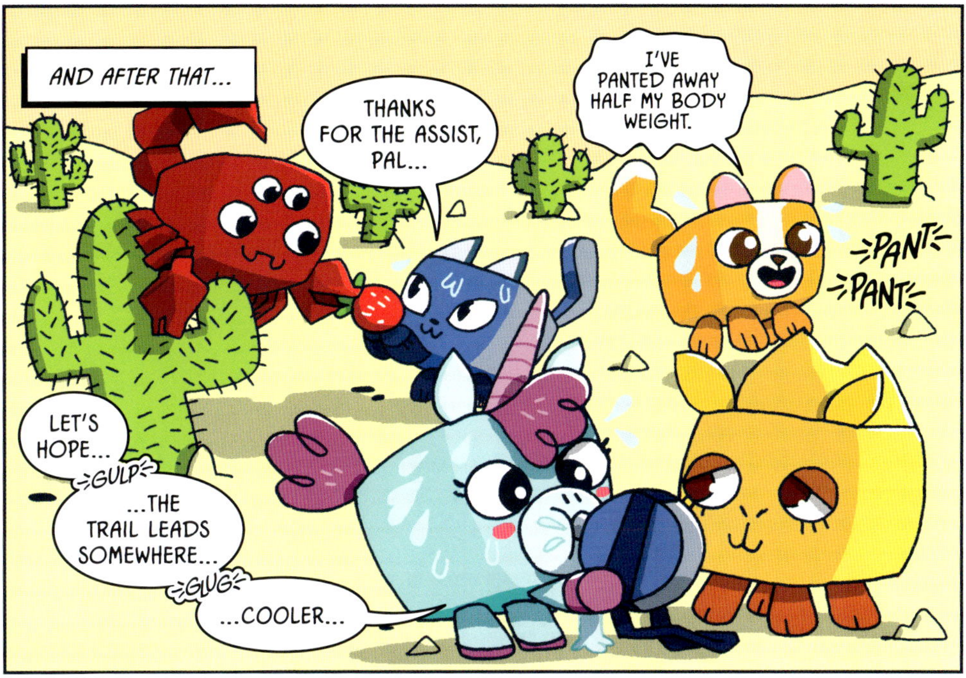
AND AFTER THAT...
THANKS FOR THE ASSIST, PAL...
I'VE PANTED AWAY HALF MY BODY WEIGHT.
PANT
PANT
LET'S HOPE...
GULP
...THE TRAIL LEADS SOMEWHERE...
GLUG
...COOLER...

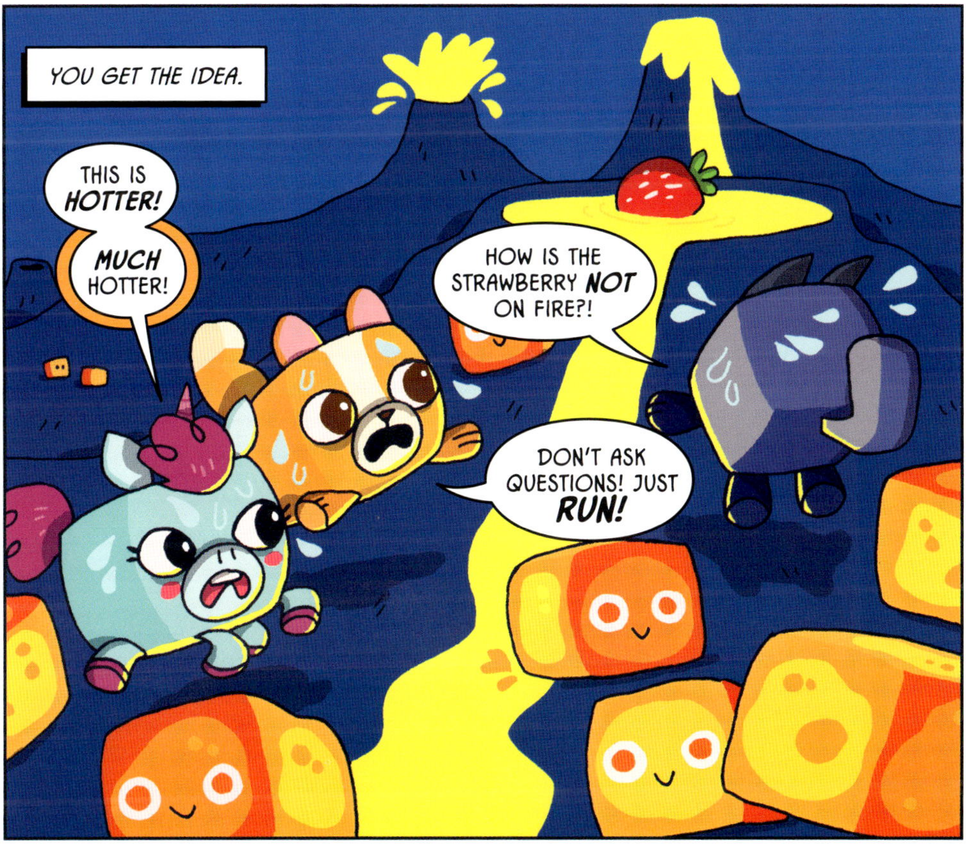
YOU GET THE IDEA.
THIS IS HOTTER!
MUCH HOTTER!
HOW IS THE STRAWBERRY NOT ON FIRE?!
DON'T ASK QUESTIONS! JUST RUN!

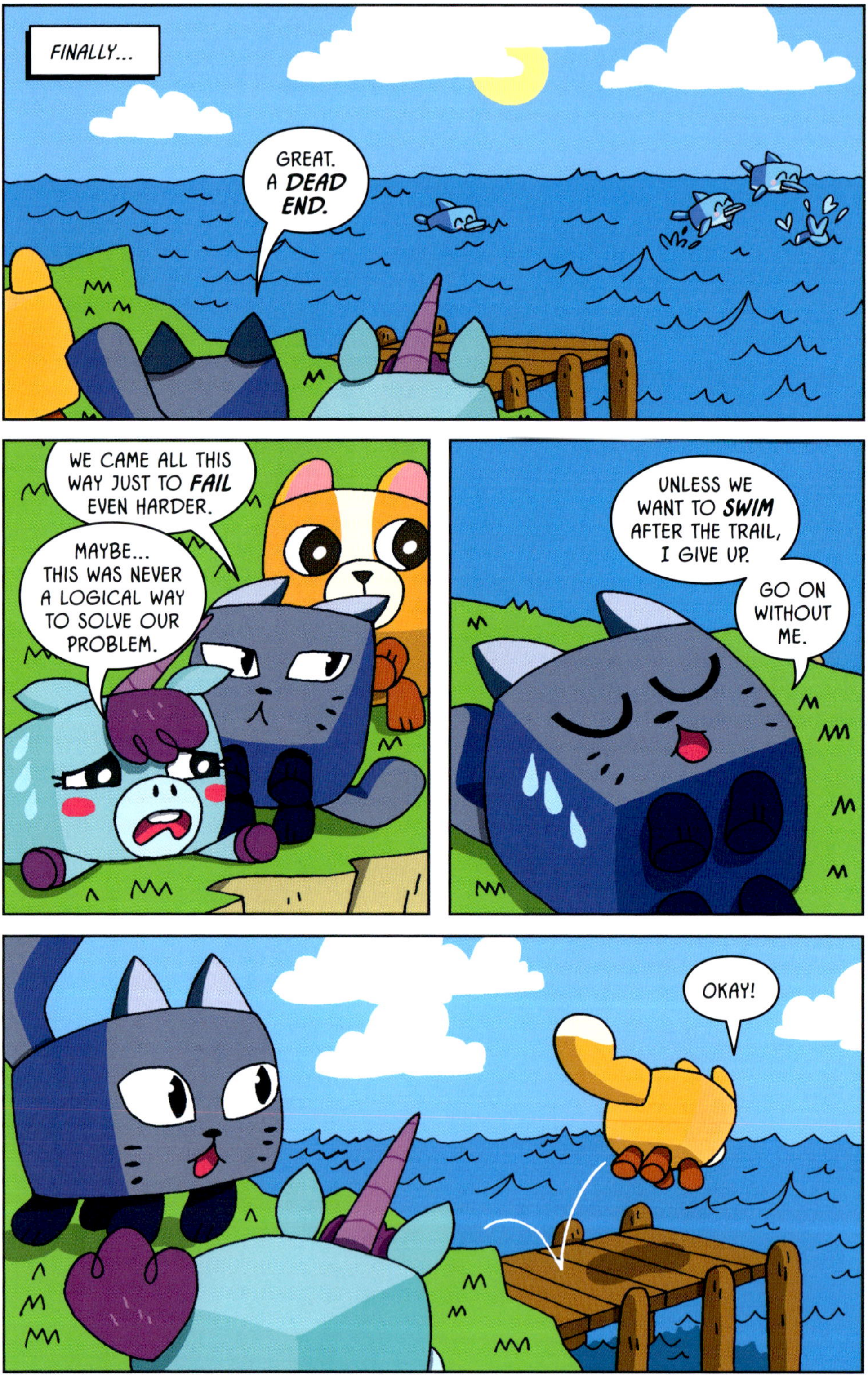
FINALLY...
GREAT. A DEAD END.
WE CAME ALL THIS WAY JUST TO FAIL EVEN HARDER.
MAYBE... THIS WAS NEVER A LOGICAL WAY TO SOLVE OUR PROBLEM.
UNLESS WE WANT TO SWIM AFTER THE TRAIL, I GIVE UP.
GO ON WITHOUT ME.
OKAY!

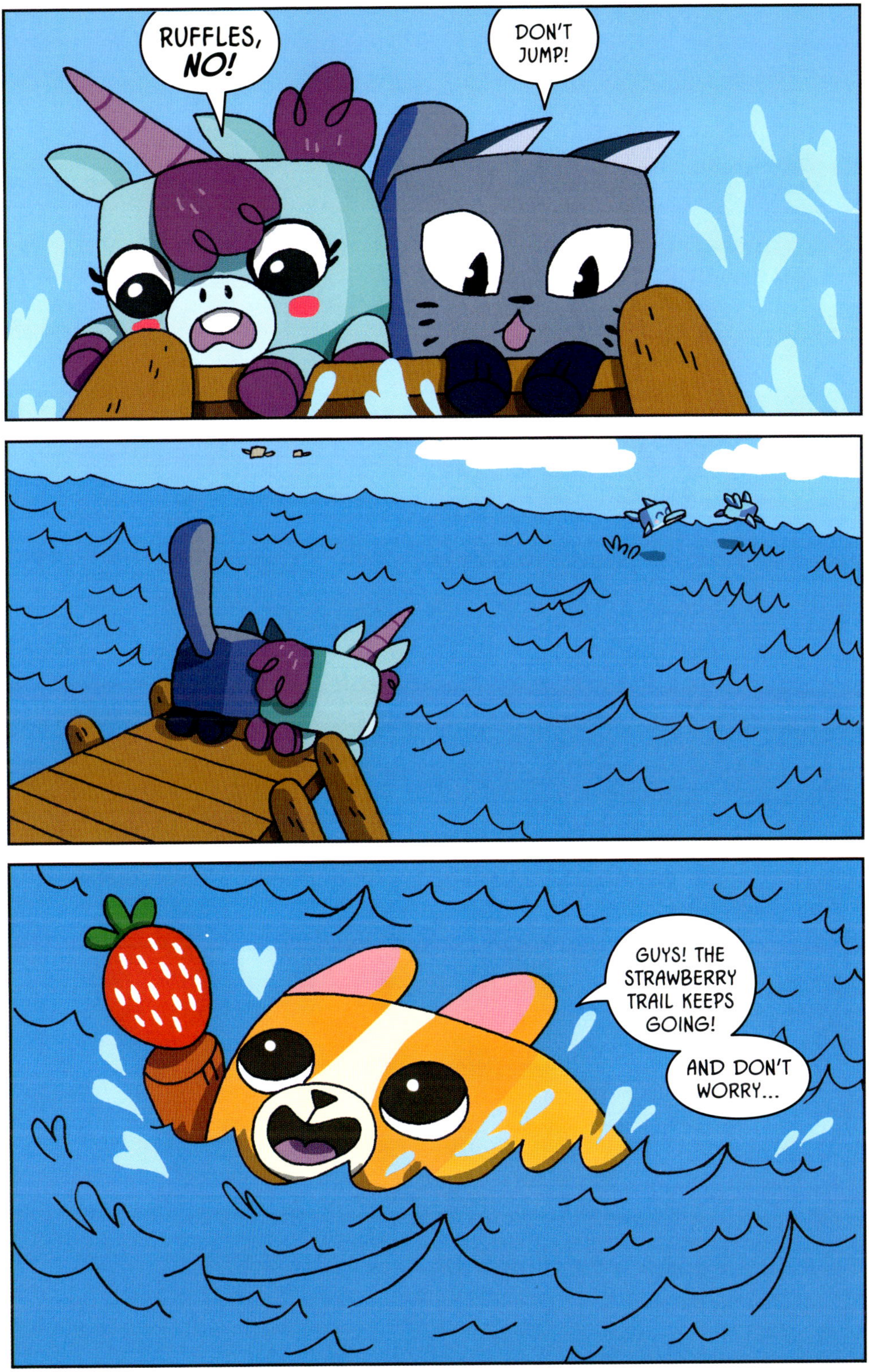
RUFFLES, NO!
DON'T JUMP!
GUYS! THE STRAWBERRY TRAIL KEEPS GOING!
AND DON'T WORRY...

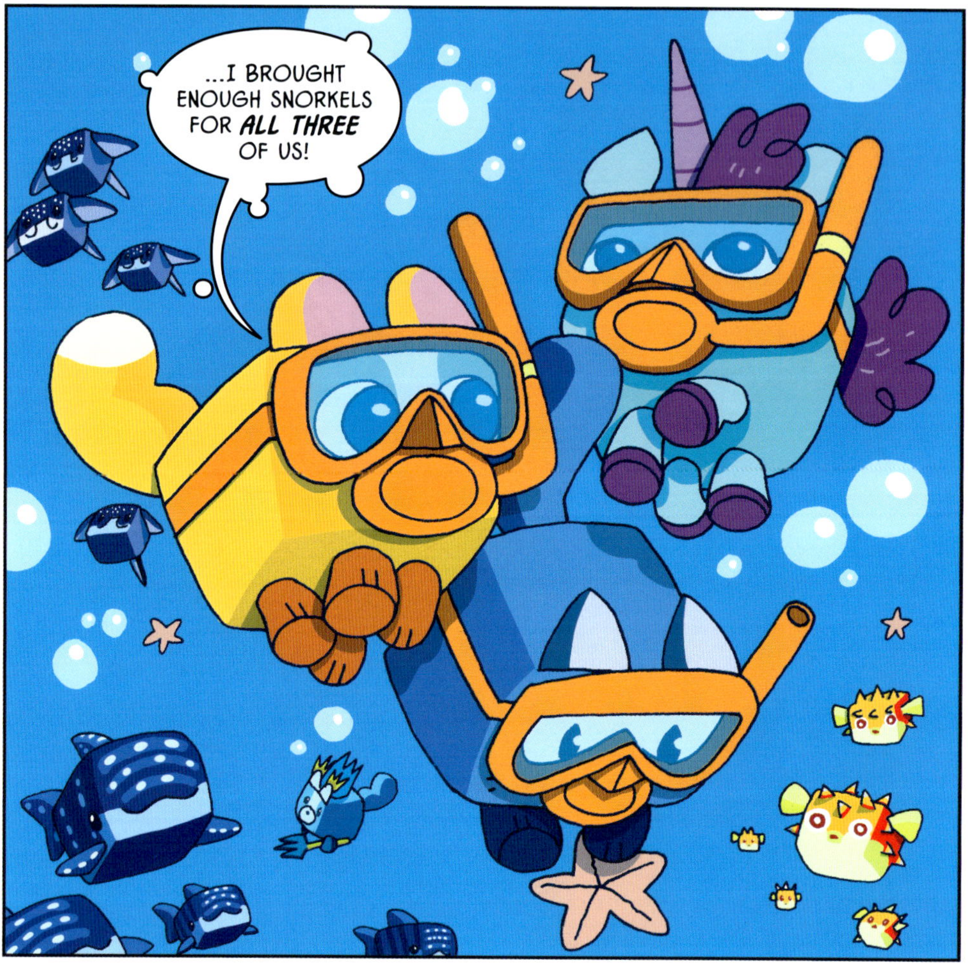
...I BROUGHT ENOUGH SNORKELS FOR ALL THREE OF US!

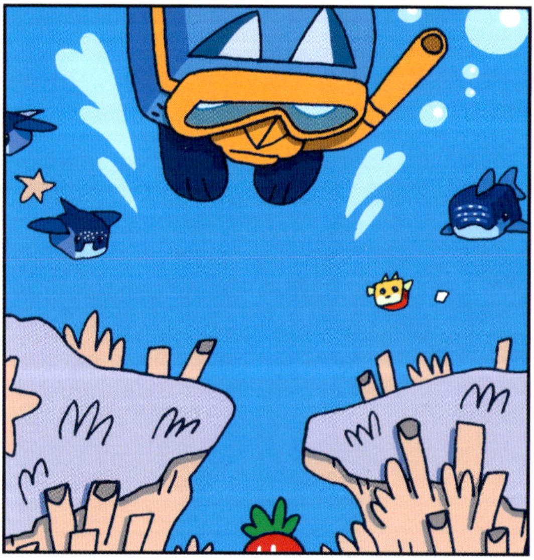

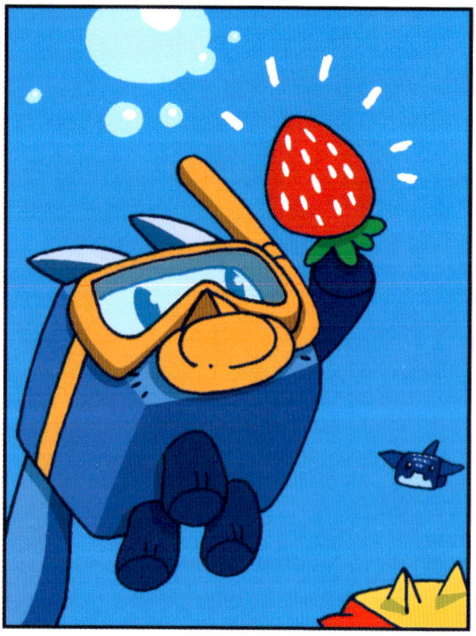

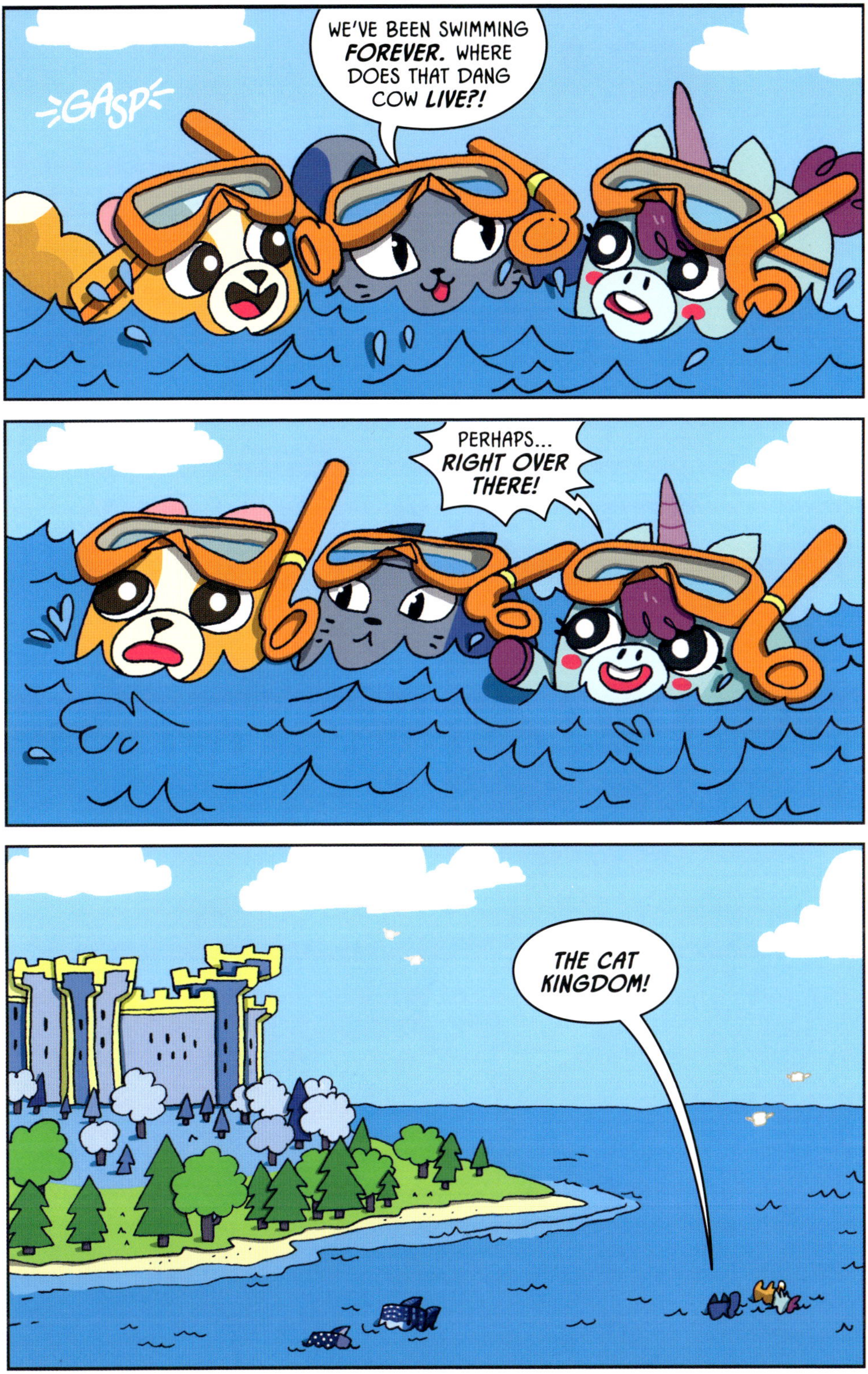
GASP
WE'VE BEEN SWIMMING FOREVER. WHERE DOES THAT DANG COW LIVE?!
PERHAPS... RIGHT OVER THERE!
THE CAT KINGDOM!

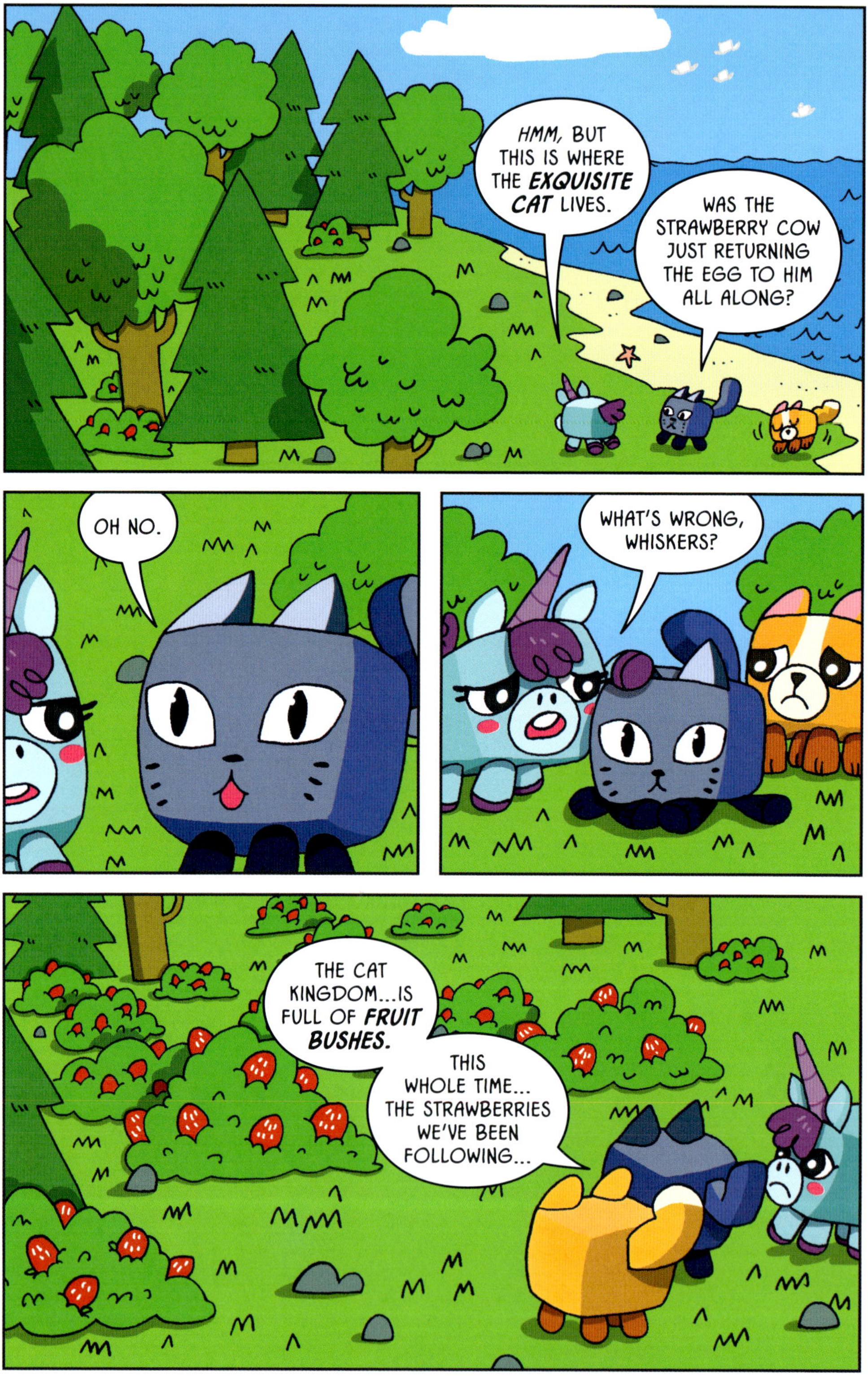
HMM, BUT THIS IS WHERE THE EXQUISITE CAT LIVES.
WAS THE STRAWBERRY COW JUST RETURNING THE EGG TO HIM ALL ALONG?
OH NO.
WHAT'S WRONG, WHISKERS?
THE CAT KINGDOM...IS FULL OF FRUIT BUSHES.
THIS WHOLE TIME... THE STRAWBERRIES WE'VE BEEN FOLLOWING...

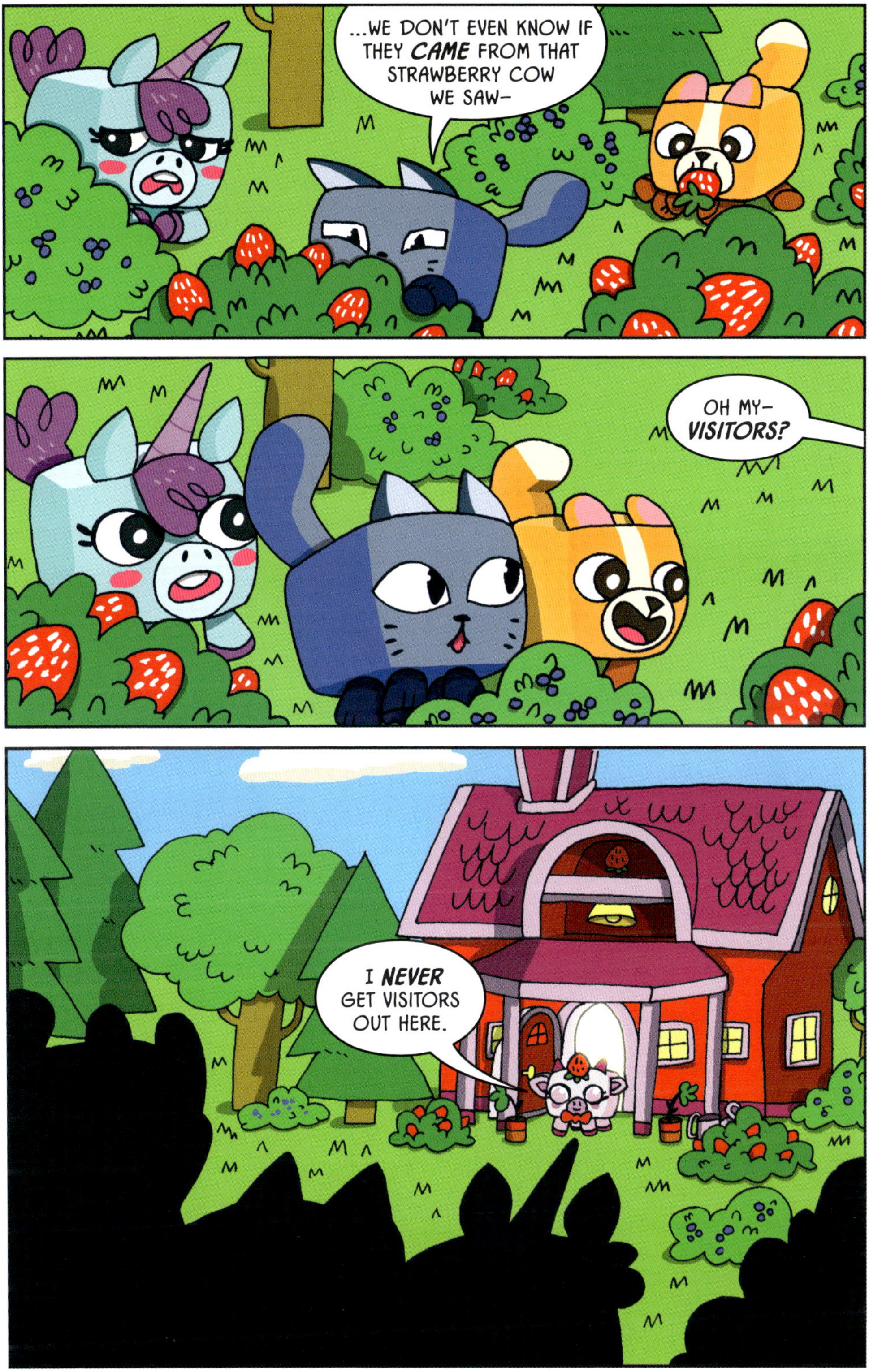
...WE DON'T EVEN KNOW IF THEY *CAME* FROM THAT STRAWBERRY COW WE SAW–
OH MY– *VISITORS?*
I *NEVER* GET VISITORS OUT HERE.

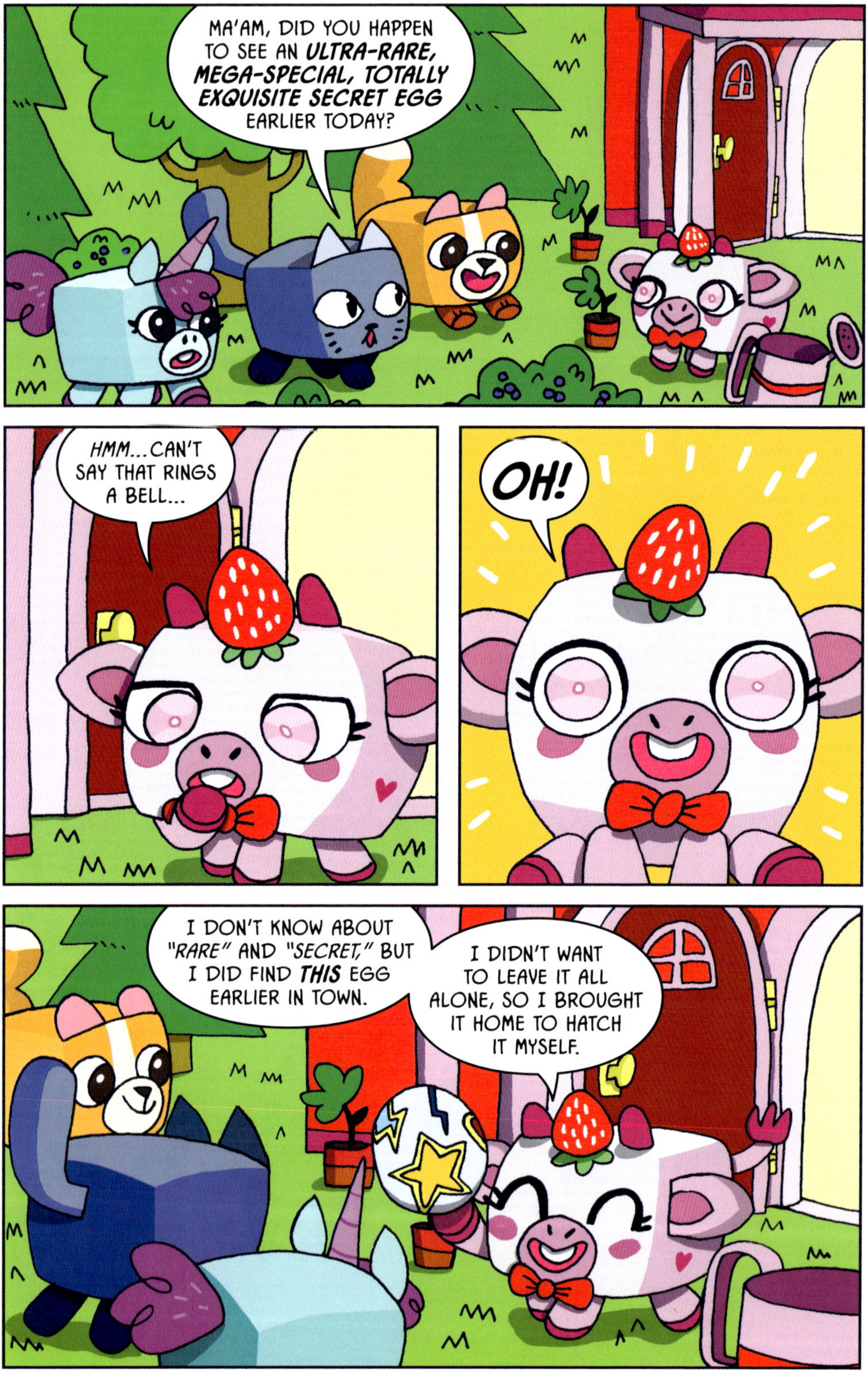
MA'AM, DID YOU HAPPEN TO SEE AN ULTRA-RARE, MEGA-SPECIAL, TOTALLY EXQUISITE SECRET EGG EARLIER TODAY?
HMM...CAN'T SAY THAT RINGS A BELL...
OH!
I DON'T KNOW ABOUT "RARE" AND "SECRET," BUT I DID FIND THIS EGG EARLIER IN TOWN.
I DIDN'T WANT TO LEAVE IT ALL ALONE, SO I BROUGHT IT HOME TO HATCH IT MYSELF.

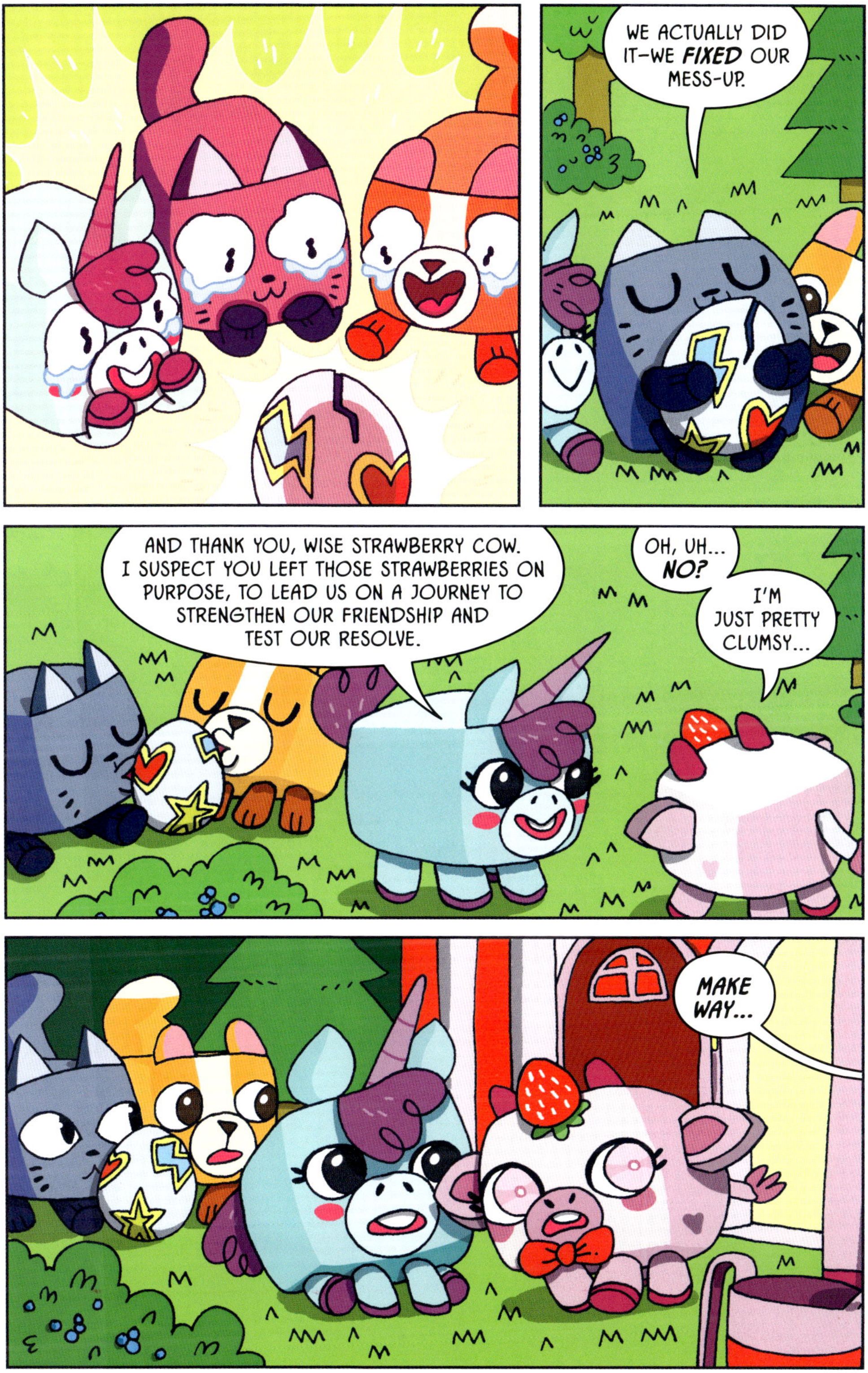
WE ACTUALLY DID IT—WE *FIXED* OUR MESS-UP.
AND THANK YOU, WISE STRAWBERRY COW. I SUSPECT YOU LEFT THOSE STRAWBERRIES ON PURPOSE, TO LEAD US ON A JOURNEY TO STRENGTHEN OUR FRIENDSHIP AND TEST OUR RESOLVE.
OH, UH... *NO?*
I'M JUST PRETTY CLUMSY...
MAKE WAY...

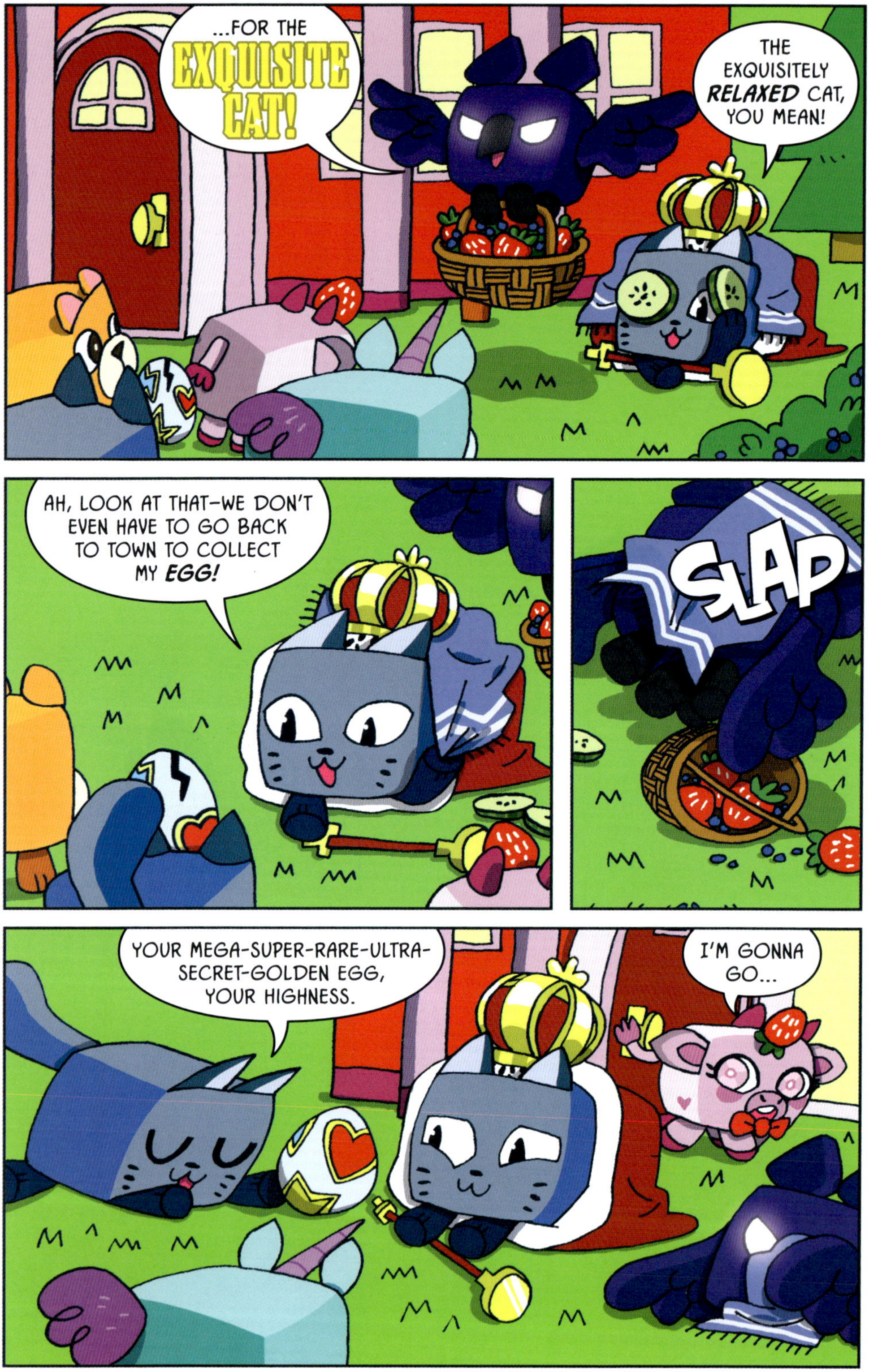
...FOR THE
EXQUISITE CAT!
THE EXQUISITELY *RELAXED* CAT, YOU MEAN!
AH, LOOK AT THAT—WE DON'T EVEN HAVE TO GO BACK TO TOWN TO COLLECT MY *EGG!*
SLAP
YOUR MEGA-SUPER-RARE-ULTRA-SECRET-GOLDEN EGG, YOUR HIGHNESS.
I'M GONNA GO...

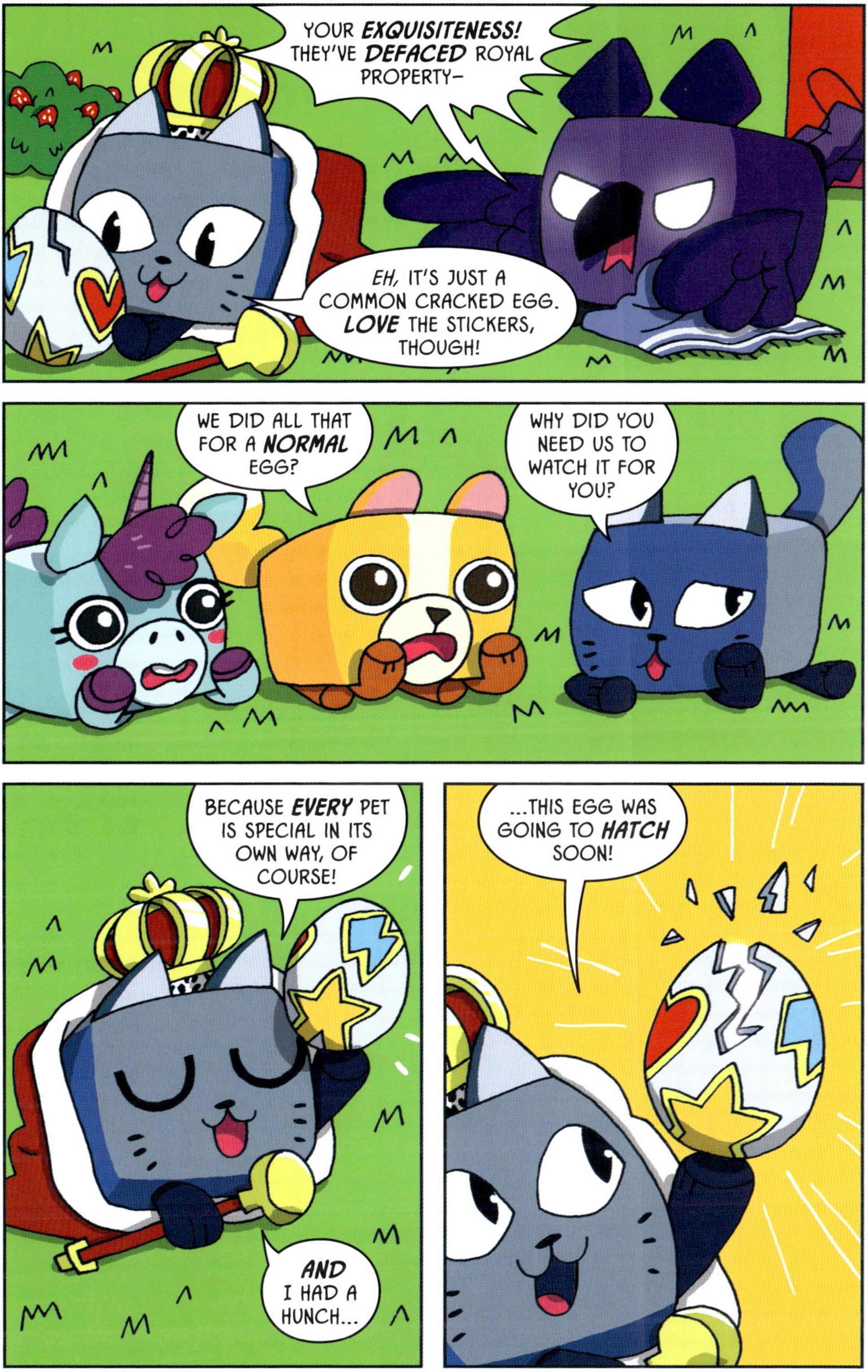
YOUR **EXQUISITENESS!** THEY'VE **DEFACED** ROYAL PROPERTY–
EH, IT'S JUST A COMMON CRACKED EGG. **LOVE** THE STICKERS, THOUGH!
WE DID ALL THAT FOR A **NORMAL** EGG?
WHY DID YOU NEED US TO WATCH IT FOR YOU?
BECAUSE **EVERY** PET IS SPECIAL IN ITS OWN WAY, OF COURSE!
AND I HAD A HUNCH...
...THIS EGG WAS GOING TO **HATCH** SOON!

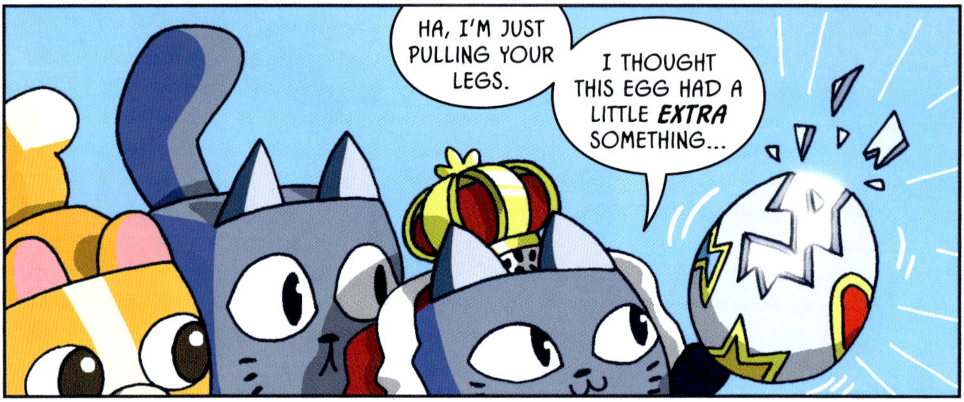
HA, I'M JUST PULLING YOUR LEGS.
I THOUGHT THIS EGG HAD A LITTLE EXTRA SOMETHING...

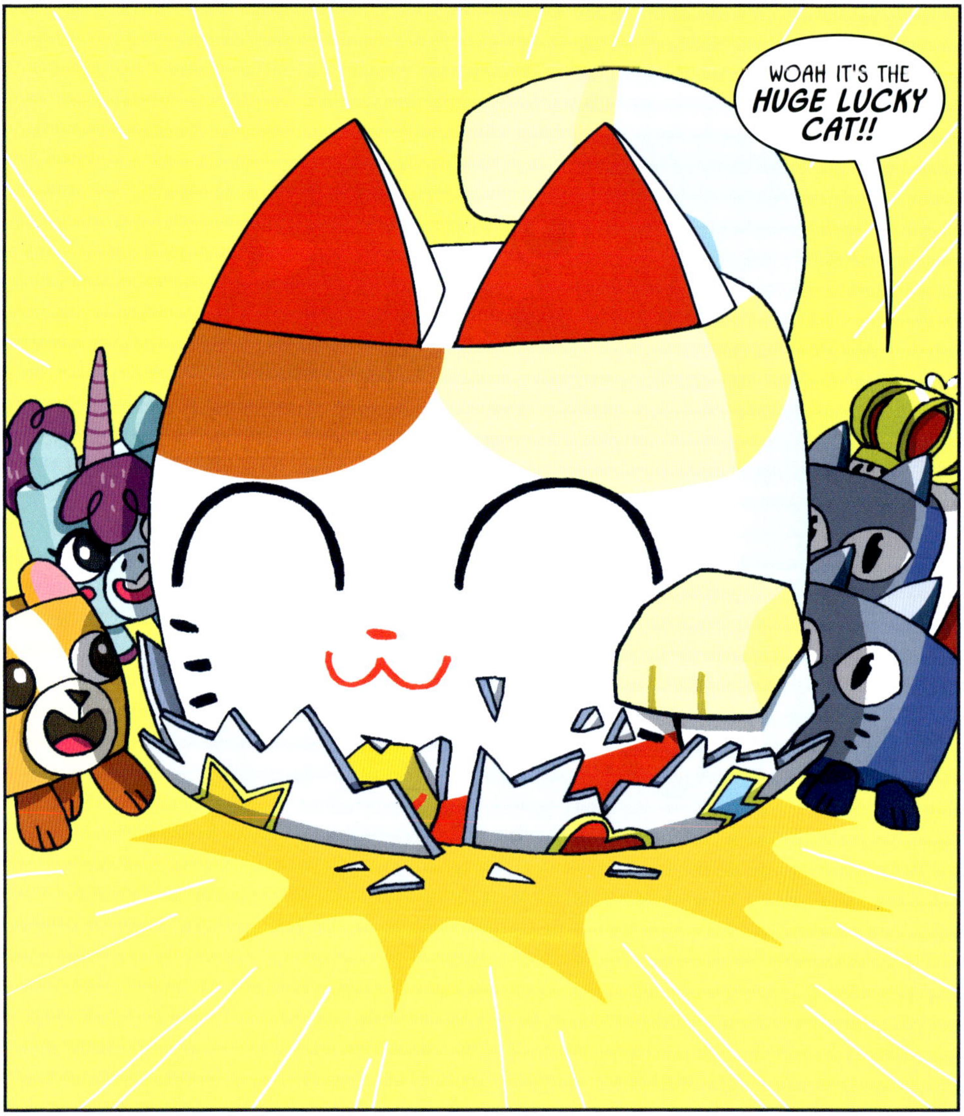
WOAH IT'S THE HUGE LUCKY CAT!!

PART 2
COIN CRAZE

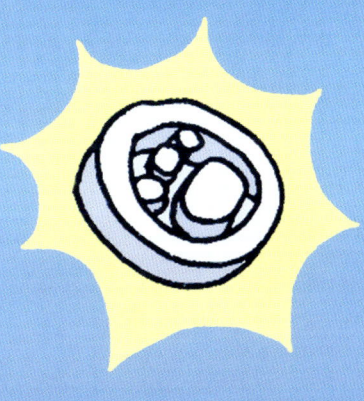

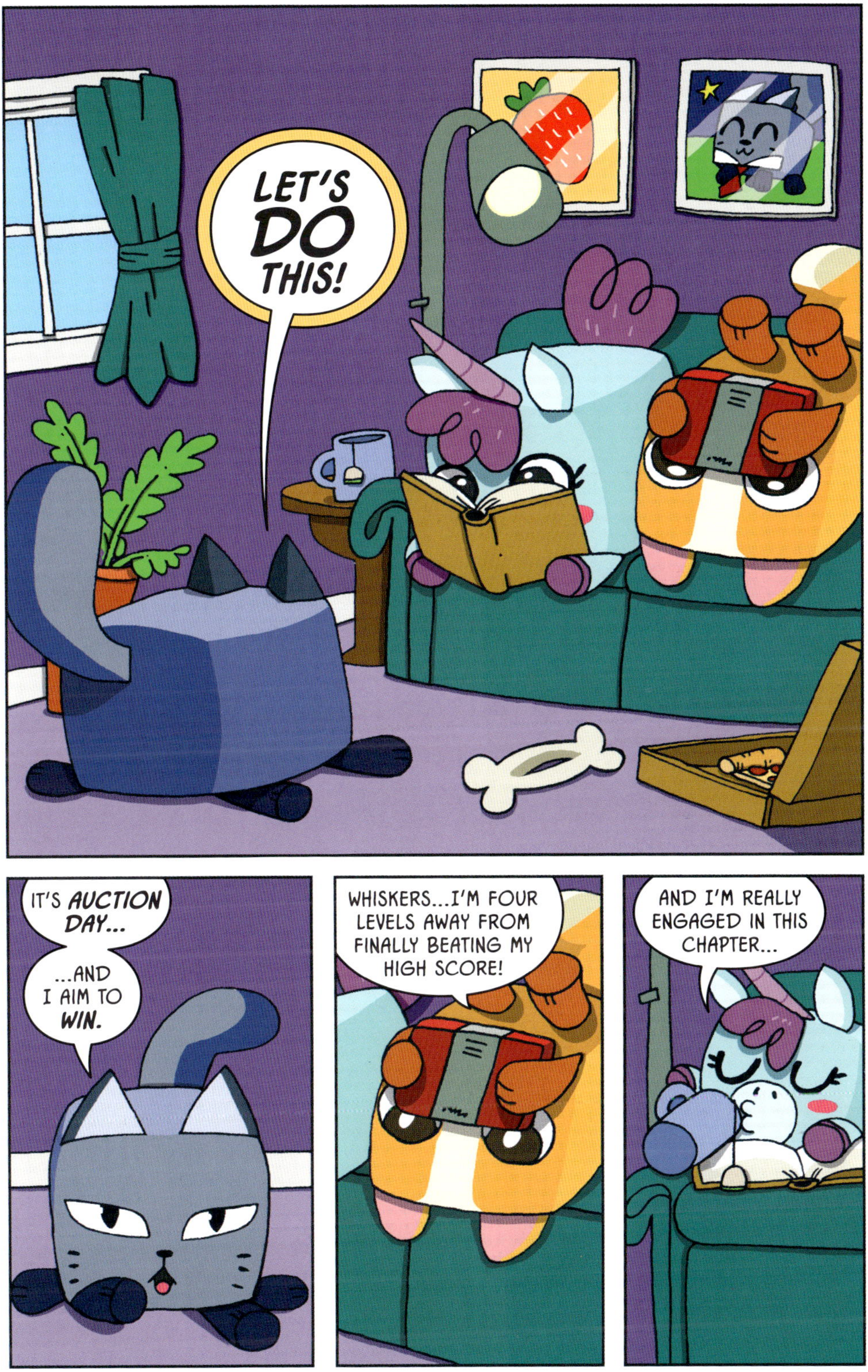
LET'S DO THIS!
IT'S AUCTION DAY...
...AND I AIM TO WIN.
WHISKERS...I'M FOUR LEVELS AWAY FROM FINALLY BEATING MY HIGH SCORE!
AND I'M REALLY ENGAGED IN THIS CHAPTER...

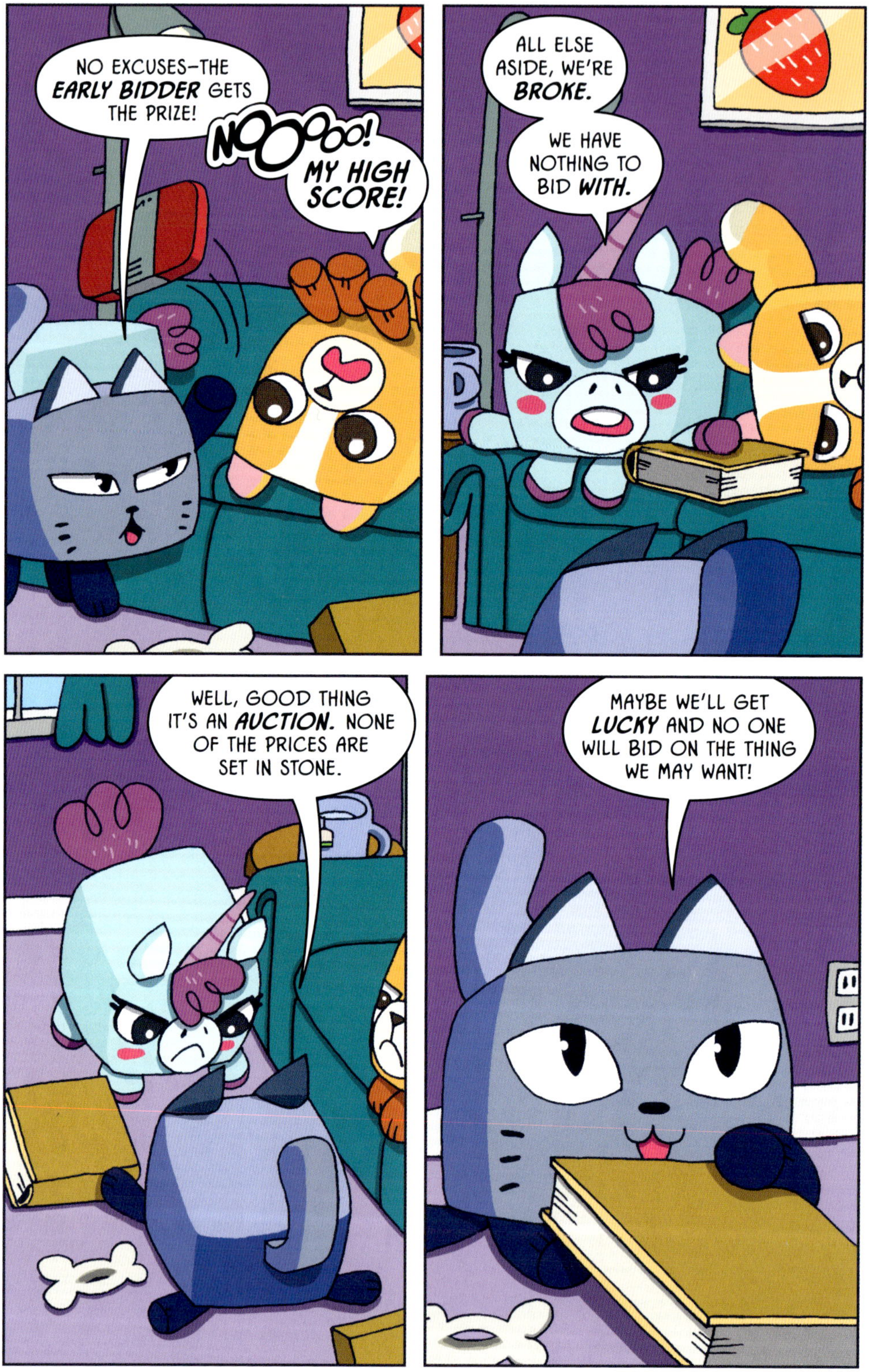
NO EXCUSES—THE *EARLY BIDDER* GETS THE PRIZE!
NOOOoo! *MY HIGH SCORE!*
ALL ELSE ASIDE, WE'RE *BROKE.*
WE HAVE NOTHING TO BID *WITH.*
WELL, GOOD THING IT'S AN *AUCTION.* NONE OF THE PRICES ARE SET IN STONE.
MAYBE WE'LL GET *LUCKY* AND NO ONE WILL BID ON THE THING WE MAY WANT!

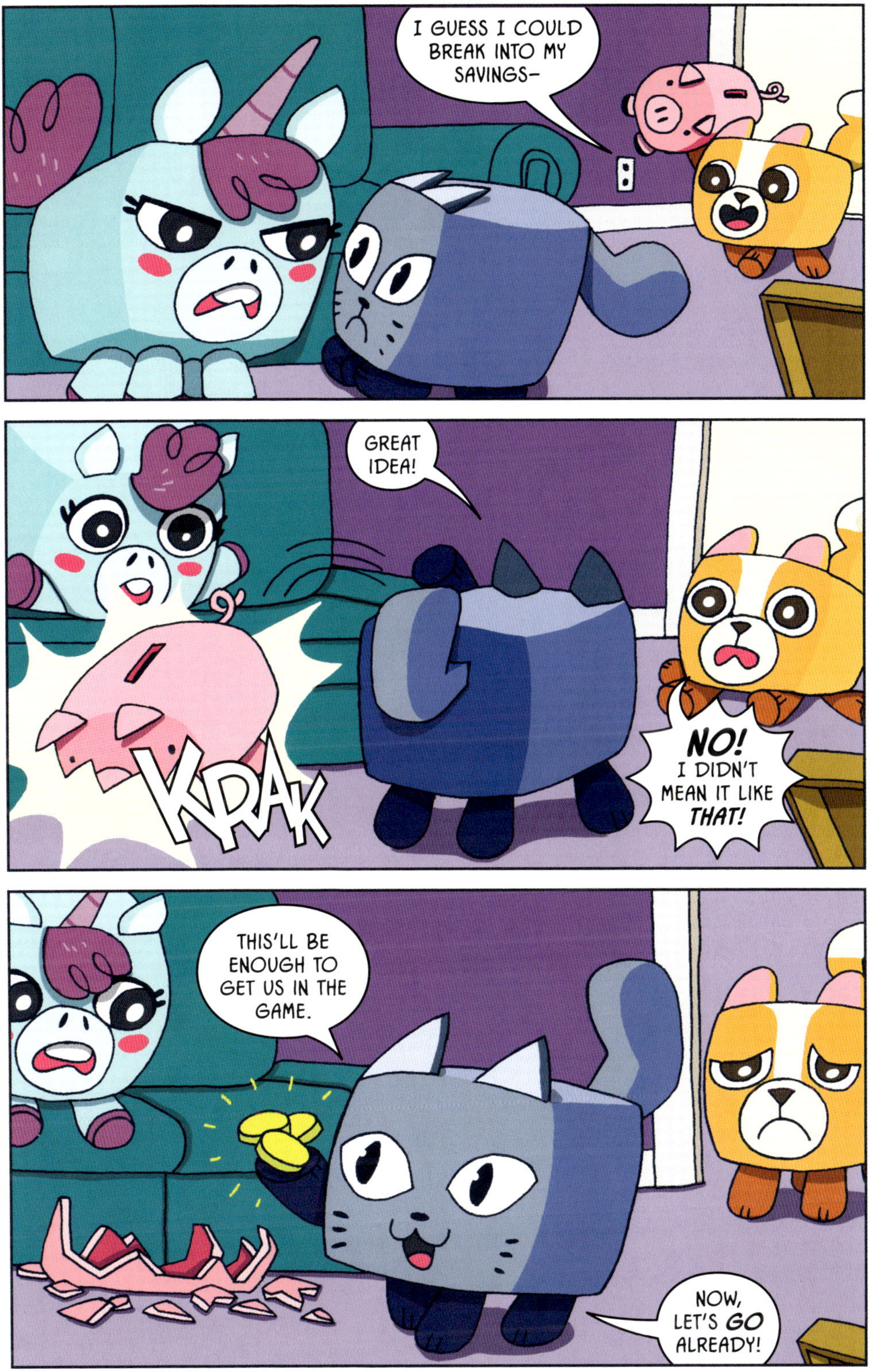
I GUESS I COULD BREAK INTO MY SAVINGS–
GREAT IDEA!
KRAK
NO! I DIDN'T MEAN IT LIKE THAT!
THIS'LL BE ENOUGH TO GET US IN THE GAME.
NOW, LET'S GO ALREADY!

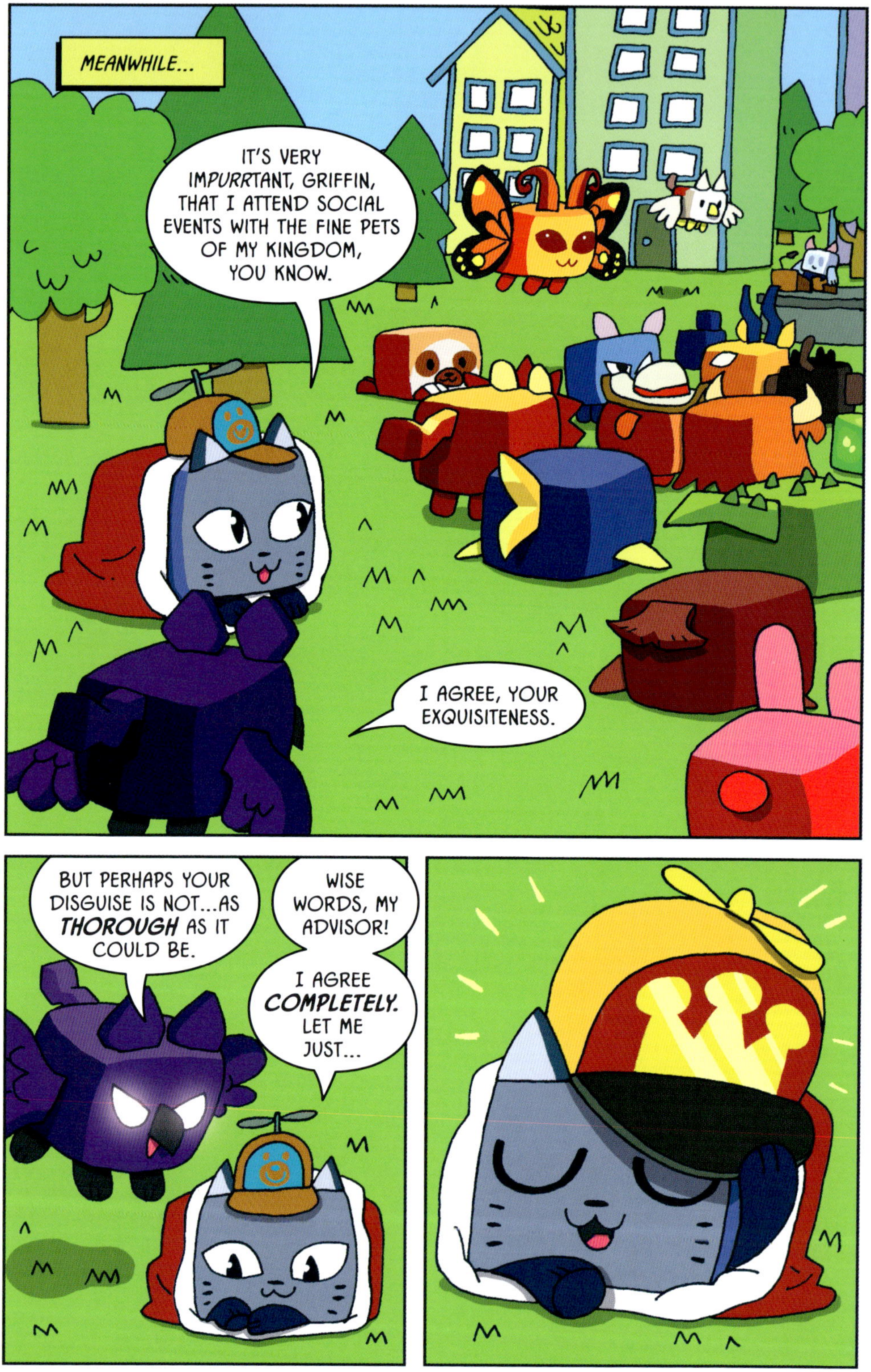
MEANWHILE...
IT'S VERY IMPURRTANT, GRIFFIN, THAT I ATTEND SOCIAL EVENTS WITH THE FINE PETS OF MY KINGDOM, YOU KNOW.
I AGREE, YOUR EXQUISITENESS.
BUT PERHAPS YOUR DISGUISE IS NOT...AS **THOROUGH** AS IT COULD BE.
WISE WORDS, MY ADVISOR!
I AGREE **COMPLETELY.** LET ME JUST...

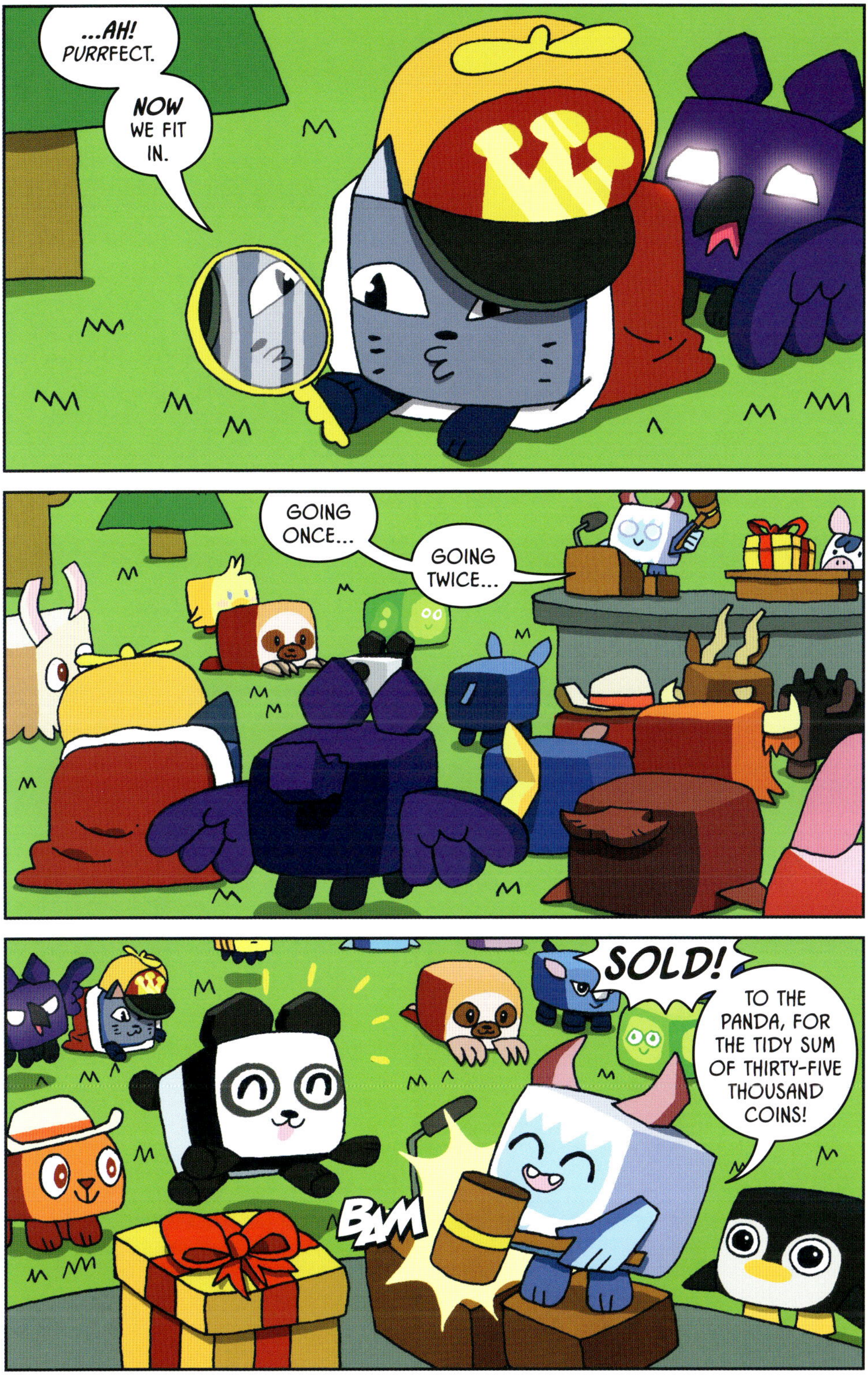
...AH! PURRFECT.
NOW WE FIT IN.
GOING ONCE...
GOING TWICE...
SOLD!
TO THE PANDA, FOR THE TIDY SUM OF THIRTY-FIVE THOUSAND COINS!
BAM

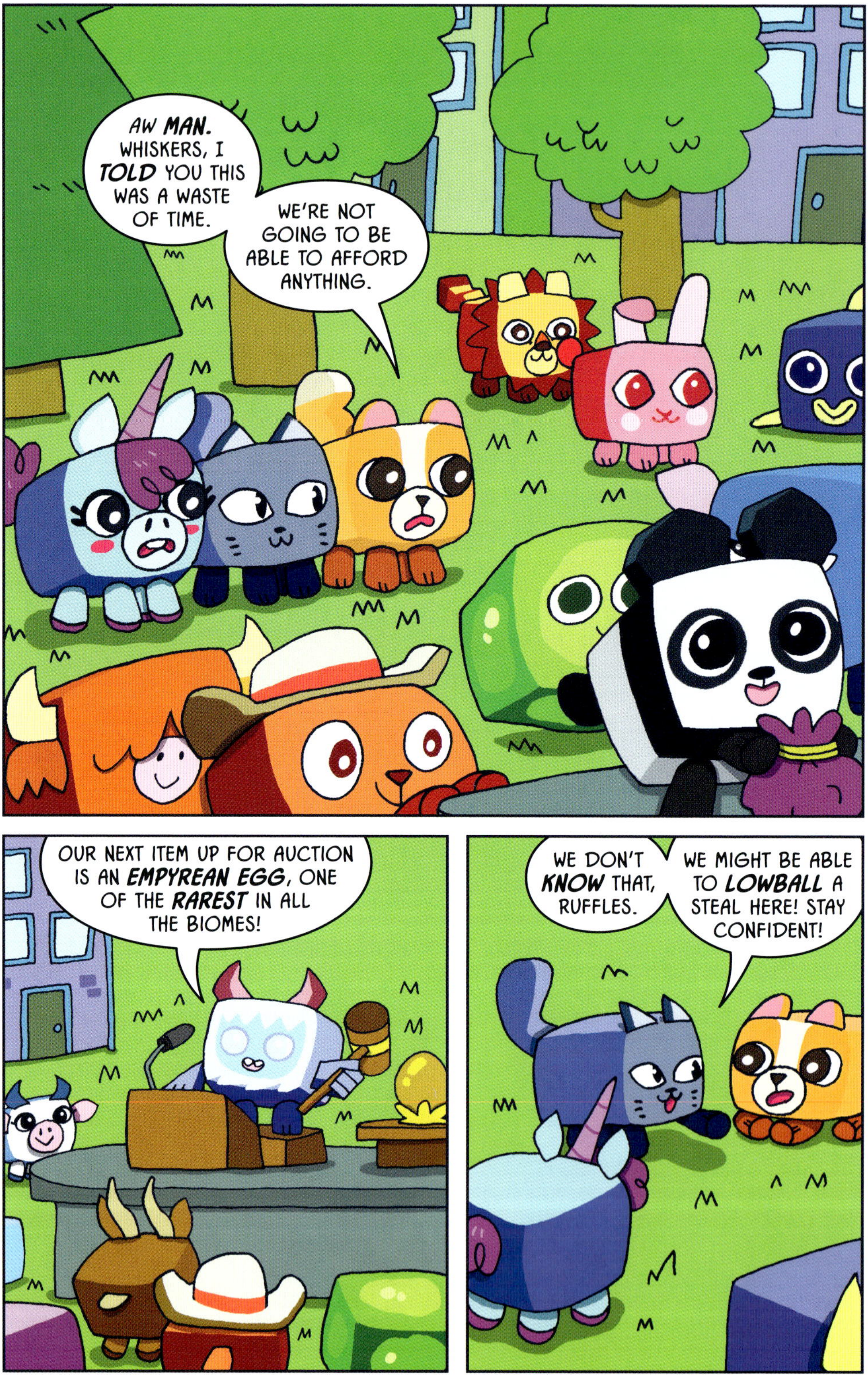
AW MAN. WHISKERS, I TOLD YOU THIS WAS A WASTE OF TIME.
WE'RE NOT GOING TO BE ABLE TO AFFORD ANYTHING.
OUR NEXT ITEM UP FOR AUCTION IS AN EMPYREAN EGG, ONE OF THE RAREST IN ALL THE BIOMES!
WE DON'T KNOW THAT, RUFFLES.
WE MIGHT BE ABLE TO LOWBALL A STEAL HERE! STAY CONFIDENT!

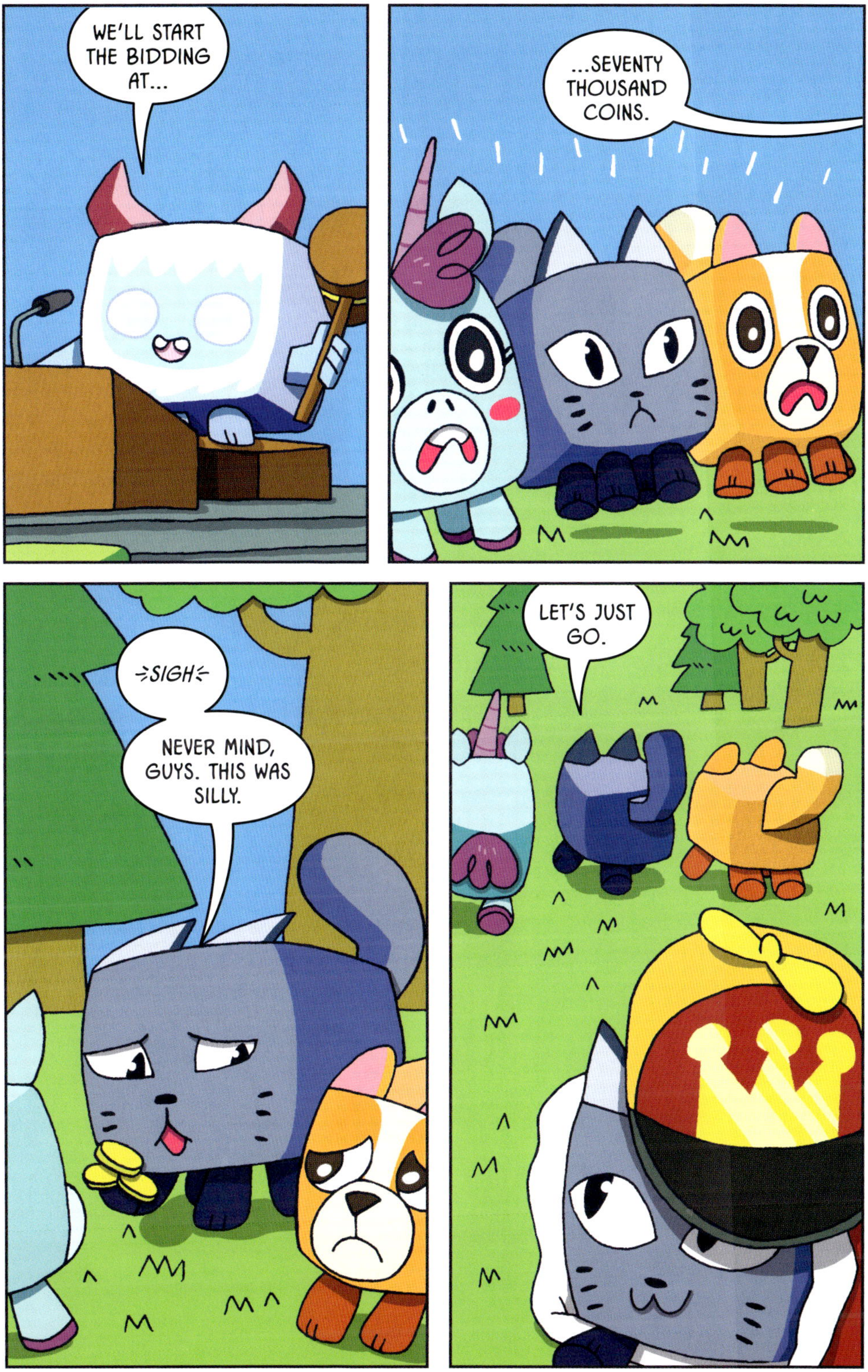
WE'LL START THE BIDDING AT...
...SEVENTY THOUSAND COINS.
SIGH
NEVER MIND, GUYS. THIS WAS SILLY.
LET'S JUST GO.

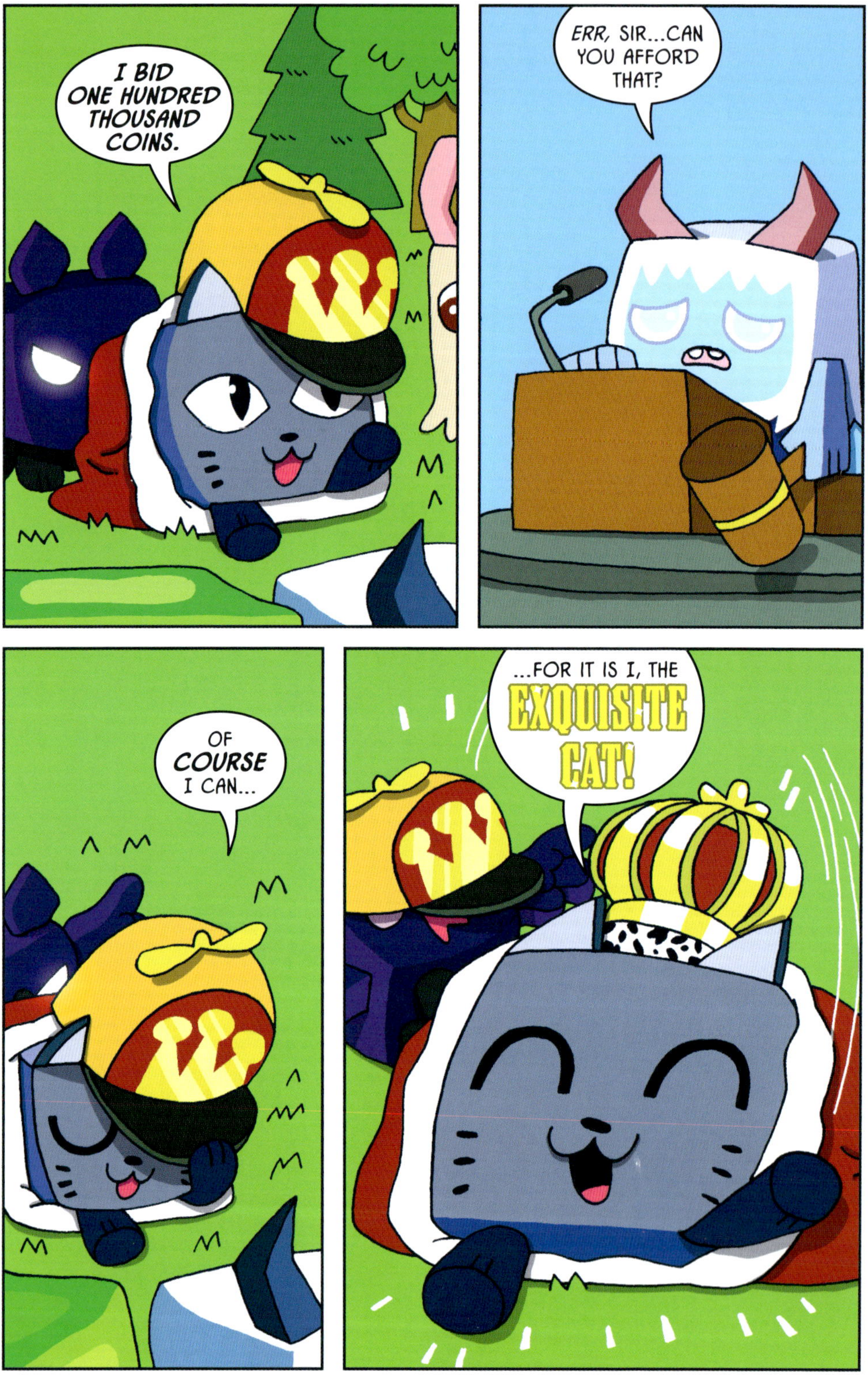
I BID ONE HUNDRED THOUSAND COINS.
ERR, SIR...CAN YOU AFFORD THAT?
OF COURSE I CAN...
...FOR IT IS I, THE EXQUISITE CAT!

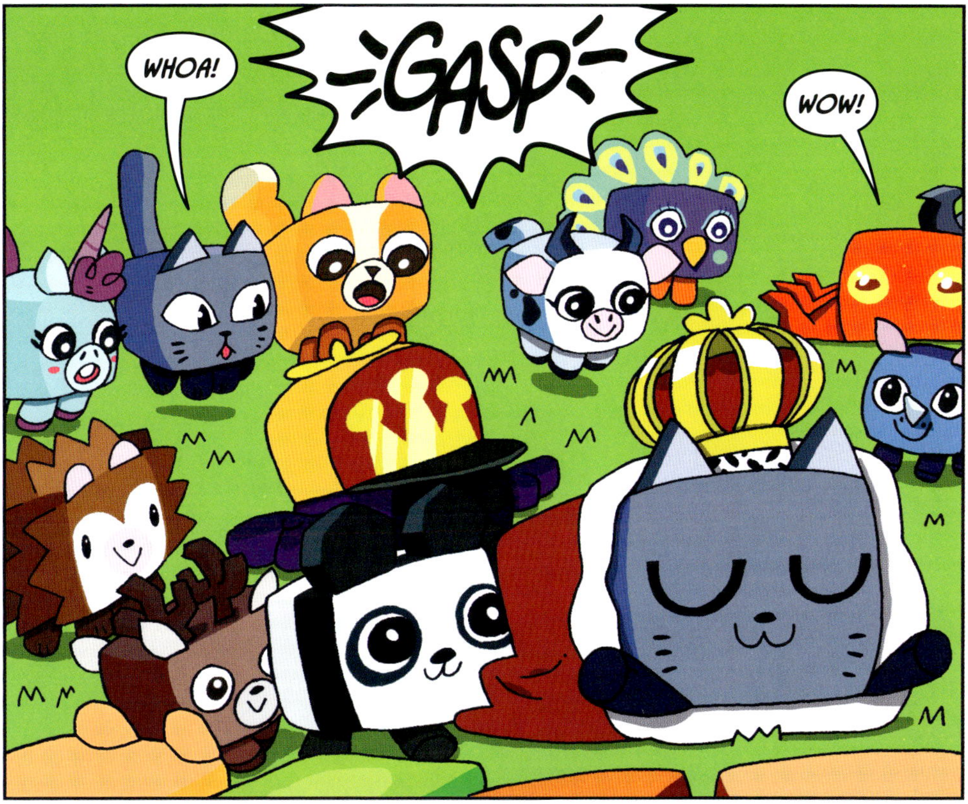
WHOA!
GASP
WOW!

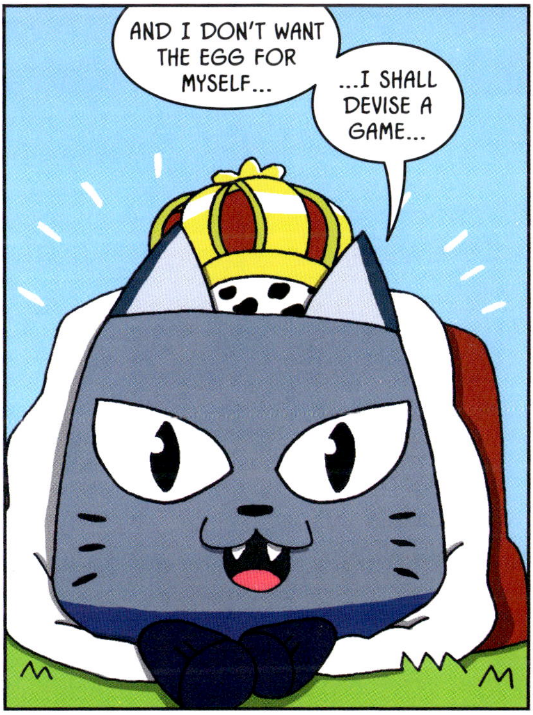
AND I DON'T WANT THE EGG FOR MYSELF...
...I SHALL DEVISE A GAME...

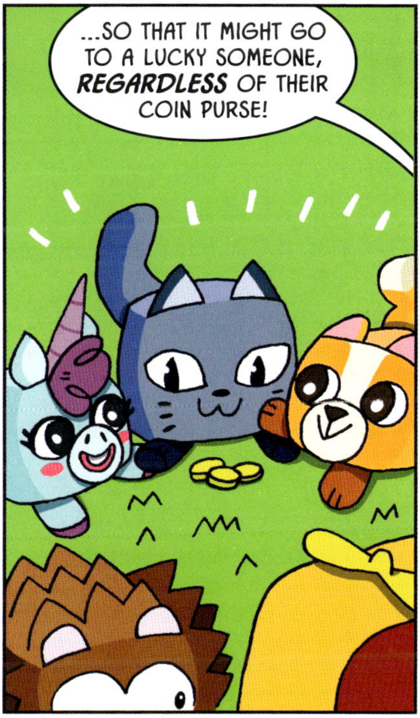
...SO THAT IT MIGHT GO TO A LUCKY SOMEONE, **REGARDLESS** OF THEIR COIN PURSE!

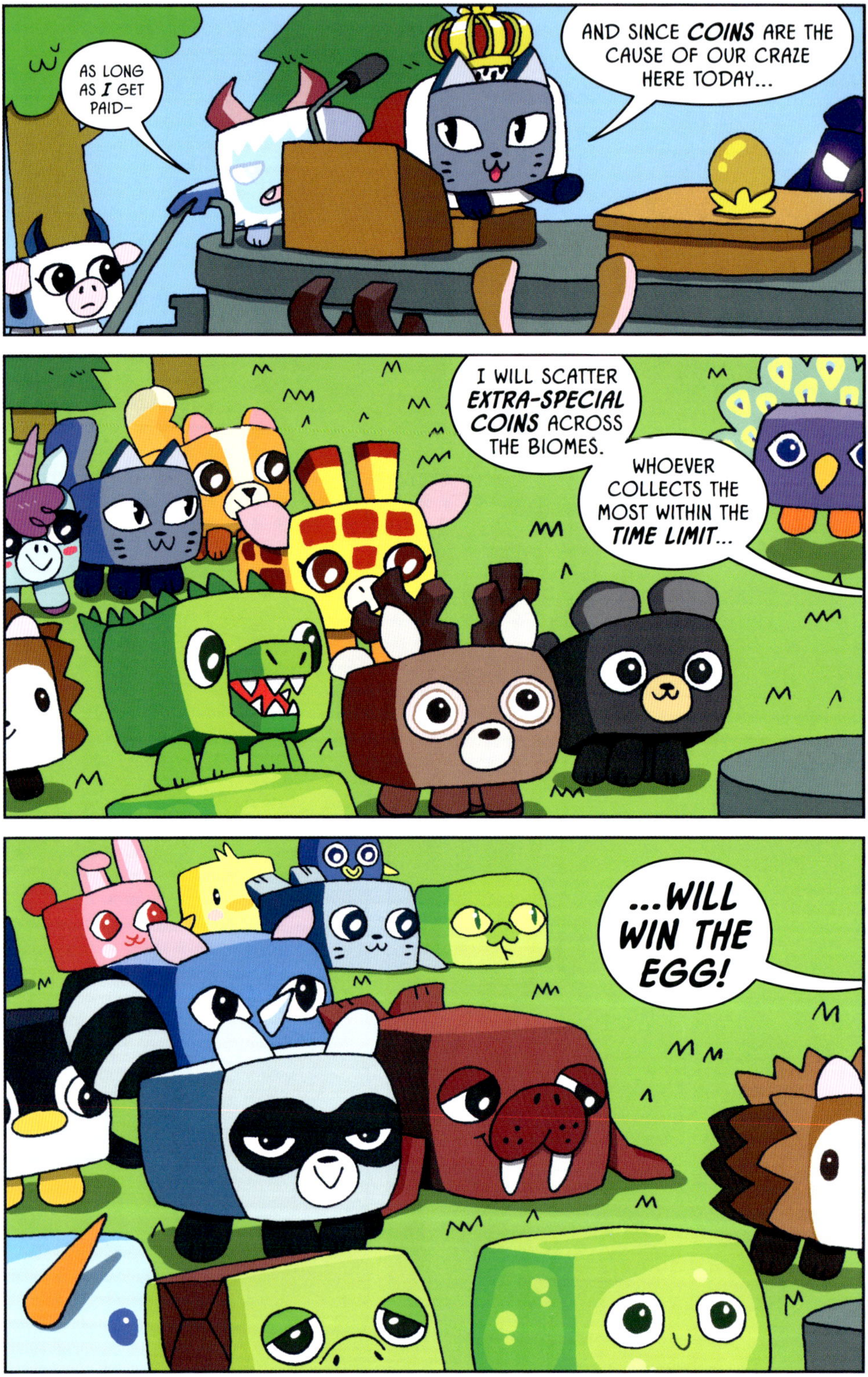
AS LONG AS *I* GET PAID–
AND SINCE **COINS** ARE THE CAUSE OF OUR CRAZE HERE TODAY...
I WILL SCATTER **EXTRA-SPECIAL COINS** ACROSS THE BIOMES.
WHOEVER COLLECTS THE MOST WITHIN THE **TIME LIMIT**...
...WILL WIN THE EGG!

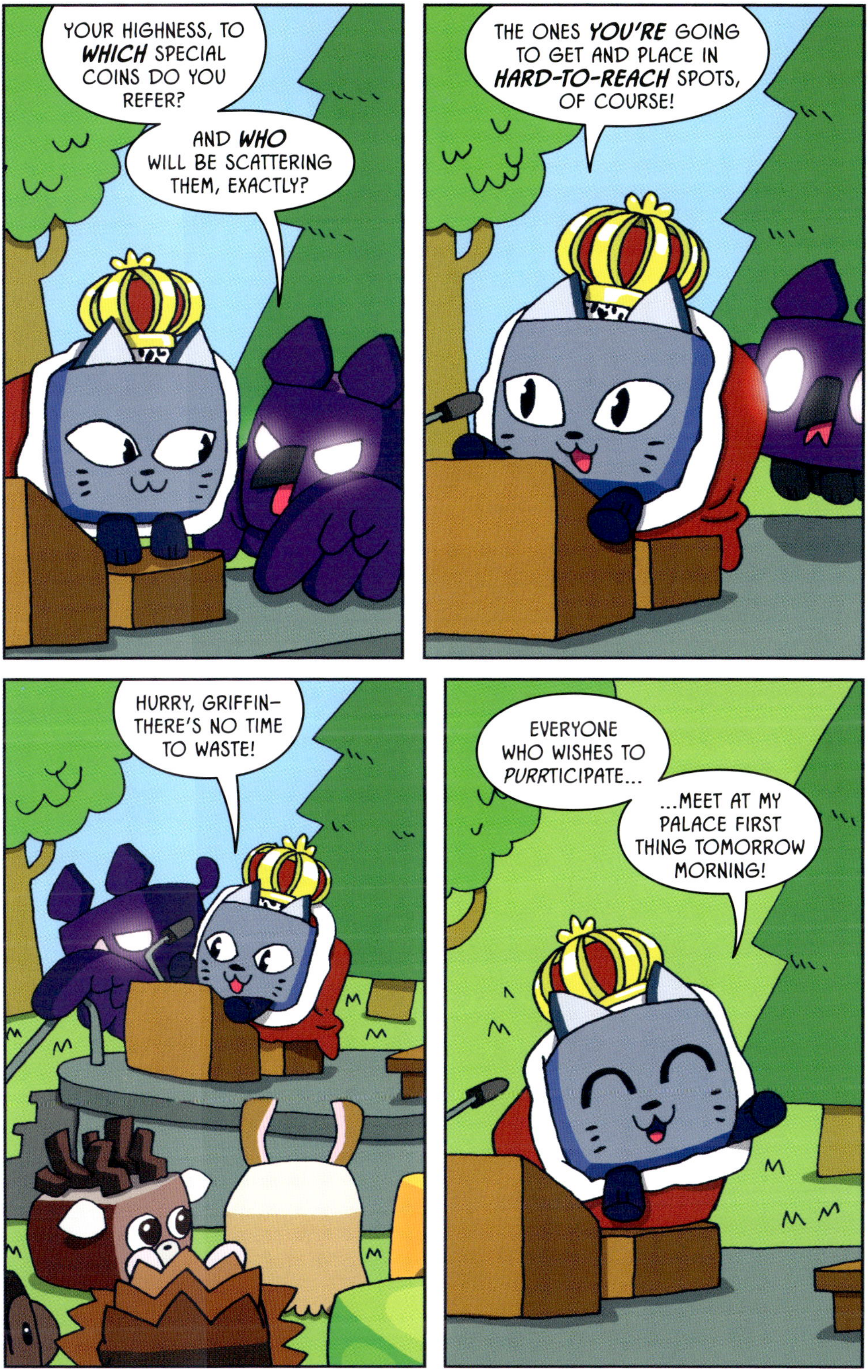
YOUR HIGHNESS, TO ***WHICH*** SPECIAL COINS DO YOU REFER?
AND ***WHO*** WILL BE SCATTERING THEM, EXACTLY?
THE ONES ***YOU'RE*** GOING TO GET AND PLACE IN ***HARD-TO-REACH*** SPOTS, OF COURSE!
HURRY, GRIFFIN–THERE'S NO TIME TO WASTE!
EVERYONE WHO WISHES TO *PURR*TICIPATE...
...MEET AT MY PALACE FIRST THING TOMORROW MORNING!

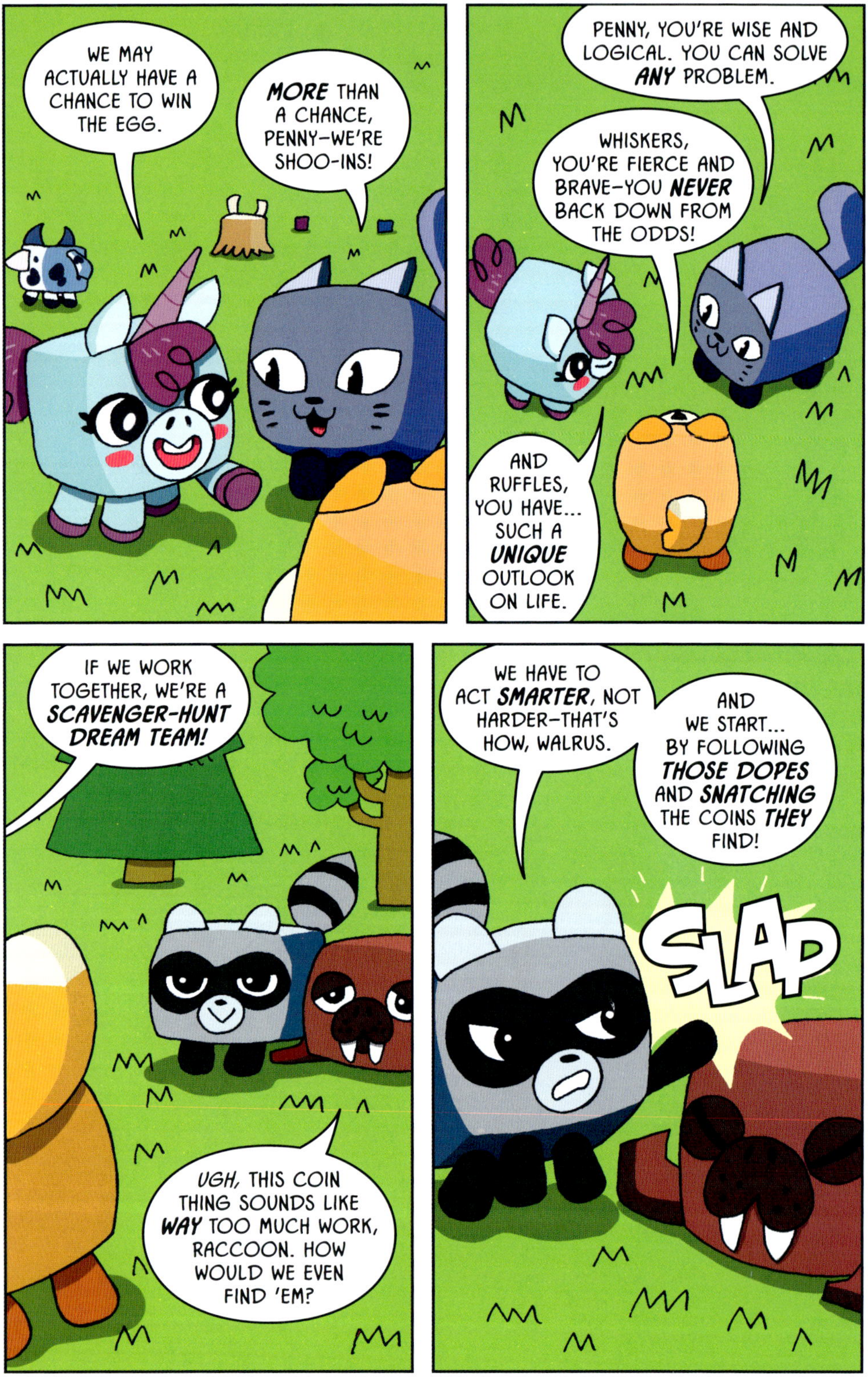
WE MAY ACTUALLY HAVE A CHANCE TO WIN THE EGG.
MORE THAN A CHANCE, PENNY—WE'RE SHOO-INS!
PENNY, YOU'RE WISE AND LOGICAL. YOU CAN SOLVE **ANY** PROBLEM.
WHISKERS, YOU'RE FIERCE AND BRAVE—YOU **NEVER** BACK DOWN FROM THE ODDS!
AND RUFFLES, YOU HAVE... SUCH A **UNIQUE** OUTLOOK ON LIFE.
IF WE WORK TOGETHER, WE'RE A **SCAVENGER-HUNT DREAM TEAM!**
UGH, THIS COIN THING SOUNDS LIKE **WAY** TOO MUCH WORK, RACCOON. HOW WOULD WE EVEN FIND 'EM?
WE HAVE TO ACT **SMARTER**, NOT HARDER—THAT'S HOW, WALRUS.
AND WE START... BY FOLLOWING **THOSE DOPES** AND **SNATCHING** THE COINS **THEY** FIND!
SLAP

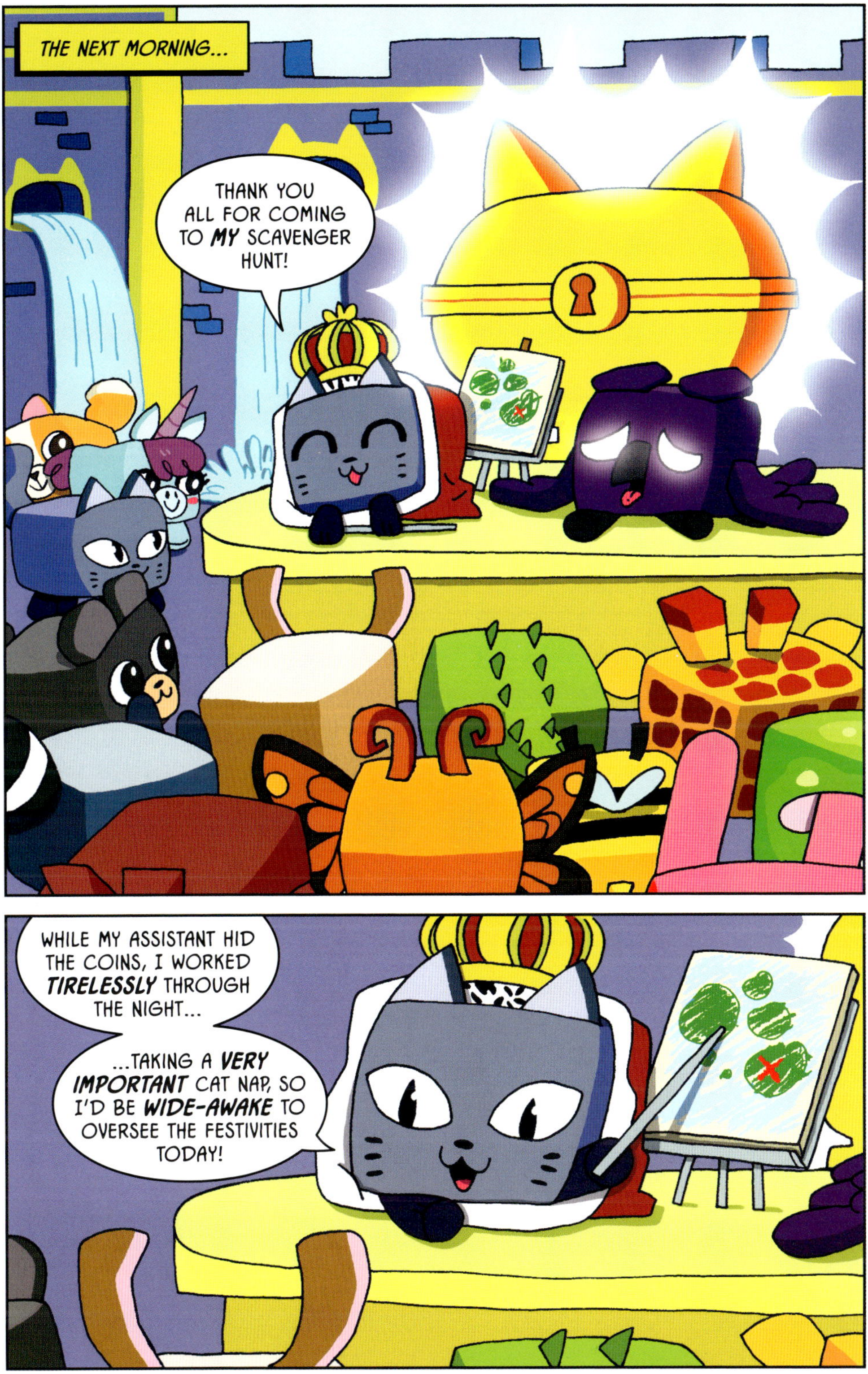
THE NEXT MORNING...
THANK YOU ALL FOR COMING TO *MY* SCAVENGER HUNT!
WHILE MY ASSISTANT HID THE COINS, I WORKED *TIRELESSLY* THROUGH THE NIGHT...
...TAKING A *VERY IMPORTANT* CAT NAP, SO I'D BE *WIDE-AWAKE* TO OVERSEE THE FESTIVITIES TODAY!

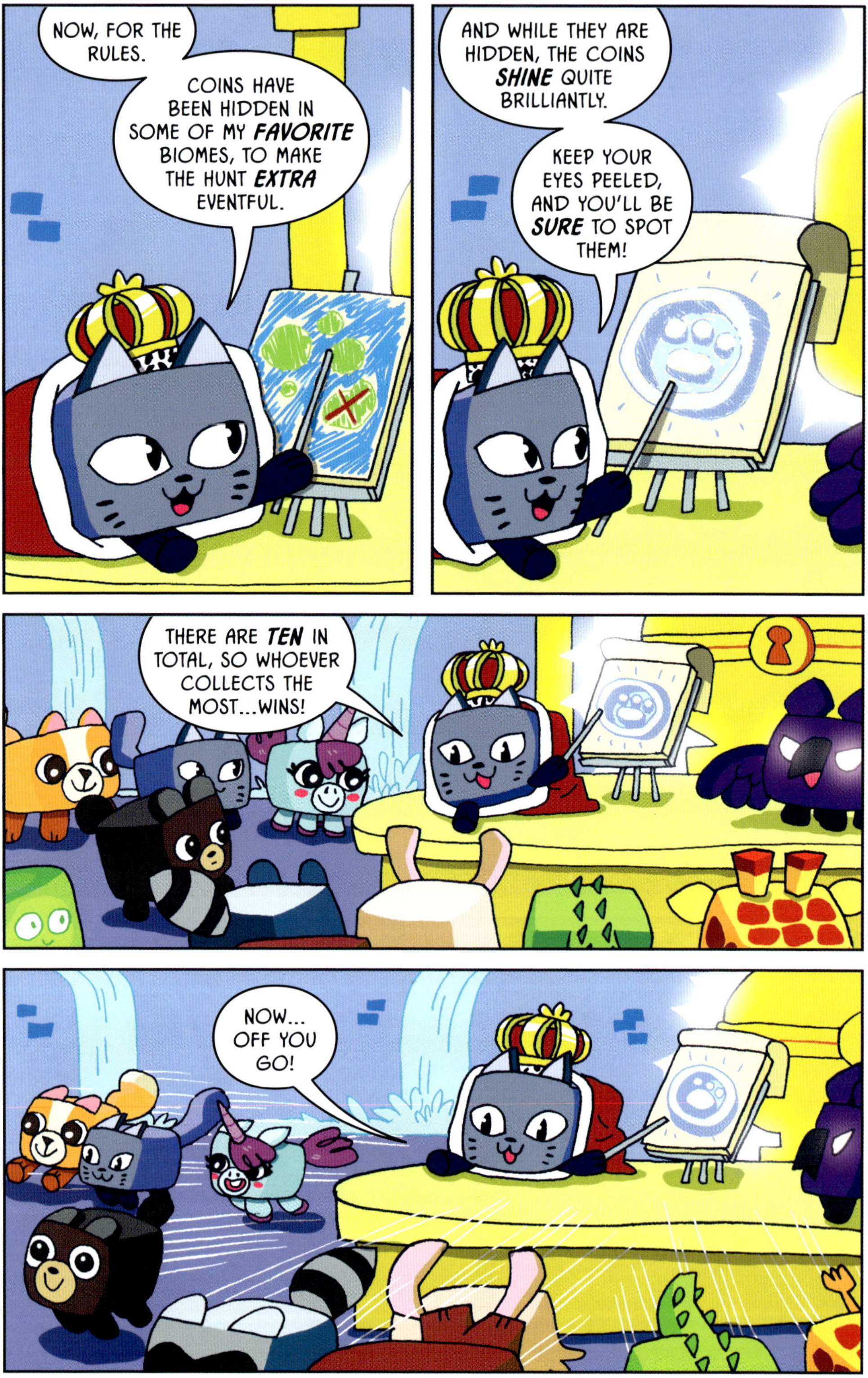
NOW, FOR THE RULES.
COINS HAVE BEEN HIDDEN IN SOME OF MY *FAVORITE* BIOMES, TO MAKE THE HUNT *EXTRA* EVENTFUL.
AND WHILE THEY ARE HIDDEN, THE COINS *SHINE* QUITE BRILLIANTLY.
KEEP YOUR EYES PEELED, AND YOU'LL BE *SURE* TO SPOT THEM!
THERE ARE *TEN* IN TOTAL, SO WHOEVER COLLECTS THE MOST...WINS!
NOW... OFF YOU GO!

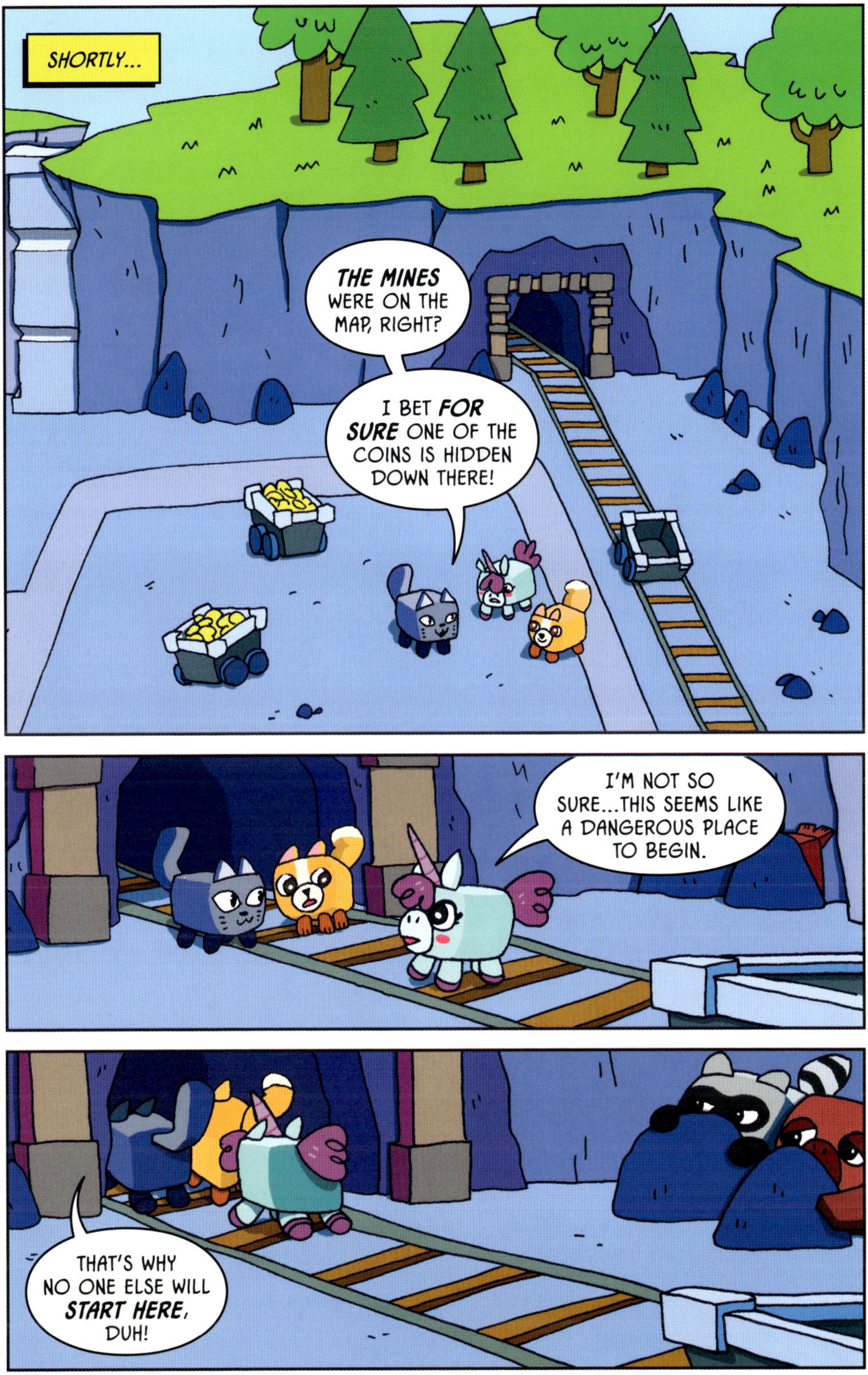
SHORTLY...
THE MINES WERE ON THE MAP, RIGHT?
I BET FOR SURE ONE OF THE COINS IS HIDDEN DOWN THERE!
I'M NOT SO SURE...THIS SEEMS LIKE A DANGEROUS PLACE TO BEGIN.
THAT'S WHY NO ONE ELSE WILL START HERE, DUH!

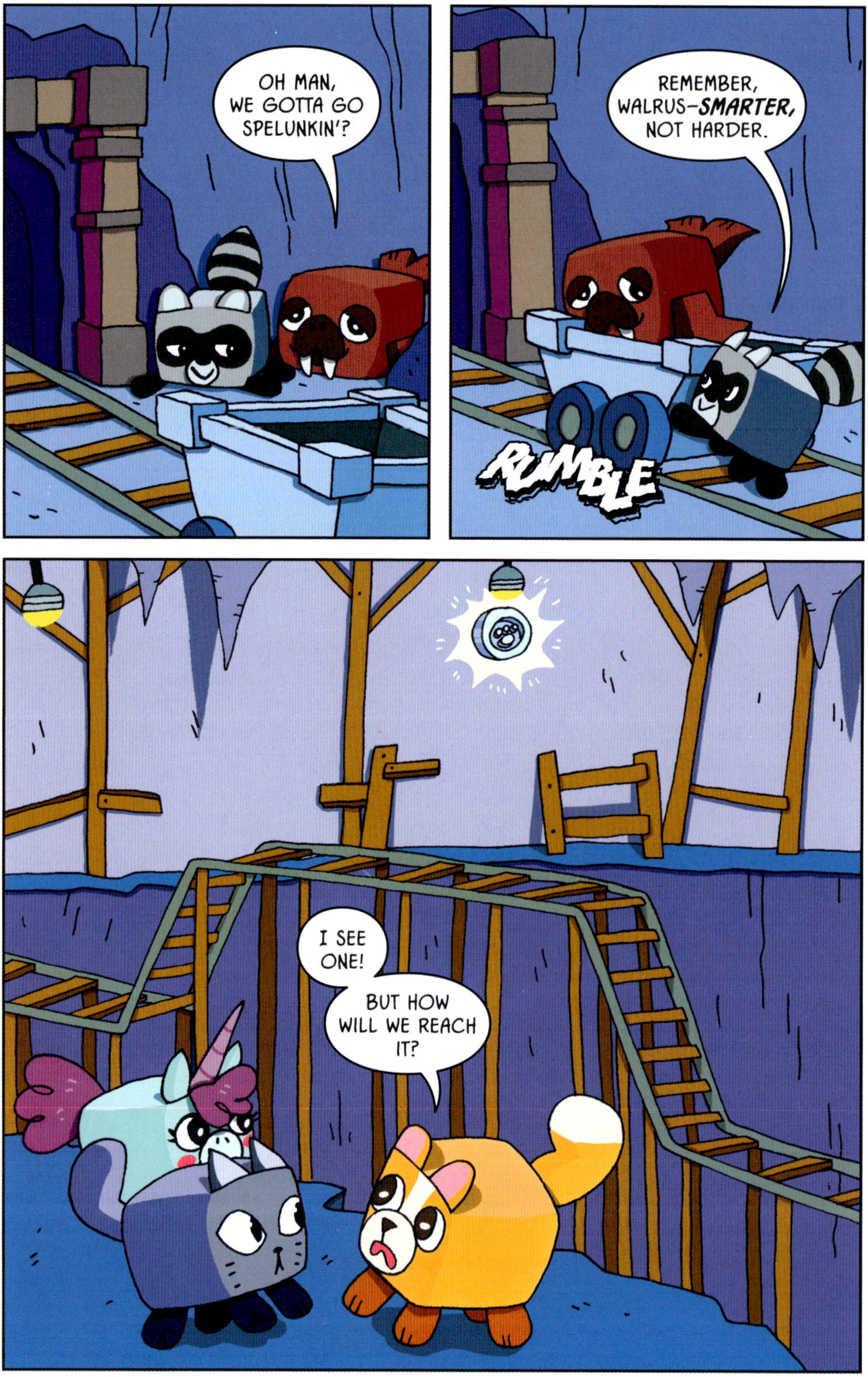
OH MAN, WE GOTTA GO SPELUNKIN'?
REMEMBER, WALRUS–SMARTER, NOT HARDER.
RUMBLE
I SEE ONE!
BUT HOW WILL WE REACH IT?

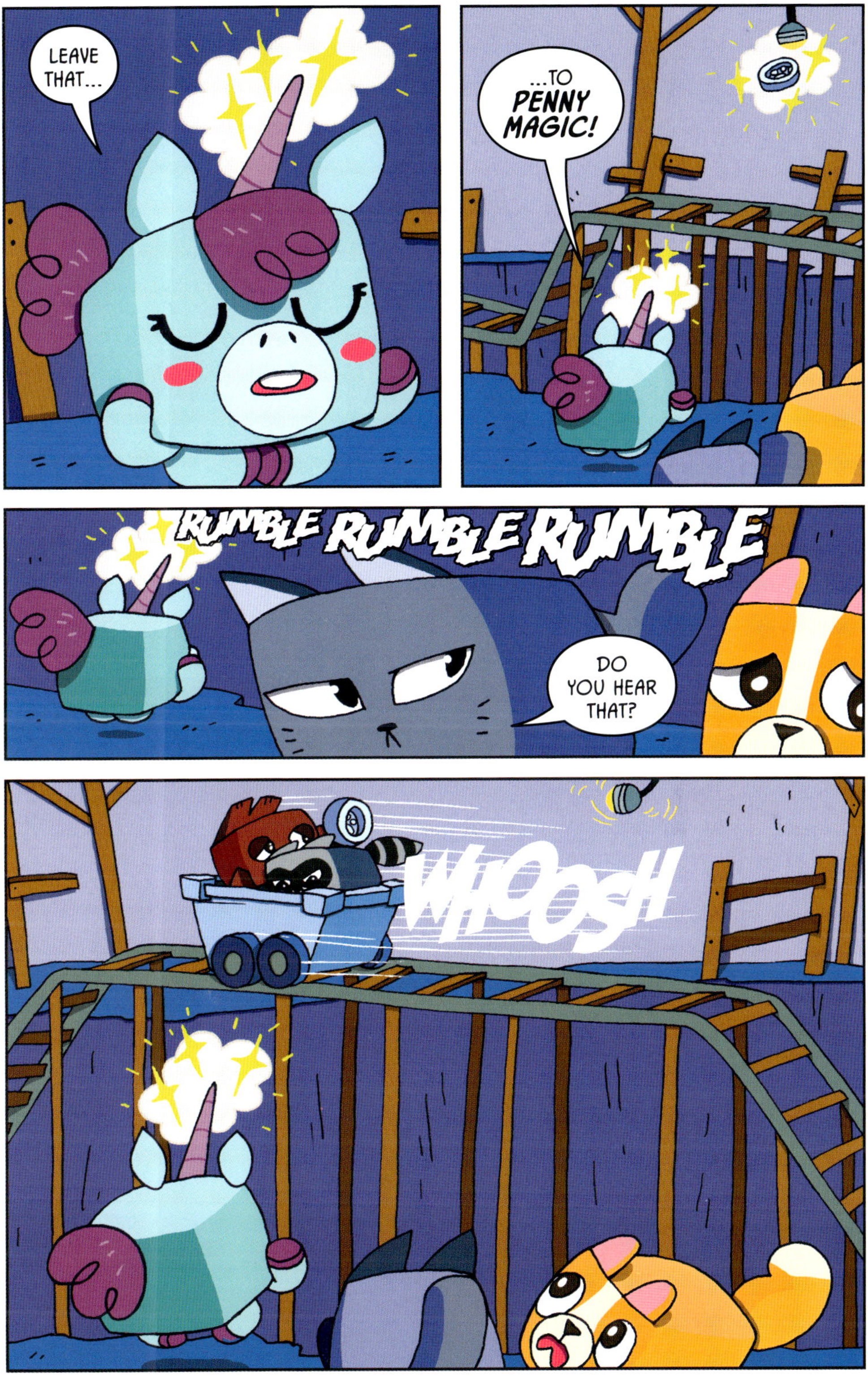
LEAVE THAT...
...TO PENNY MAGIC!
RUMBLE RUMBLE RUMBLE
DO YOU HEAR THAT?
WHOOSH

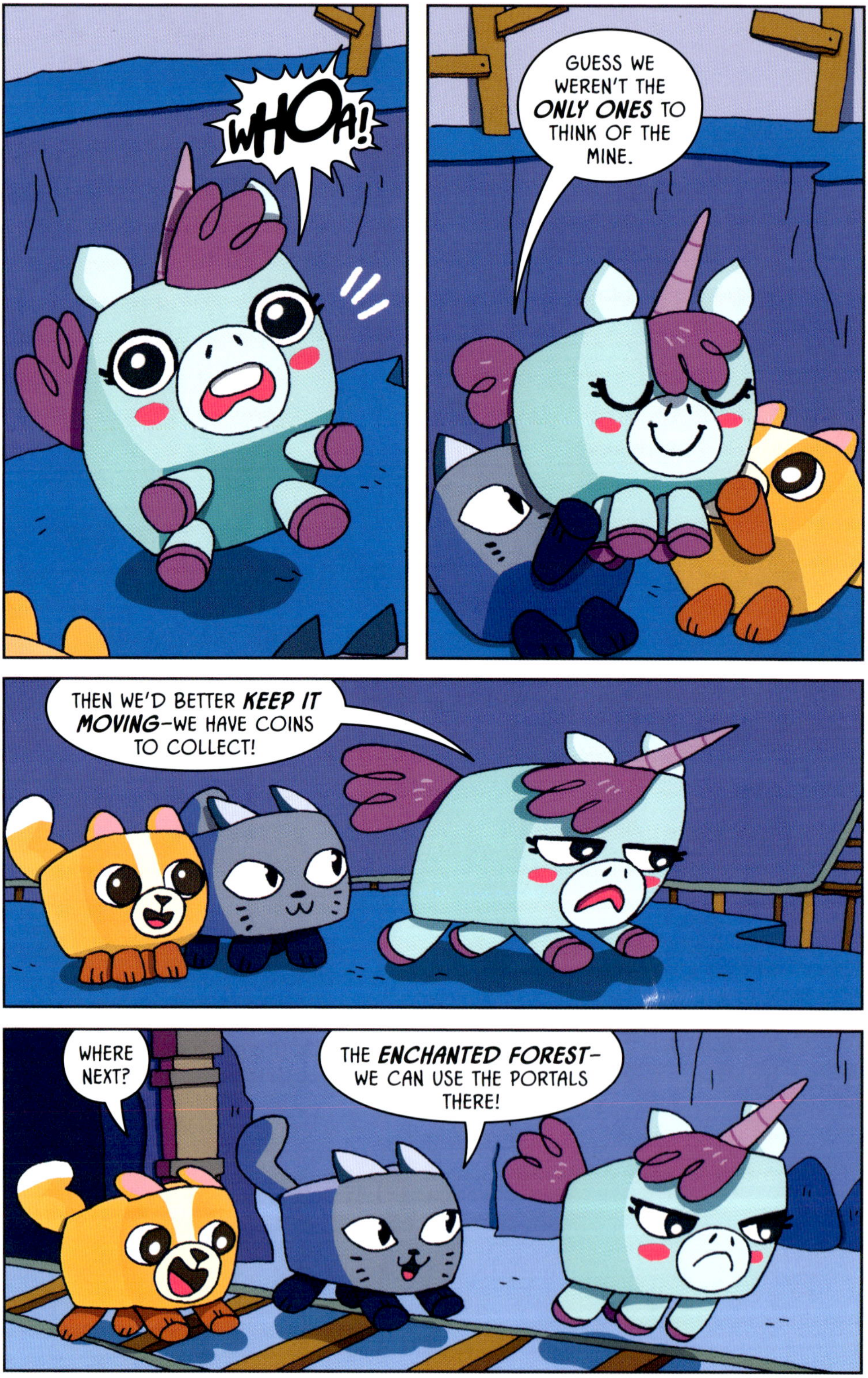
WHOA!
GUESS WE WEREN'T THE ONLY ONES TO THINK OF THE MINE.
THEN WE'D BETTER KEEP IT MOVING–WE HAVE COINS TO COLLECT!
WHERE NEXT?
THE ENCHANTED FOREST–WE CAN USE THE PORTALS THERE!

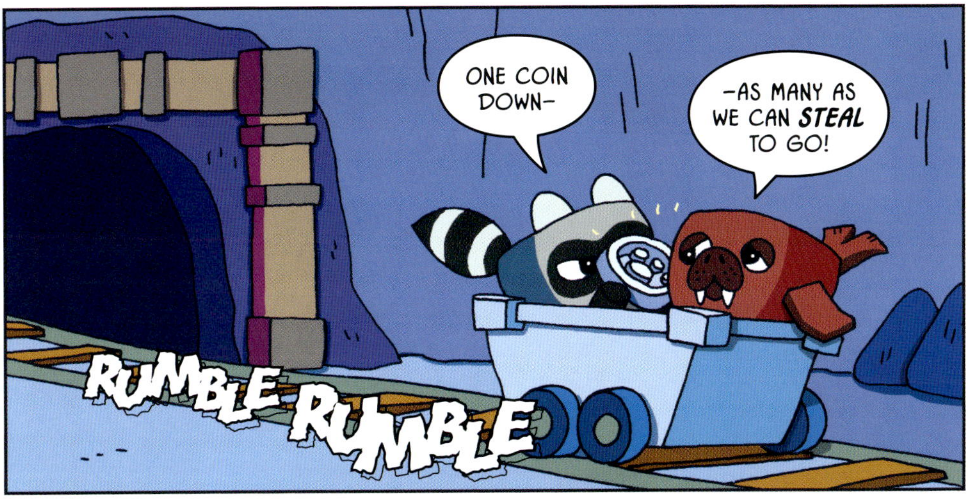
ONE COIN DOWN–
–AS MANY AS WE CAN STEAL TO GO!
RUMBLE RUMBLE

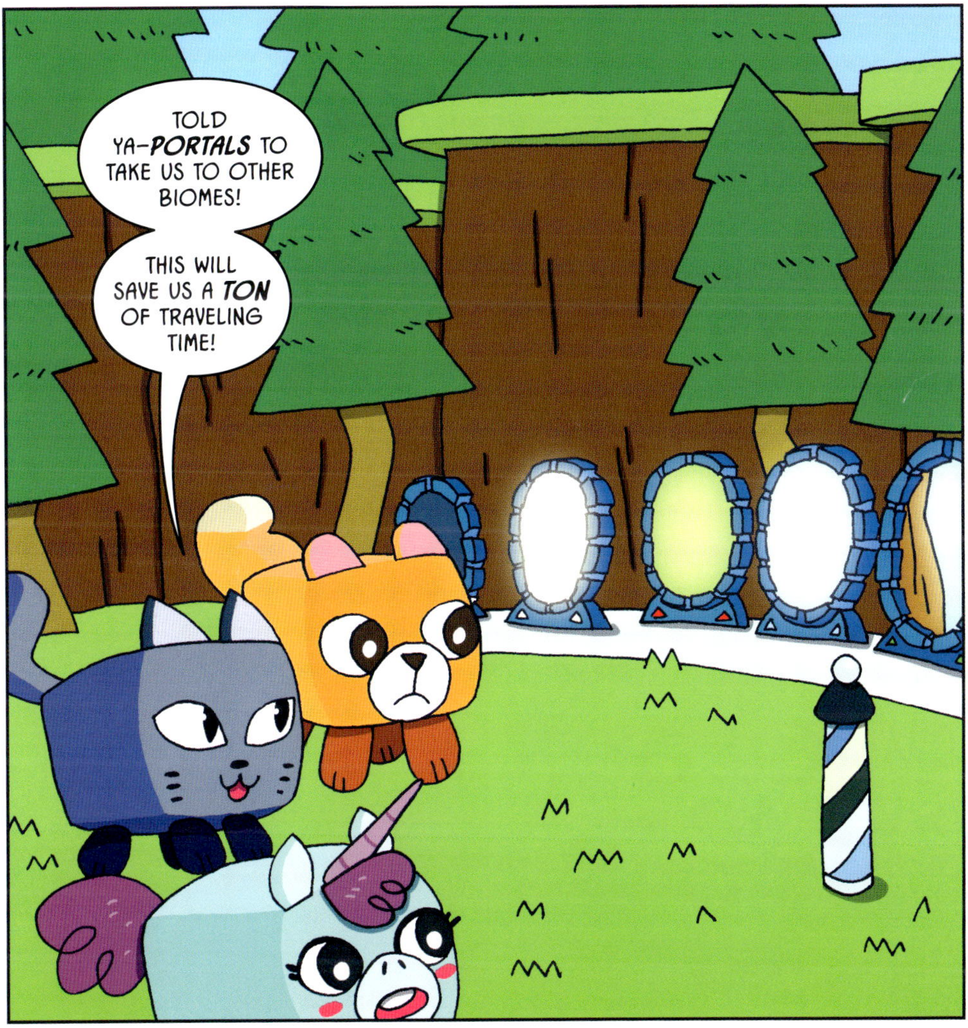
TOLD YA–PORTALS TO TAKE US TO OTHER BIOMES!
THIS WILL SAVE US A TON OF TRAVELING TIME!

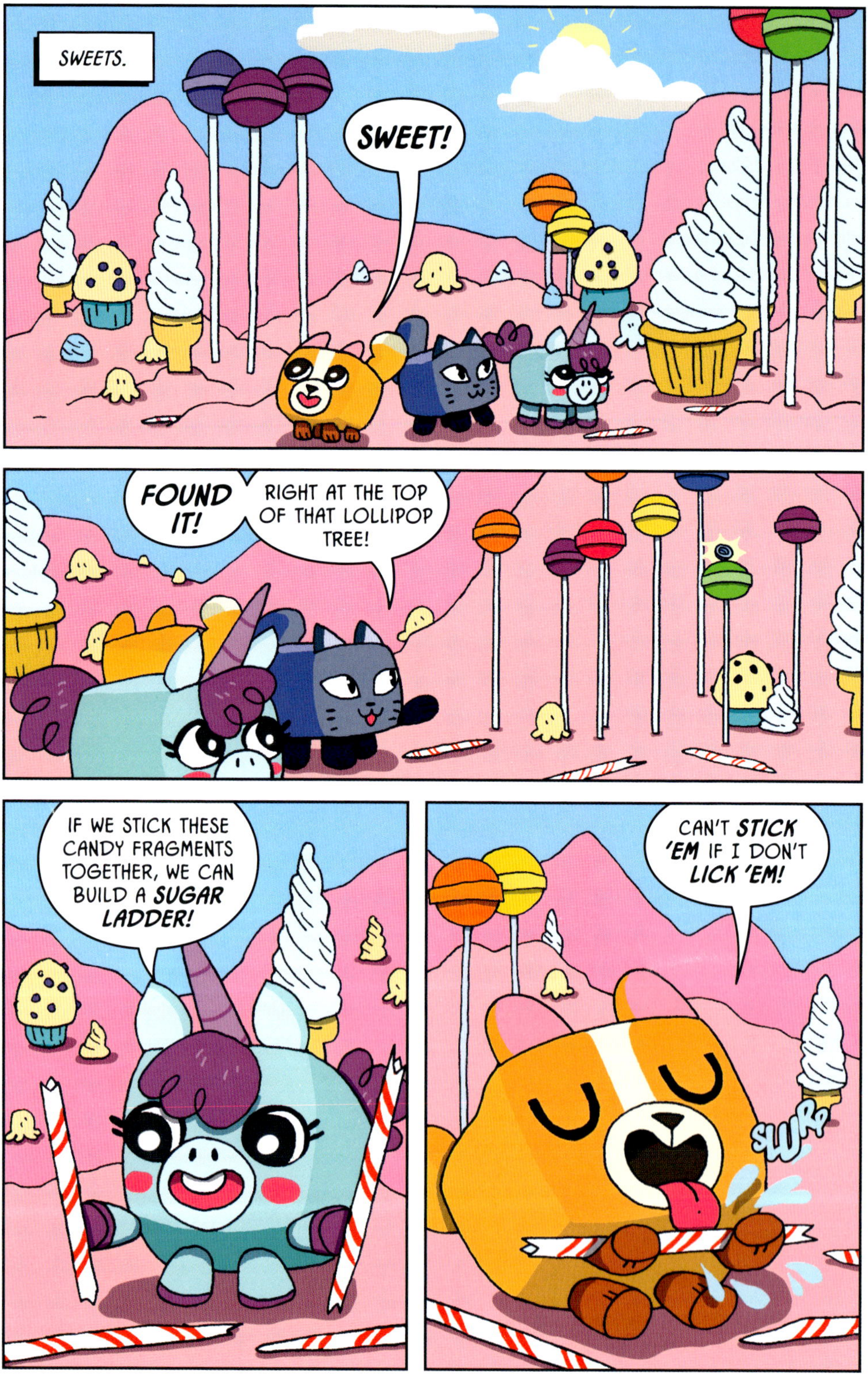

SWEETS.
SWEET!
FOUND IT!
RIGHT AT THE TOP OF THAT LOLLIPOP TREE!
IF WE STICK THESE CANDY FRAGMENTS TOGETHER, WE CAN BUILD A SUGAR LADDER!
CAN'T STICK 'EM IF I DON'T LICK 'EM!
SLURP

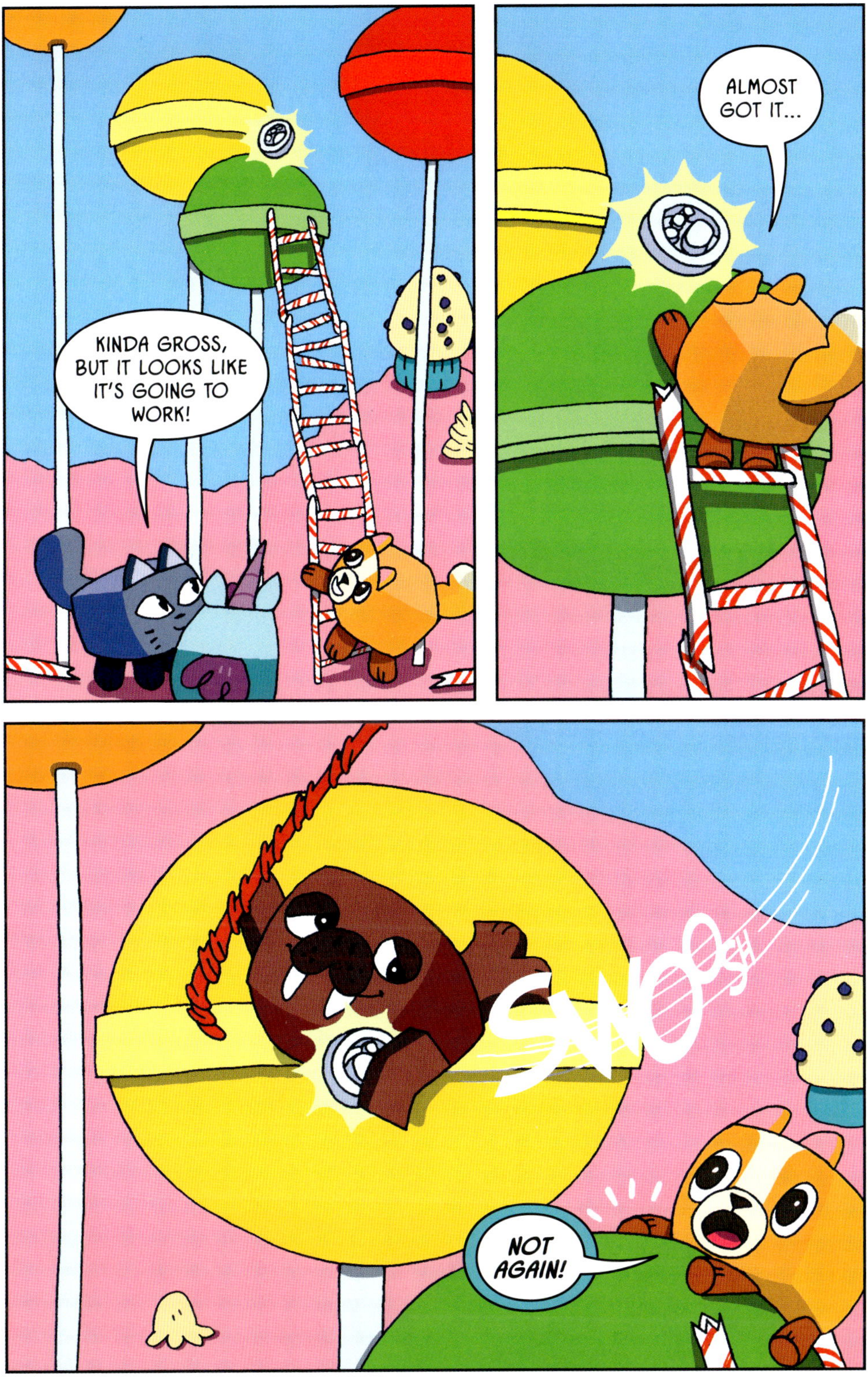
KINDA GROSS, BUT IT LOOKS LIKE IT'S GOING TO WORK!
ALMOST GOT IT...
SWOOSH
NOT AGAIN!

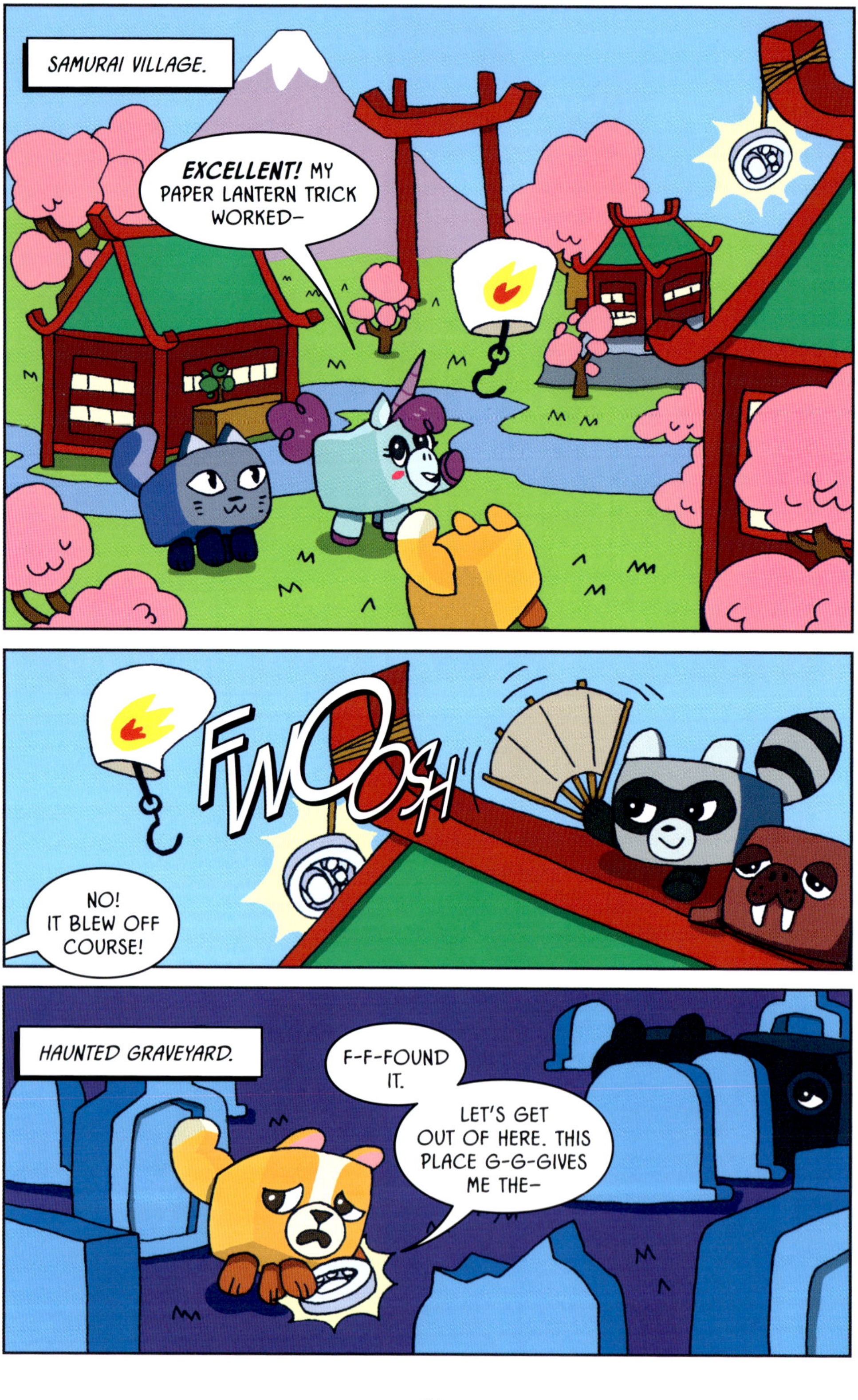
SAMURAI VILLAGE.
EXCELLENT! MY PAPER LANTERN TRICK WORKED–
FWOOSH
NO! IT BLEW OFF COURSE!
HAUNTED GRAVEYARD.
F-F-FOUND IT.
LET'S GET OUT OF HERE. THIS PLACE G-G-GIVES ME THE–

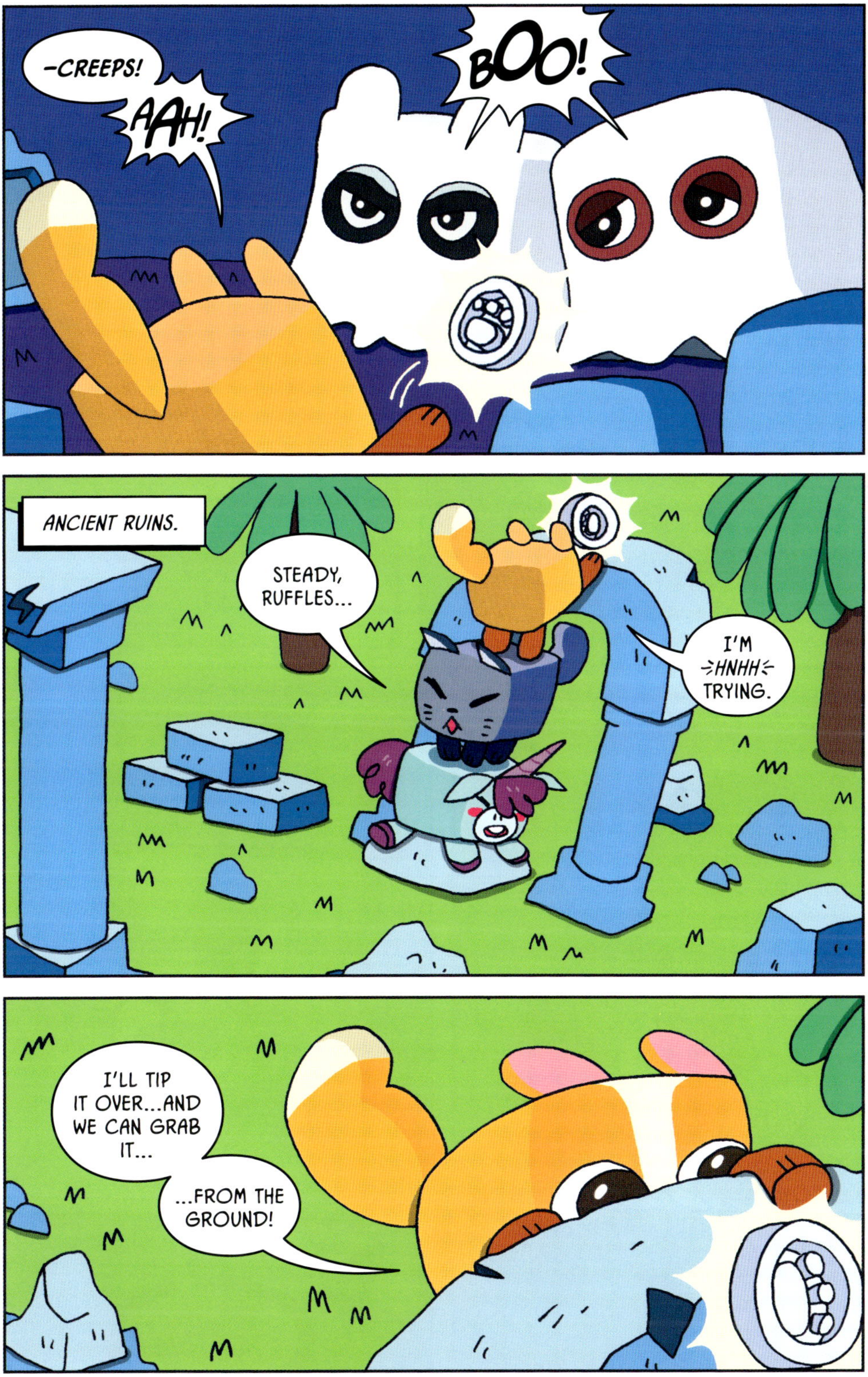
-CREEPS!
AAH!
BOO!
ANCIENT RUINS.
STEADY, RUFFLES...
I'M ≡HNHH≡ TRYING.
I'LL TIP IT OVER...AND WE CAN GRAB IT...
...FROM THE GROUND!

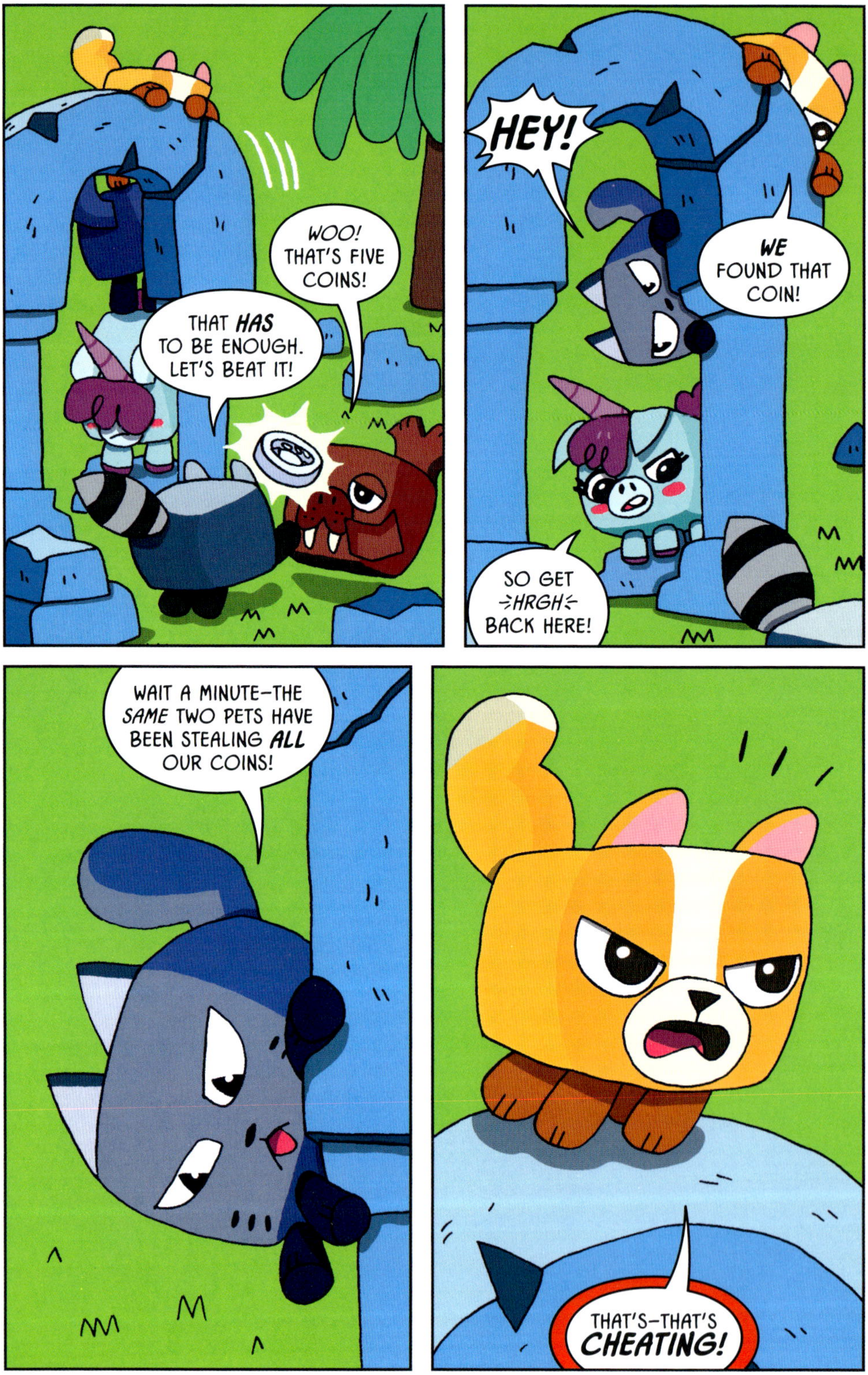
WOO! THAT'S FIVE COINS!
THAT *HAS* TO BE ENOUGH. LET'S BEAT IT!
HEY!
WE FOUND THAT COIN!
SO GET *HRGH* BACK HERE!
WAIT A MINUTE—THE *SAME* TWO PETS HAVE BEEN STEALING *ALL* OUR COINS!
THAT'S—THAT'S *CHEATING!*

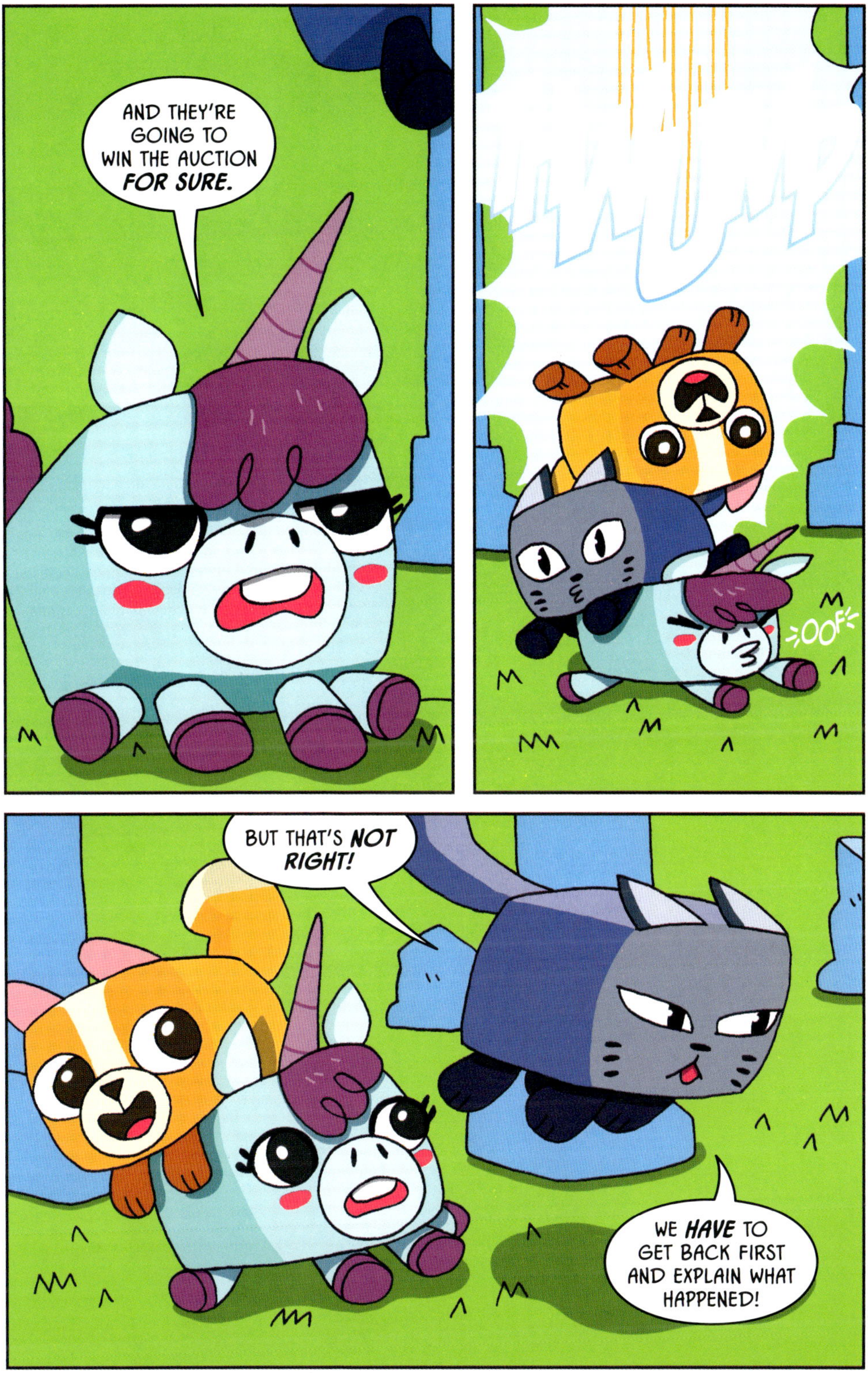
AND THEY'RE GOING TO WIN THE AUCTION FOR SURE.
OOF
BUT THAT'S NOT RIGHT!
WE HAVE TO GET BACK FIRST AND EXPLAIN WHAT HAPPENED!

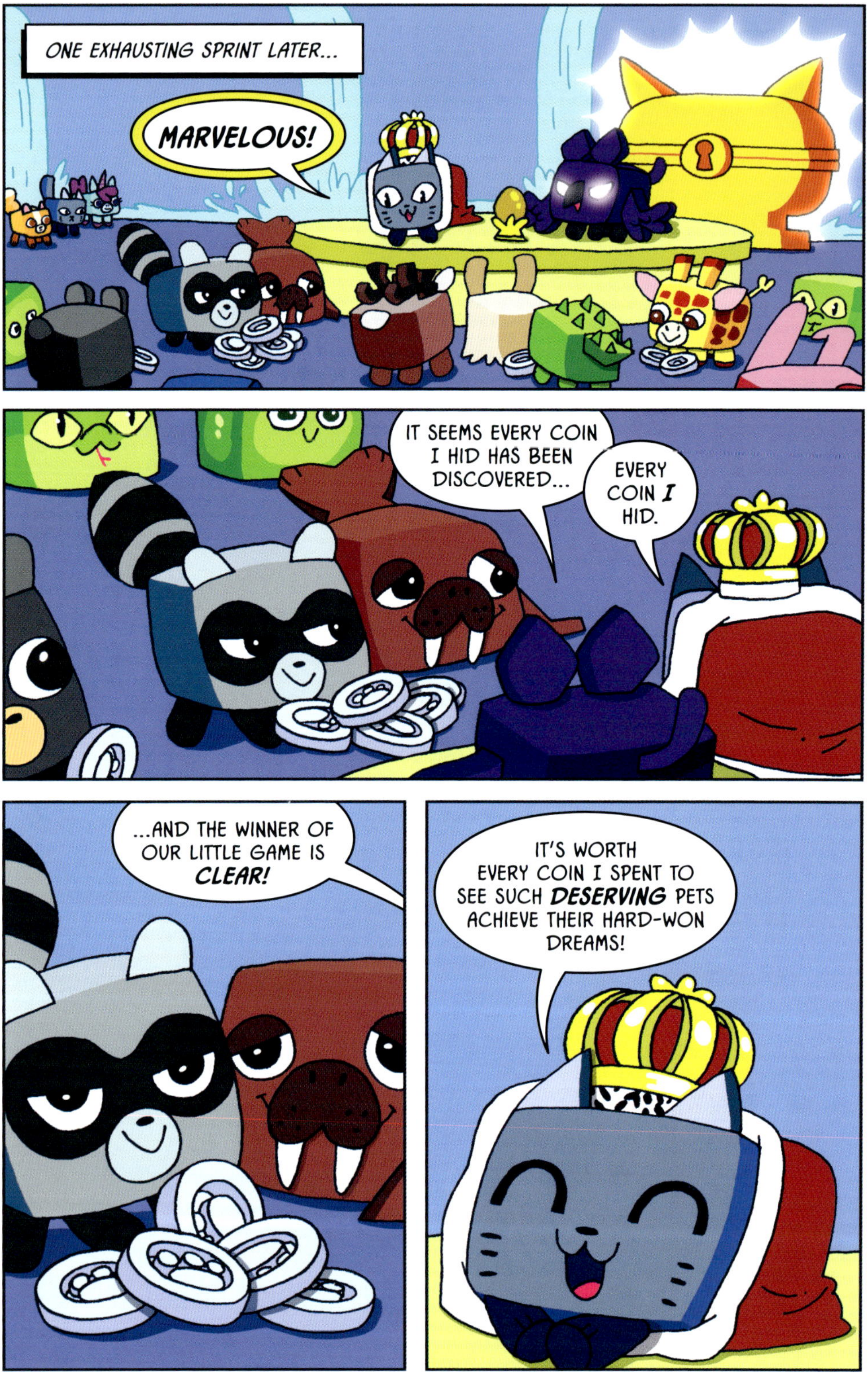
ONE EXHAUSTING SPRINT LATER...
MARVELOUS!
IT SEEMS EVERY COIN I HID HAS BEEN DISCOVERED...
EVERY COIN I HID.
...AND THE WINNER OF OUR LITTLE GAME IS CLEAR!
IT'S WORTH EVERY COIN I SPENT TO SEE SUCH DESERVING PETS ACHIEVE THEIR HARD-WON DREAMS!

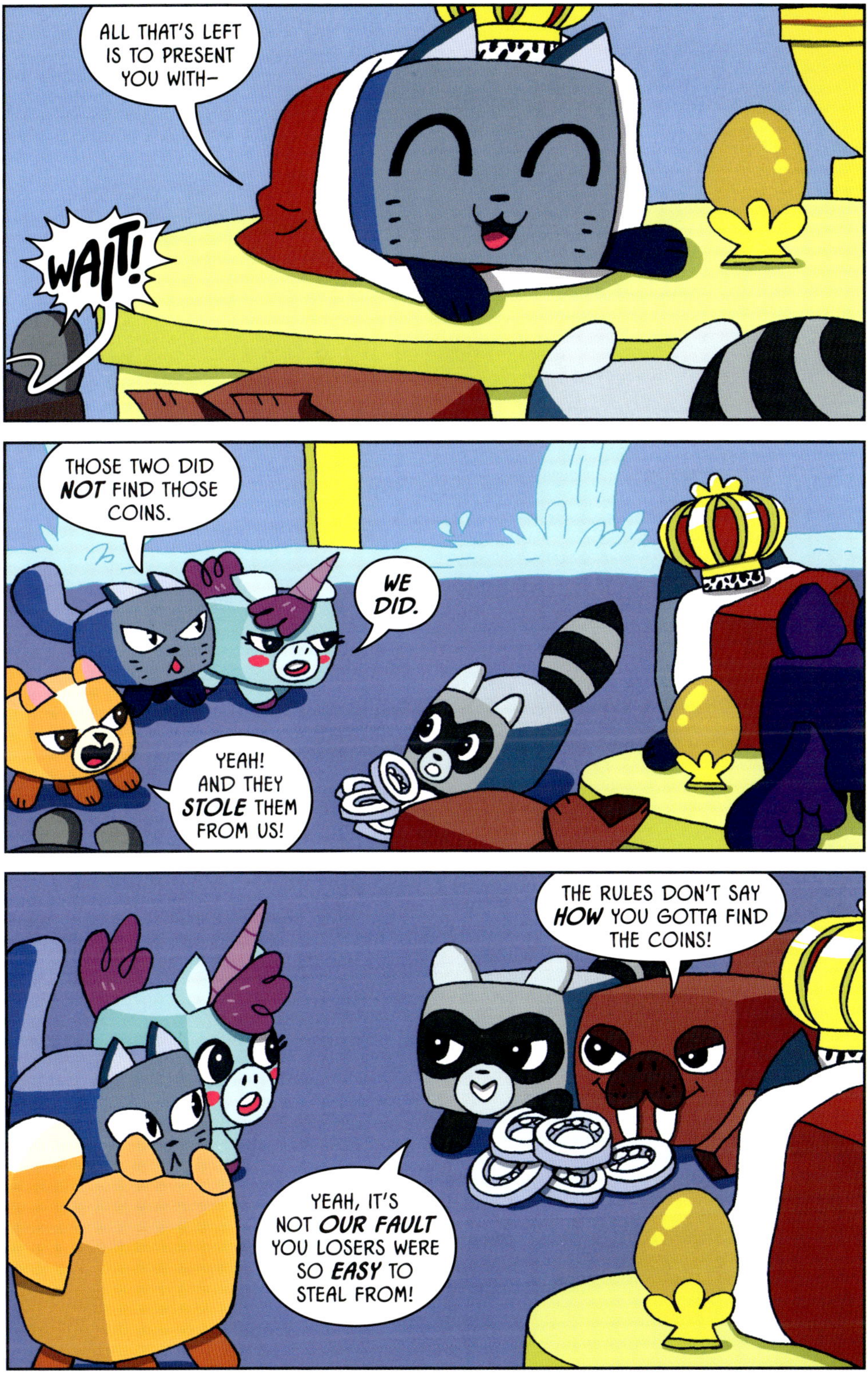
ALL THAT'S LEFT IS TO PRESENT YOU WITH–
WAIT!
THOSE TWO DID NOT FIND THOSE COINS.
WE DID.
YEAH! AND THEY STOLE THEM FROM US!
THE RULES DON'T SAY HOW YOU GOTTA FIND THE COINS!
YEAH, IT'S NOT OUR FAULT YOU LOSERS WERE SO EASY TO STEAL FROM!

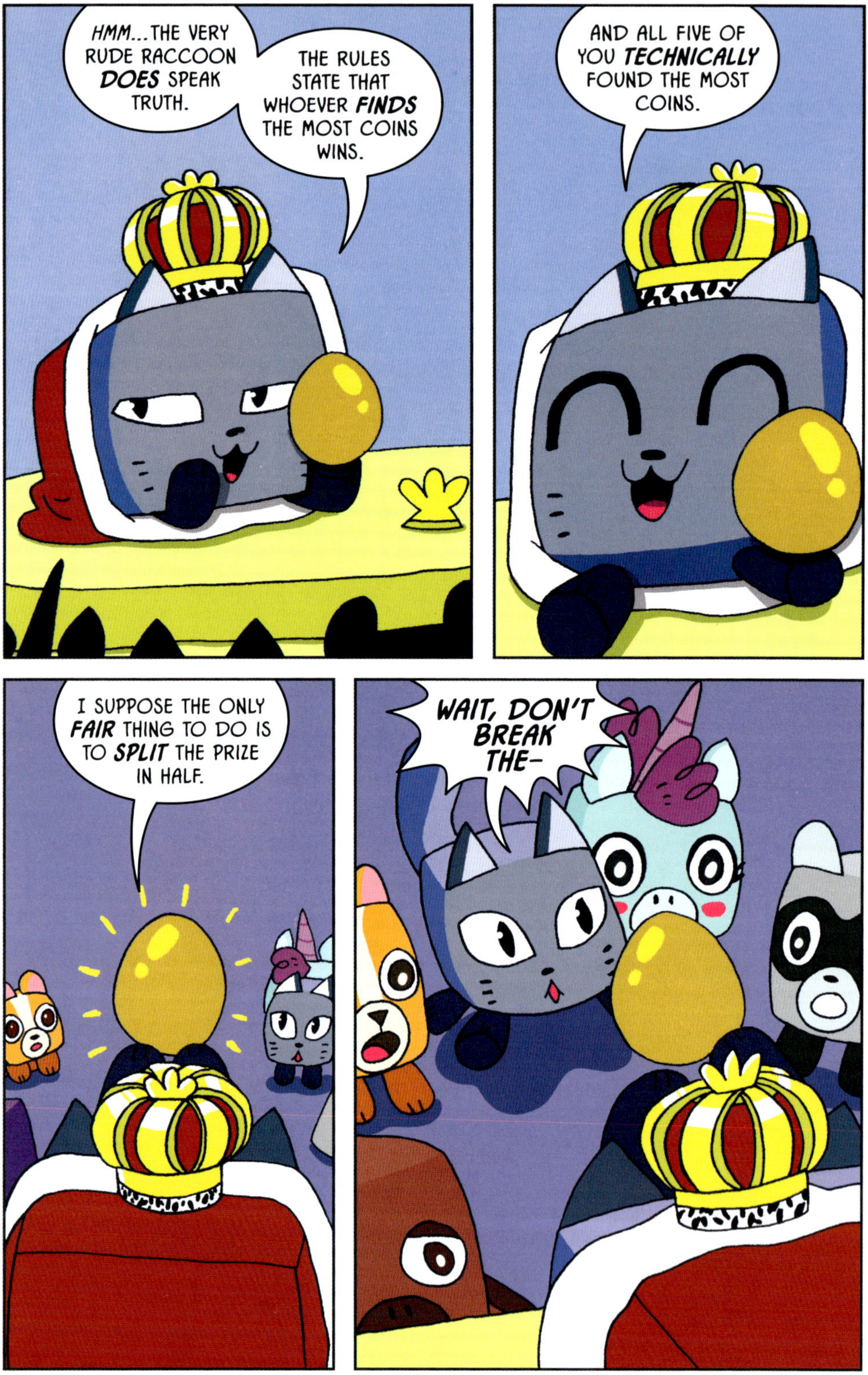
HMM...THE VERY RUDE RACCOON DOES SPEAK TRUTH.
THE RULES STATE THAT WHOEVER FINDS THE MOST COINS WINS.
AND ALL FIVE OF YOU TECHNICALLY FOUND THE MOST COINS.
I SUPPOSE THE ONLY FAIR THING TO DO IS TO SPLIT THE PRIZE IN HALF.
WAIT, DON'T BREAK THE–

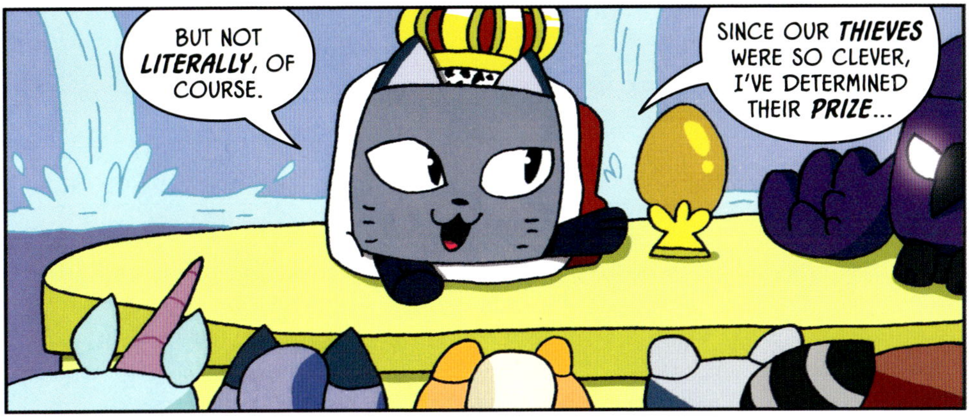
BUT NOT LITERALLY, OF COURSE.
SINCE OUR THIEVES WERE SO CLEVER, I'VE DETERMINED THEIR PRIZE...

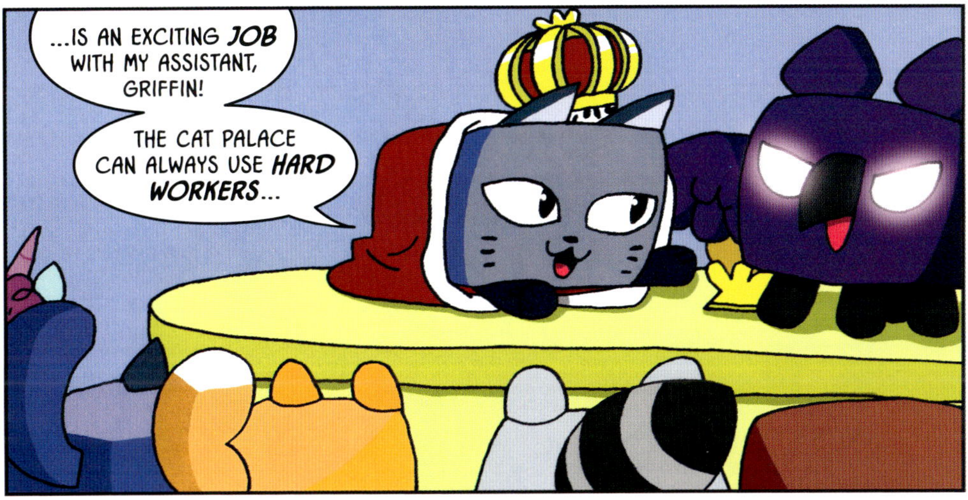
...IS AN EXCITING JOB WITH MY ASSISTANT, GRIFFIN!
THE CAT PALACE CAN ALWAYS USE HARD WORKERS...

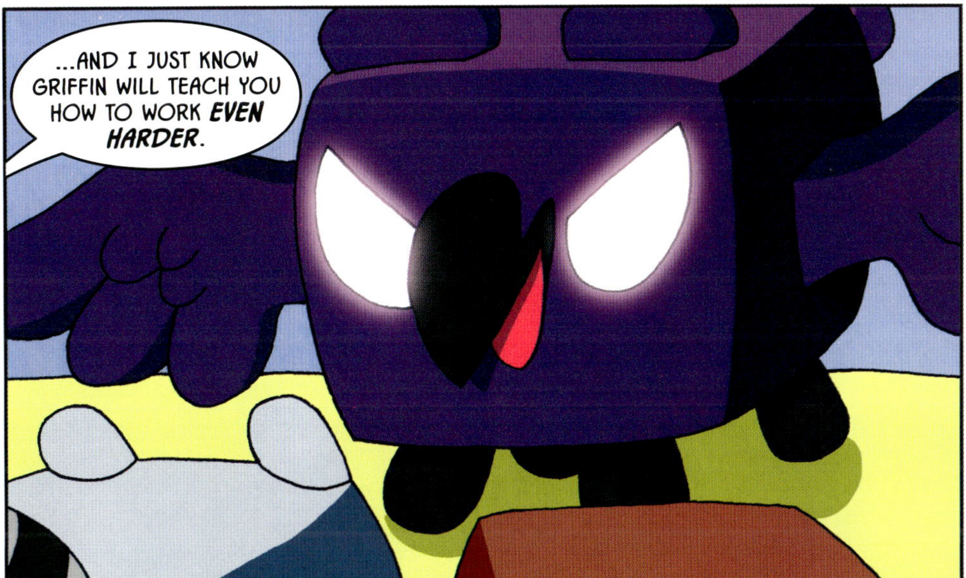
...AND I JUST KNOW GRIFFIN WILL TEACH YOU HOW TO WORK EVEN HARDER.

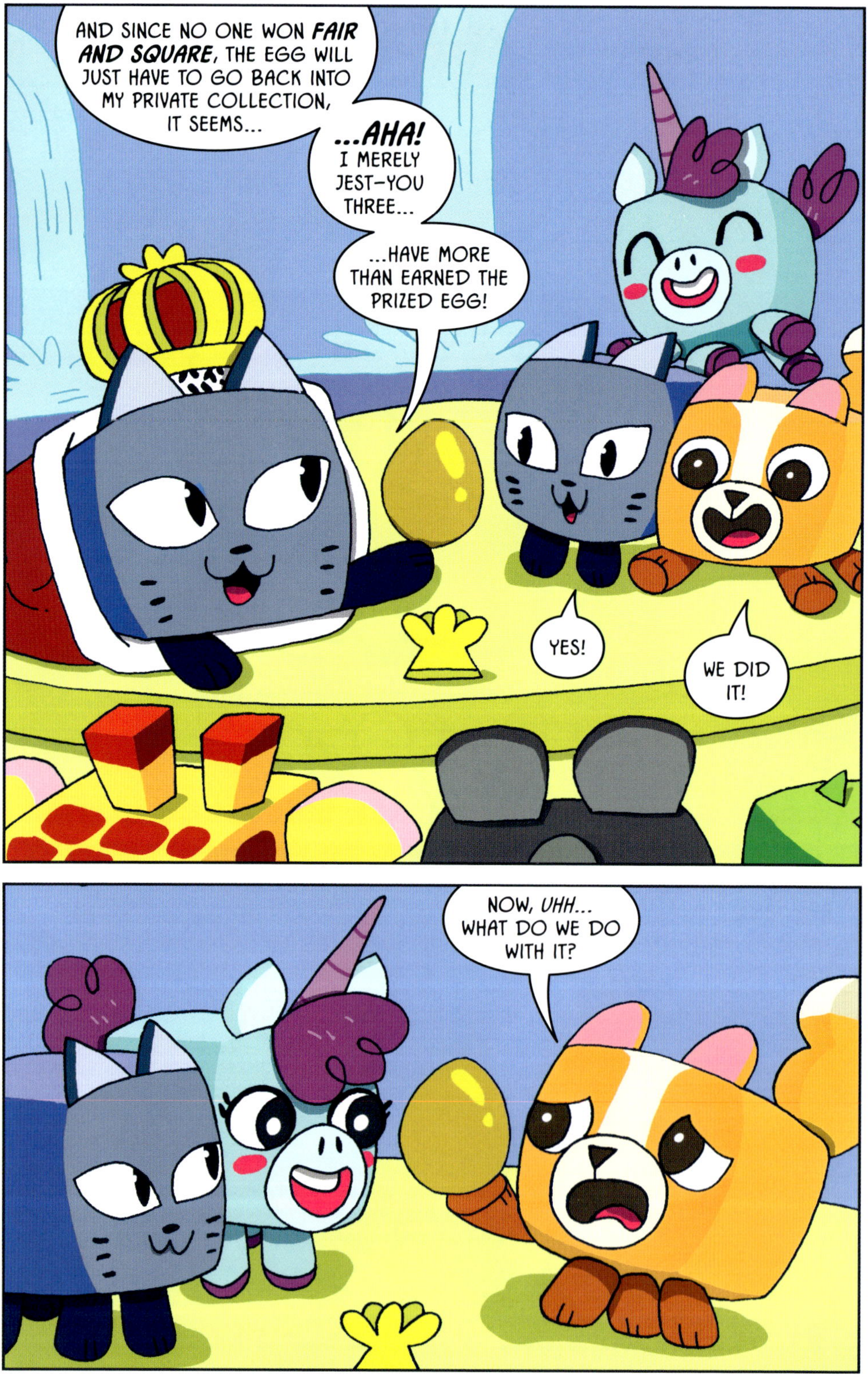
AND SINCE NO ONE WON FAIR AND SQUARE, THE EGG WILL JUST HAVE TO GO BACK INTO MY PRIVATE COLLECTION, IT SEEMS...
...AHA! I MERELY JEST—YOU THREE...
...HAVE MORE THAN EARNED THE PRIZED EGG!
YES!
WE DID IT!
NOW, UHH... WHAT DO WE DO WITH IT?

PART 3
MAP MADNESS

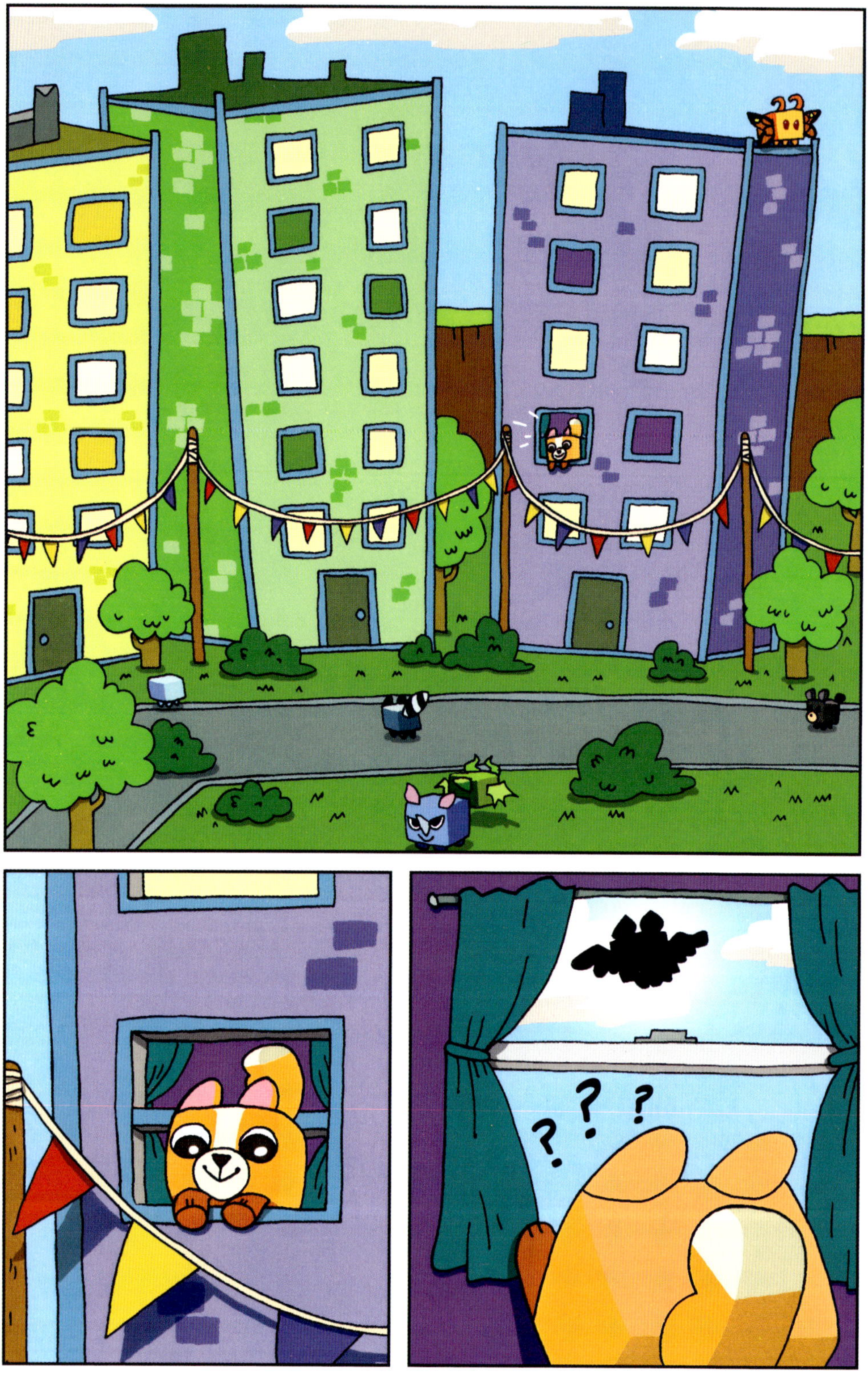

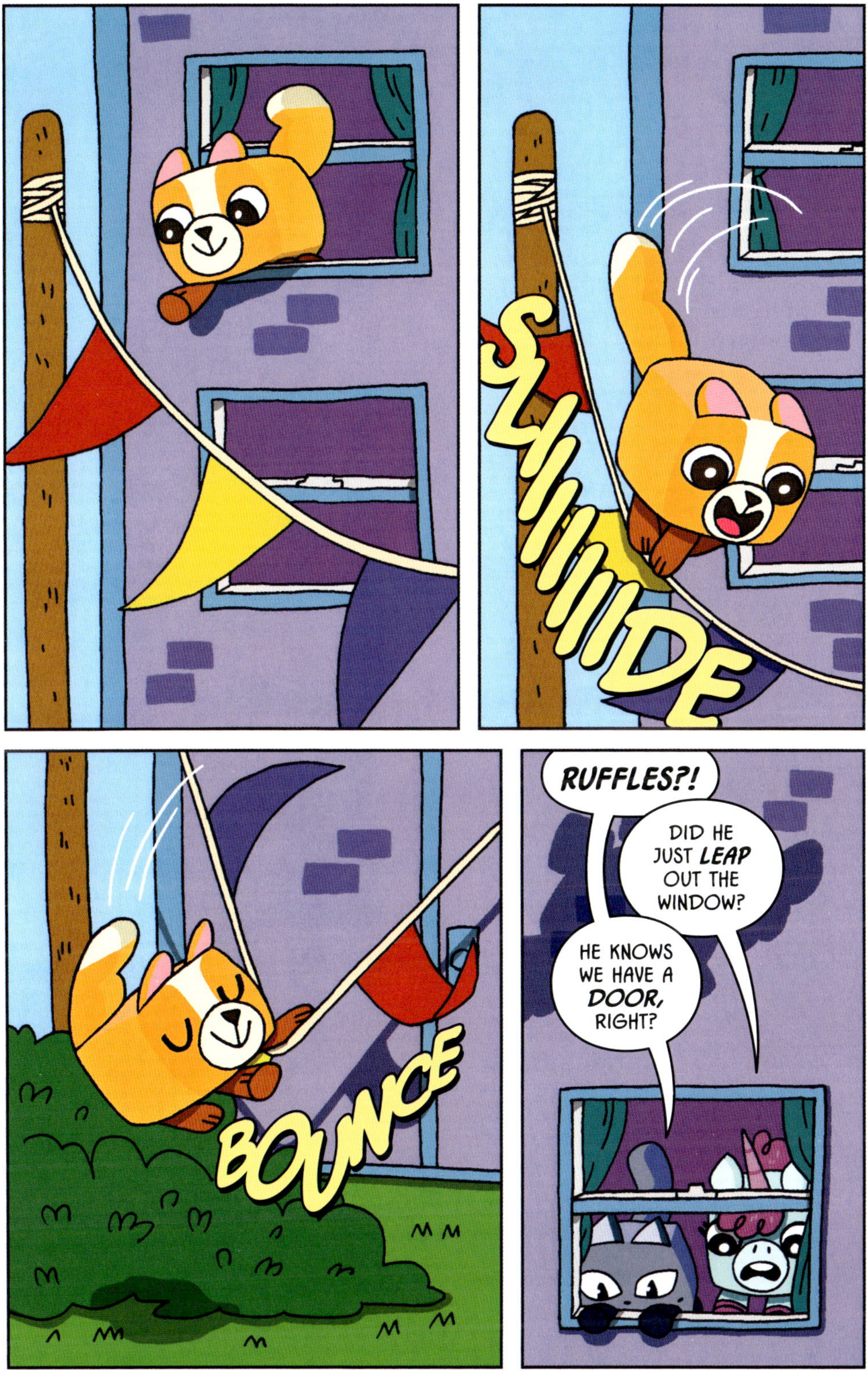
SHHHHIIIIDE
BOUNCE
RUFFLES?!
DID HE JUST LEAP OUT THE WINDOW?
HE KNOWS WE HAVE A DOOR, RIGHT?

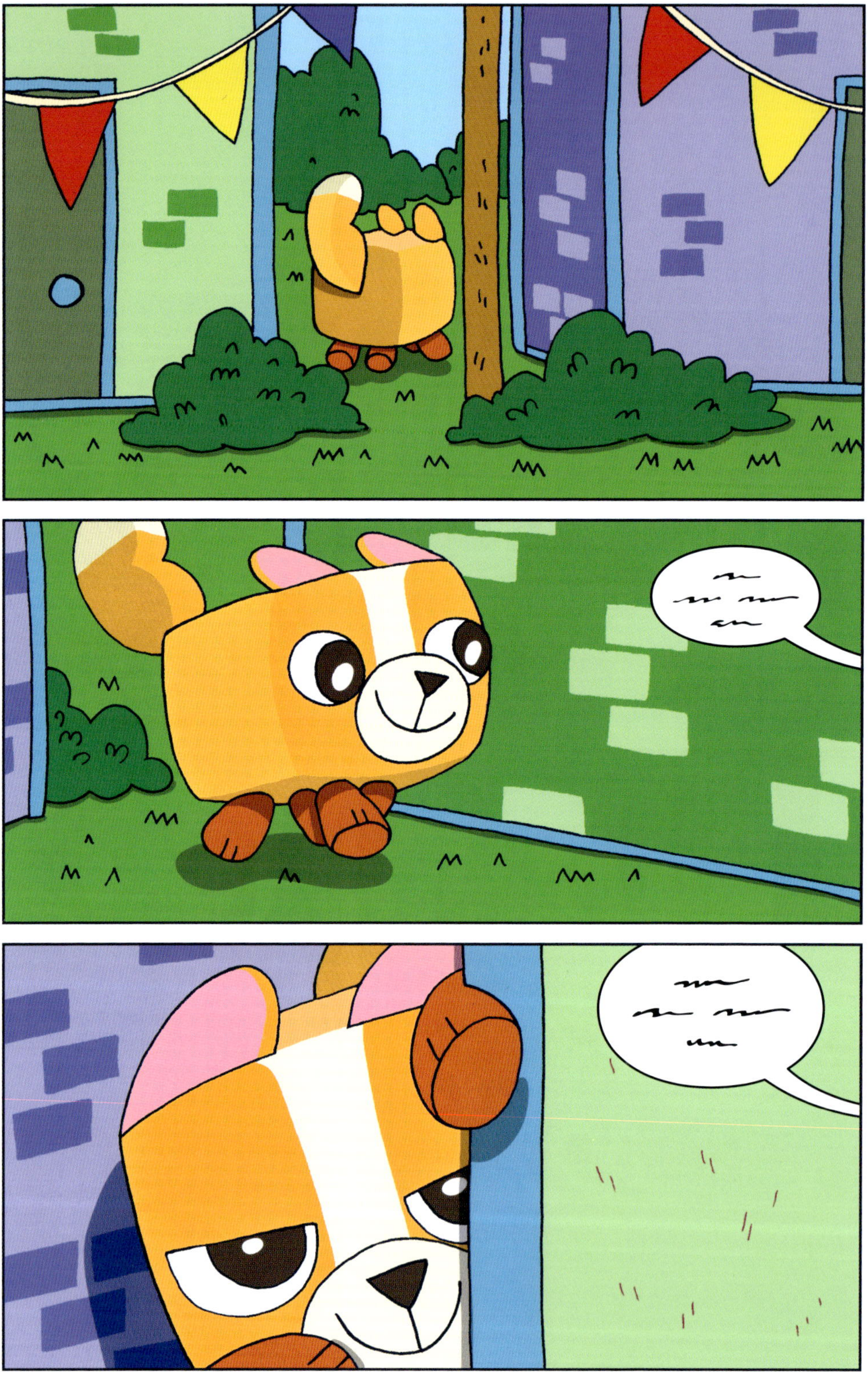

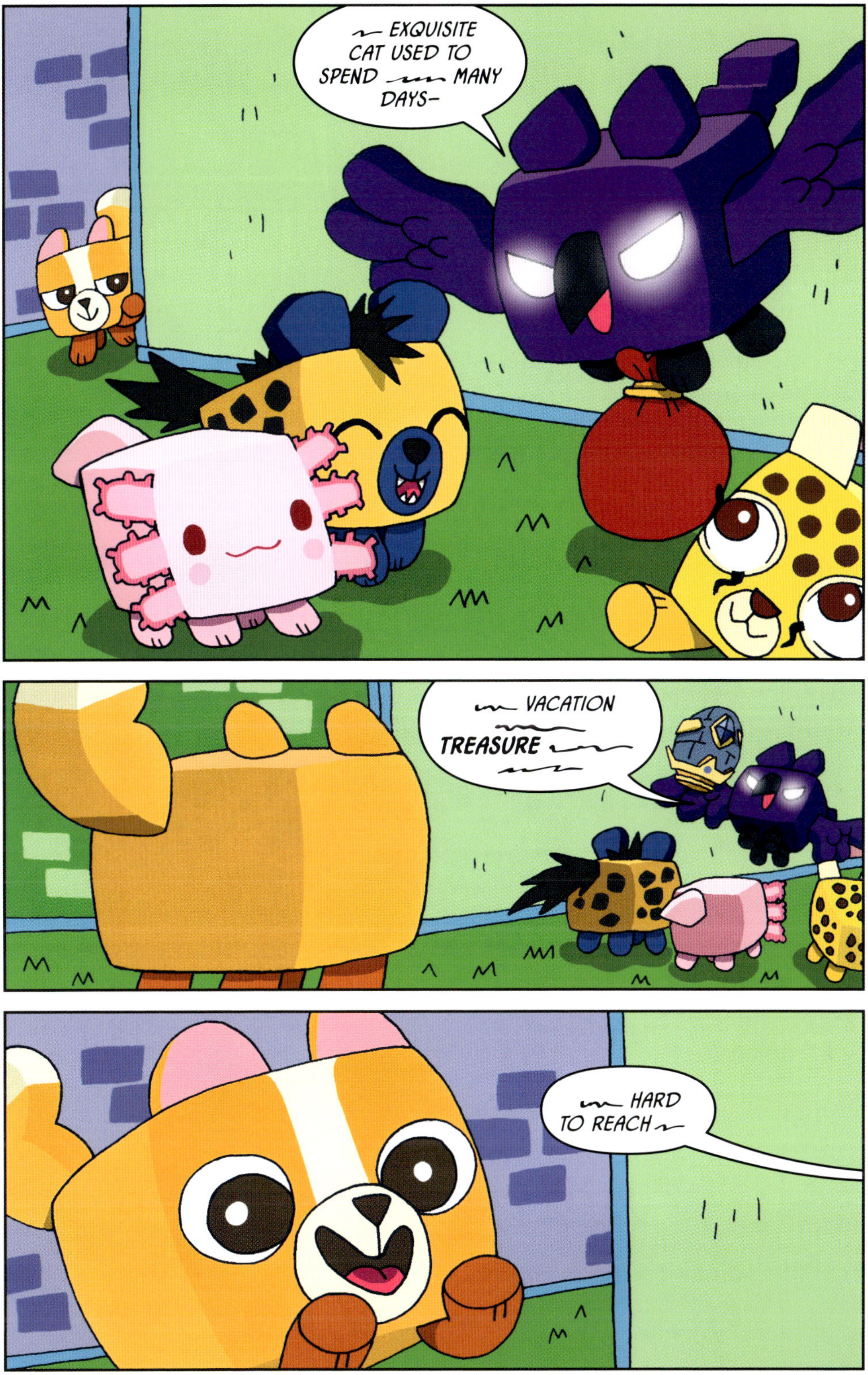
EXQUISITE CAT USED TO SPEND MANY DAYS–
VACATION TREASURE
HARD TO REACH

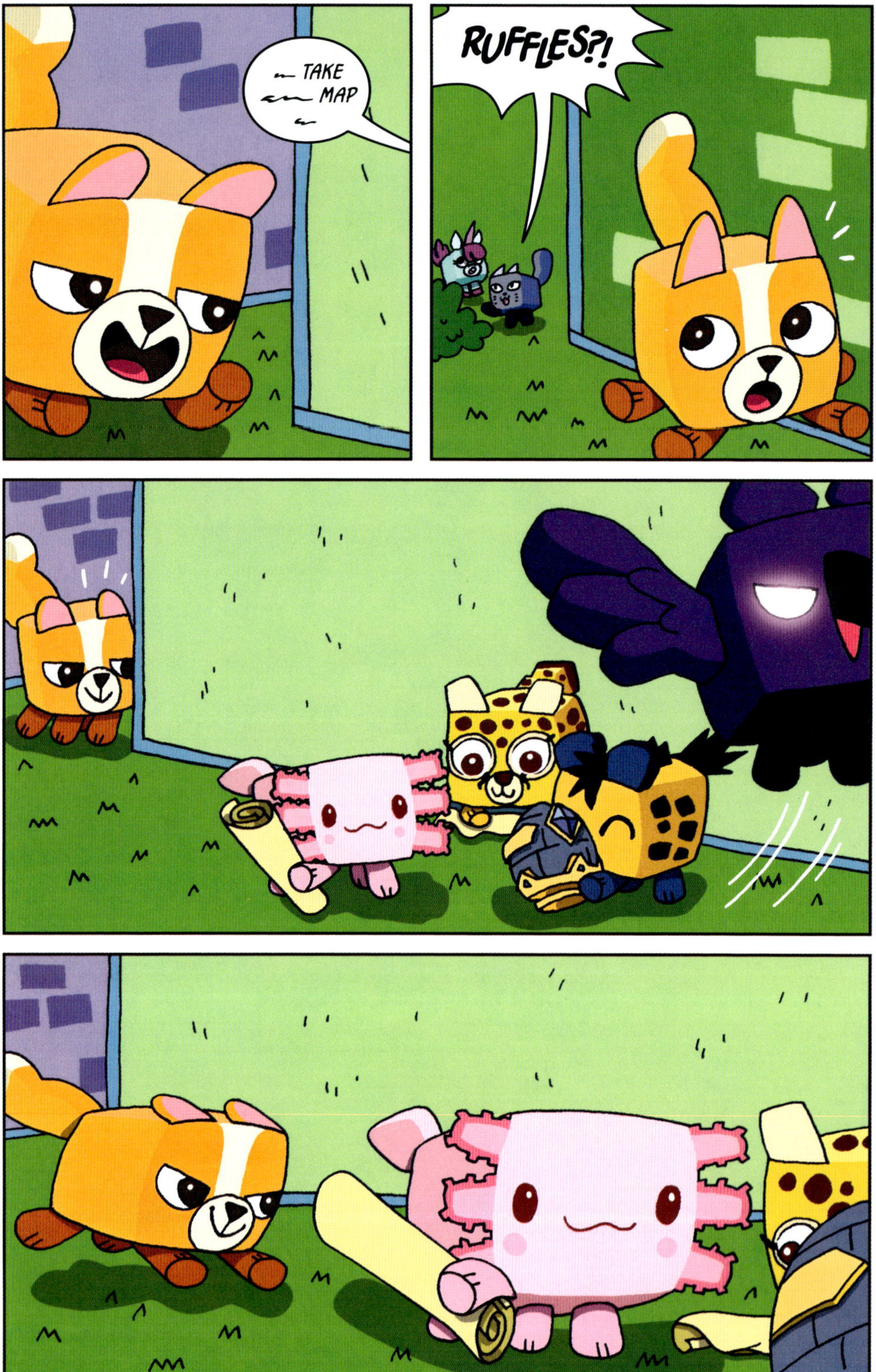

TAKE MAP
RUFFLES?!

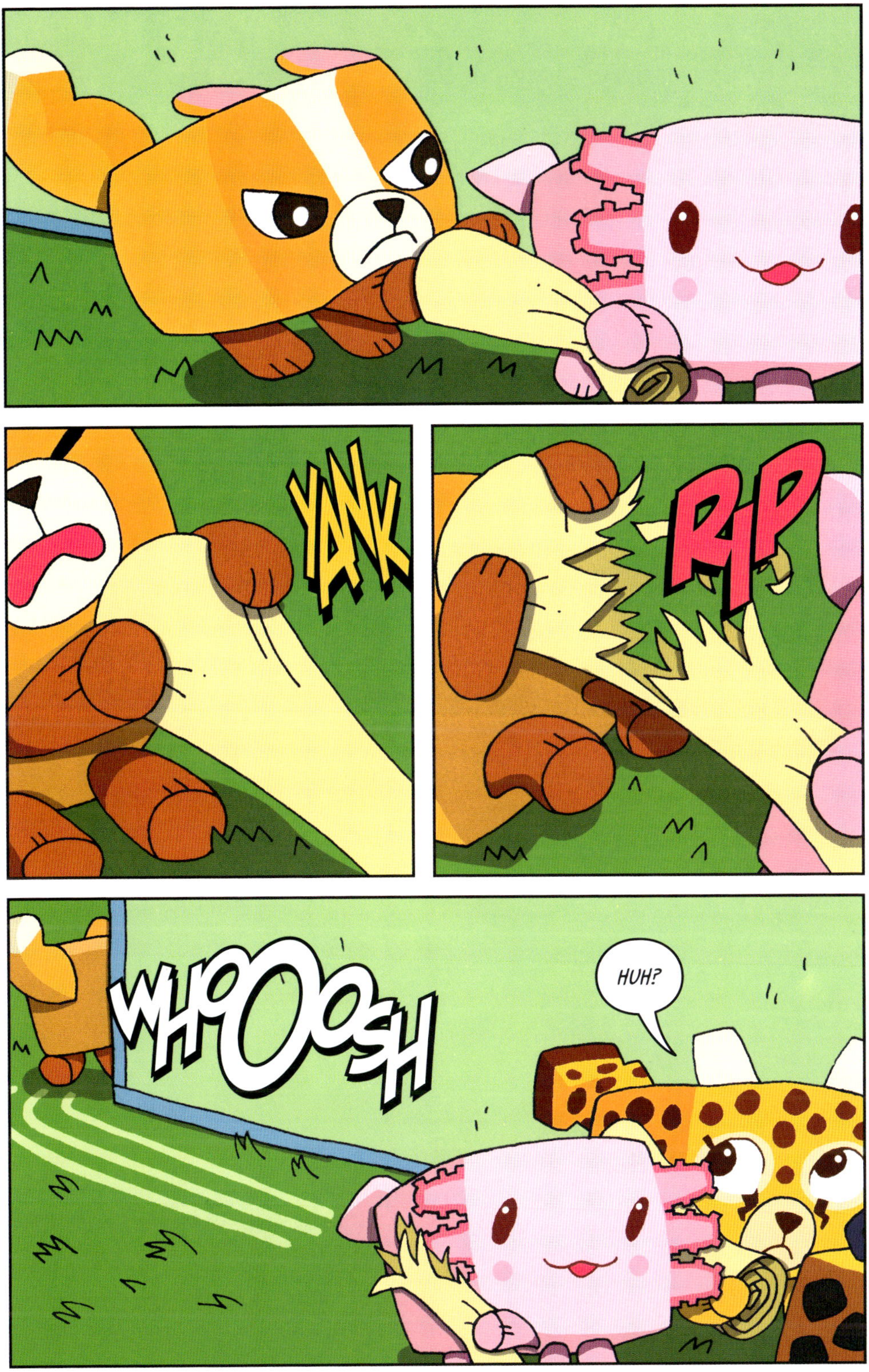
YANK
RIP
WHOOOSH
HUH?

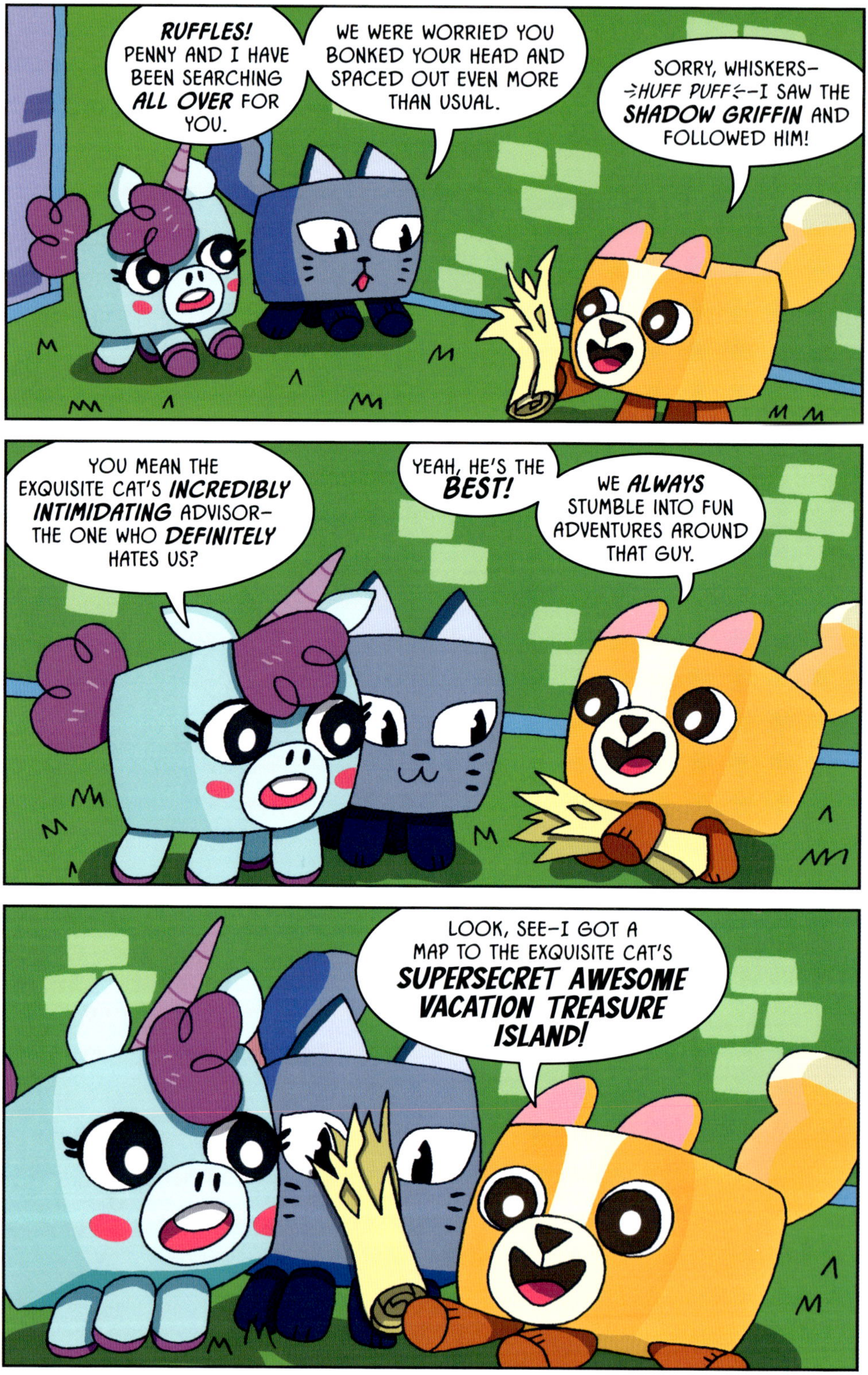
RUFFLES! PENNY AND I HAVE BEEN SEARCHING ALL OVER FOR YOU.
WE WERE WORRIED YOU BONKED YOUR HEAD AND SPACED OUT EVEN MORE THAN USUAL.
SORRY, WHISKERS- HUFF PUFF -I SAW THE SHADOW GRIFFIN AND FOLLOWED HIM!
YOU MEAN THE EXQUISITE CAT'S INCREDIBLY INTIMIDATING ADVISOR- THE ONE WHO DEFINITELY HATES US?
YEAH, HE'S THE BEST!
WE ALWAYS STUMBLE INTO FUN ADVENTURES AROUND THAT GUY.
LOOK, SEE-I GOT A MAP TO THE EXQUISITE CAT'S SUPERSECRET AWESOME VACATION TREASURE ISLAND!

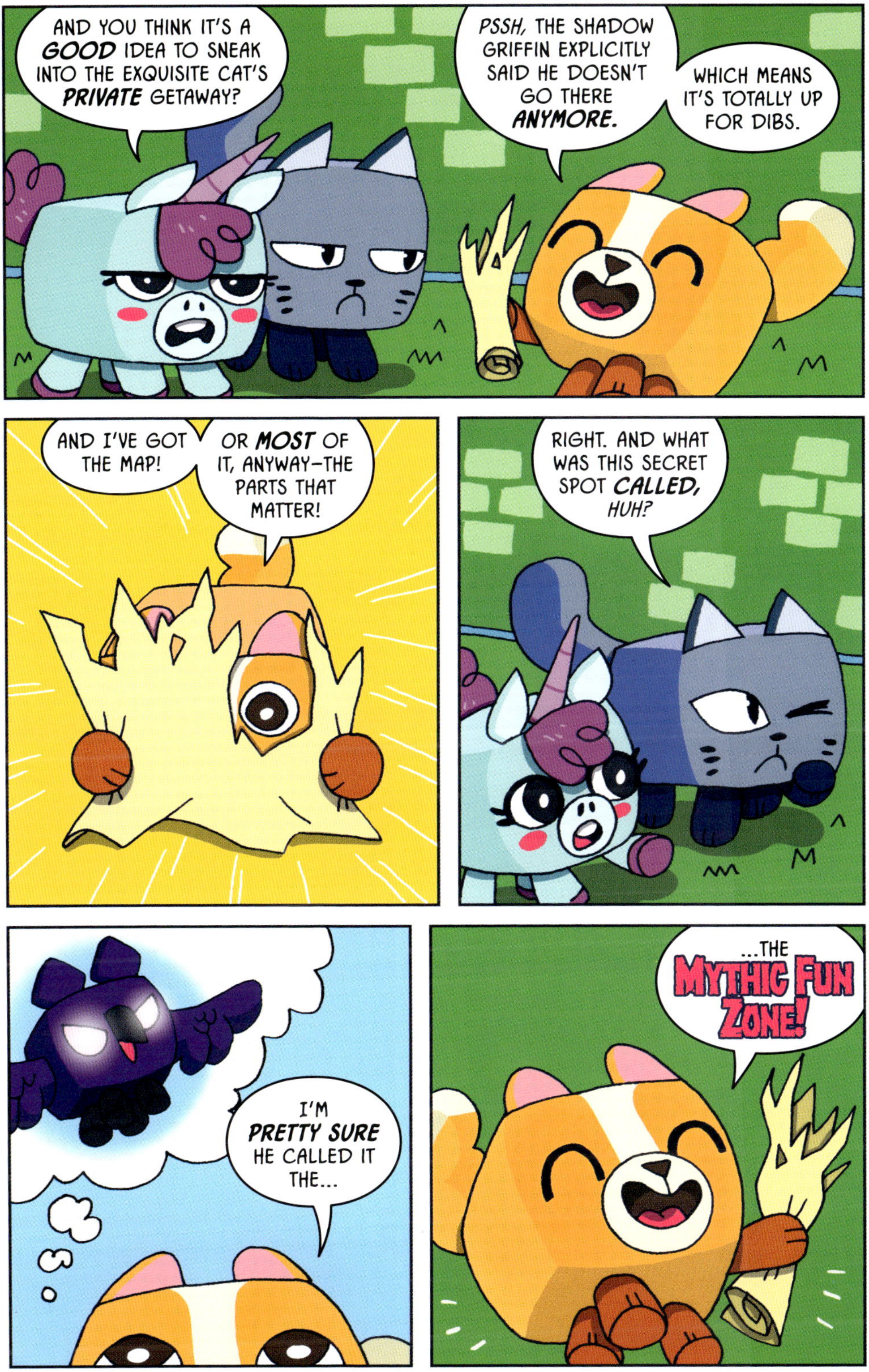
AND YOU THINK IT'S A GOOD IDEA TO SNEAK INTO THE EXQUISITE CAT'S PRIVATE GETAWAY?
PSSH, THE SHADOW GRIFFIN EXPLICITLY SAID HE DOESN'T GO THERE ANYMORE.
WHICH MEANS IT'S TOTALLY UP FOR DIBS.
AND I'VE GOT THE MAP!
OR MOST OF IT, ANYWAY—THE PARTS THAT MATTER!
RIGHT. AND WHAT WAS THIS SECRET SPOT CALLED, HUH?
I'M PRETTY SURE HE CALLED IT THE...
...THE MYTHIC FUN ZONE!

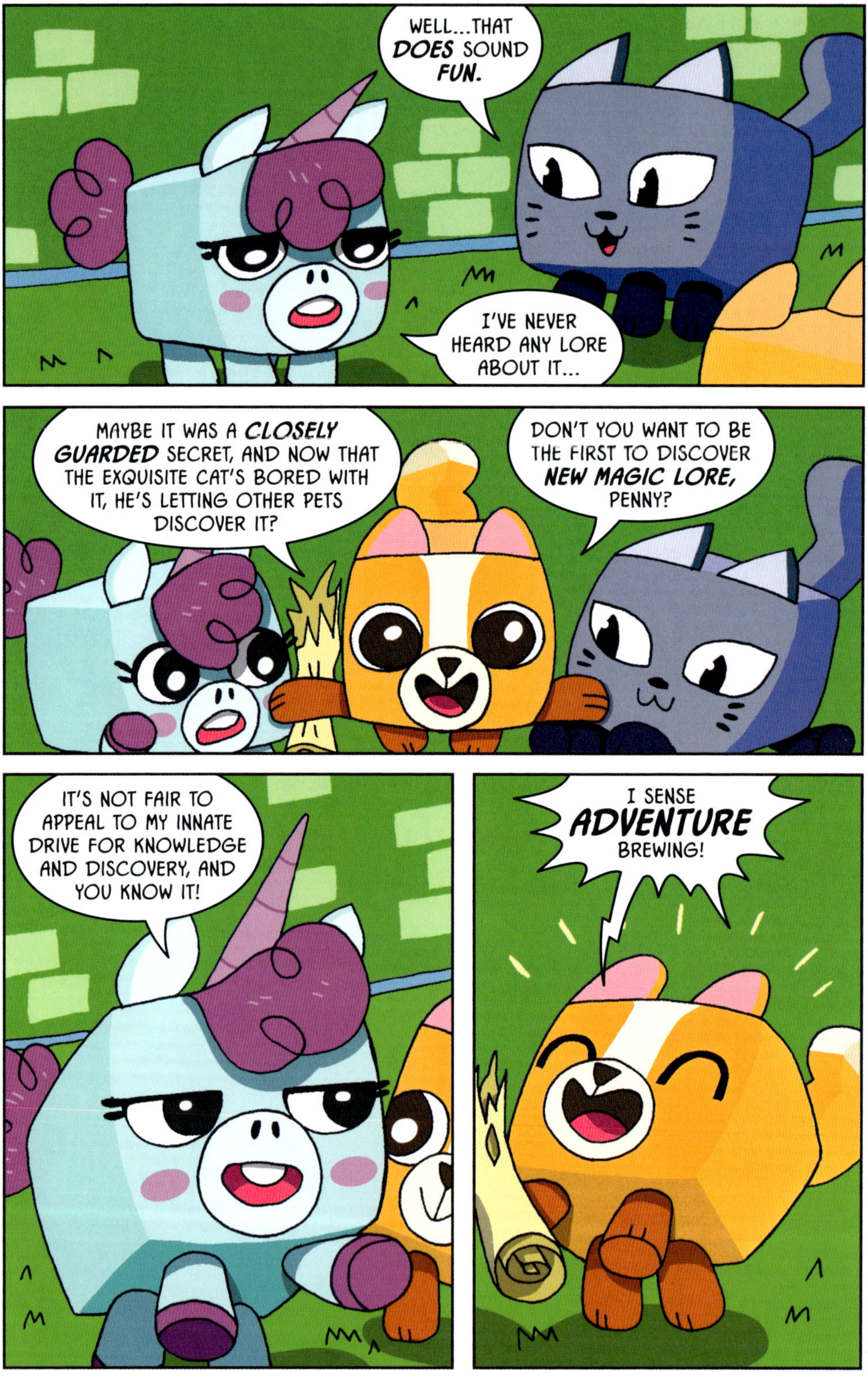
WELL...THAT DOES SOUND FUN.
I'VE NEVER HEARD ANY LORE ABOUT IT...
MAYBE IT WAS A CLOSELY GUARDED SECRET, AND NOW THAT THE EXQUISITE CAT'S BORED WITH IT, HE'S LETTING OTHER PETS DISCOVER IT?
DON'T YOU WANT TO BE THE FIRST TO DISCOVER NEW MAGIC LORE, PENNY?
IT'S NOT FAIR TO APPEAL TO MY INNATE DRIVE FOR KNOWLEDGE AND DISCOVERY, AND YOU KNOW IT!
I SENSE ADVENTURE BREWING!

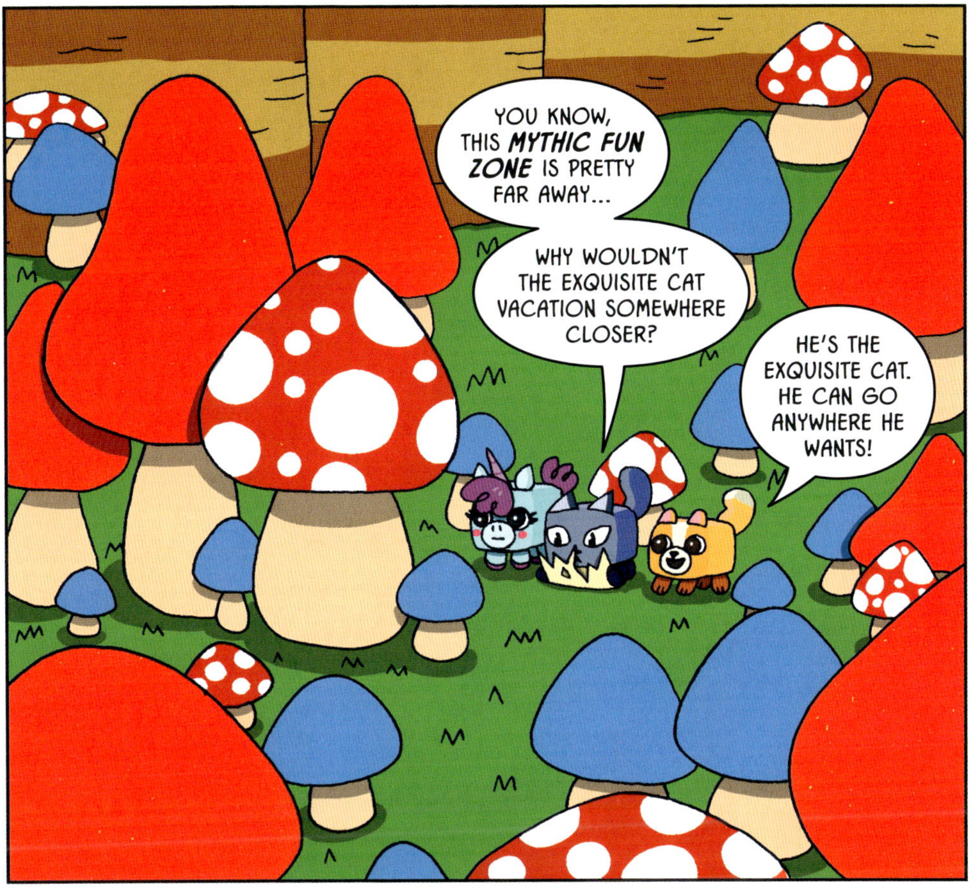
YOU KNOW, THIS MYTHIC FUN ZONE IS PRETTY FAR AWAY...
WHY WOULDN'T THE EXQUISITE CAT VACATION SOMEWHERE CLOSER?
HE'S THE EXQUISITE CAT. HE CAN GO ANYWHERE HE WANTS!

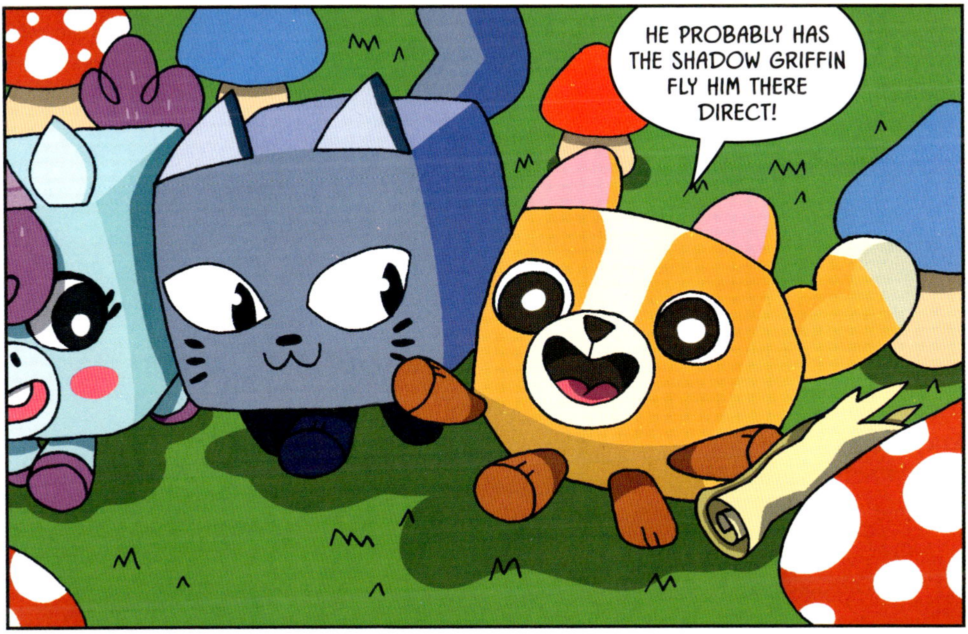
HE PROBABLY HAS THE SHADOW GRIFFIN FLY HIM THERE DIRECT!

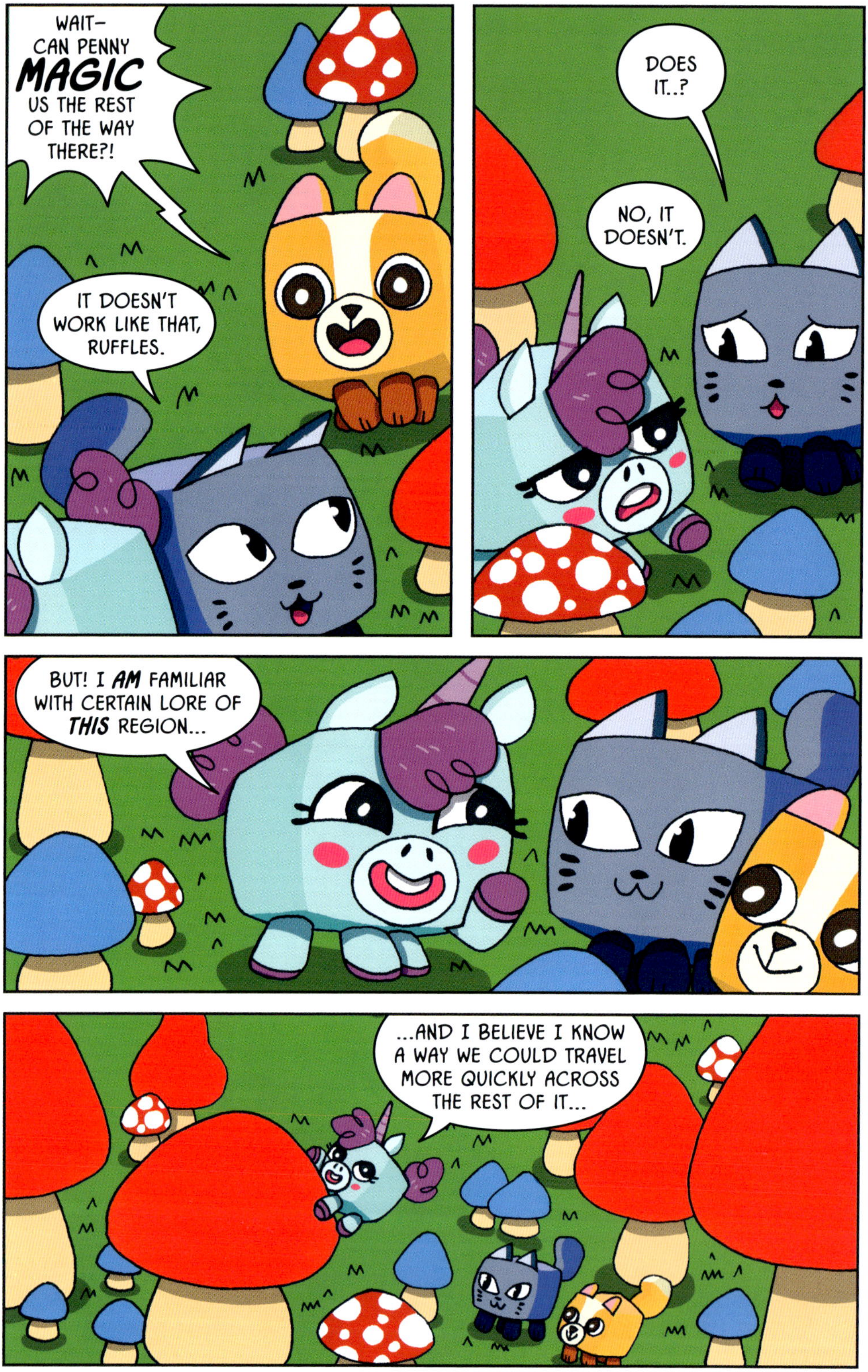
WAIT— CAN PENNY MAGIC US THE REST OF THE WAY THERE?!
IT DOESN'T WORK LIKE THAT, RUFFLES.
DOES IT..?
NO, IT DOESN'T.
BUT! I AM FAMILIAR WITH CERTAIN LORE OF THIS REGION...
...AND I BELIEVE I KNOW A WAY WE COULD TRAVEL MORE QUICKLY ACROSS THE REST OF IT...

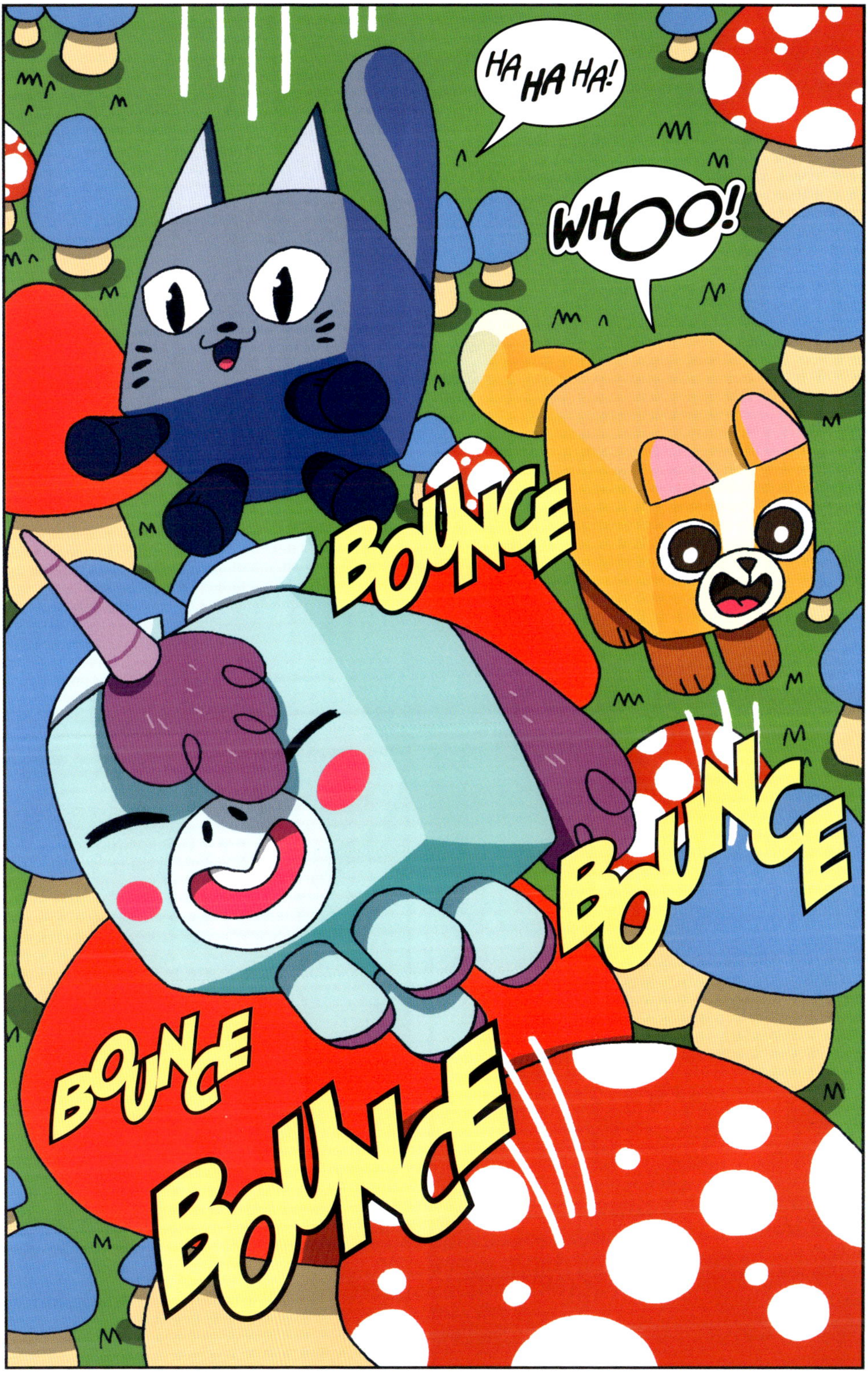
HA HA HA!
WHOO!
BOUNCE
BOUNCE
BOUNCE
BOUNCE

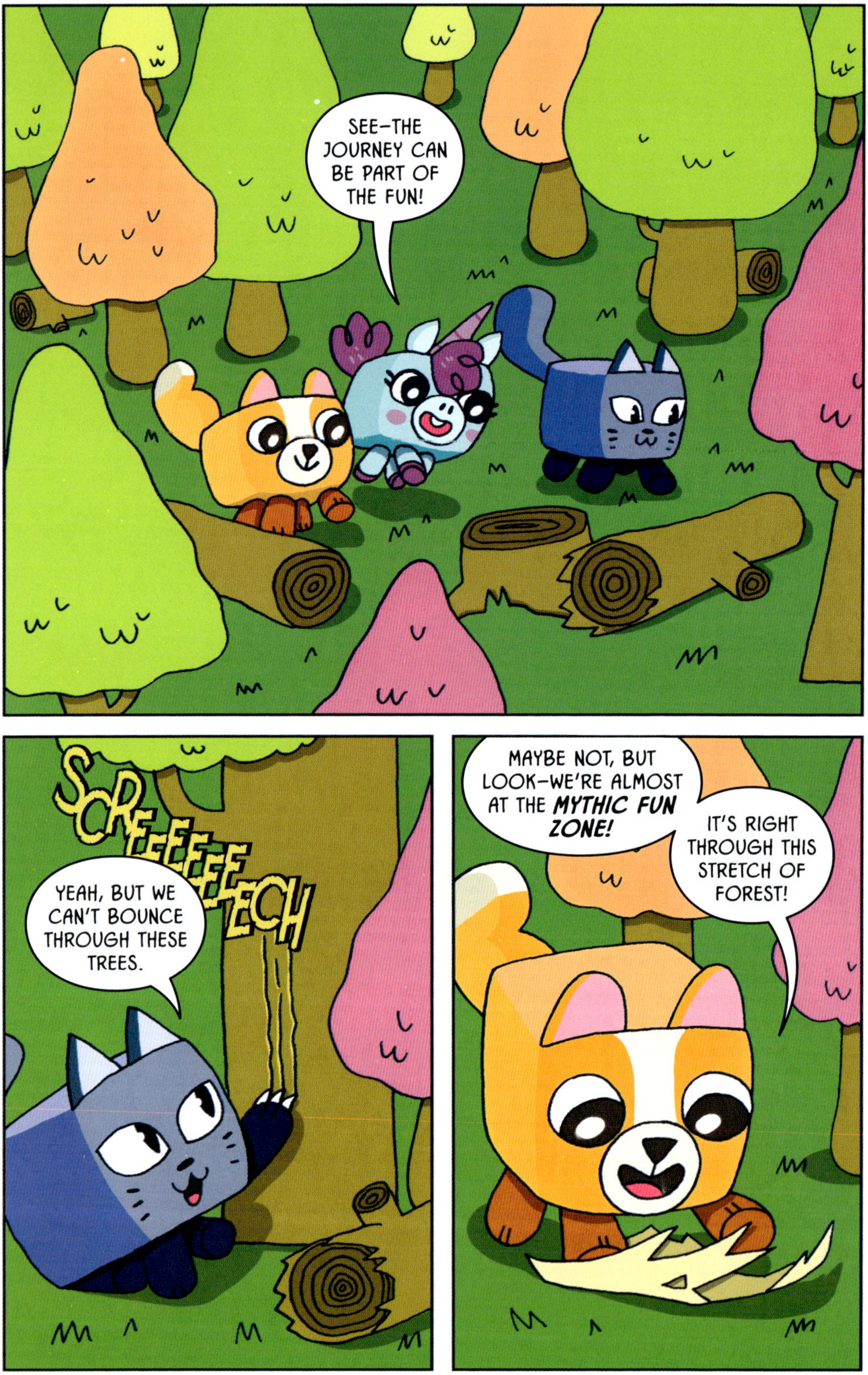
SEE—THE JOURNEY CAN BE PART OF THE FUN!
SCREEEEEEECH
YEAH, BUT WE CAN'T BOUNCE THROUGH THESE TREES.
MAYBE NOT, BUT LOOK—WE'RE ALMOST AT THE *MYTHIC FUN ZONE!*
IT'S RIGHT THROUGH THIS STRETCH OF FOREST!

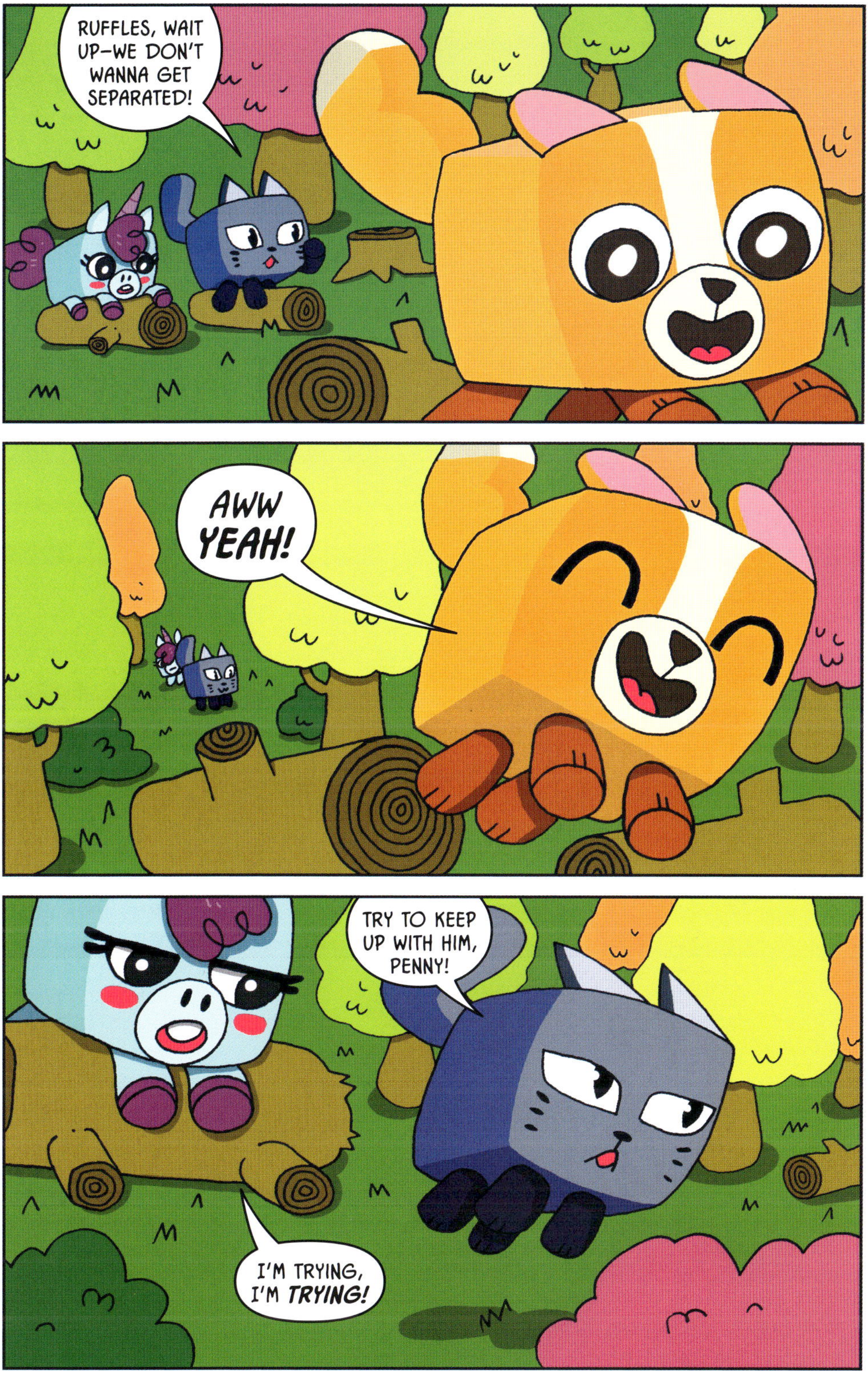
RUFFLES, WAIT UP—WE DON'T WANNA GET SEPARATED!
AWW YEAH!
TRY TO KEEP UP WITH HIM, PENNY!
I'M TRYING, I'M *TRYING!*

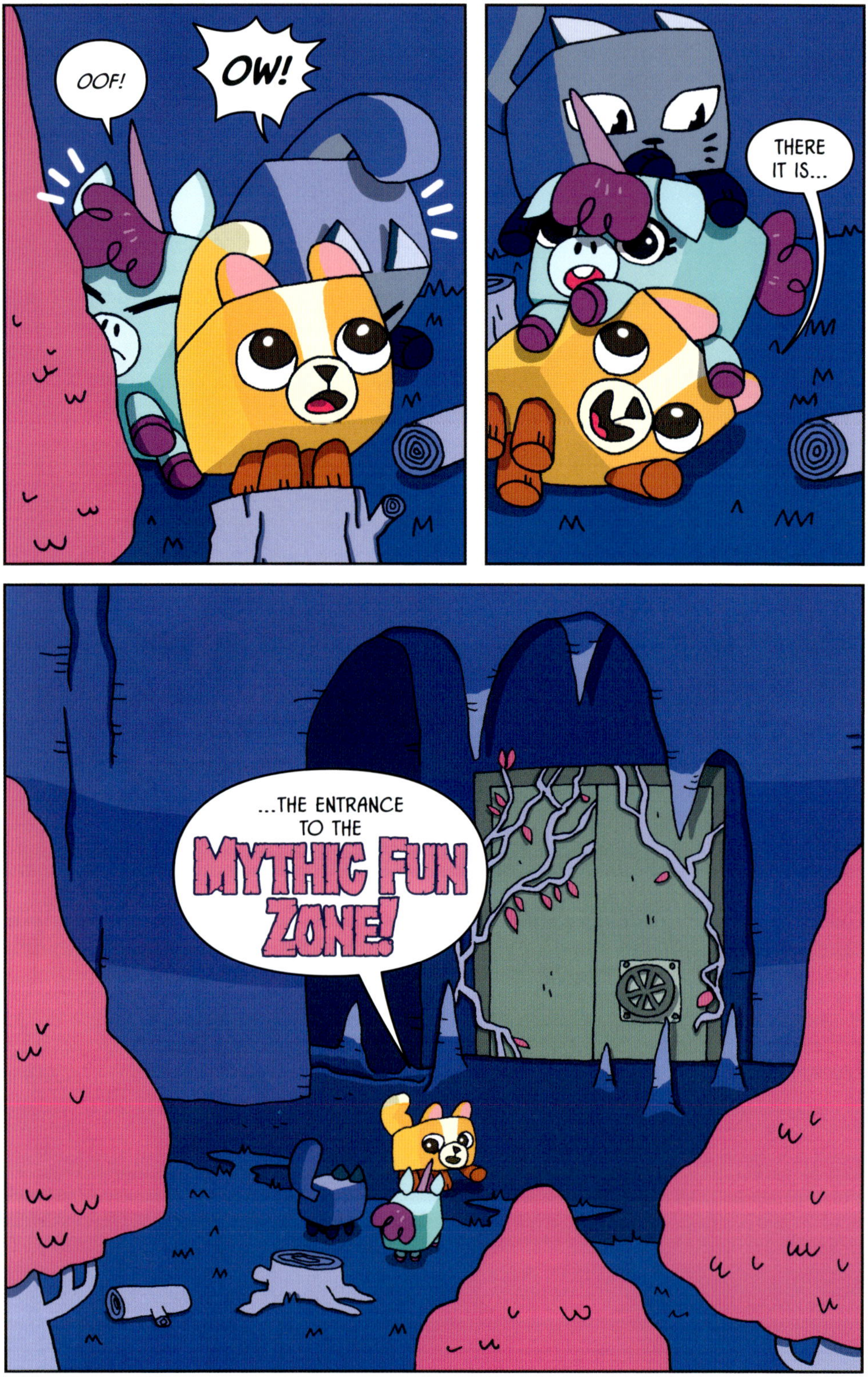
OOF!
OW!
THERE IT IS...
...THE ENTRANCE TO THE
MYTHIC FUN ZONE!

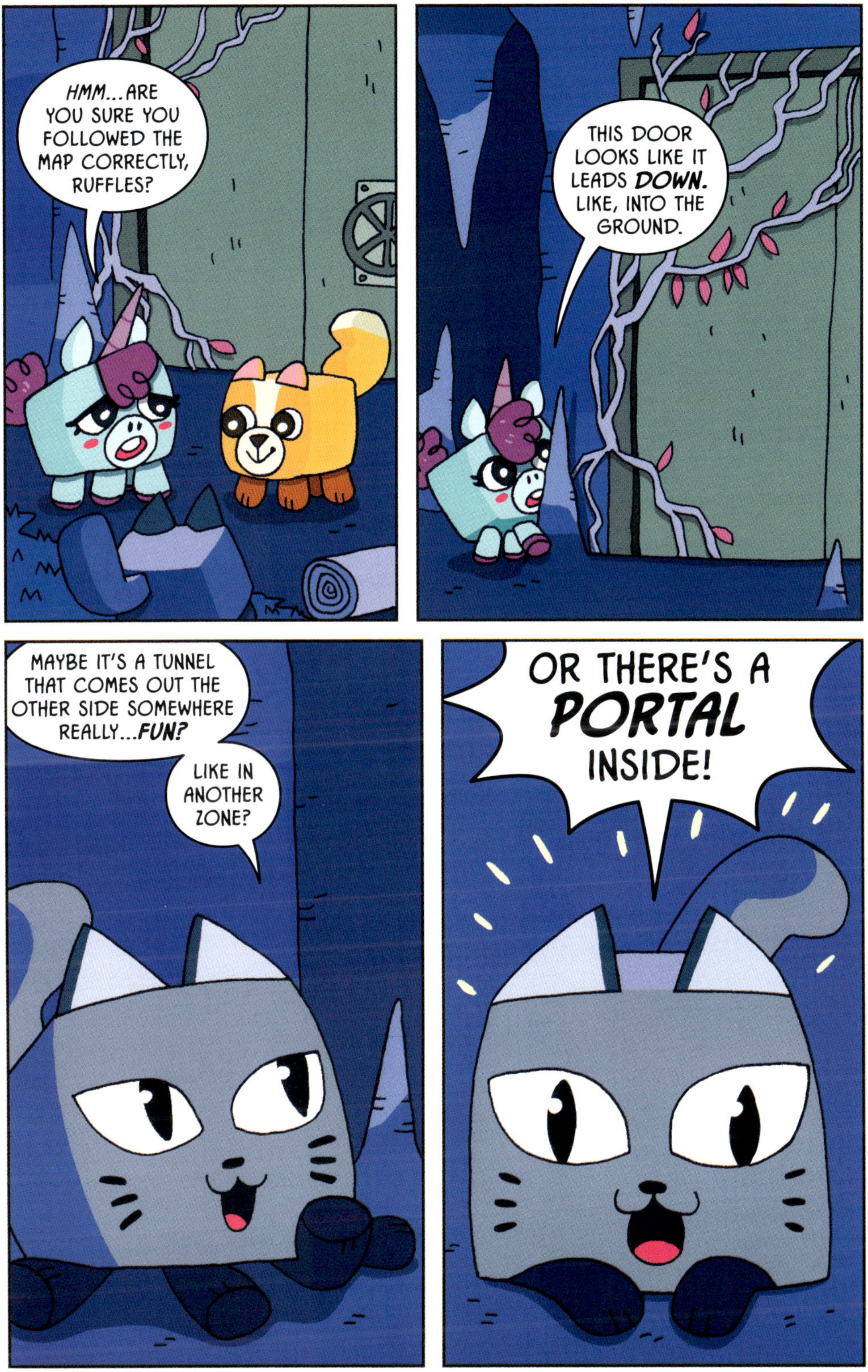
HMM...ARE YOU SURE YOU FOLLOWED THE MAP CORRECTLY, RUFFLES?
THIS DOOR LOOKS LIKE IT LEADS DOWN. LIKE, INTO THE GROUND.
MAYBE IT'S A TUNNEL THAT COMES OUT THE OTHER SIDE SOMEWHERE REALLY...FUN?
LIKE IN ANOTHER ZONE?
OR THERE'S A PORTAL INSIDE!

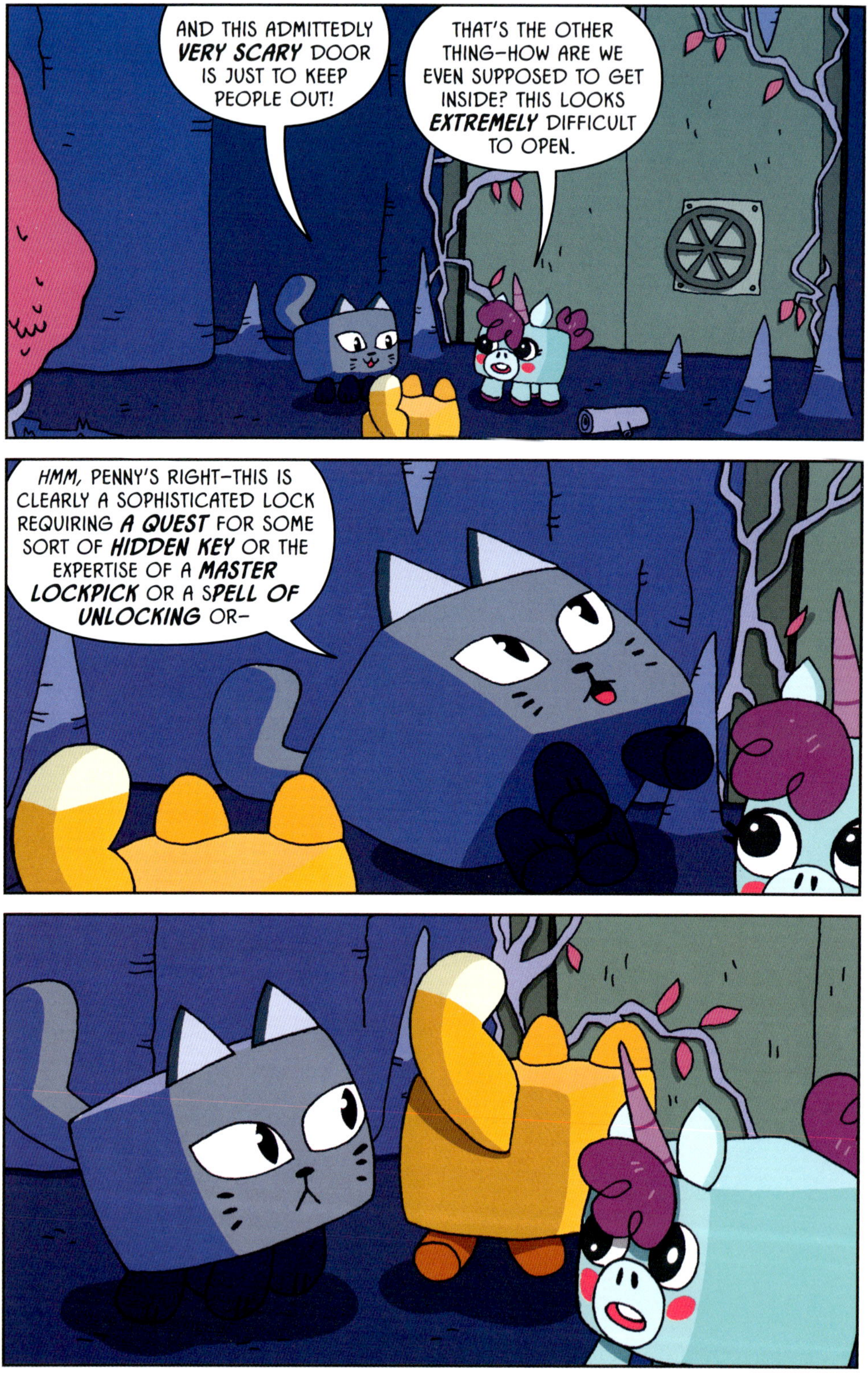
AND THIS ADMITTEDLY ***VERY SCARY*** DOOR IS JUST TO KEEP PEOPLE OUT!
THAT'S THE OTHER THING—HOW ARE WE EVEN SUPPOSED TO GET INSIDE? THIS LOOKS ***EXTREMELY*** DIFFICULT TO OPEN.
HMM, PENNY'S RIGHT—THIS IS CLEARLY A SOPHISTICATED LOCK REQUIRING ***A QUEST*** FOR SOME SORT OF ***HIDDEN KEY*** OR THE EXPERTISE OF A ***MASTER LOCKPICK*** OR A ***SPELL OF UNLOCKING*** OR—

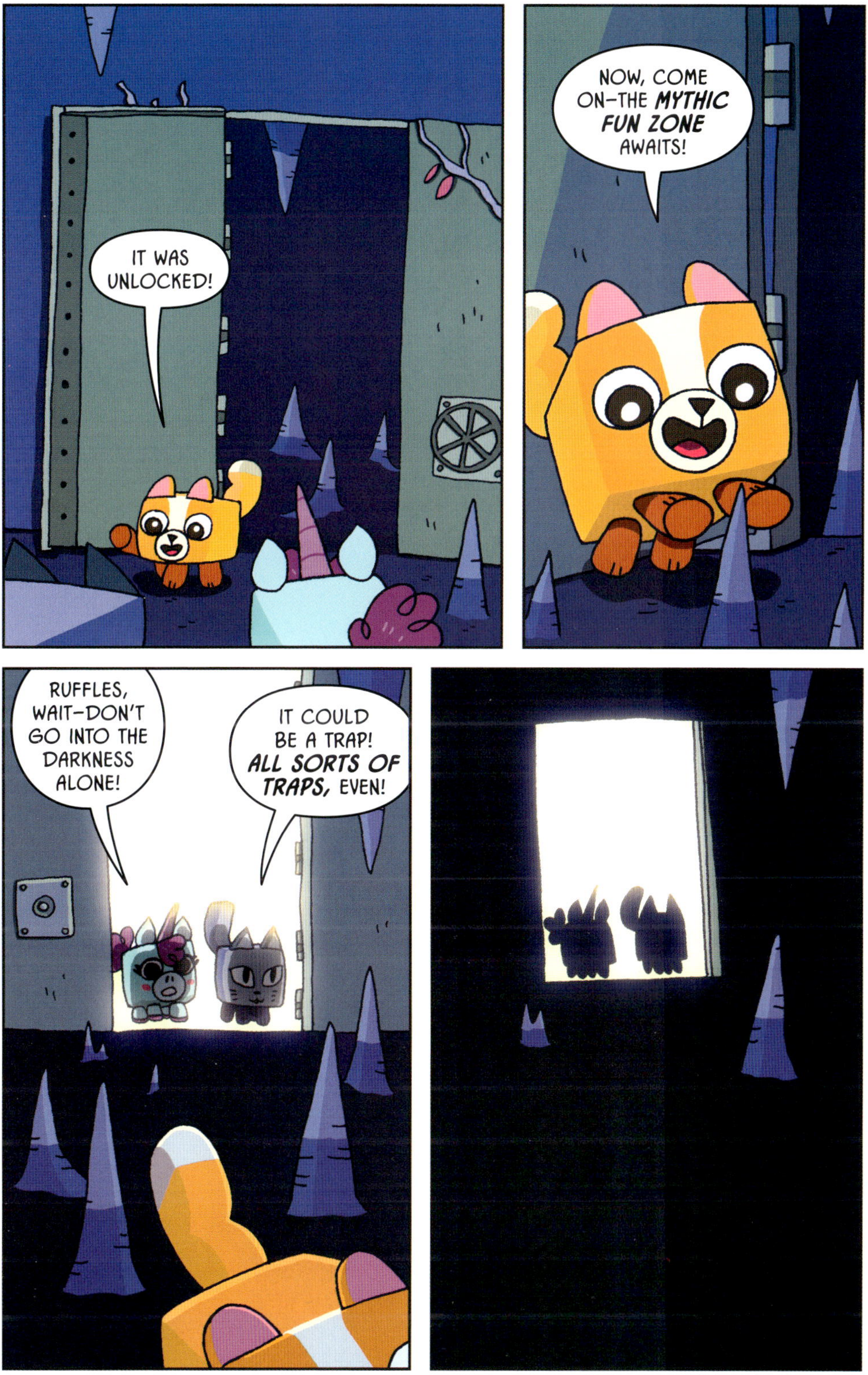
IT WAS UNLOCKED!
NOW, COME ON—THE MYTHIC FUN ZONE AWAITS!
RUFFLES, WAIT—DON'T GO INTO THE DARKNESS ALONE!
IT COULD BE A TRAP! ALL SORTS OF TRAPS, EVEN!

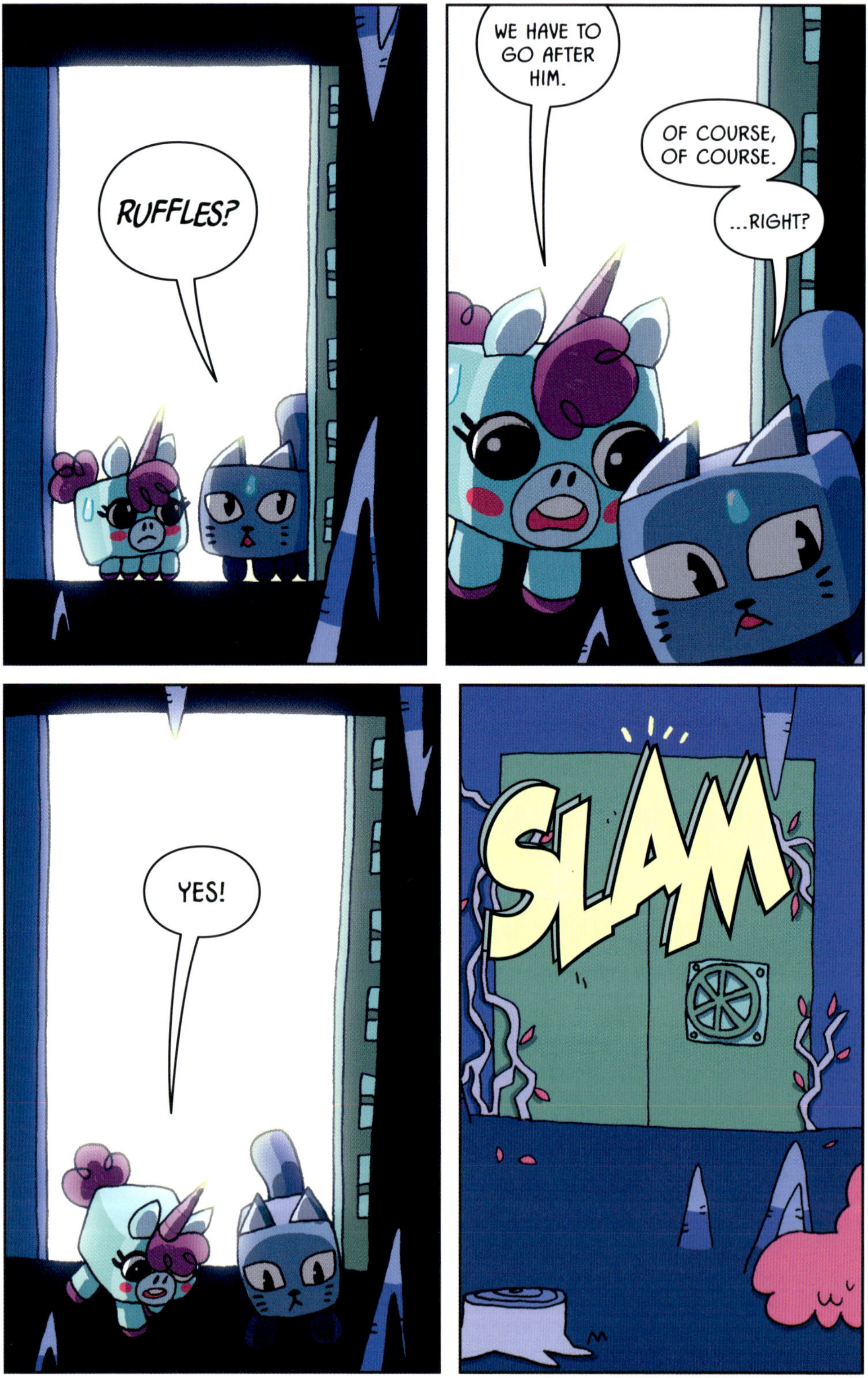
RUFFLES?
WE HAVE TO GO AFTER HIM.
OF COURSE, OF COURSE.
...RIGHT?
YES!
SLAM

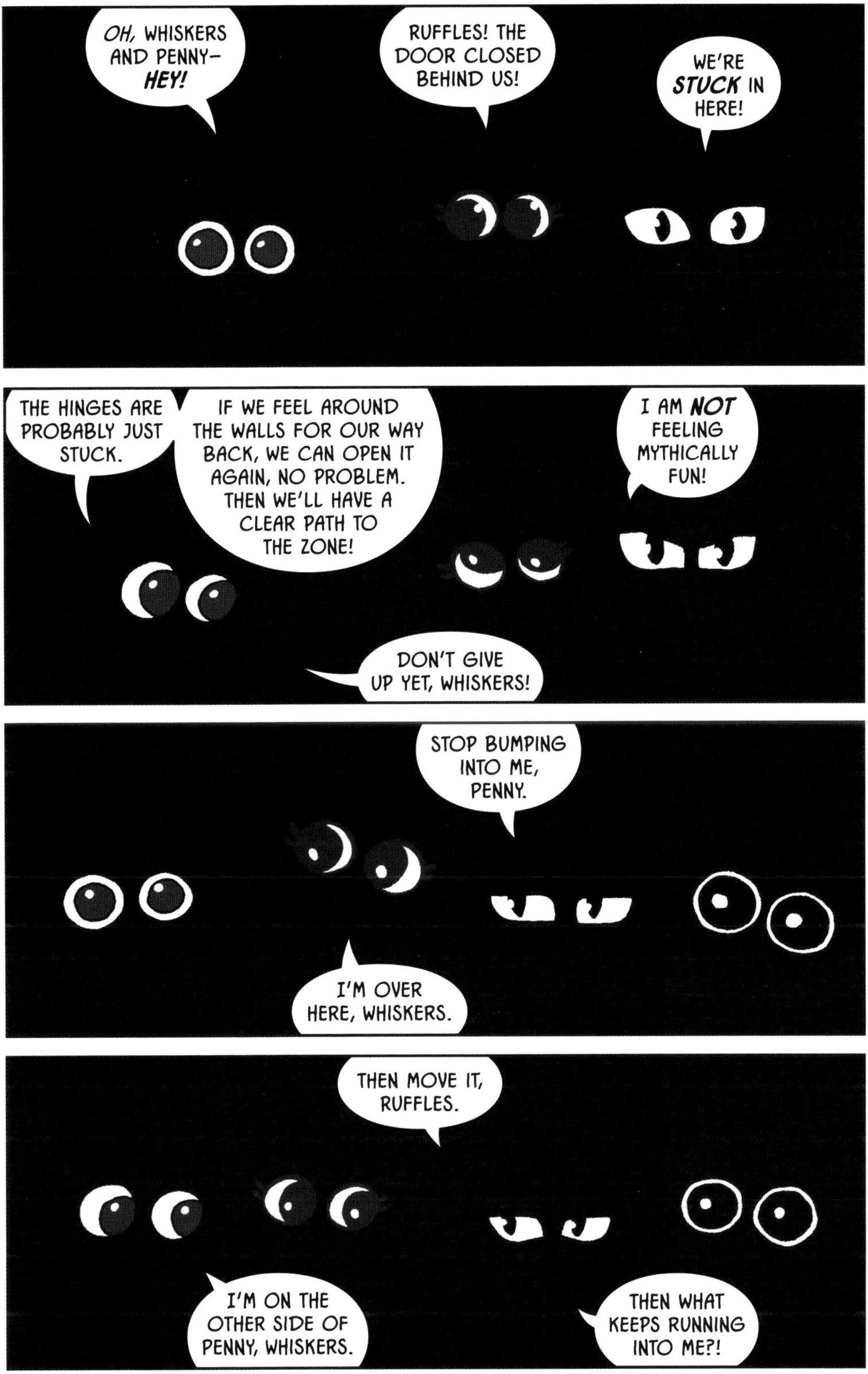
OH, WHISKERS AND PENNY— *HEY!*
RUFFLES! THE DOOR CLOSED BEHIND US!
WE'RE *STUCK* IN HERE!
THE HINGES ARE PROBABLY JUST STUCK.
IF WE FEEL AROUND THE WALLS FOR OUR WAY BACK, WE CAN OPEN IT AGAIN, NO PROBLEM. THEN WE'LL HAVE A CLEAR PATH TO THE ZONE!
I AM *NOT* FEELING MYTHICALLY FUN!
DON'T GIVE UP YET, WHISKERS!
STOP BUMPING INTO ME, PENNY.
I'M OVER HERE, WHISKERS.
THEN MOVE IT, RUFFLES.
I'M ON THE OTHER SIDE OF PENNY, WHISKERS.
THEN WHAT KEEPS RUNNING INTO ME?!

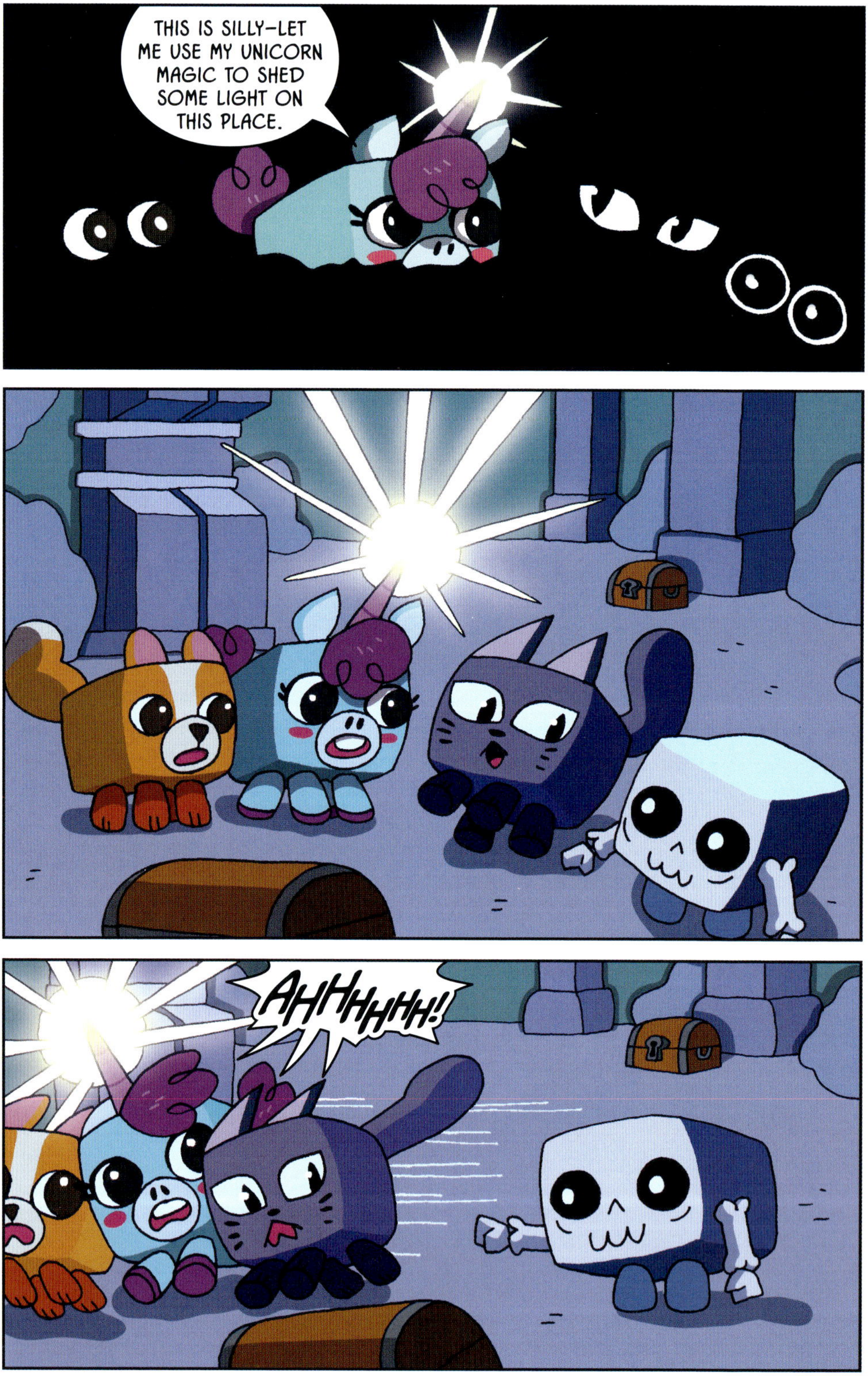
THIS IS SILLY–LET ME USE MY UNICORN MAGIC TO SHED SOME LIGHT ON THIS PLACE.
AHHHHHH!

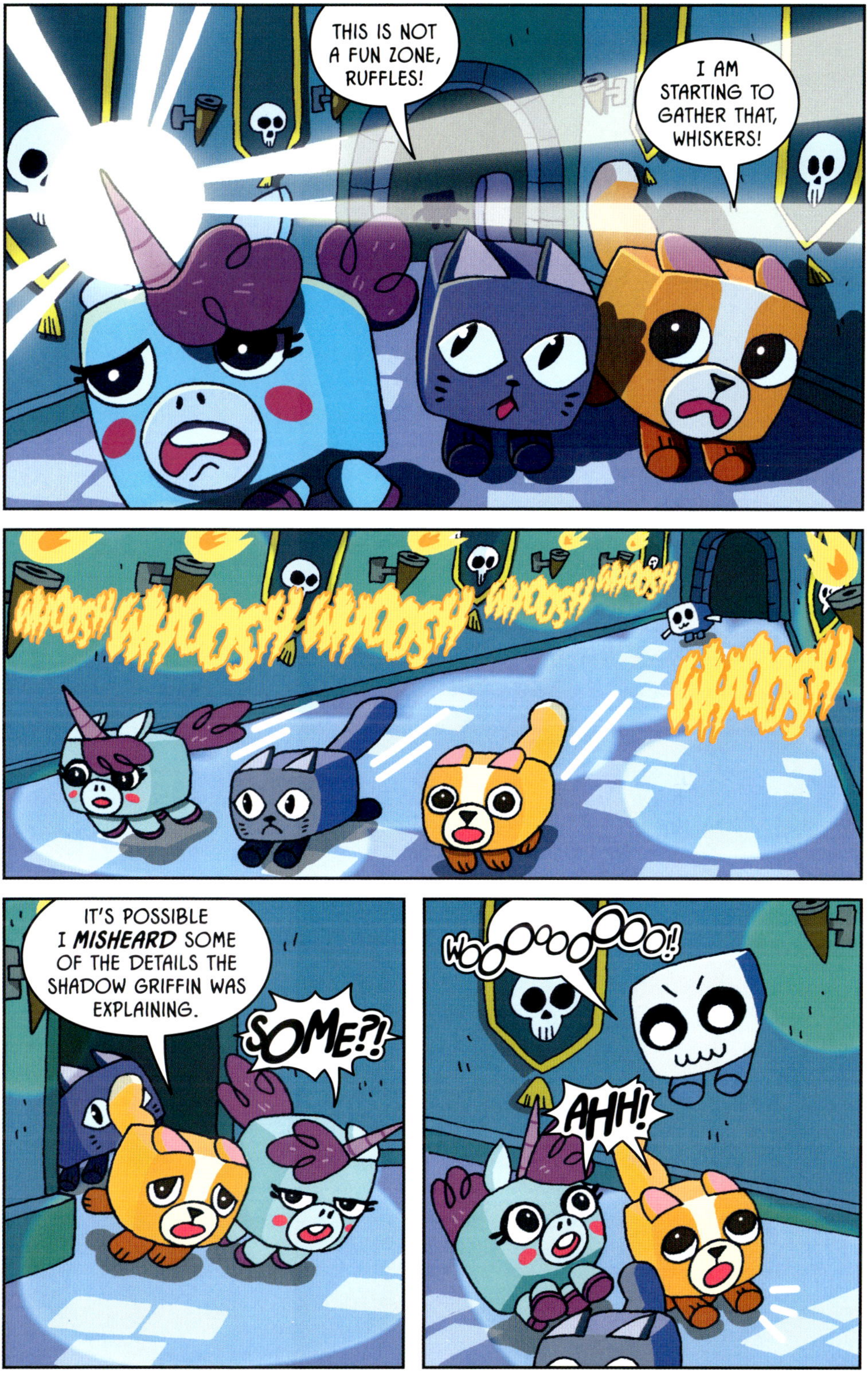
THIS IS NOT A FUN ZONE, RUFFLES!
I AM STARTING TO GATHER THAT, WHISKERS!
WHOOSH WHOOSH WHOOSH WHOOSH WHOOSH
WHOOSH
IT'S POSSIBLE I **MISHEARD** SOME OF THE DETAILS THE SHADOW GRIFFIN WAS EXPLAINING.
SOME?!
WOOOOOOOOO!
AHH!

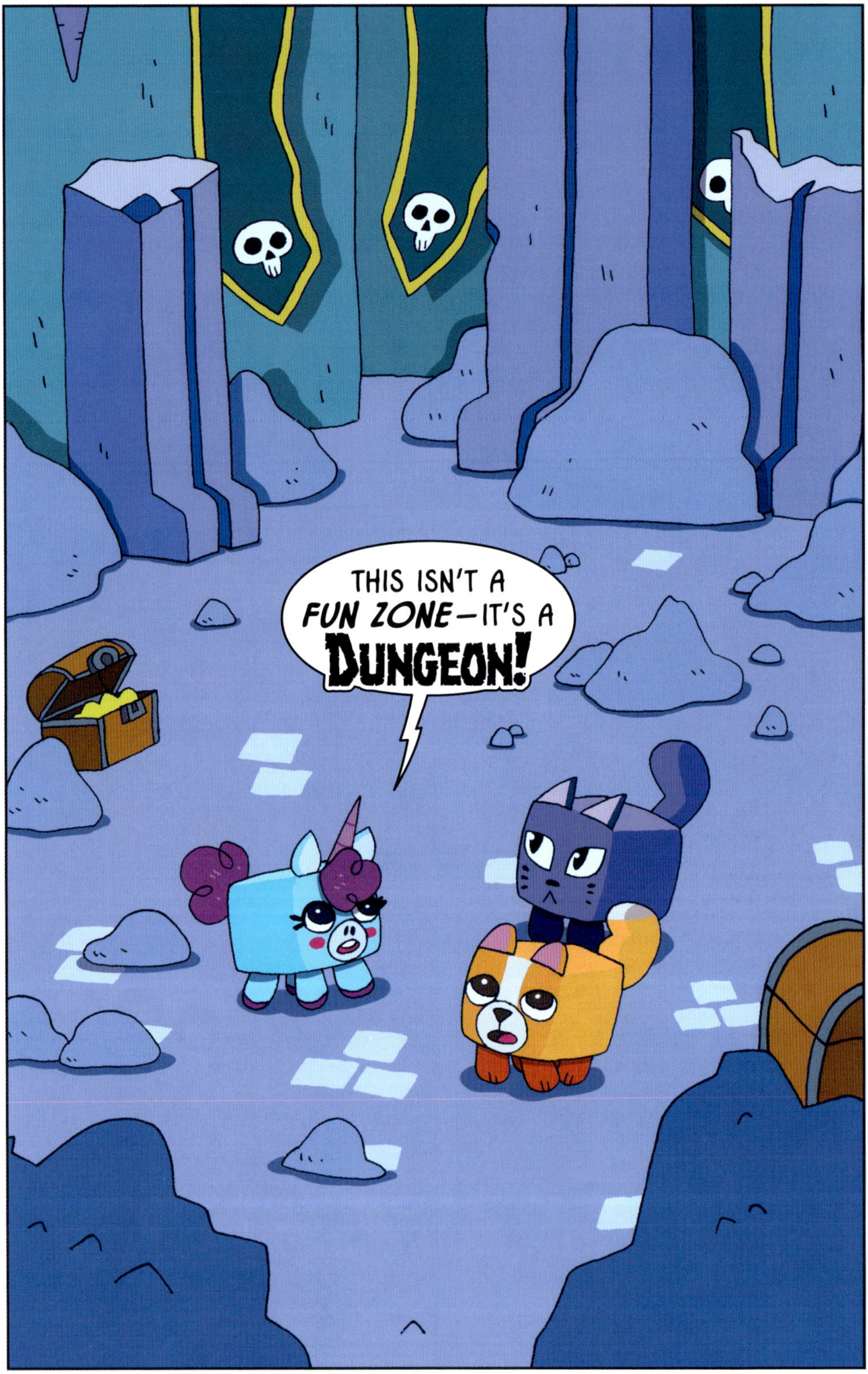
THIS ISN'T A FUN ZONE—IT'S A DUNGEON!

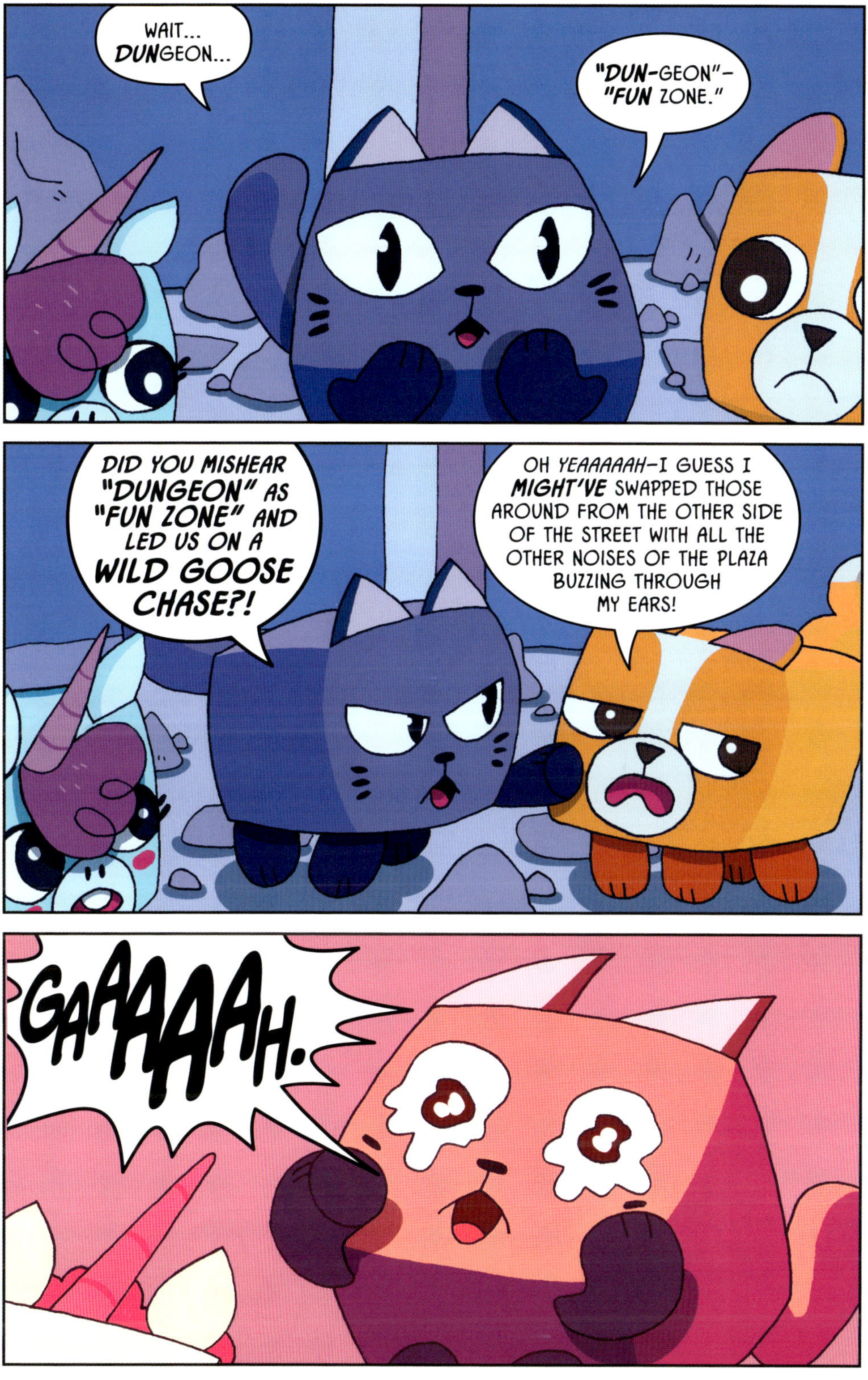
WAIT... DUNGEON...
"DUN-GEON"— "FUN ZONE."
DID YOU MISHEAR "DUNGEON" AS "FUN ZONE" AND LED US ON A WILD GOOSE CHASE?!
OH YEAAAAAH—I GUESS I MIGHT'VE SWAPPED THOSE AROUND FROM THE OTHER SIDE OF THE STREET WITH ALL THE OTHER NOISES OF THE PLAZA BUZZING THROUGH MY EARS!
GAAAAAH.

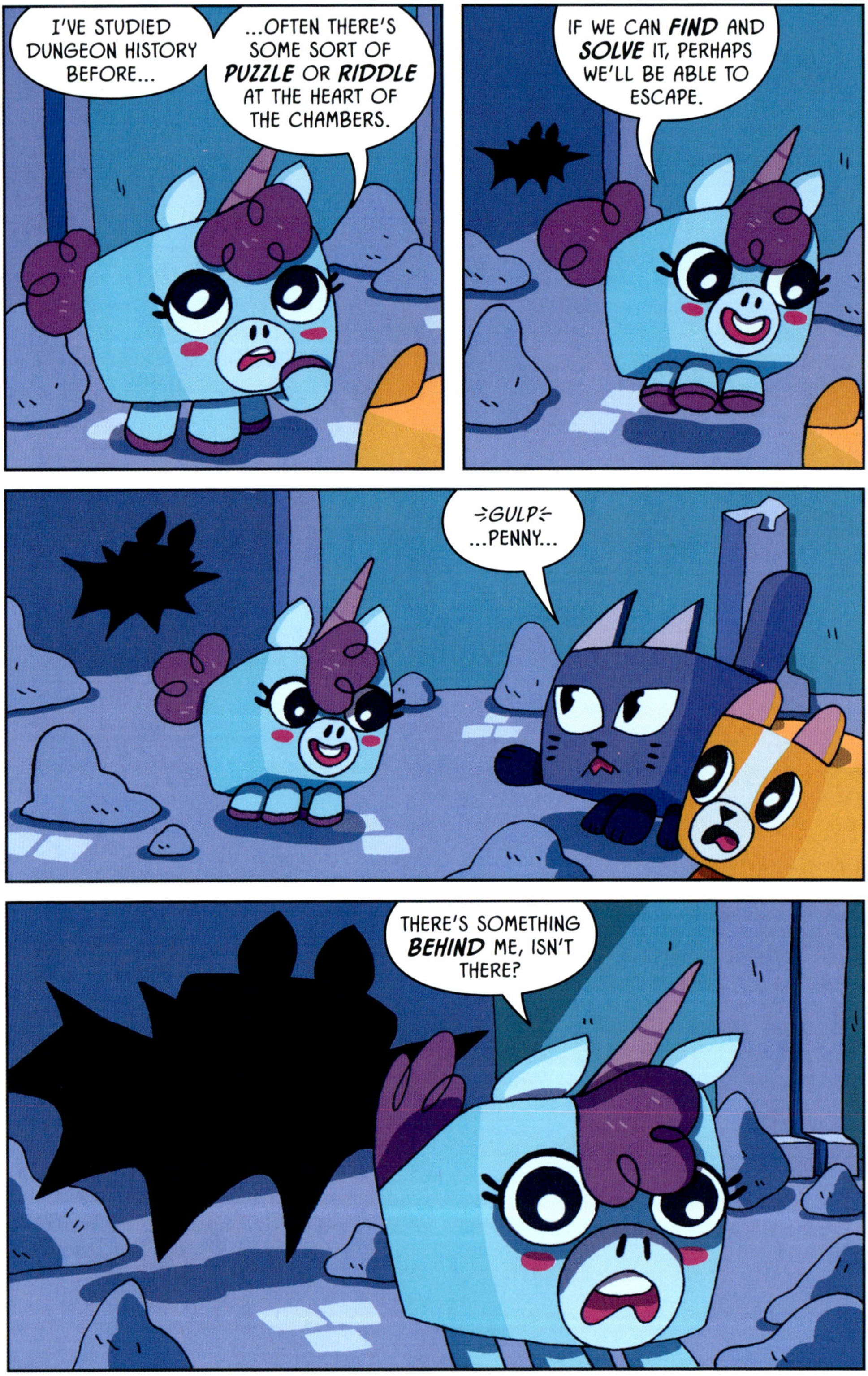
I'VE STUDIED DUNGEON HISTORY BEFORE...
...OFTEN THERE'S SOME SORT OF **PUZZLE** OR **RIDDLE** AT THE HEART OF THE CHAMBERS.
IF WE CAN **FIND** AND **SOLVE** IT, PERHAPS WE'LL BE ABLE TO ESCAPE.
GULP
...PENNY...
THERE'S SOMETHING **BEHIND** ME, ISN'T THERE?

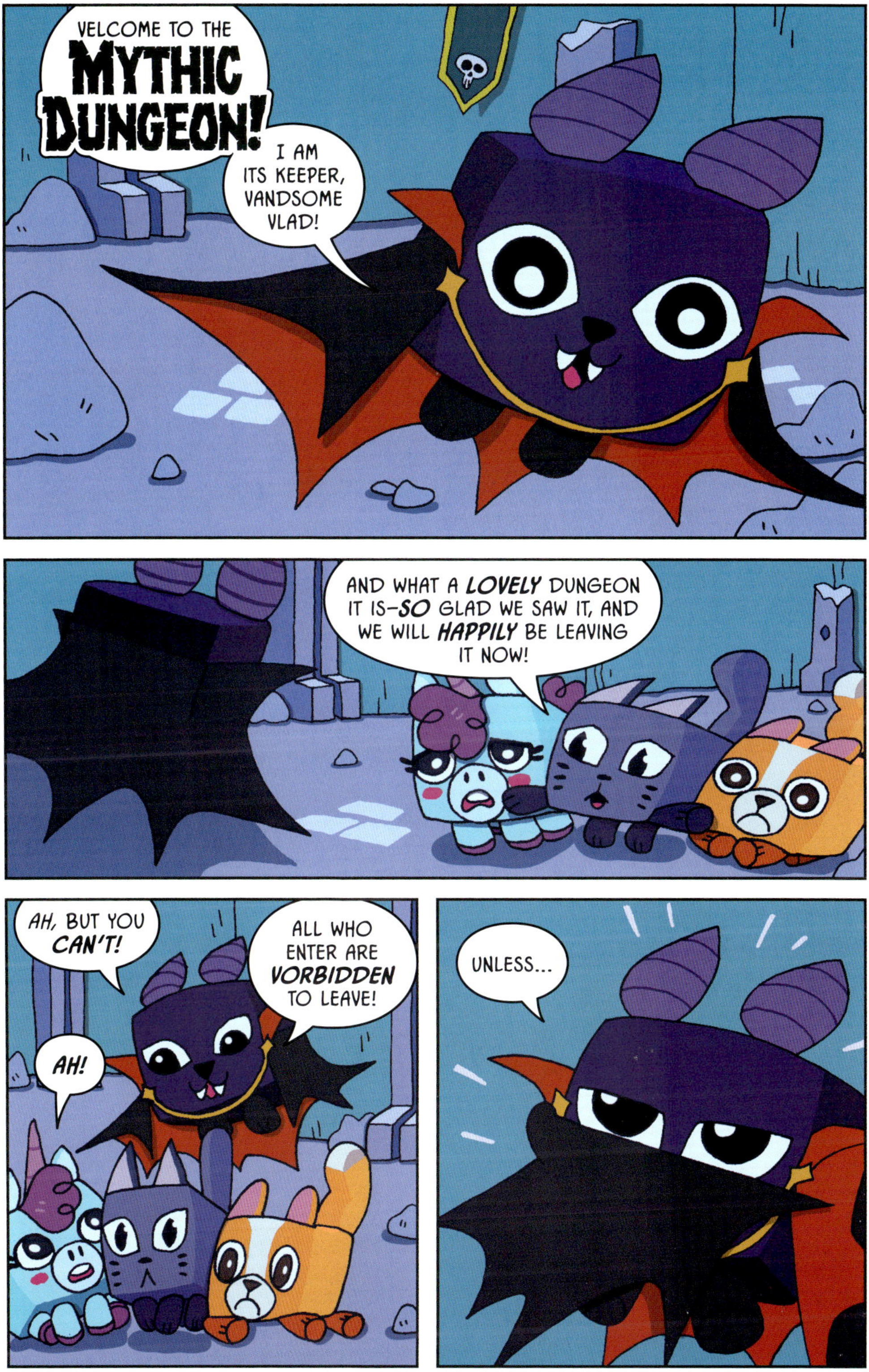
VELCOME TO THE MYTHIC DUNGEON!
I AM ITS KEEPER, VANDSOME VLAD!
AND WHAT A LOVELY DUNGEON IT IS—SO GLAD WE SAW IT, AND WE WILL HAPPILY BE LEAVING IT NOW!
AH, BUT YOU CAN'T!
ALL WHO ENTER ARE VORBIDDEN TO LEAVE!
AH!
UNLESS...

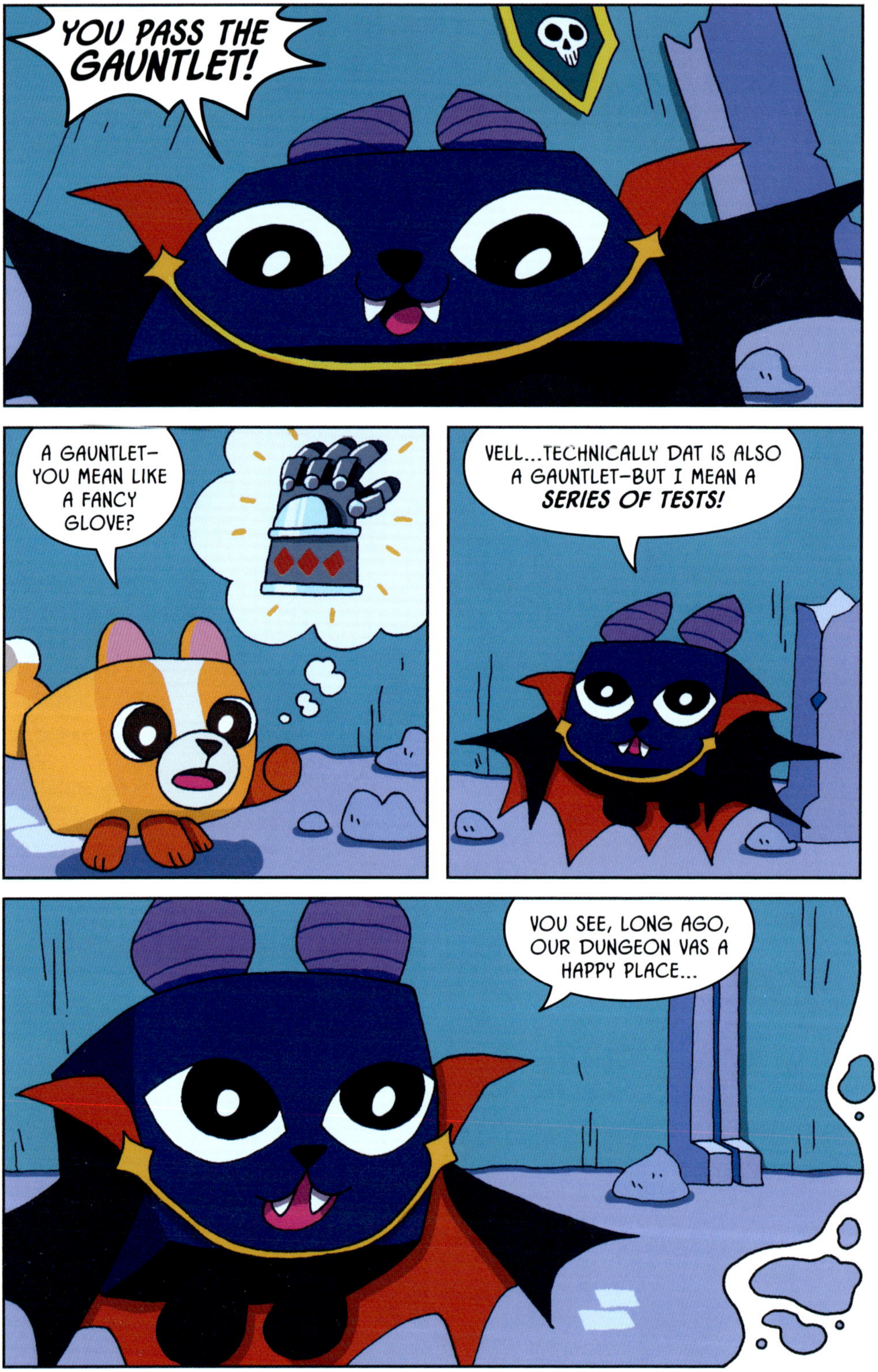
YOU PASS THE GAUNTLET!
A GAUNTLET– YOU MEAN LIKE A FANCY GLOVE?
VELL...TECHNICALLY DAT IS ALSO A GAUNTLET–BUT I MEAN A ***SERIES OF TESTS!***
YOU SEE, LONG AGO, OUR DUNGEON VAS A HAPPY PLACE...

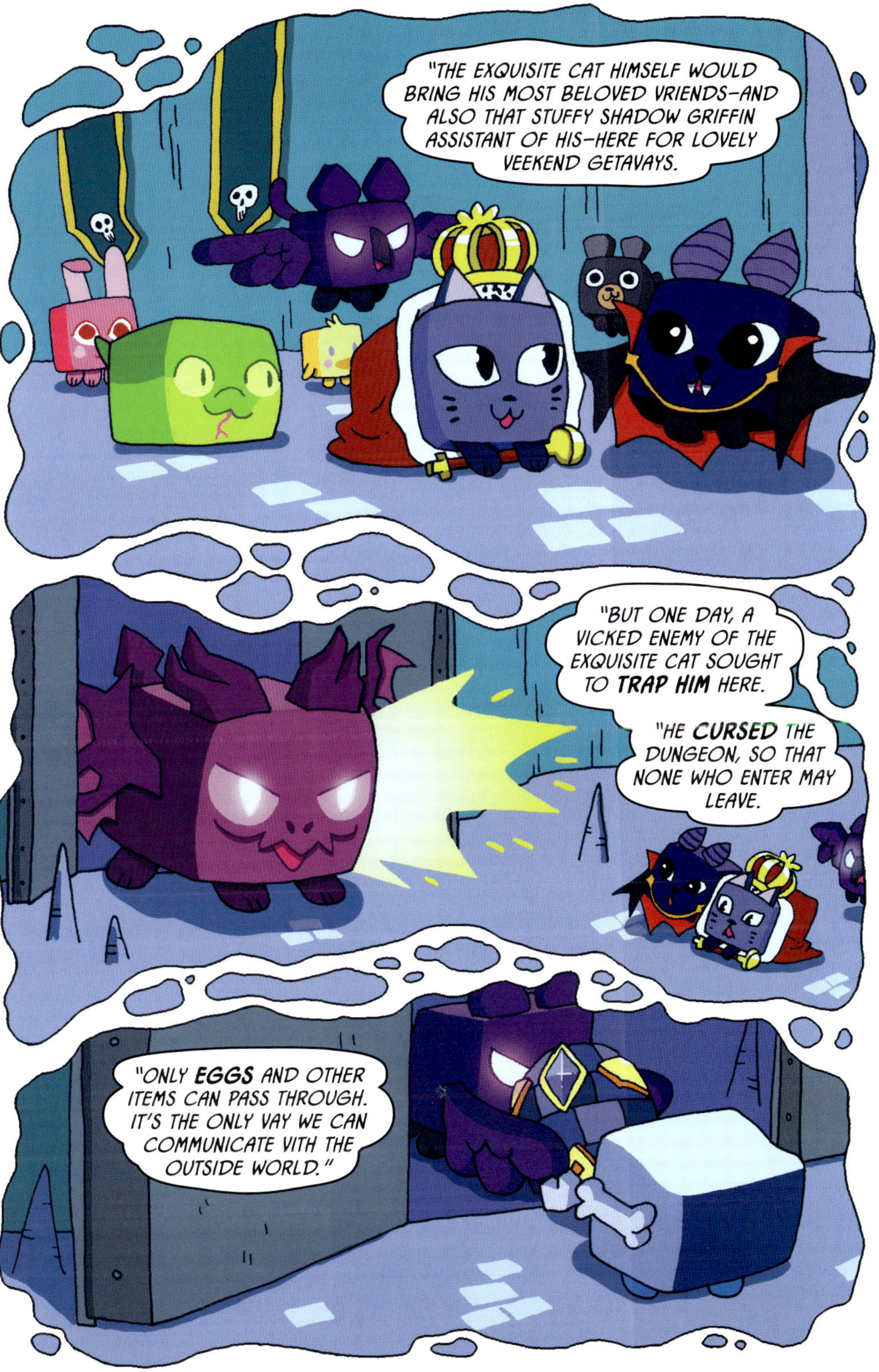
"THE EXQUISITE CAT HIMSELF WOULD BRING HIS MOST BELOVED VRIENDS—AND ALSO THAT STUFFY SHADOW GRIFFIN ASSISTANT OF HIS—HERE FOR LOVELY VEEKEND GETAVAYS.
"BUT ONE DAY, A VICKED ENEMY OF THE EXQUISITE CAT SOUGHT TO **TRAP HIM** HERE.
"HE **CURSED** THE DUNGEON, SO THAT NONE WHO ENTER MAY LEAVE.
"ONLY **EGGS** AND OTHER ITEMS CAN PASS THROUGH. IT'S THE ONLY VAY WE CAN COMMUNICATE VITH THE OUTSIDE WORLD."

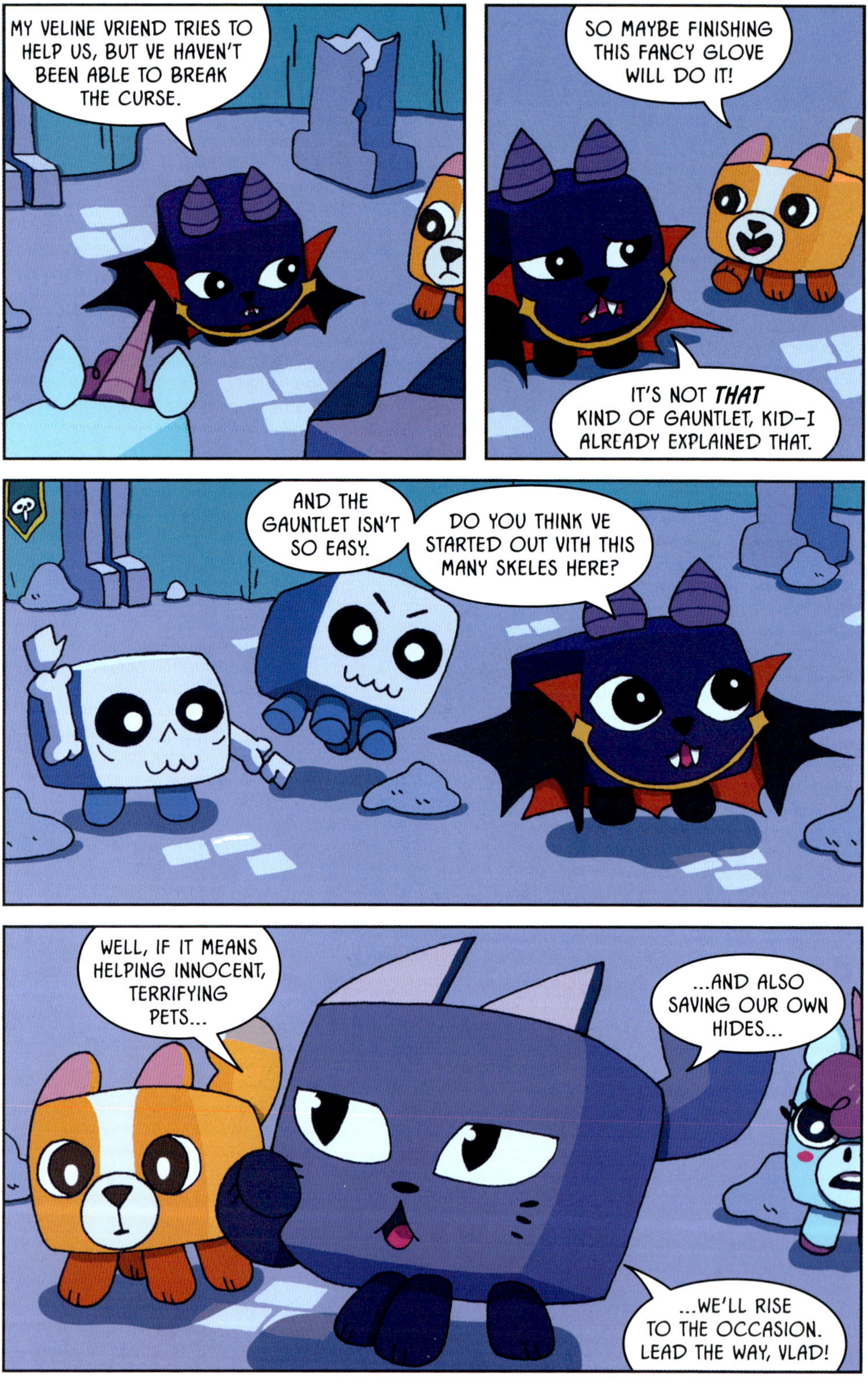
MY VELINE VRIEND TRIES TO HELP US, BUT VE HAVEN'T BEEN ABLE TO BREAK THE CURSE.
SO MAYBE FINISHING THIS FANCY GLOVE WILL DO IT!
IT'S NOT **THAT** KIND OF GAUNTLET, KID–I ALREADY EXPLAINED THAT.
AND THE GAUNTLET ISN'T SO EASY.
DO YOU THINK VE STARTED OUT VITH THIS MANY SKELES HERE?
WELL, IF IT MEANS HELPING INNOCENT, TERRIFYING PETS...
...AND ALSO SAVING OUR OWN HIDES...
...WE'LL RISE TO THE OCCASION. LEAD THE WAY, VLAD!

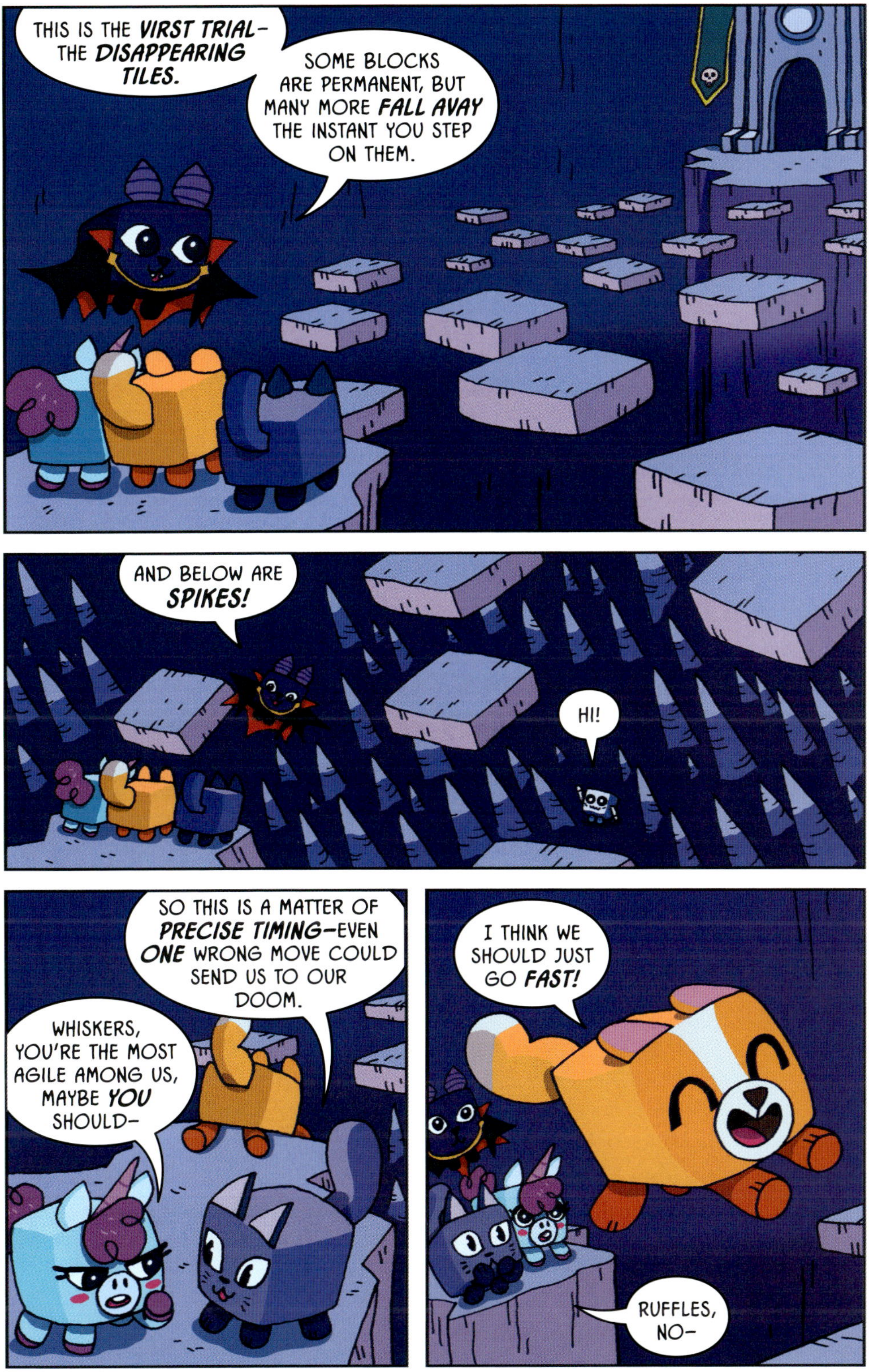
THIS IS THE VIRST TRIAL—THE DISAPPEARING TILES.
SOME BLOCKS ARE PERMANENT, BUT MANY MORE FALL AVAY THE INSTANT YOU STEP ON THEM.
AND BELOW ARE SPIKES!
HI!
SO THIS IS A MATTER OF PRECISE TIMING—EVEN ONE WRONG MOVE COULD SEND US TO OUR DOOM.
WHISKERS, YOU'RE THE MOST AGILE AMONG US, MAYBE YOU SHOULD—
I THINK WE SHOULD JUST GO FAST!
RUFFLES, NO—

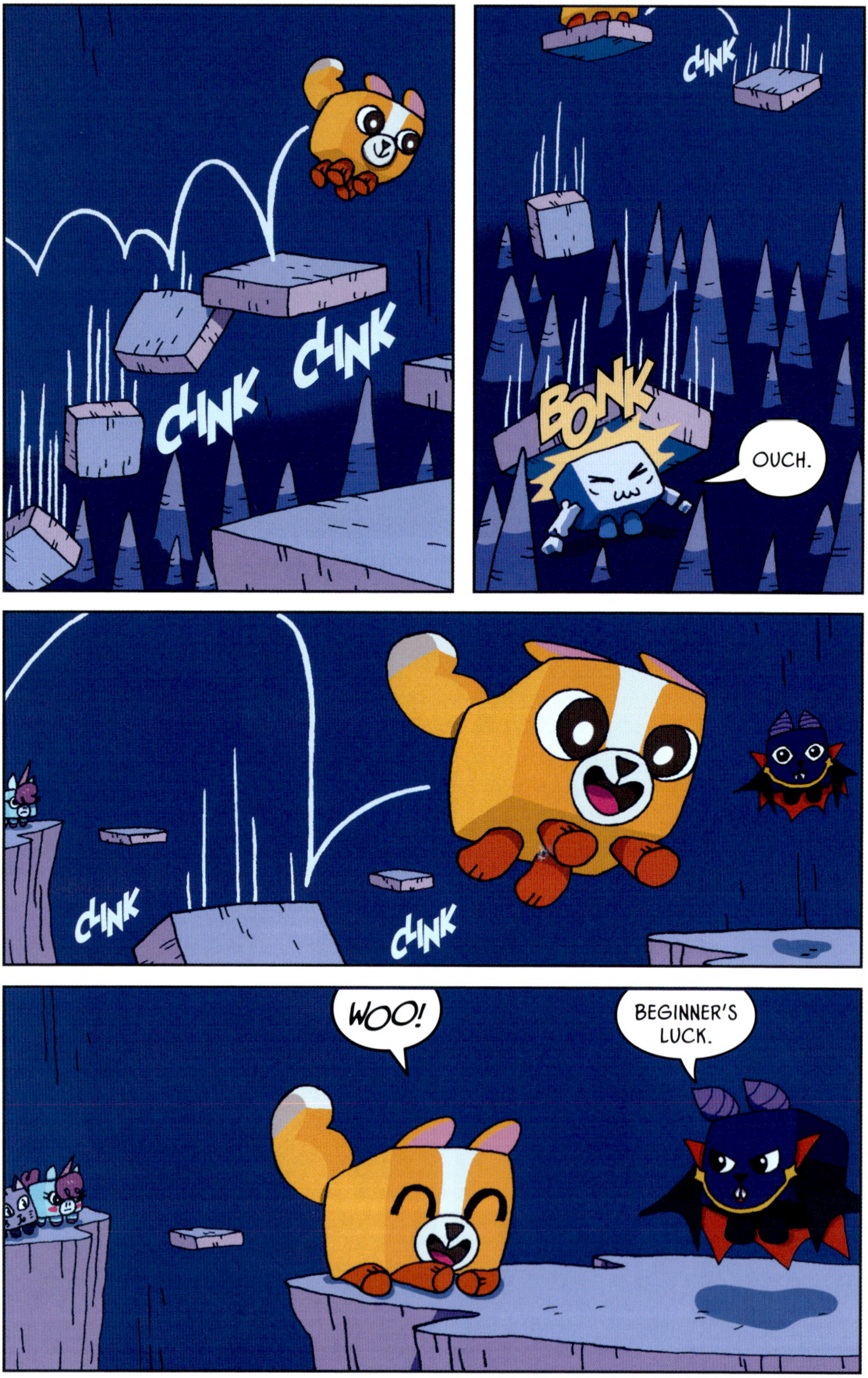
CLINK
CLINK
CLINK
BONK
OUCH.
CLINK
CLINK
WOO!
BEGINNER'S LUCK.

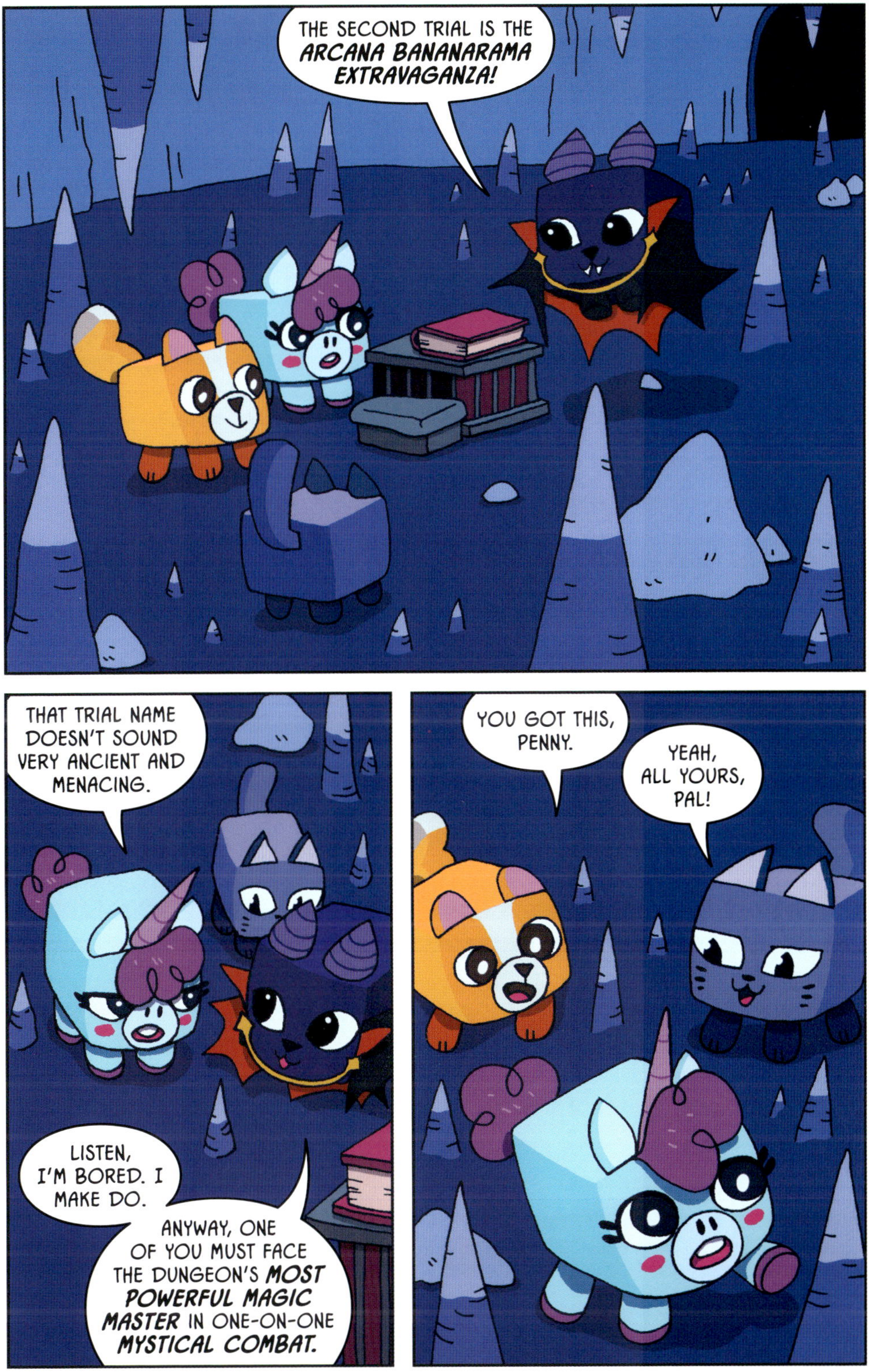
THE SECOND TRIAL IS THE ***ARCANA BANANARAMA EXTRAVAGANZA!***
THAT TRIAL NAME DOESN'T SOUND VERY ANCIENT AND MENACING.
LISTEN, I'M BORED. I MAKE DO.
ANYWAY, ONE OF YOU MUST FACE THE DUNGEON'S ***MOST POWERFUL MAGIC MASTER*** IN ONE-ON-ONE ***MYSTICAL COMBAT.***
YOU GOT THIS, PENNY.
YEAH, ALL YOURS, PAL!

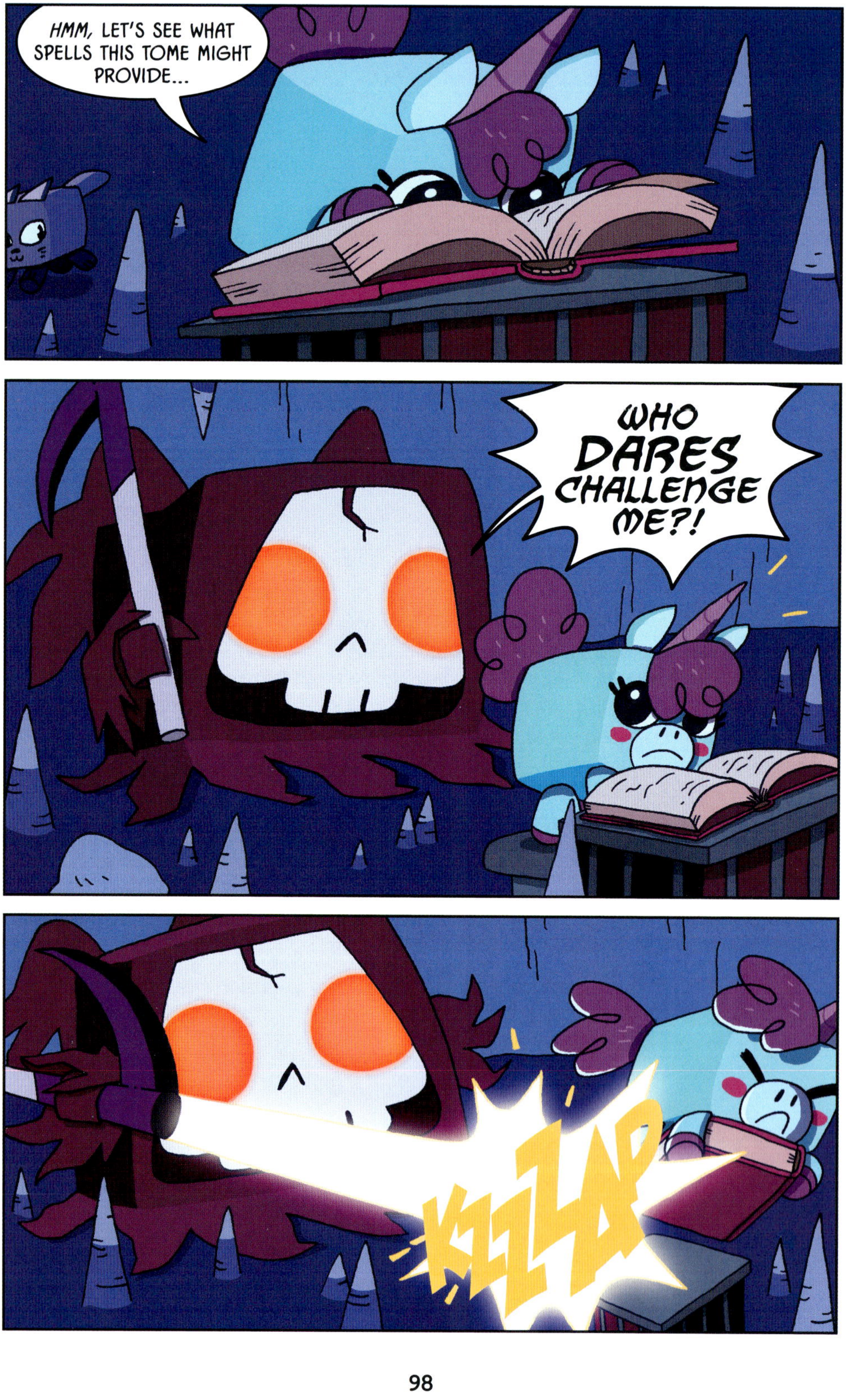
HMM, LET'S SEE WHAT SPELLS THIS TOME MIGHT PROVIDE...
WHO DARES CHALLENGE ME?!
KZZZAP

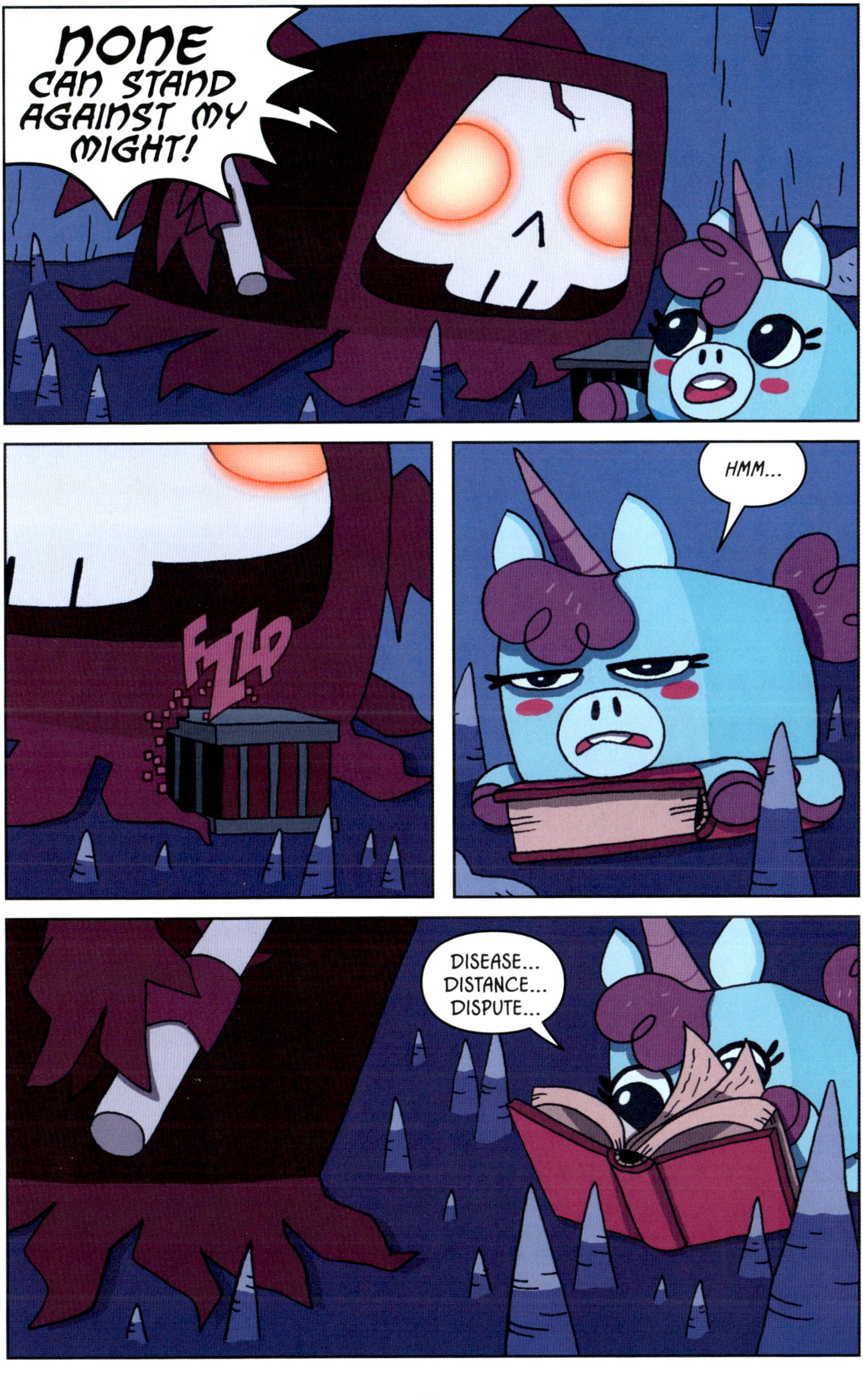
NONE CAN STAND AGAINST MY MIGHT!
FZZAP
HMM...
DISEASE... DISTANCE... DISPUTE...

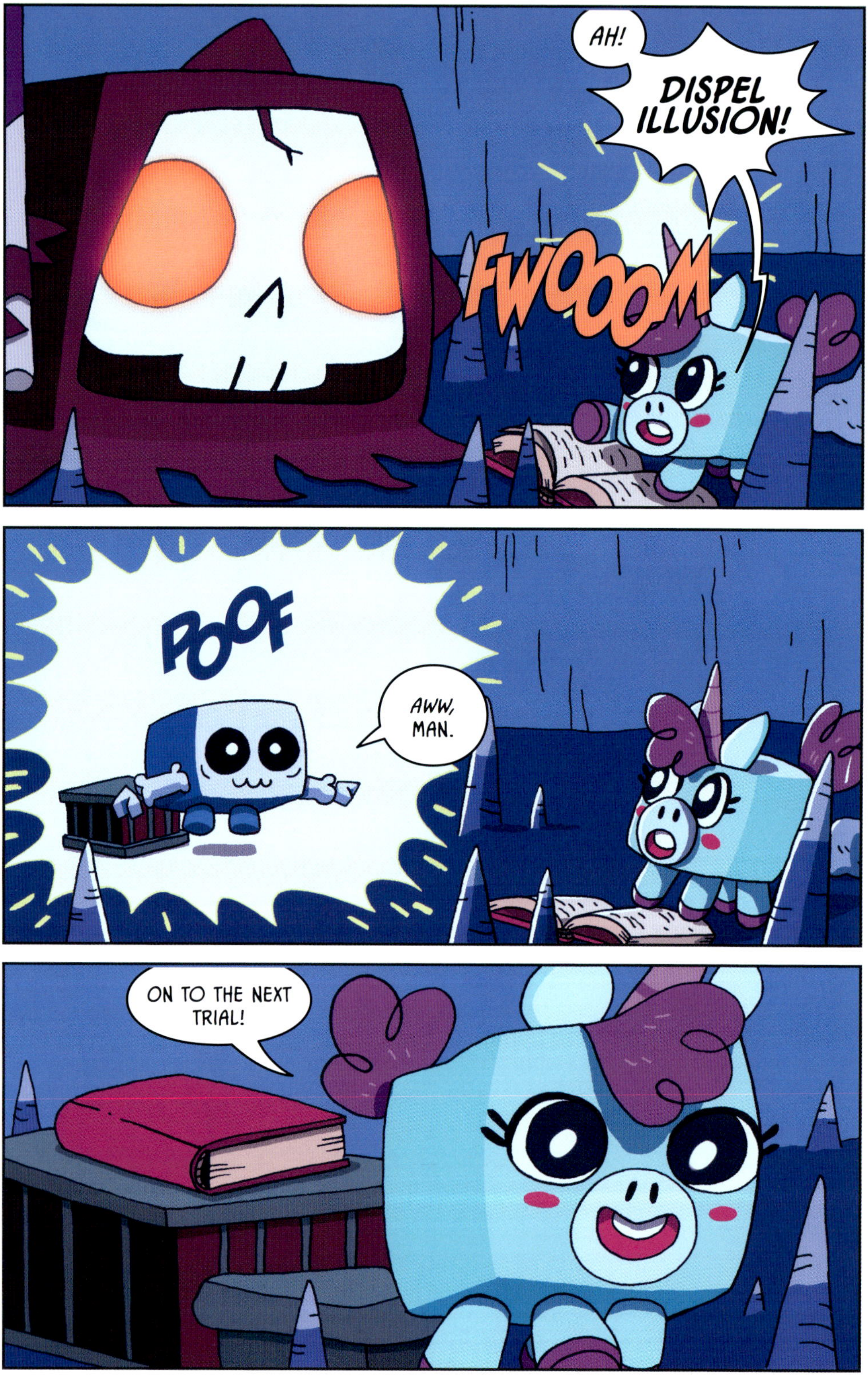
AH!
DISPEL ILLUSION!
FWOOOOM
POOF
AWW, MAN.
ON TO THE NEXT TRIAL!

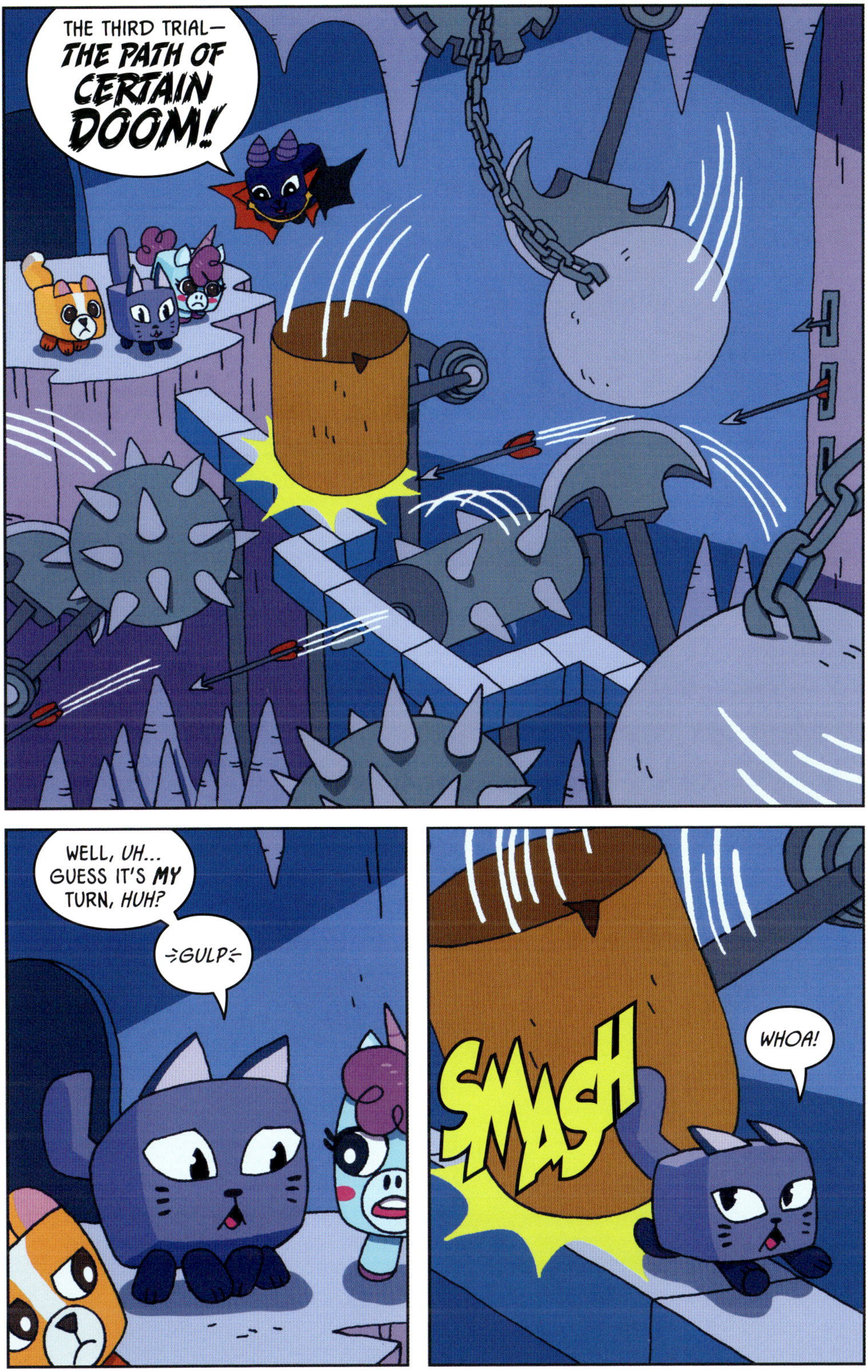
THE THIRD TRIAL—
THE PATH OF CERTAIN DOOM!
WELL, UH... GUESS IT'S MY TURN, HUH?
GULP
SMASH
WHOA!

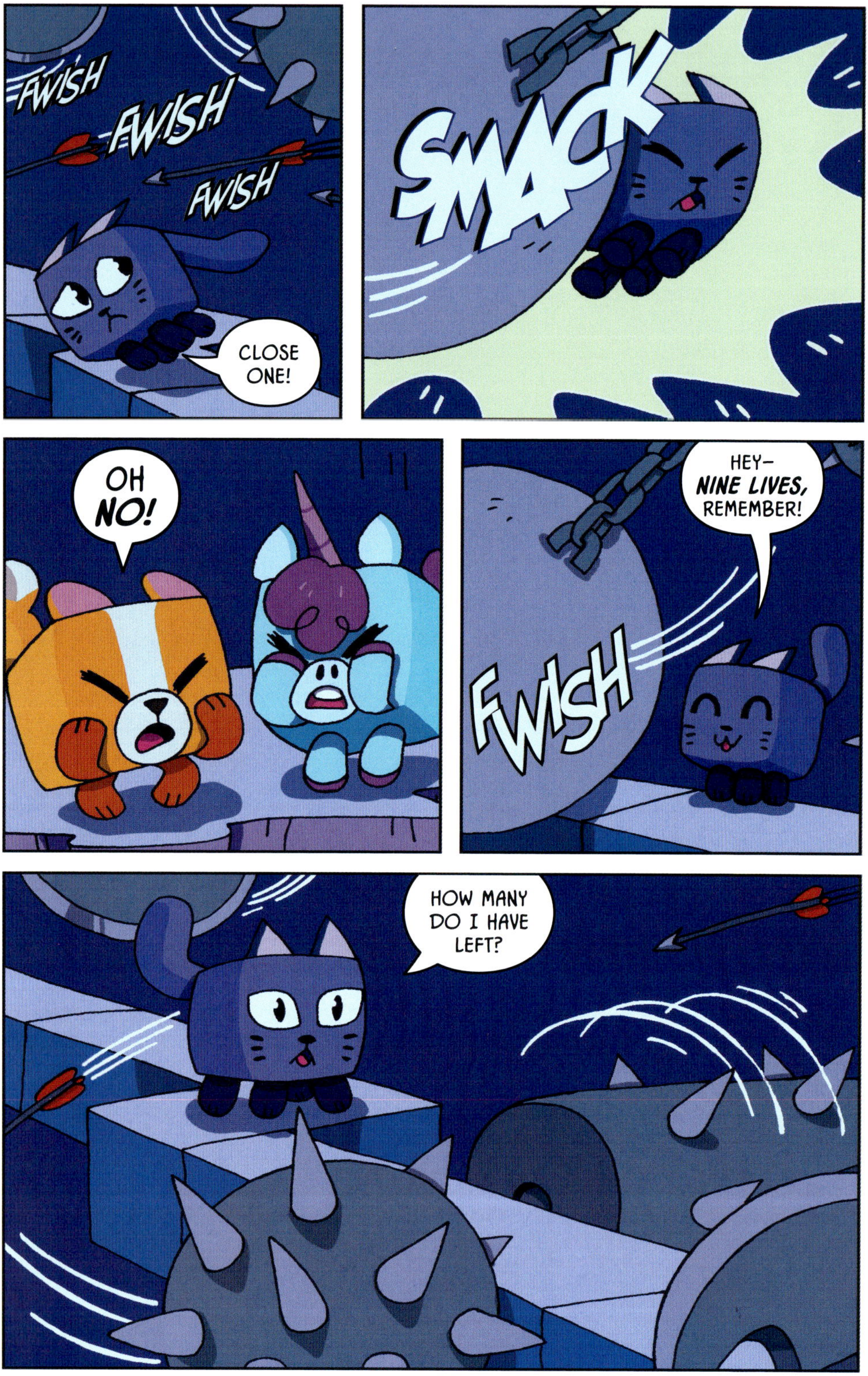
FWISH
FWISH
FWISH
CLOSE ONE!
SMACK
OH NO!
HEY— NINE LIVES, REMEMBER!
FWISH
HOW MANY DO I HAVE LEFT?

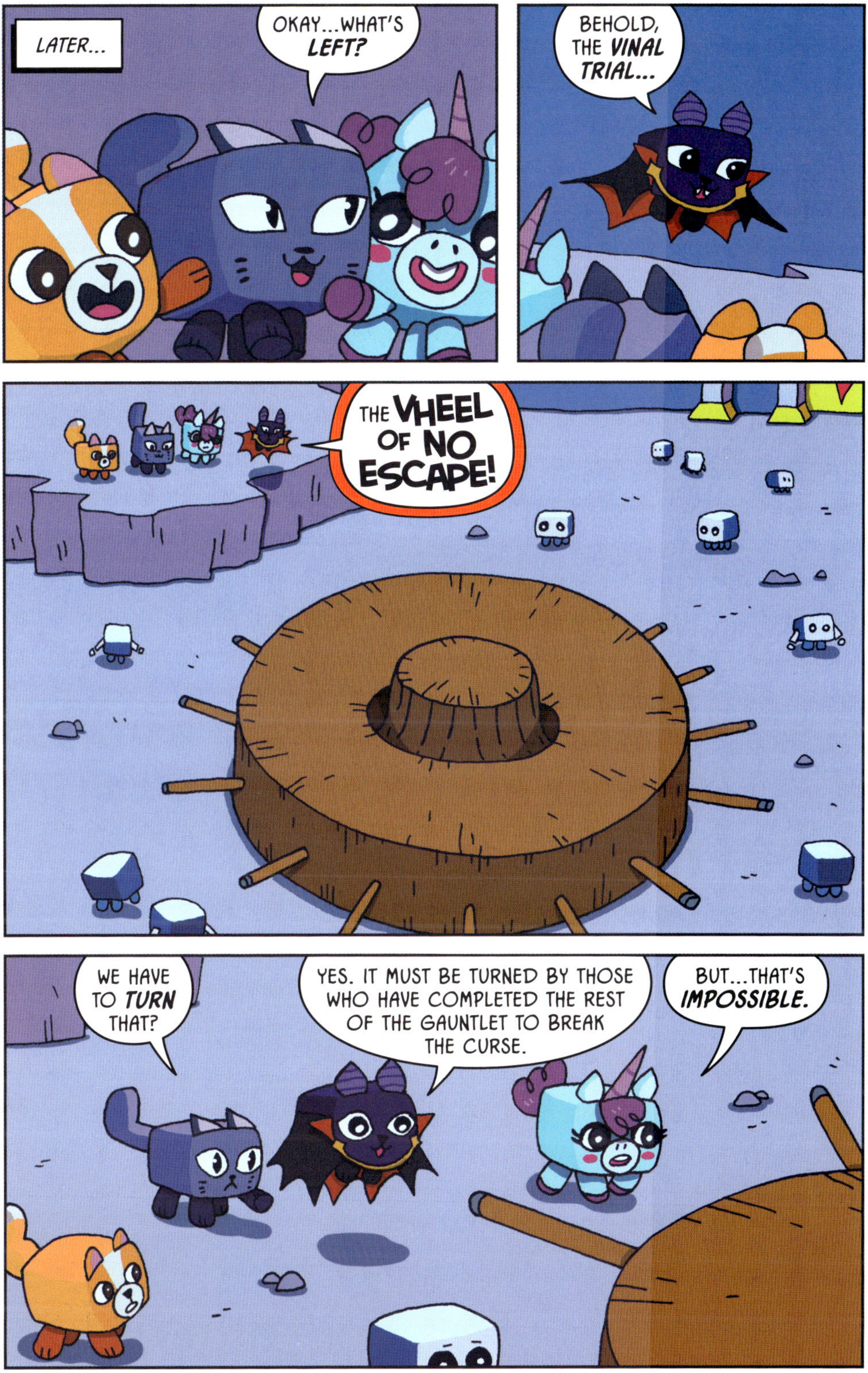
LATER...
OKAY...WHAT'S LEFT?
BEHOLD, THE VINAL TRIAL...
THE VHEEL OF NO ESCAPE!
WE HAVE TO TURN THAT?
YES. IT MUST BE TURNED BY THOSE WHO HAVE COMPLETED THE REST OF THE GAUNTLET TO BREAK THE CURSE.
BUT...THAT'S IMPOSSIBLE.

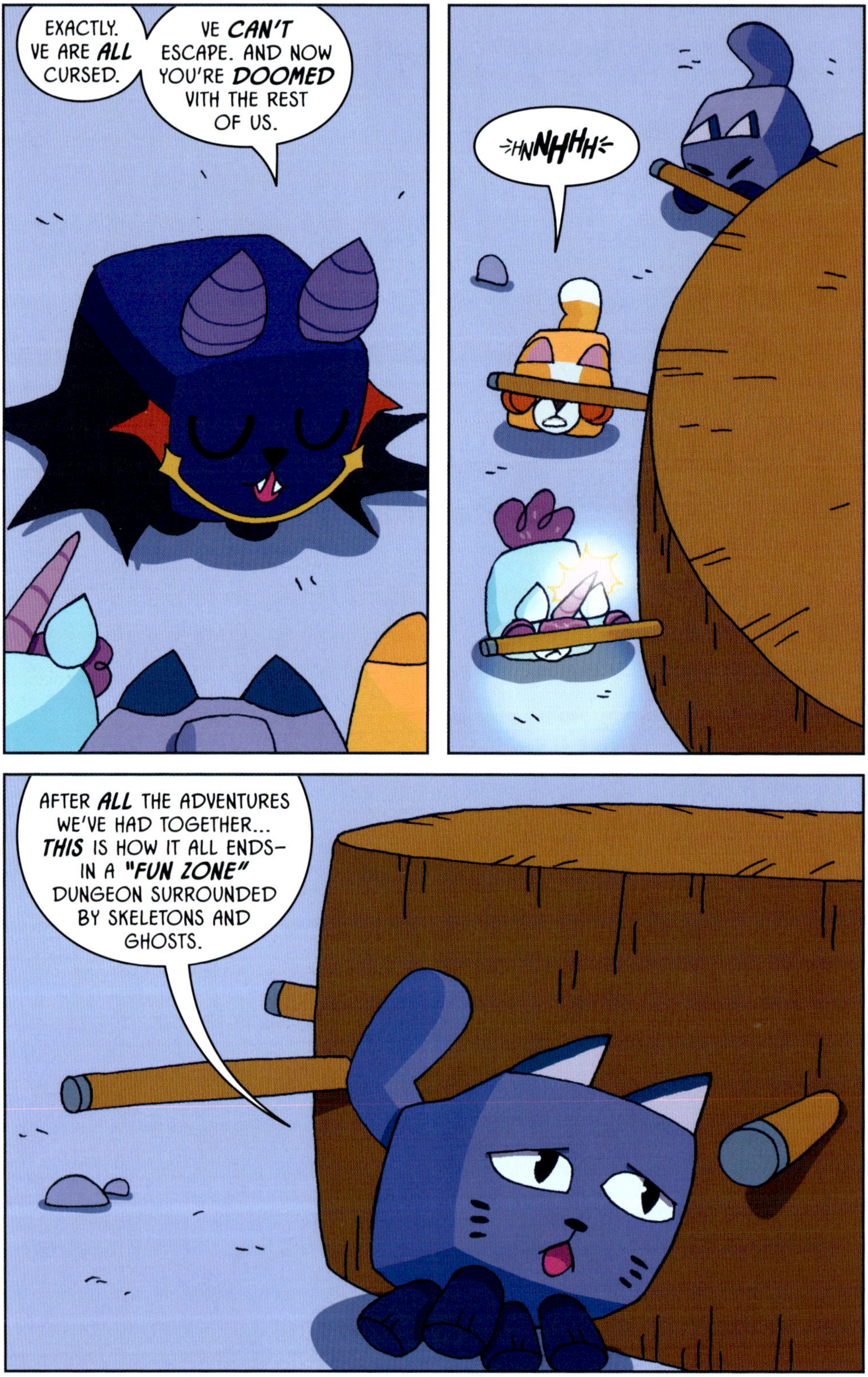
EXACTLY. VE ARE ALL CURSED.
VE CAN'T ESCAPE. AND NOW YOU'RE DOOMED VITH THE REST OF US.
HNNHHH
AFTER ALL THE ADVENTURES WE'VE HAD TOGETHER... THIS IS HOW IT ALL ENDS— IN A "FUN ZONE" DUNGEON SURROUNDED BY SKELETONS AND GHOSTS.

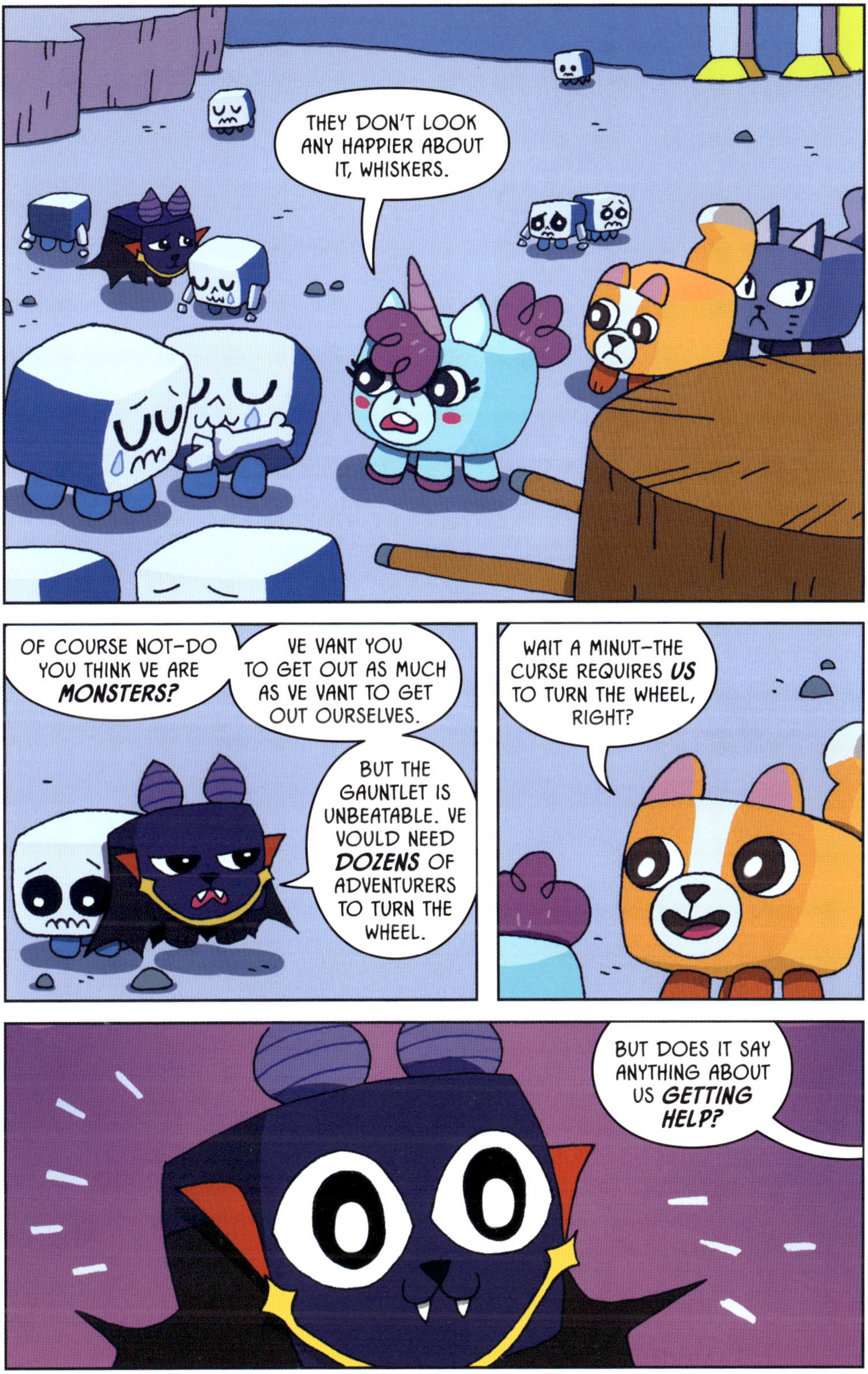
THEY DON'T LOOK ANY HAPPIER ABOUT IT, WHISKERS.
OF COURSE NOT—DO YOU THINK VE ARE **MONSTERS?**
VE VANT YOU TO GET OUT AS MUCH AS VE VANT TO GET OUT OURSELVES.
BUT THE GAUNTLET IS UNBEATABLE. VE VOULD NEED **DOZENS** OF ADVENTURERS TO TURN THE WHEEL.
WAIT A MINUT—THE CURSE REQUIRES **US** TO TURN THE WHEEL, RIGHT?
BUT DOES IT SAY ANYTHING ABOUT US **GETTING HELP?**

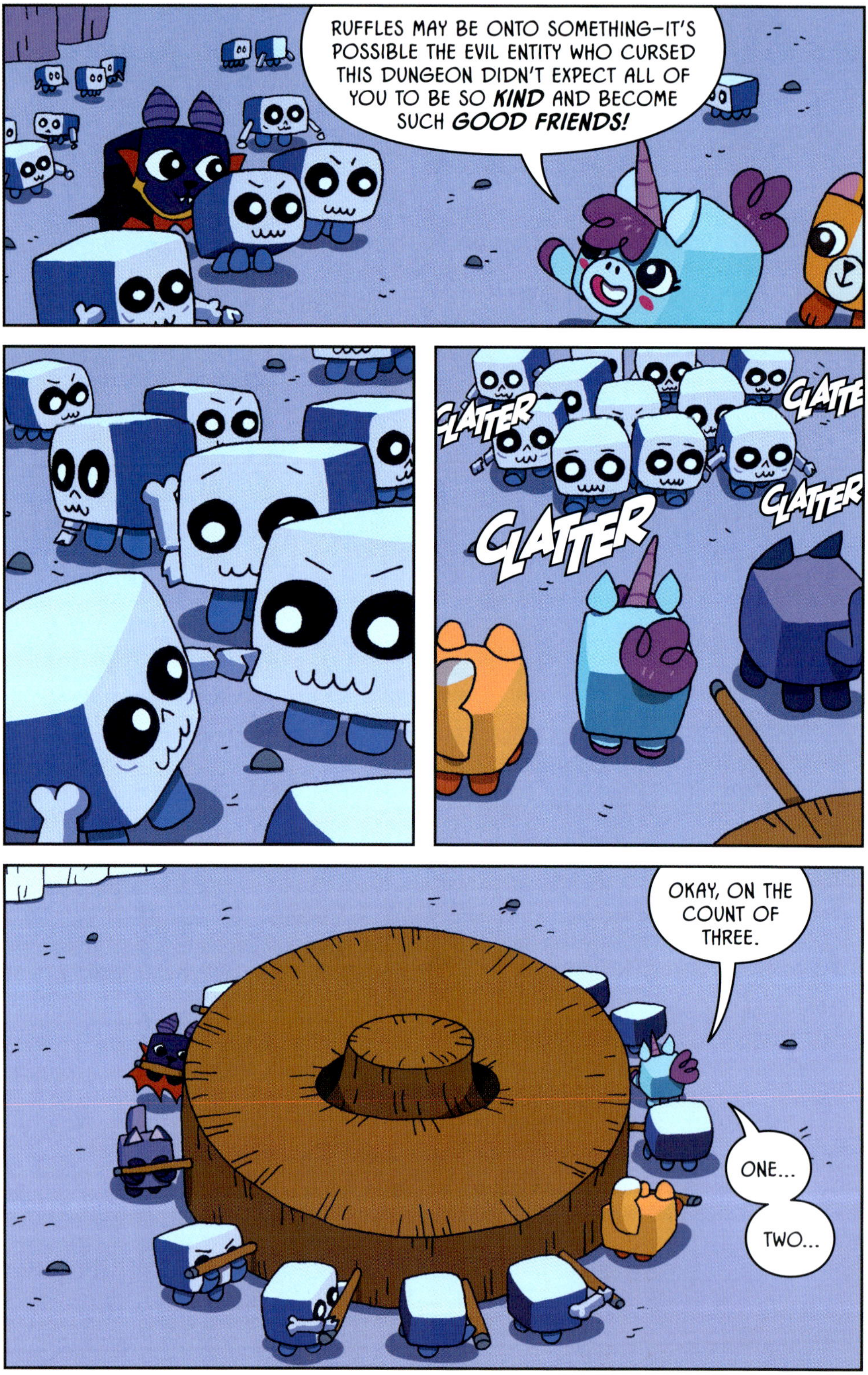
RUFFLES MAY BE ONTO SOMETHING—IT'S POSSIBLE THE EVIL ENTITY WHO CURSED THIS DUNGEON DIDN'T EXPECT ALL OF YOU TO BE SO **KIND** AND BECOME SUCH **GOOD FRIENDS!**
CLATTER
CLATTER
CLATTER
CLATTER
OKAY, ON THE COUNT OF THREE.
ONE...
TWO...

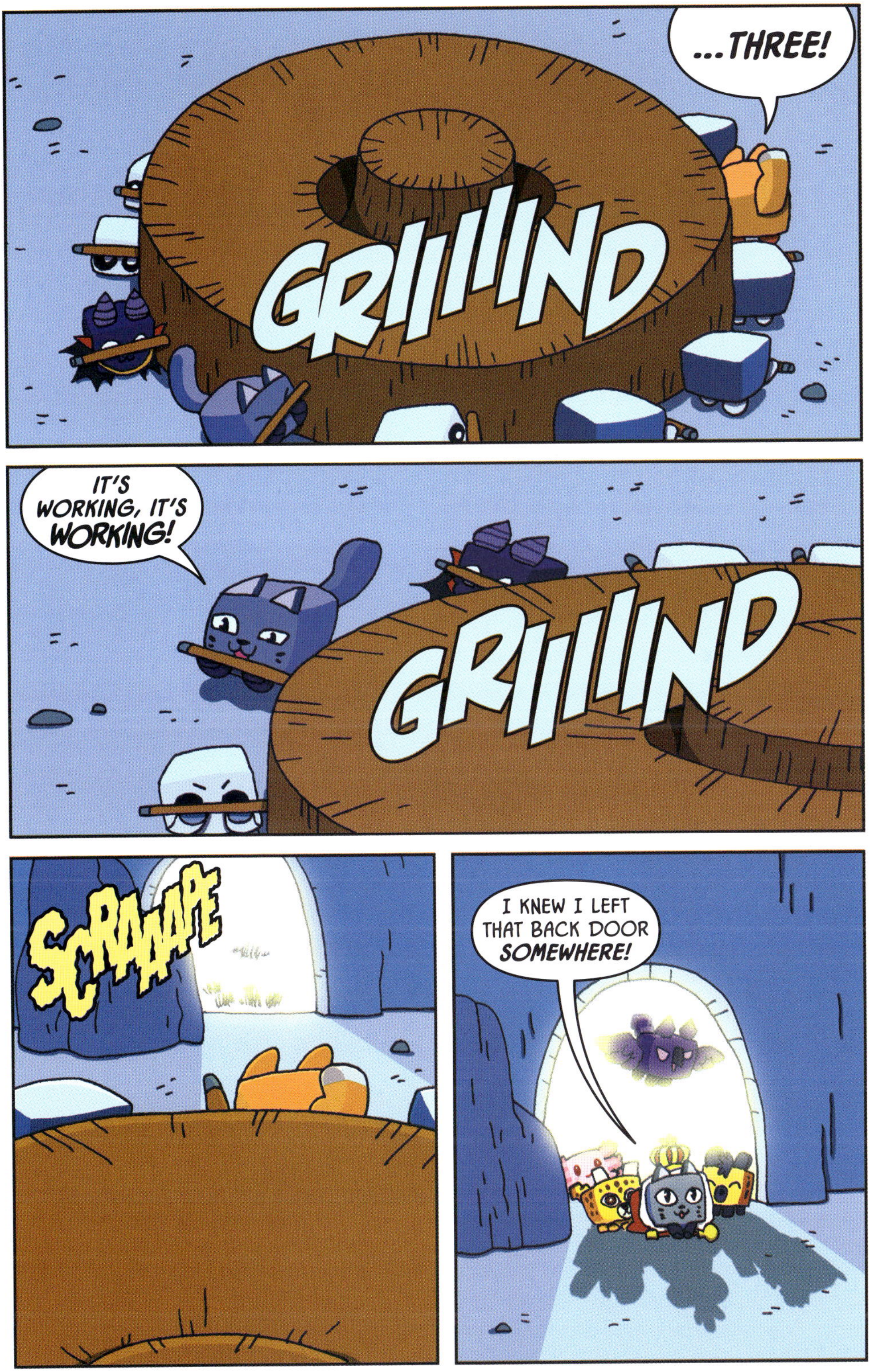
...THREE!
GRIIIIND
IT'S WORKING, IT'S WORKING!
GRIIIIND
SCRAAAPE
I KNEW I LEFT THAT BACK DOOR SOMEWHERE!

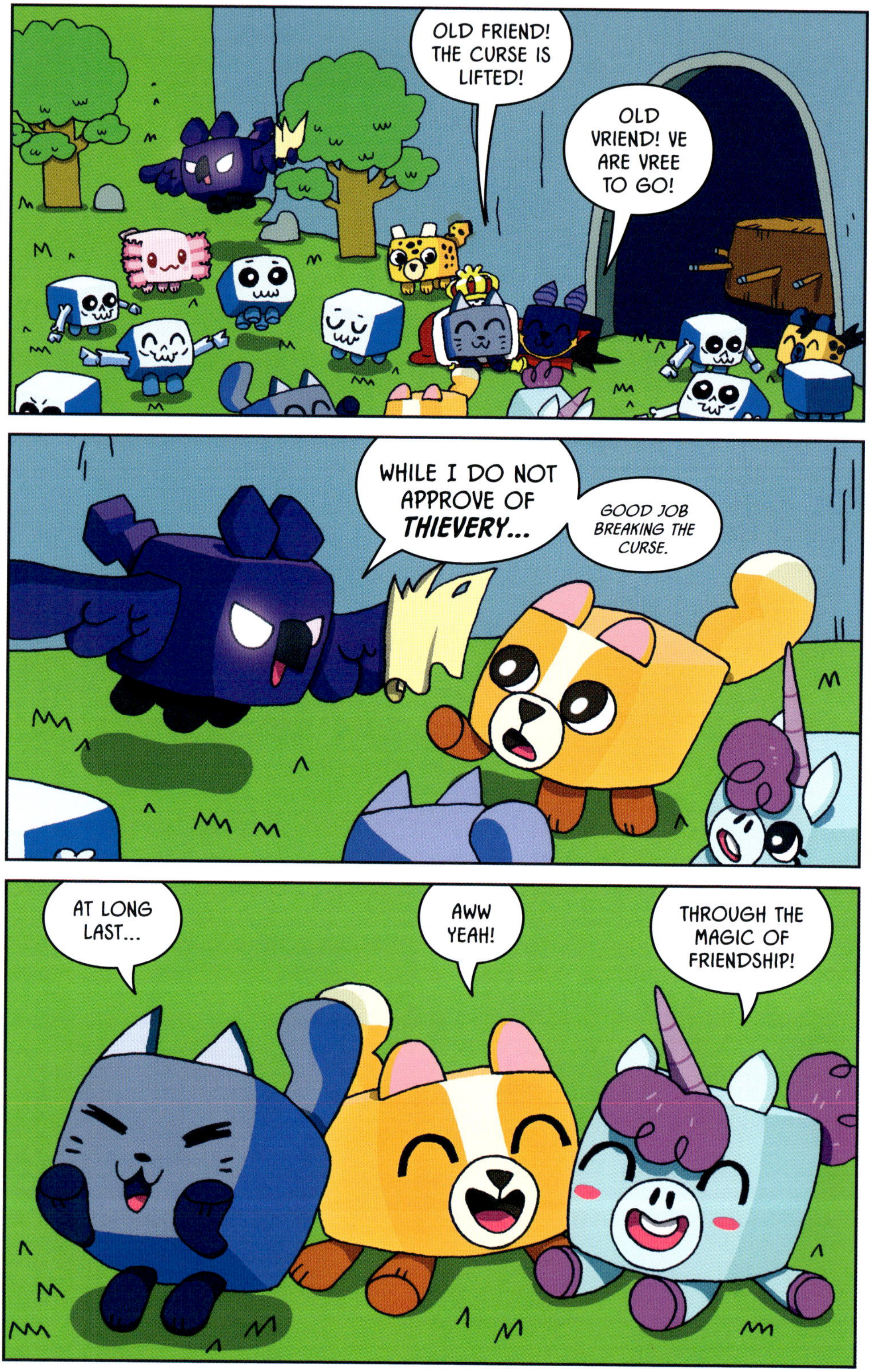
OLD FRIEND! THE CURSE IS LIFTED!
OLD VRIEND! VE ARE VREE TO GO!
WHILE I DO NOT APPROVE OF **THIEVERY...**
GOOD JOB BREAKING THE CURSE.
AT LONG LAST...
AWW YEAH!
THROUGH THE MAGIC OF FRIENDSHIP!

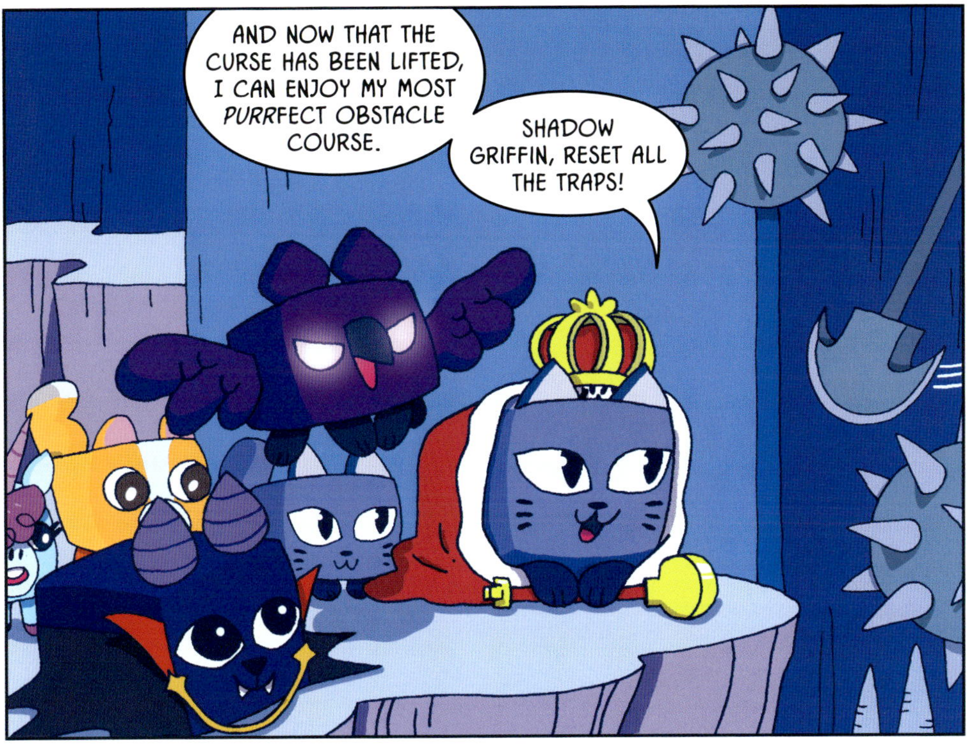
AND NOW THAT THE CURSE HAS BEEN LIFTED, I CAN ENJOY MY MOST *PURR*FECT OBSTACLE COURSE.
SHADOW GRIFFIN, RESET ALL THE TRAPS!

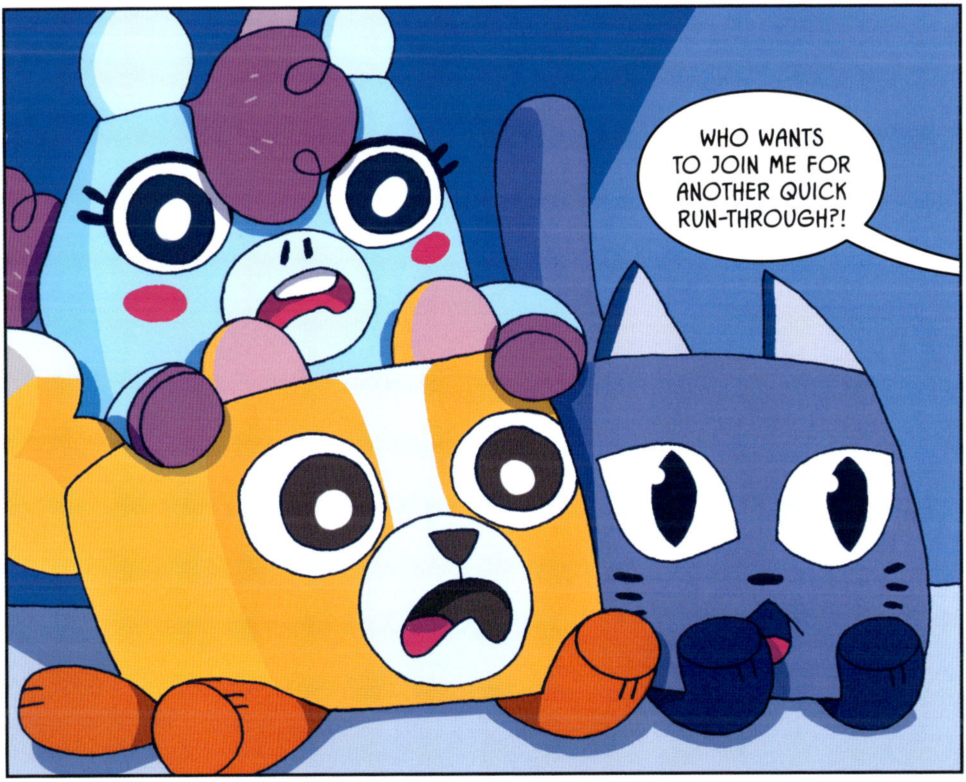
WHO WANTS TO JOIN ME FOR ANOTHER QUICK RUN-THROUGH?!

THE END

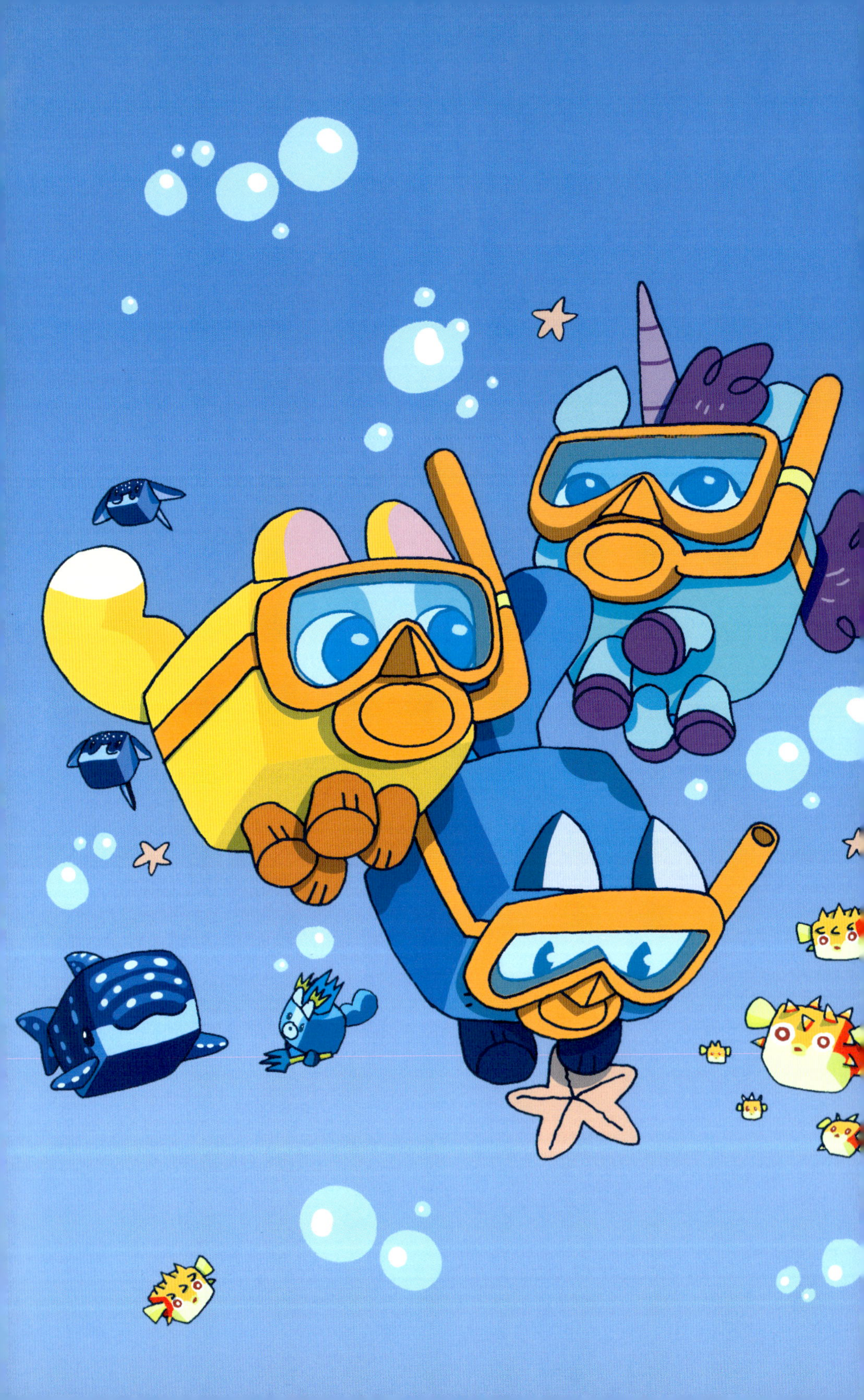

MIKE LAUGHEAD

is a comics creator and illustrator of children's books, T-shirts, book covers, and other fun things in the children's market. He has been doing that for almost twenty years. Mike is also an illustration instructor at Brigham Young University-Idaho. He resides in Idaho with his amazing wife and three wonderful daughters. To see his portfolio, visit ShannonAssociates.com/MikeLaughead.

STEVE FOXE

Steve Foxe is the author of over 75 comics and children's books, including *X-Men '92: House of XCII*, *Archer & Armstrong Forever*, *Rainbow Bridge*, *Party & Prey*, *Adventure Kingdom*, and the *Spider-Ham* series from Scholastic. He is the co-creator of Razorblades: The Horror Magazine alongside James Tynion IV, and is the editor of the Eisner-nominated *The Department of Truth* at Image Comics. In the world of licensed kids' books, he has written for properties like Pokémon, Mario, LEGO City, Batman, Justice League, Baby Shark, and many more.

He lives somewhere cold, where he tweets about comics, scary movies, his boyfriend, and their dog at @steve_foxe.

WANT MORE PET SIMULATOR STORIES?

Check out what the pets are up to in *Two Tales of Teamwork,*

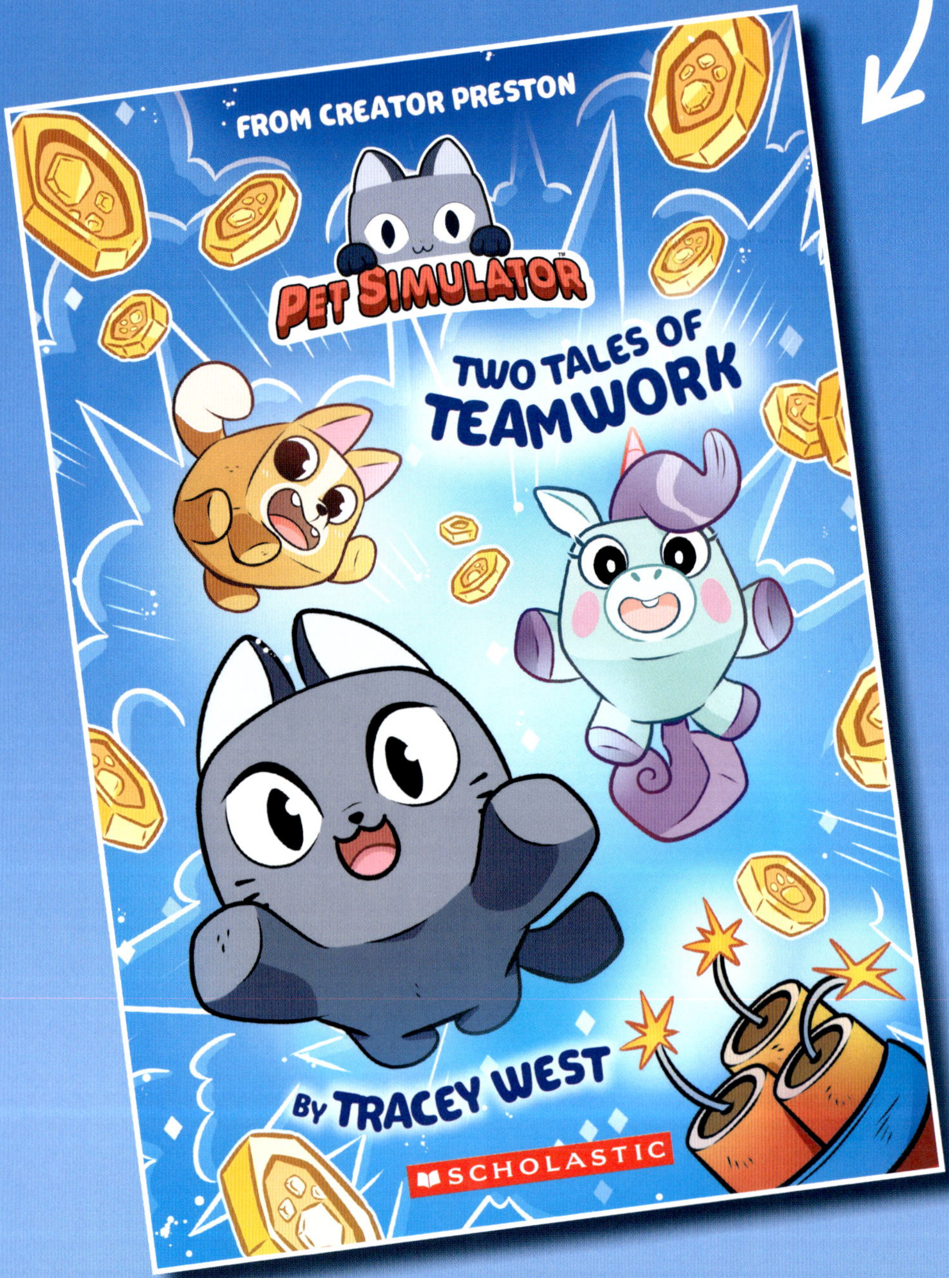
FROM CREATOR PRESTON
PET SIMULATOR
TWO TALES OF TEAMWORK
BY TRACEY WEST
SCHOLASTIC

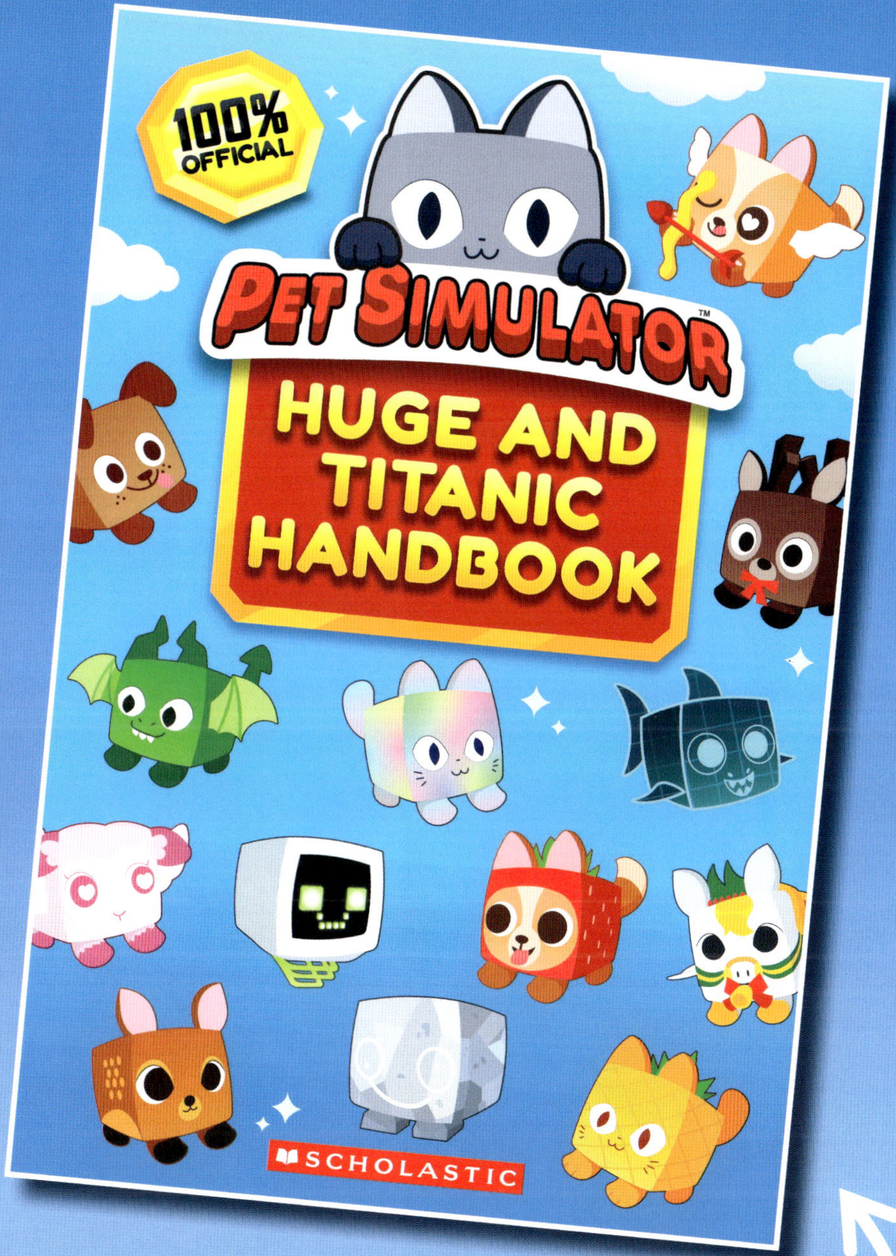
100% OFFICIAL
PET SIMULATOR™
HUGE AND TITANIC HANDBOOK
SCHOLASTIC

and learn cool facts with
the *Huge and Titanic Handbook*!

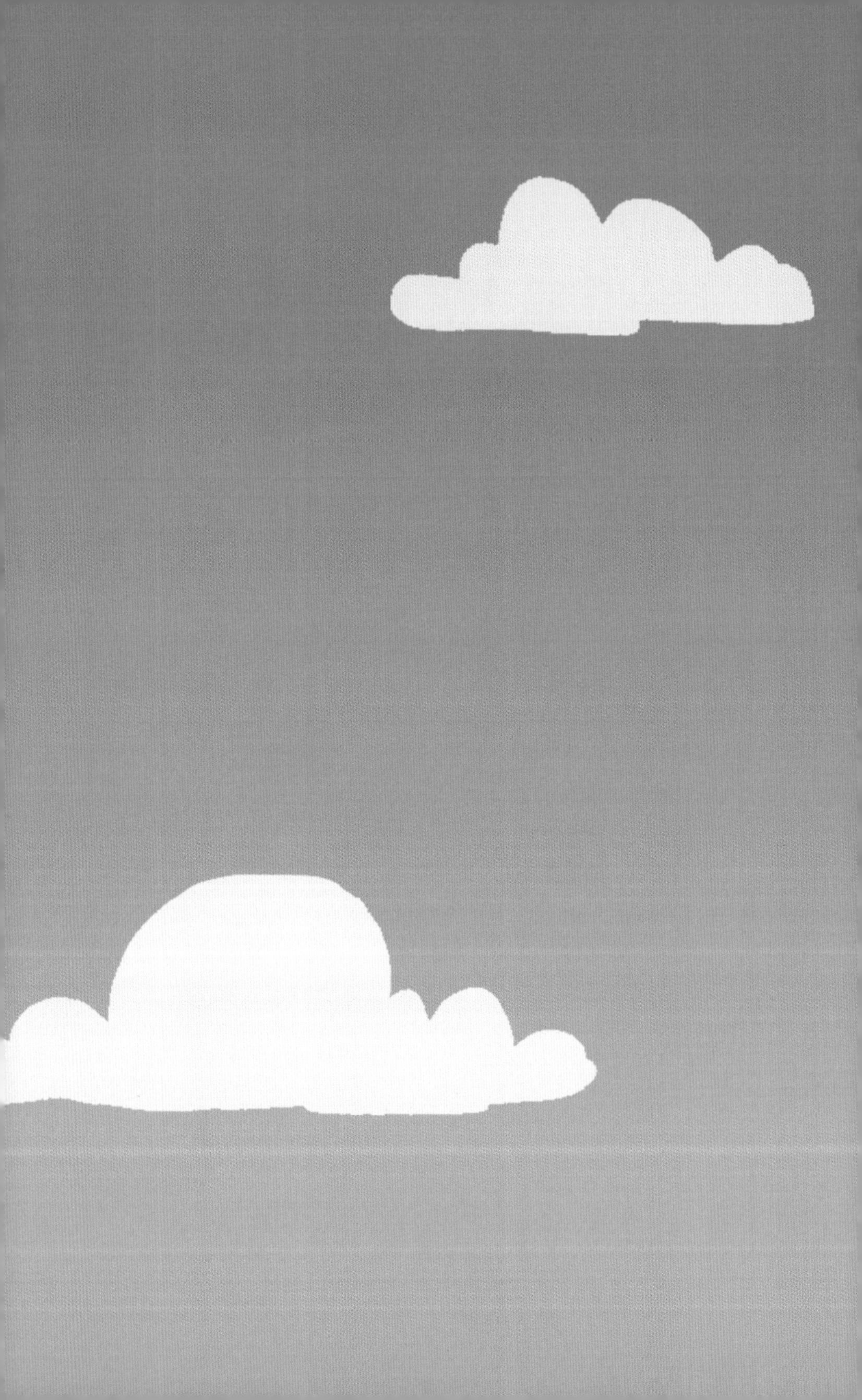

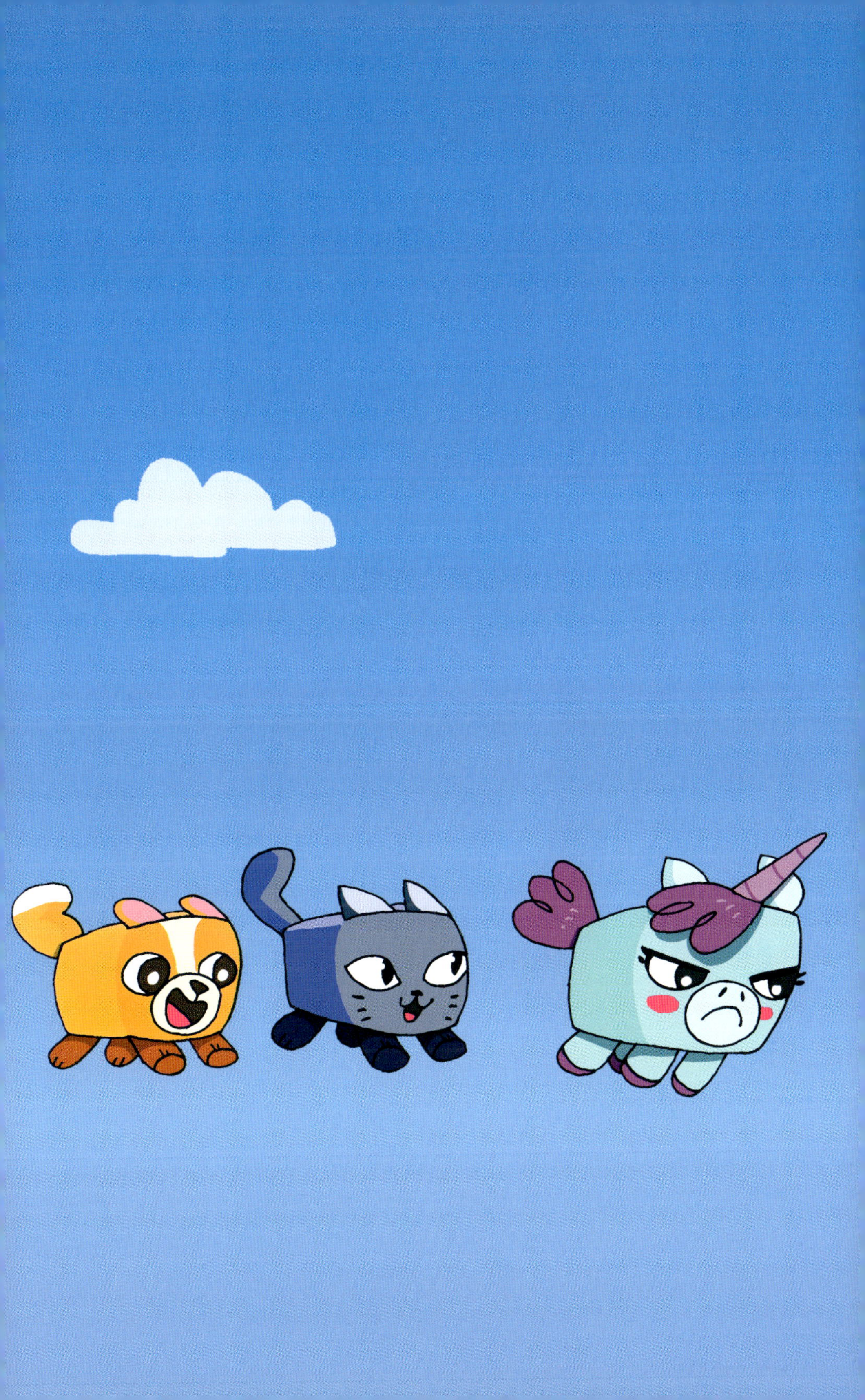

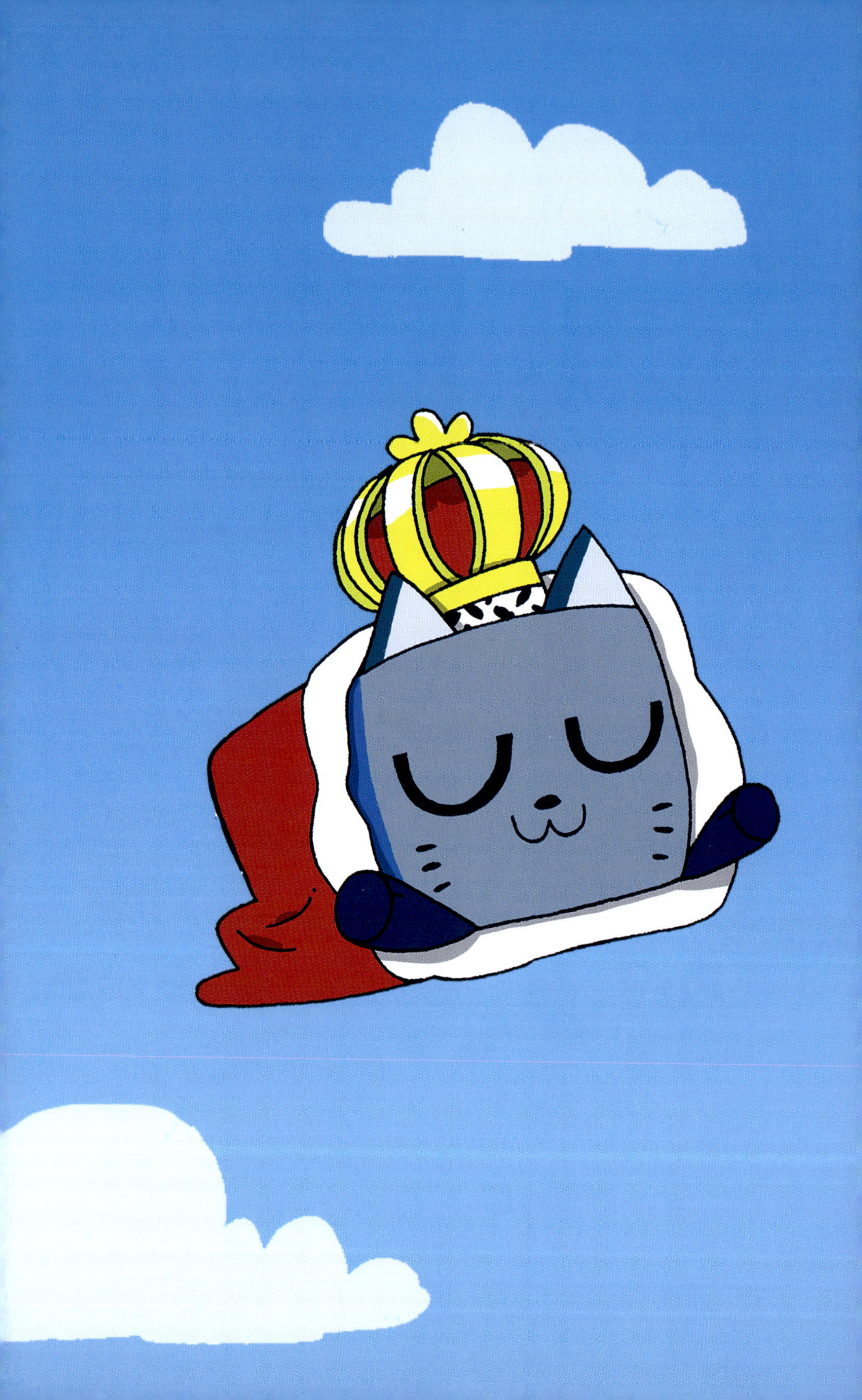

Now it's time for you to play the game and start collecting your own pets!

Check out the website below and expand your pet collection:

playpetsim.com

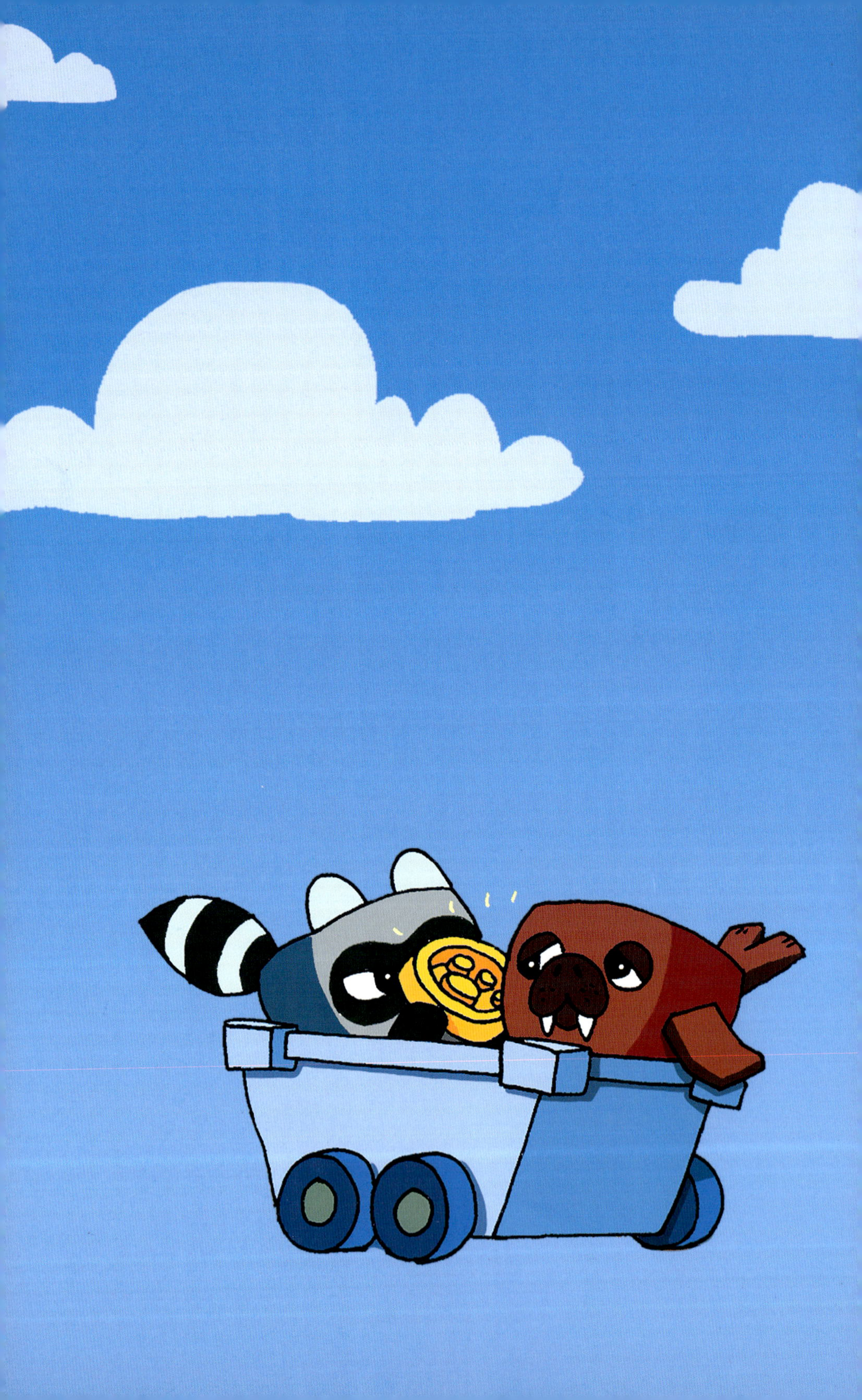